Putting on the Style

Sunday Times bestselling author Freda Lightfoot was born in Lancashire. She always dreamed of becoming a writer but this was considered a rather exotic ambition. She has been a teacher, bookseller in the Lake District, then a smallholder and began her writing career by publishing over forty short stories and articles before finding her vocation as a novelist. She has since written over forty-eight novels, mostly sagas and historical fiction. She now spends warm winters living in Spain, and the rainy summers in Britain.

Also by Freda Lightfoot

Lakeland Sagas

Lakeland Lily
The Bobbin Girls
Kitty Little
Gracie's Sin
Daisy's Secret

A Champion Street Market Saga

Putting on the Style
Fools Fall in Love
That'll be the Day
Candy Kisses
Who's Sorry Now
Lonely Teardrops

A Salford Saga

Ruby McBride
The Favourite Child
The Castlefield Collector
Dancing on Deansgate

The Poor House Lane Sagas

The Girl From Poor House Lane
The Child from Nowhere
The Woman from Heartbreak House

FREDA LIGHTFOOT

Putting on the Style

CANELO

First published in the United Kingdom in 2006 by Hodder & Stoughton

This edition published in the United Kingdom in 2021 by

Canelo
31 Helen Road
Oxford OX2 0DF
United Kingdom

Print ISBN 978 1 80032 489 3
Ebook ISBN 978 1 78863 668 1

This book is a work of fiction. Names, characters, businesses, organizations, places and events are either the product of the author's imagination or are used fictitiously. Any resemblance to actual persons, living or dead, events or locales is entirely coincidental.

Look for more great books at www.canelo.co

Printed and bound in Great Britain by Clays Ltd, Elcograf S.p.A.

1

Chapter One

1953

Dena knew the instant she heard the splash that her young brother was dead, that the last gurgling sounds he made as he fought for life would live forever in her mind.

Their assailants had sprung from the darkness, little more than shadows, jumping out upon them to attack with feet and fists, battering and thumping, punching and kicking. She could hear those same feet now running, fading away into the darkness, although not before they'd given her a good beating too, pummelling her in the stomach, kicking her in the back and legs when she fell, so that she feared they might not stop till she too was a goner. Now, with only the distant sounds of the city washing over her, and the wind whistling under the canal bridge Dena risked moving a leg, terrified it might be broken because she had to get up. She had to save him.

'*Pete! Pete!*'

Every muscle screamed out in agony as she struggled to reach the edge of the bank, desperately trying to penetrate the inky blackness. Dena sent up a silent prayer that she might find his cheery face laughing up at her, see her little brother swimming to the bank. Pete was a good swimmer, better than her, yet instinct told her that he could not have survived such a terrible beating. Even so, without pausing for thought she jumped into the water, ready to give her own life to save his.

How long she searched, diving in the filthy water again and again, calling his name, crying and screaming for him, Dena

I

couldn't rightly have said. Until she was floundering for air, her lungs choked with oil, muck and filth, legs tangled in weed and old rope and bits of tyres, and she too was in danger of drowning. Until she was finally forced to drag herself out and collapse exhausted on the towpath.

She was too late to save her young brother. Far, far too late!

If only she'd managed to protect him. He was ten years old and she'd promised her mam that she'd take good care of him. Oh, if only they hadn't taken this shortcut. 'Mam, I wish you'd come to fetch us,' Dena sobbed. 'I wish we hadn't come this way.' But they'd been hungry for their tea on this cold January evening, tired after a long day working on the market. She did not allow herself to consider that as a skinny thirteen-year-old, Dena had little hope of protecting him against such an attack.

The pair of them had emerged from under the canal bridge, giggling and laughing, about to turn off the towpath and make a dash up Barber's Court when the gang had pounced. They'd grabbed Pete by the scruff of the neck and started bouncing him between them like a rubber ball.

He'd sworn at them, and tried to fend them off. He'd always been good with his fists had Pete, but that seemed to inflame them all the more. There were too many of them and the ruthless thugs set about beating him senseless. Even when he fell to the ground they dragged him to his feet just so they could knock him down again, chuckling maliciously as they did so.

Dena's own screams, her frantic efforts to reach him, had all been in vain. She'd been held fast, slammed back against the wall under the bridge by two of the gang, their cowardly faces hidden beneath balaclavas while she was made to watch the punishment meted out to an innocent boy as if it were a performance to be proud of.

She'd seen little in the darkness, couldn't identify a single one of them, nothing but a huddle of figures with their backs to her, fists and feet flying. They could have been any one of a number of gangs who roamed these streets. She saw the flash of a blade, heard the crunch of knuckle on bone and Pete's low groans of agony, his gasps for breath and desperate pleas begging for mercy.

But his assailants spoke not a single word throughout, which added to the sense of nightmare of the whole episode, like watching a scene in a black and white film. Dena couldn't take in what her own eyes were telling her. There was no sense of reality, the eerie silence punctuated only by grunts and callous laughter. She felt utterly helpless. And then came that last terrified scream which had echoed beneath the bridge and over the water before being sharply cut off, followed a few minutes later by a soul-sinking splash as they dumped his body into the filthy canal.

Now, as she lay bruised and damaged, alone on the towpath, there was nothing but the sound of her own weeping.

–

Alice Dobson did not take the news of her son's probable drowning well, but then what mother would? At first, she refused to believe it, accusing Dena of spinning some fanciful yarn, or of telling nasty tales about her brother. Even the sight of her daughter gasping for breath, having run the rest of the way home, covered with cuts and bruises and soaked through to the skin didn't penetrate her dazed mind. 'If this is one of your daft squabbles…'

'Mam, we have to do something. We need help. He's likely a goner but…' Alice refused to listen, just carried on making tea, setting the table, even told Dena to wash her hands. Her mother liked things to be all nice and proper.

Dena walked out, went herself to the police station to report the accident. That's how she described it to the sergeant, taking care not to give away too many particulars. The last thing they needed was for her to start mouthing off about their Pete being beaten up. Whichever gang had done this terrible thing wouldn't take kindly to her shopping them to the police, and would more than likely come back to give her a second pasting if she was stupid enough as to try, or else start harassing Mam. You learned to keep your mouth shut in this neighbourhood.

The desk sergeant peered over his spectacles at the stick-thin girl before him, dressed in a thin cotton frock and tatty cardigan that offered no protection against a cold winter's night, and felt a wave of pity for her. She couldn't be more than eleven or twelve at most, and was clearly genuinely distressed, her tears making clean tracks in the dirt on her face.

And what a face! He'd seen more waifs and strays standing before his desk than he cared to remember but there was something utterly innocent about this face. It was captivating, almost angelic. Was it the perfect oval shape and pointed chin, the small, straight nose or those dark curling lashes wet with tears, which gave it such an ethereal beauty? The chestnut brown eyes had gold flecks in them and gazed up at him so trustingly, imploring him to help as if the simple presence of a police uniform could put right all the ills of the world.

The sergeant cleared his throat. She could be spinning him a yarn, deliberately sent to lure a force of police to go chasing off in one direction while the rest of her gang did their worst in another. You had to be cautious in this job, and not be taken in by some sob story told by an urchin, however angelic. They were often the worst liars of all. 'He fell in, you say? What were you doing playing by the canal? Has your mother not told you how dangerous that is?'

'We live in Barber's Court.'

The sergeant sniffed his disdain, knowing the area well. A stinking hole if ever there was one. Should be raised to the ground in this new, post-war world, and hopefully soon would be. Though the folk who lived there would no doubt mess up a new place just as bad.

She must have read the disdain in his eyes because she said with some spirit, 'I don't always look like this. We're respectable in our house. Tablecloths and everything.'

The sergeant instantly felt ashamed. Many people had fallen on hard times during the war. Houses were hard to come by, either

4

decent or otherwise, and too many women had been widowed. 'You must be used to that towpath then, living down there. Happen he's swum down the canal for a bit, got out some place else. Is your mam out looking for him? She'll give him jip when she catches him, eh?'

Dena shook her head, dark tendrils of wet hair showering him with water. He saw then that she was shivering, her teeth chattering with cold, and realised in a flash that she must have jumped in and tried to save the lad herself. He picked up his phone and began to dial. This accident clearly needed urgent attention.

–

It was over a week before they found him. When Dena heard the knock on the door she guessed instantly who it was. Usually that all too familiar sound heralded yet another complaint about her tearaway brother, some mischief he'd been up to. Perhaps tying dustbin lids to door handles, breaking someone's windows with his cricket ball, or chucking mud at folk's clean washing. Mrs Emmett next door had once made him wash two of her pillowcases as punishment for his naughtiness, but Pete had only thought it funny that his own filthy hands had made the washing water so dirty the pillowcases had come out worse.

But despite his bad behaviour, and what lad living in these rough streets of Manchester wasn't a bit on the wild side at times, his heart was in the right place. Maybe he would have been easier to cope with if their dad hadn't been killed in the war, gone down with his ship before even his son was born. There were times when Pete could have done with a father's guiding hand but at least he didn't steal or lie or hurt people.

He was funny and affectionate, always with a grin on his cheeky face. And underneath that cocky exterior, that brash, devil-may-care façade which he used as a shield to protect himself, underneath all of that he was soft as butter.

5

He'd willingly set to and make tea if Mam was having one of her 'turns'. He'd run her errands, fetch her knitting and endlessly charm her so that he was easily her favourite.

And he was always at the market early every Saturday morning to help Barry Holmes load up the fruit and veg for his stall, for all he was only ten years old. Pete worked hard all day and stayed late to stack away the trestles that Barry used without a word of complaint, pocketing his few shillings in wages with one of his famous wide grins. He was scruffy and untidy, and would do anything to avoid having his neck washed, but he readily tolerated the nagging of an older sister.

But no more. Dena knew in her heart that this knock was different from the others. Her young brother would never work the market again, nor have his neck scrubbed on a Saturday night.

She pulled open the door and silently invited the two policemen to step inside.

'Is your mam in?' the sergeant asked, his voice carrying that special hushed tone that people adopted when the news was bad. 'You'd best fetch her, love.'

'I don't need fetching, I'm here. Say what you've got to say then take your mucky feet off my clean doorstep and sling your hook.'

The sergeant backed off a pace, although he wasn't on her doorstep, having planted his booted feet on the clean linoleum since the door opened directly into a living-kitchen. His mate was and quickly stepped back into a puddle, which made matters worse.

Both officers punctiliously wiped their feet while Dena softly closed the door behind them.

Alice Dobson made no attempt to offer them a seat as she normally would have done, nor did she order Dena to run and put on the kettle. Satisfied that she'd made it very clear to them how she was known for keeping a clean house, thank you very much, even if she did live in one of the worst courts Manchester could offer, she returned to staring into a blazing fire. The small room was stiflingly hot but she sat like stone, hands neatly folded on her lap, her lips as tightly curled as her brown hair which she had permanently waved every two or three months.

The sergeant cleared his throat, as always hating this part of his job. 'I'm sorry love but we need an identification.'

Alice jerked up her head and looked into the round face filled with compassion. She wore a thick navy cardigan and woollen skirt pulled so far down over her plump knees that only a pair of thick ankles and carpet slippers could be seen. The over-heated room, sour with the smell of poverty, seemed to suck the air from Dena's lungs as she watched and waited, what felt like a lifetime, for her mother to take in the significance of this remark.

Then something in her expression seemed to collapse as finally Alice faced the truth that her son was indeed dead, and she began to whimper. 'No, no, I can't. I can't. Don't ask me.'

She let out a terrible wail, flung herself at Dena and slapped her hard across the face. 'You did this. This is all your fault, you little *bitch*!' And then she burst into noisy, gulping sobs.

Chapter Two

There was a stiff breeze blowing on this cold January morning, bristling the hairs on the scavenging dogs and cats round the fish market, sending scraps of tattered brown paper bags and rotting cabbage leaves scurrying the length of Champion Street. Because of the cold weather the outdoor market was quieter than usual, most folk taking refuge inside the market hall. The old Victorian, iron-framed building was heaving with people, the wind blowing in through the big double doors, making old ladies tighten their headscarves as they bought skeins of wool to knit socks for their old man, or a nice bit of crumbly Lancashire for his tea.

And when they were done and their shopping baskets filled with onions, potatoes and a big green cabbage from Holmes's Fruit and Veg, a couple of Poulson's best meat and potato pies and a string of shiny red polony sausage from Ramsay's Pork Butchers, they'd sigh with relief and go off to the market cafe for a cuppa and a bacon butty.

A good half of Belle Garside's customers visited the cafe as much for a gossip and to see her pretty young waitress's bright, cheerful smile as to enjoy the excellent food. They loved simply to have it light up their lives for a few precious moments.

This morning they were destined to be disappointed. Some folk glanced in the cafe and, seeing Dena wasn't present, changed their minds and went and bought a hot potato from Benny's cart instead. Others didn't linger for that extra cup, nor order a slice of Belle's delicious apple pie in order to have a repeat performance of that bewitching smile.

Belle noticed the fall-off in trade and blamed Dena for it, deeply irritated by the girl's absence since it badly affected her profits. She did have another waitress, but Joan Chapman somehow didn't have the pulling power of the younger girl, being swarthy skinned with boyishly cropped dark hair and was also married with three kids. She made wonderful pies and cakes did Joan, but didn't cause any hearts to beat faster.

'Where the hell is the silly child? The minute she shows her face, she's sacked, do you hear me?' Belle roared.

'You can't do that, she's just lost her brother.' This from her younger son Kenny, who fancied Dena.

'By heck, what's this, not going soft are you? I thought you hated the little tyke.'

'I do, I mean – I did. Used to get up my nose good and proper.'

Belle chuckled, a deep throaty sound, the kind that could bring a man to his knees if the moment was right. 'I seem to remember that he objected to you lusting after his big sister, wasn't that the way of it? Thought she could do better, eh? Silly little brat.'

'I weren't lusting after her. I like her that's all. Any quarrel I had with Pete has nothing to do wi' Dena. Our Carl can't – couldn't – stand him neither. But I could help you this morning, if you'd let me,' Kenny offered, judging it wise to change the subject. He didn't care to have his personal feelings picked over by anyone, least of all by his nosy mother.

Belle was outraged.

'I'll have no son of mine waiting table in a miserable market cafe, nor plunging his hands in washing-up water. That's not why I work my fingers to the bone every day of my life.'

Kenny snorted with laughter, knowing this for a wild exaggeration of the truth. Belle's fingers, tipped with long pointed fingernails and painted pillar-box red had never risked so much as a chip to her perfect nail varnish which she carefully renewed every day. But he couldn't accuse her of not being a worker. She was usually at the cafe by six-thirty at the latest, ready to serve breakfast to the early workers by seven, rain or shine, every single morning, winter and summer.

Her first task each day was to supervise the preparation of the morning's baking, carried out by the ever reliable put-upon Joan assisted by various part-time girls during the course of a week. But they'd all know about it soon enough if the produce didn't reach Belle's stringent standards.

Not a scrap of dough or pastry ever tarnished his mother's lovely hands. She could occasionally be seen wielding a frying pan or kettle but, generally speaking, Belle preferred to confine her role to pouring out the odd cup of tea, flirting with her customers and relieving them of their hard-earned brass, while looking decorative and glamorous.

'I don't see anything wrong in me helping with the washing up, just till Dena shows up,' Kenny said. He'd do anything for the chance of seeing her, even resort to this most hated of tasks.

Belle slapped two fried eggs and a couple of bacon rashers on to a plate already well loaded with sausages, tomatoes and fried bread, and with a wiggle of her comfortably rounded hips, placed it before Alec Hall who was taking his usual morning break from his music stall.

'There you are chuck, don't say I don't spoil you.' She leaned over his shoulder as she put down the plate, bestowing upon him an alluring smile while allowing ample time for him to appreciate her cleavage. 'I want that Guy Mitchell record, 'She Wears Red Feathers', ooh, I love it, don't you? I'll pick it up next time I'm passing.'

'I'll have it wrapped ready for you, Belle.'

'With me usual discount, I hope.'

He winked at her. 'I'm sure we can come to some arrangement that suits us both.'

'Cheeky monkey!'

Task completed, the smile instantly vanished as she returned to berating her son, who was being uncharacteristically helpful this morning when usually she couldn't get him to lift a finger. Which brought to mind her elder son, with whom she had no problems in that direction. A real worker was Carl, ambitious, with very firm ideas on how things should be done.

'Where's our Carl? Don't just stand there like a lump of cold porridge, go and find him. Get yourself out of here and do some proper work for a change, why don't you? Man's work. I wasn't brought in with the morning fish, I know why you hang around the cafe all the time, for all you might protest your innocence.'

Kenny looked instantly sheepish and half turned away so his mother wouldn't see the warm flush he could feel creeping up his neck. 'All right, all right, I was going anyway.'

'I'll let you know when she turns up.' Belle smirked, knowing she really shouldn't tease the poor lad.

'It don't matter. I've no reason to hang around, no reason at all.' And Kenny slunk away, hands in his pockets, all gangly-limbs and hunched shoulders.

But he didn't get far. As he turned to leave the market hall just by Winnie Watkin's fabric stall, he saw her. Something lurched inside him, filling him with a wave of nervousness that made him feel sick. She was so lovely he couldn't imagine ever growing tired of looking at her. Her cheeks were all pink, her shiny chestnut brown curls tousled by the wind. She was dressed in a grey skirt and white blouse, and her old navy school cardigan with the sleeves pulled up to hide the holes in the elbows. He saw Winnie put out a hand to offer a word of sympathy as she passed by.

Pushing back his shoulders and flicking back the untidy thatch of fair hair that fell over his brow, of which he was inordinately proud, Kenny casually sauntered over. 'Hello, Dena.'

She looked suddenly flustered. 'I know, I know, don't tell me, I'm late.'

'No, it's not that, I were just…'

'Don't go on at me please, Kenny, I've enough on me plate right now. Sorry Winnie, I'll have to run. Talk to you later.'

'Rightio, love – and remember – I'm here if you want me. Keep your pecker up, girl.'

Dena didn't even glance his way as she dashed past, too concerned with the reception awaiting her at the cafe no doubt, bracing herself to face his mother. Kenny felt a kick of disappointment deep in his belly. So far he was getting nowhere with Dena

Dobson, but he meant one day for his luck to change. He meant to make her his.

–

Dena had scarcely noticed him. She was still haunted by the moment when she'd gazed upon the white face of her dead brother. After this most unpleasant duty had been carried out, the kindly sergeant had held her head while she vomited down the police station toilet, telling her what a brave girl she was, and how no young lass of her age should have to go through such a nasty experience.

Dena felt she hadn't had any choice but to be brave. If her mother refused to identify Pete, who else was there?

Mrs Emmett from next door had very kindly accompanied her to the police station, and seen her safely home again afterwards, weeping all the way. But Dena had gone alone into that awful room to view the body of her brother, save for the sergeant.

The moment seemed to mark the pattern of her life from then on. Whatever it was that needed doing, Dena was always the one to do it.

Alice seemed to withdraw from the world, spending most of her time sitting in her chair staring silently into the fire, although there were many days when she didn't bother to get out of bed at all. And her stillness was unnerving. Apart from her hysterical outburst on the day the police called with the dreadful news, from which Dena still bore the bruises, she hadn't shed a single tear.

Dena was dreading the funeral, had put proper notice in the paper, believing it only right and proper that some effort be made to tell her mother's family, who might not even know they had grandchildren, let alone that one of them was dead.

She'd tackled Alice about this. 'Do you know where they live now? Would you like me to write, or to go and find them? They're still family, after all?'

'I have no family.'

'Yes, you have, Mam. I remember you telling me all about them once. You always said that you got on with your brother best of the lot. He must be me Uncle Eric. Wouldn't you like to see him again, at least?'

'Don't call him that. He's no uncle to you. My so-called family have never shown any interest in either me or my children, so they can stay out of my life,' Alice snapped, and there was an end of the matter.

Alice Dobson had come down in the world and married beneath her, so far as her family were concerned. At turned twenty-eight she'd almost given up all hope of marriage when she'd fallen in love with a plumber's mate some years younger than herself, not even properly qualified when she'd first met him. Alice had never regretted her decision because he'd made her happy.

Maurice Dobson had been a loving husband and a good provider and she hadn't felt in the least bit deprived. Later, he'd joined the Merchant Navy and done well for himself. But her family had written her off, and made no contact with her since, not even by letter.

There had been a time when Alice had longed to have her mother by her side, when she'd given birth to Dena for one, and in those first difficult months following with a new baby. She'd sent a card announcing the birth but had received no reply, which had caused much heartache and tears.

Now she had no idea whether her parents were even still alive, and probably that was for the best. They'd only find fault and say she'd got what she deserved.

She would have preferred to have started her married life in a large comfortable terraced house in John Street, but had to settle for a two up and two down on Duke Street where they were bombed out back in 1941 during the Christmas Blitz. They'd been lucky to escape with their lives, being in the air-raid shelter on Lower Byrom Street at the time. Since then they'd flitted from house to house, each one cheaper than the one before.

But with her husband away at war Alice had somehow learned to cope alone, a skill she'd perfected in recent years.

Following Maurice's tragic death in 1943 while she was pregnant with Pete, their situation had worsened considerably. For the first time in her married life, Alice had been forced to seek employment to supplement the inadequate widow's pension. Even so, she'd only ever worked part-time, helping out in various shops over the years, and always choosing the smartest in St Anne's Square, King Street, or the better part of Deansgate. It was her way of hanging on to her precious respectability.

With a father who was a bank clerk, and a mother on every charity committee in Chorlton, not for a moment did she want her employers to know how far down the social ladder she had fallen.

Alice had once dreamed of getting full-time work in Pauldens, or at Kendals the famous department store, selling hats, or shoes, or else serving on the perfume counter. She'd applied for several advertised positions but never struck lucky.

And with a new baby and a young child to care for, a war still raging across Europe, life hadn't been easy.

Now they were reduced to this miserable hovel in Barber's Court where she was forced to share a bed with her daughter and Pete had used a put-me-up in the kitchen.

Even after the war hopes of securing a better job that would enable her to take her family out of Barber's Court, into one of the new council houses or flats starting to be built on blitzed sites, never materialised. Once the men had come back from their war service, jobs seemed harder to come by, and Alice had lost heart.

Naturally, as soon as they were old enough the children had helped family finances by taking Saturday jobs on Champion Street Market. It was never really enough and she would miss Pete's contribution.

Now, sadly, all of Alice's dreams were as dead as her beloved son. No priority would be given to a widow with only one daughter, not with the current housing shortage. She'd been let down by everyone and really had nothing left to live for; didn't care any more what happened to her.

Pete was given a miserable funeral with the rain sheeting down and pitifully few wreaths on his small cheap coffin. Not a single member of Alice's family turned up. No letter, no card of condolence, not even a bunch of flowers.

Alice stood silent and grim-faced throughout the painful ceremony, entirely without emotion, frozen in shock, aware of her daughter sobbing but unable to respond to it. Weeping wouldn't bring back her darling Pete, would it? Besides, Dena was alive, so what did she have to complain about?

And wasn't it all her own fault? Hadn't the stupid girl failed to look after him? Hadn't she been told to always keep a careful watch over her younger brother? Clearly she hadn't done so, and now he was dead. Alice found that very hard to forgive.

So if that knowledge brought the girl pain and suffering, or meant that she'd have to work a bit harder to make up for his loss in future, what of it? Wasn't it only what she deserved?

Chapter Three

Dena didn't need her mother to blame her for Pete's death, she'd already taken full responsibility for the tragedy, making no allowances for her own youth and physical inadequacy against the gang. The thought of her failure to protect her brother tormented her by day and kept her awake half the night.

If only she'd gone the long way round, walked home along Liverpool Road and kept to main thoroughfares where there were at least lamps lit. The fact they'd run down that ginnel, along the towpath and under the canal bridge a dozen times a week for as long as she could remember seemed no excuse at all to her young logic.

She was consumed by guilt, not only because she was alive and Pete was dead, but also for all the times when she'd spoken sharply to him, when she hadn't had the patience to endure his stupid jokes and silly teasing. Why hadn't she shown him more affection, made it clear how important he was to her, how very much she had loved him?

It felt for a while as if her tears might never stop, her anguish never ease but there did finally come a day when Dena felt she'd run dry of all emotion and had no more tears left to shed. She was exhausted by her grief and although the pain remained deep inside her, she felt the need to return to some sort of routine. Anything to focus her mind away from that burden of guilt and loss. Besides, they still needed to eat, to wash their clothes and keep clean. And Mam was making no effort at all.

It was perfectly clear that from now on if something needed doing, Dena would be the one to do it.

She would get up every morning, see to the fire, sweep and tidy up then take breakfast and a mug of tea up to her mam in bed, knowing it could still be there when she got back from school.

On her way home she would pick up a few essentials from the corner shop: bread, potatoes, milk if she could afford it. They lived largely on bacon and mash, vegetable soup and dripping butties. Finding anything decent they could afford to eat was becoming a serious problem as there was barely any money coming into the house now that her mother had given up work.

Alice was entitled, as a war widow, to a small pension, which covered the cost of the rent but little else, beyond putting the odd shilling or two into the electric metre. Could Dena even hope to provide the rest from what she earned working on the Saturday market?

She wondered if should look for another job in the evenings to earn a bit more, once she felt up to it. But then who would make tea for Mam and keep her company, help her get ready for bed and make her cocoa? She couldn't ask too much of her neighbour, Mrs Emmett, kind as the old woman was. She had a sick husband to care for. Besides, Dena also worried about how she would ever find the energy on top of all the washing and other chores that she had to do in the evening?

It was no comfort that she didn't have to tidy up after her little brother any more, messy child that he was. Oh, wouldn't she welcome tripping over his football or picking up his dirty socks? How she missed his cheerful face, even his daft pranks. She'd give anything to find a frog in her bed or her shoe laces in a knot, a couple of his favourite tricks.

And even if her mother did little herself about the house, she was quick to spot any flaws in Dena's routine.

'Have you donkey-stoned that doorstep?'

'Yes, Mam.'

'Well, don't forget to wipe down those window-sills.'

'I'll do them tonight, Mam.'

'I can hardly see out of these windows, they're that mucky.'

'I did them only last week, but I'll do them again if you like, Mam.'

'Get off to school, don't stand about here all morning, arguing and wasting time. I hope you've got clean underwear on. I don't want you shaming me if you fall under a bus and have to be taken to hospital.'

'No, Mam. I mean yes I have, Mam. I'll ask Mrs Emmett to look in at dinner time.'

'Nosy old git!'

'I don't know what we'd do without her. I'm off now, all right?'

'I told you to go ten minutes ago.'

'Ta-ra then.'

Mrs Emmett met her at the door as she was leaving. 'Don't worry chuck. You're a good lass, you. And your mam's a survivor, make no mistake about that. She'll come out of this.'

Dena gave a wan smile. 'I've left some soup on the stove but I doubt she'll be bothered to warm it up. She's no appetite at all.'

'Don't you fret. I'll make sure she eats something and check she doesn't want for anything. I shall enjoy a bit of a camp over a nice cup of tea.'

Dena went off to school content that she'd done all she could. But how to get her mother back to work? That was the biggest problem.

–

Her one other source of support, in addition to old Mrs Emmett, proved to be Barry Holmes for whom her brother had worked so diligently on his fruit and veg stall. He was there at her brother's funeral, had given her shoulder a sympathetic squeeze and offered to help in any way he could.

One afternoon after school, feeling particularly low, Dena decided to take him up on his offer. Rain was sheeting down and the prospect of returning home to precious little food in the larder and her mother's endless complaints all suddenly seemed too much to bear. She needed a friend in that moment, someone who had known and loved Pete as much as she did.

She ran through the streets, splashed uncaring through puddles as thunder clapped and lightening rent the air. Dena was soaked to the skin by the time she arrived at the outside market where Barry had his stall, but would readily have gone through brimstone and hell-fire for the sight of a welcoming face at the end of it.

He didn't see her at first as he stood beating his arms with his gloved hands and stamping his feet in a bid to keep warm as he stood under the dripping canvas; the sound of the rain hammering on the cobbles blotting out her approach.

When he did see her, his round homely face lit up. 'Dena, what the devil are you doing here? You look like a drowned rat, or more likely a stray kitten dragged out of the cut.'

Dena chuckled. 'I reckon I come pretty close to both.'

He was at once all action. 'Here, give us a hand. I were planning on packing up anyway. Who is going to come looking for tatties and beetroot in weather like this, eh?'

He giggled boyishly at her and instantly started to carefully pack away apples, oranges, strings of onions and great green orbs of Savoy cabbage. Dena helped, working quickly alongside him with professional ease so that in no time at all the boxes of fruit and sacks of potatoes were carefully stowed away in his van.

Dena liked Barry Holmes. She didn't know how old he was, oldish, or so he seemed to her and not particularly good-looking being short and chunky, his face somewhat plain with a sloping forehead and long nose. His upper lip was almost invisible and the full lower one looked as if he were pouting half the time. Nevertheless, the small dark eyes peering short-sightedly at her with deep concern from behind his spectacles, seemed to represent instant reassurance and security.

'Right, we'll just take this lot round to the warehouse. I never leave them in the van overnight in case they get nicked. You can't trust anyone round here. Pinch the skin off your rice pudding some of 'em. Then you must come to mine for a cuppa and a nice toasted muffin. What d'you say to that, chuck? That'll warm the cockles.'

Dena beamed and nodded happily.

–

Dena always felt honoured by Barry's friendship. He wasn't a particularly sociable creature. Living alone since his mother died and being something of a private individual he seemed to prefer his own company much of the time, apart from the boxing club on a Friday where he coached his boys.

Pete had been a member. There was nothing her little brother had enjoyed more than to give that old punchbag a good pummelling. He'd looked up to Barry, following him everywhere like an adoring lap dog.

And was it any wonder? Barry Holmes seemed to represent the father figure both she and her little brother had missed. Dena's own memories of her father had grown hazy and vague after all these years, and Pete had had none at all. Barry was the best replacement they could find.

He'd led such an exciting life, once having worked on the North Pier at Blackpool where he'd tried his hand at all manner of activities from running a flea circus, being a caller for housey-housey, and even performing with a Punch and Judy show. Dena loved nothing better than to listen to his stories. Barry Holmes could be very entertaining when he'd a mind to be, showing a caustic wit and dry sense of humour.

She suspected that he was ashamed of having come down in the world to something so mundane as a market stall. But he sold first-class fruit and veg and had become another of Champion Street Market's colourful characters with his famous bowler hat and carnation in his buttonhole. Even when he was working on his allotment he would have the bowler hat perched on the back of his round head. It always made her laugh to see it as he dug up leeks and potatoes in his old gardening jacket and muddy wellies. No cloth cap for Barry.

Dena was very fond of him.

They soon unloaded the stuff into his warehouse and the moment they reached his house he quickly ushered her inside, insisting she go upstairs and change into some dry clothes.

'You'll find a dressing gown behind the bathroom door, chuck. Put that on and fetch your wet togs down with you.'

Minutes later she was sitting on a stool by his fire, warmly wrapped in a plaid dressing gown that smelled of shaving soap and his favourite Woodbine cigarettes. Not at all unpleasant. And while her clothes steamed on the clothes rack, Barry whistled happily to himself in the back kitchen as he filled the kettle.

He'd made no mention of the cuts and bruises on her face, obviously accepting that she'd come by them trying to save her brother from drowning.

'Would you like raspberry jam on your toasted muffins, chuck? Course you would. Now where did I put that toasting fork?'

Dena felt a lovely curl of happiness deep inside. How wonderful to have someone look after her for a change. She almost felt like crying but then kindness always made her weep and really she mustn't. She'd done too much crying lately and was making her eyes all sore. 'Can I help?'

'No, you just sit still and get warm, cherub. Uncle Barry will see to everything. We'll have you warmed up in no time. Switch the wireless on, it'll happen be Dick Barton soon.'

'No, it won't, that's on later. Anyway, I'm happy sitting here admiring your ornaments and pictures.'

His house was surprisingly grand for all it was situated in Champion Street, close to the market. He had a front parlour as well as a living room, and she'd caught a glimpse of darkly polished mahogany furniture, a green tiled fireplace with a prettily decorated fire screen in front of it, and a comfy three-piece suite as they'd passed the open door. His mam had always kept it nice, and she supposed Barry continued to do so out of respect to her memory. No one was ever invited into the front room. Presumably he saved it for special occasions like Christmas. Dena thought that proved Barry Holmes must be quite well off.

Anyway, Dena felt more at ease on this stool by the black leaded Lancashire range, toasting herself against the bright fire at its heart.

While she waited she studied the black and white photographs of Blackpool on the cream flock wallpaper. It was a place she'd never visited but dreamed of doing so one day, just for the fun of it. She meant to ride on the big dipper and paddle in the sea, eat Blackpool rock and go right up to the top of the tower.

She'd never even seen the sea. Mam didn't approve of getting messed up with sand, or riding in dirty, smoky trains. There was a great deal her mother didn't approve of, come to think of it.

–

They sat cosily together remembering old times, and while they ate toasted muffins dripping with butter and raspberry jam, and Dena drank two full mugs of tea, she talked and Barry listened.

For the first time she felt able to express out loud her grief and misery over losing her brother, and the horror of seeing him drown in the canal. Even so, she was careful not to make any mention of the bullying and beating that had preceded the drowning. She'd buried that deep inside herself, a secret to keep forever. Dena wanted no repercussions, no bully-boys coming after her and Mam.

'I miss him so much, Barry.'

'Aye,' he said sadly. 'So do I. Right little star was your Pete. One of me best lads. Never a word of complaint, no matter what the weather he was there every Saturday morning, bright and sharp as a new pin, eager to get on with the job. Remember that time he dropped that box of apples and sent them rolling everywhere. Little tinker wasn't watching what he was doing. I'll swear he nicked one.'

'Our Pete didn't steal.'

Barry gave her an old-fashioned look, but said nothing. Dena had adored her younger brother, had seen no wrong in him. But then happen she had a point. 'He wasn't a bad lad, better than most anyway.'

'Mr George trusted him to mind his shop for him, if he wanted to nip out for a pint at dinner time.'

Barry nodded. 'And Mr George's baker's shop was never broken into as many others were, that's true.'

'He'd give our Pete a couple of Eccles cakes in payment.' As memories flooded back, Dena continued in a low voice, 'Mam used to go every Wednesday to buy us a big custard tart each. Our Pete loved custard tarts.'

'Aye, he always were a greedy little tyke!' Barry wiped away a stray tear. 'Here lass, sup up. I'll make us a fresh pot.'

And over a third cup Dena opened her heart further and told him how worried she was about her mother. 'She just seems to have collapsed in upon herself. Given up her job and never stirs a foot from her chair, not even to lift a duster, and you know how she loved cleaning her house. Mam always likes things just so and my efforts never seem to please her somehow. I don't know what to do for the best.'

'You need help, love, that's what. You can't possibly manage on your own, young lass like you.'

She felt better just for having talked, never mind the good meal he'd given her. It was as if she did have a friend after all, someone she could rely on to be there if she needed a shoulder to cry on.

'You can always come and have a natter with me anytime,' Barry told her as she prepared to leave. 'My door's always open for a friend. And put something on them bruises. They look proper nasty.'

So he had noticed after all. Life suddenly seemed much less bleak.

Chapter Four

Kenny slouched into the kitchen of his home, leaving the front door wide open behind him as he trod mud over the new red carpet with little blue and green dots and lines. A voice barked in loud disapproval. 'Were you born in a field? Shut that door.'

Ignoring his brother, half hidden behind the *Manchester Evening News*, Kenny made no move to obey but flung himself down on the green moquette sofa and propped his feet up on the Long Tom coffee table.

'Shut it yourself,' he muttered, his mouth taking on its accustomed expression of scorn as his brother heaved a furious sigh and kicked the door closed behind him. Carl was like an old mother hen at times, nag, nag, nag, just like his flaming mother.

As Carl returned to his seat, snatching up the paper he'd cast aside, he slapped Kenny's feet off the table as Belle was forever doing. His mother was always going on at him for what she termed his slovenly behaviour; for spitting or slouching, farting or belching. All perfectly normal activities in Kenny's view! Daft cow! Now she'd even got Carl doing it. He got up again and set off for the door.

'Where you going now?'

Kenny grunted. 'Out!'

'You've only just this minute come in.'

'Well now I'm flaming going out again, somewhere I'll get a better welcome than here in me own home.'

Carl lifted one large, booted foot, effectively blocking his exit. 'Not yet you're not, not till you've done your chores and had some tea. Mam'll be home in a minute.'

Kenny had never willingly done any chores in his entire life and had no intention of starting now. Besides, he'd left school now so Carl couldn't push him around any longer. He was a working man, at least he would be once he'd found himself a job. Nor would his mam care whether he had any tea or not. They were hardly the sort of family to go in for sitting round a table using knives and forks. A bag of chips would do him later. But he made no attempt to say any of this to Carl. Tension between the two brothers was ever high, one or the other of them likely to fly off the handle at the least provocation.

Carl had adopted this parental role years ago and Kenny hated him for having the extra couple of years, and the build, to exert that sort of power. With his dark good looks he was a favourite with the women. They seemed to like his foreign-looking olive skin and untidy black curls, even that big square jaw of his. And when he won all those prizes in the boxing ring, they fell over themselves to get noticed.

Carl could do no wrong in his mam's eyes, whereas Belle scarcely seemed to notice that her younger son even existed. And if she did, it was only to give him an ear bashing for some supposed fault. Kenny hated him for that too.

And just like their mam, Carl only ever saw the worst in him. Half expecting disaster to strike at any moment where Kenny was concerned; in his view was mean and sadistic. Picking a fight with his brother, however, did not appeal. With the physique of the talented amateur boxer he undoubtedly was, Kenny always thought twice before taking him on as an opponent at the best of times, and today Kenny had no wish to risk any bruises marring his good looks. He was hoping to spot Dena later, and she'd be sure to notice and make some sarcastic comment if she thought he'd been fighting.

Trying to impress Dena Dobson was far more difficult than he'd expected. More often than not she'd walk past him without even a glance in his direction, more than a little galling. But he meant to make her take notice of him, one way or another.

25

Blue eyes burning with resentment Kenny sat down again, managing to express his displeasure by leaving a smear of mud on the new fluffy green rug. Then realising his mam would thump him for messing it up, he tried to rub at the dirty mark with his heel.

'Leave off, you're making it worse,' Carl shouted. 'Why can't you just sit still and read the paper or listen to the wireless for five minutes without fidgeting or being a nuisance?' he said, and clipped him round the ear.

Kenny shot to his feet. 'Right, that's it! I've had enough of this.'

This time the booted foot rested against his stomach to shove him firmly back on to the sofa and hold him there. 'You'll sit till I say you can move. I was wanting a word.'

'I'm taking no orders from you.'

Carl smiled. It was not a pleasant sight. 'Aye, you are mate. Tomorrow I've fixed you an interview for a job so you'll get up early, wash behind your ears and try to pretend you're human, right?'

Kenny inwardly groaned. Carl had already sent him for half a dozen interviews, none of which had resulted in anything. 'What is it this time?'

'Up at the engineering works, and this time you'll show willing or I'll cut you up into little pieces and feed you to Sam Beckett's bulldog. Got that?' All said in a cheerful bantering tone but there was no denying Carl had a knack of reinforcing his power over Kenny.

Kenny allowed a few seconds to pass, as he wasn't intimidated. 'Right. Can I go now?'

Carl removed his foot. 'Where you off to, anyway?'

'Out with me mate, Chippy.'

'Doing what?'

'I dunno.'

'And where were you the other night, for instance?' Carl persisted, a quizzical expression in his dark blue eyes. 'You weren't at the club.'

'Where were you, more like?' Kenny yelled, and kicking his brother's feet to one side, marched out, this time slamming the door loudly behind him.

Kenny found Chippy, as he would expect, hanging around the empty market, digging amongst the rubbish bins in case something good had been thrown away by mistake. Chippy only had a dad, who kept forgetting to feed him. Hence his nickname. He lived largely on bags of chips from the shop on the corner, when he could find the brass to pay for them. But he was a cheerful soul and happy to go along with whatever Kenny told him to do.

Now the two lads took their bikes and rode the length of the canal towpath, first with no feet on the pedals, then with no feet and only one hand on the handlebars. Then with neither feet nor hands. By a miracle, neither of them skidded in the mud or fell into the cut, which made them feel very big and important.

After that, they broke into Barry Holmes's lock-up and helped themselves to a few apples and a couple of dirty pound notes from the cash box he kept tucked under a loose floorboard. To celebrate their own cleverness they rewarded themselves with a steak pudding and double portion of chips each.

–

The first thing Dena thought to do was to call the doctor. Like the old sergeant at the police station he was sympathetic to their plight, even if not particularly hopeful that he could do much to help. His first concern though, was for Dena.

'Good heavens, where did you get that shiner?'

Dena had no wish to tell the doctor either about the beating she and Pete had endured by the canal, nor about her mother belting her. She'd managed to hide the bruises she carried on her arms, legs and ribs, even from the police, and they'd readily accepted her brother's death as a tragic accident. But the black eye and bust lip her mother had given her was less easily explained. The sergeant had seen Alice do it, but had put it down to hysteria, not even enquiring if she'd ever hit her daughter before.

Dena judged it disloyal to her mam to tell the doctor the truth, so she claimed to have sustained the injury while searching for her brother in the canal. He looked sceptical, seemed about to ask more questions, but then changed his mind and accepted her story, giving her a pot of ointment for her split lip.

He talked to Alice for a few moments and gave her pills to help her to sleep, which Dena was instructed to count out every night to make sure she didn't take too many. Later he explained all about the new National Health Service, and had her mother fitted up with free spectacles and new false teeth, also free. Alice seemed to have taken a shine to the man and when he asked was there anything else he could get her, she suggested that National Health corsets might be a good idea.

'Now that I'm not as trim as I used to be.'

Dena was shocked to see that she even batted her eyelashes at him. Was Mam not so grief-stricken as she claimed?

The doctor tactfully pointed out that this wasn't a particularly good reason, and how the special corsets were generally handed out to people with ruptures and similar problems, just as they gave out smog masks to those with bad lungs, and wigs to people who'd lost all their hair.

'That would be a good idea,' said Alice. 'I wouldn't mind a wig. It would save me the expense of a perm every few months.'

'Mam, don't say such dreadful things!' Dena felt herself blushing with embarrassment at her mother's impudence. Had she lost her mind through all of this tragedy?

The doctor winked at Dena. 'I'm glad to see a return of your old sense of humour Mrs Dobson, and your sarcasm is well justified. Glasses and spectacles, wigs and corsets are all very well but I realise they do little to improve your financial situation. I appreciate that as you're far too proud to ask for help unless you really need it. I have trouble sometimes persuading many of my patients to ask for bread to put in their mouths. Even so I would encourage you to pursue the matter. You may well be entitled to some assistance and deserve whatever is due to you.'

'Oh, I have my pride, make no mistake about that,' said Alice sharply. 'What I'm saying is I don't want no daft handouts of any sort, only what's right and proper.'

'Everybody seems to be struggling these days. Still trying to rebuild their lives and homes after the war. It's proving to be very difficult for some. But with a new young Queen on the throne we hope for better times in future, eh? They say they're going to show the coronation on the television. Will you be able to watch it, do you think, Mrs Dobson?'

'We can't afford no television,' said Alice, in the kind of tone she might use if he'd asked if she intended to fly to the moon.

'Mam isn't fit to work just yet and I'm still at school,' Dena hastily butted in before Alice caused any further offence with that biting tongue of hers. 'The neighbours do what they can to help but it's nowhere near enough. I've been thinking that I'd best leave school early and get a job. We desperately need more money coming in.'

The doctor frowned. 'How old are you, Dena?'

'Thirteen.'

'Good Lord, you're far too young to leave school. Education is important. You need to make something of yourself, bright girl like you.'

'I'll be fourteen in a month or two.'

'Even so, you're far too young.'

What she didn't tell him was that for much of the time she was also far too hungry, because whenever they were short she was the one to go without. If it weren't for handouts from the neighbours and the vegetables she got from Barry, they'd surely starve.

Again the doctor assured Dena that her mother could well be entitled to sick benefit in this New Jerusalem currently being built by the Beveridge committee, and she agreed to ask if this was true.

Dena would have remained invisible and avoided any awkward questions from the authorities, but she dutifully presented herself at the council offices the very next morning. A snooty official looked down his nose at her before instantly ordering her off the premises. She bravely stood her ground, tried to politely inform him that her mother was ill and couldn't work, so could they please have some money to tide them over till she was well again. When the man physically ejected her from the building, threatening to call the police, Dena realised that the New Jerusalem hadn't arrived yet, not in Manchester anyway.

Chapter Five

Champion Street Market was crowded, as always on a Saturday. Stalls lined the pavement from Tonman Street to Deansgate, some little more than trestle tables piled high with goods to be picked over by bargain hunters and browsers alike. There was the pot man juggling his plates, letting one fall every now and then, just to get people's attention, before beating down his own prices and selling dozens in a mock auction.

'Look at the beautiful pattern on this tea set, every bit as pretty as your Auntie Nellie's garters. I'm not asking ten shillings – I'm not asking five shillings, or four or three shillings. Who will give me half a crown?'

He'd gathered a crowd this morning, many just for the entertainment.

On the corner sat old Mr Lee who'd been wounded in the First World War, and was still selling his matches as he had done every Saturday this last thirty-odd years. He was well loved and the place wouldn't have been the same without him.

Old men in flat caps and mufflers stood in a huddle by the ancient horse trough smoking their pipes, discussing the odds on the three-thirty or whether City would get in the cup this year. Harassed mothers kept a tight hold of their children's hands in case they should wander off and get lost in the crowds. A normal market day just like any other.

Except for Dena Dobson. Dena didn't think that life could ever be normal again, not for her at any rate. She should have been in the cafe by nine as usual, ready to serve breakfast to hungry stallholders. Instead she was sitting in a waiting room that smelled

31

of cat pee and unwashed bodies, determined to get some help for her mam.

The last thing Dena needed was to put her job at risk, but, unable to visit the council offices during the week now that she was back at school, Saturday morning had been the only appointment she could get.

She'd nearly given up when that po-faced official had thrown her out, much preferring not to draw attention to herself or to risk giving any clue as to what had really happened to her brother. But then she'd remembered something: Pete had come home from school one day with bruises on his face and knuckles. It had happened again a week or two later, and sometimes he winced when she scrubbed his knees or his neck. He'd insisted nothing was wrong but Dena was almost certain he was being bullied just before he'd died, although he wouldn't say one way or the other.

Yet he'd shown such courage, even when they were beating him to death down by the canal. Dena felt duty-bound to be equally brave, so that if Pete was watching her from heaven, he'd be proud of her.

Like it or not, she had to try again.

She needed help with the rent and rates, sick pay for Mam, or else unemployment benefit. Dena had no real idea, which if any of these would apply to them, but they definitely needed some sort of allowance to tide them over and enable her to stay on at school, and she was determined to get whatever was their due.

But underneath her bravado she was scared, and desperately anxious not to lose her Saturday job while she fought for these so-called rights of theirs.

Belle might give the impression of being full of good cheer and not one for taking life too seriously but beneath that easy-going, life-is-all-about-having-a-good-time attitude, beat a heart of pure steel. Her affection and tolerance stretched only so far as her own needs and material comforts, and those of her two sons, were concerned. These came first and last and Belle Garside would bend any rules in order to maintain this creed and her comfortable life-style.

So if her young waitress turned up late for work yet again, even if it was because of waiting in a queue at the council offices, family tragedy or no, Belle would view it as a waste of her valuable time. Time to be paying good money. She could easily take it into her head to sack her, which would be a disaster. They'd starve for sure then.

–

Dena sat in the waiting room for what seemed like hours worrying about all of this before finally being called into a tiny, windowless room, the walls painted a bilious green.

A sour-faced woman with whiskers on her chin and the shadow of a moustache above her upper lip sat opposite, and for several minutes she scrutinised Dena from head to toe through narrowed eyes while establishing her name and address. Only then did she indicate that Dena might sit on a hard wooden chair.

Her next question came like a bark of gunfire. 'Where did you get those bruises?'

Dena gave her the same story she'd told the doctor, all about trying to save her brother. The woman looked equally sceptical, a pair of dark bushy eyebrows, liberally speckled with grey, coming together in a disbelieving scowl. 'So, why can't your mother work?'

'Because she's ill.'

'What's wrong with her?'

Dena again explained. The woman's response was not one of sympathy or understanding but simply another sharp query as to why, in that case, Dena herself couldn't get a job.

'I'm only thirteen and still at school.'

The woman frowned even more. 'I expect your headmaster would agree to your leaving early, once you turn fourteen. I could give you a letter to say you need to be released as you are your family's sole means of support.'

For some reason she seemed to imagine this would solve everything.

33

'I'd really prefer to stay on and finish my education. Our doctor thinks that's important.'

The whiskers seemed to bristle as the mouth twisted into a thin-lipped smile. 'Education is wasted on girls. You'll get married and be having babies in no time, then your husband can keep you.'

Dena felt sick at this bleak prediction for her future. 'Even if I did leave school this summer, we still have to eat in the meantime, and pay the rent and, like I say, Mam's pension isn't enough to keep us.'

'Has your mother ever paid an insurance stamp?'

Dena didn't know but very much doubted it. 'She's only ever worked part-time, so happen not.'

'In that case she is not entitled to sick pay. She will just have to pull herself together, find a job, and pay into the scheme before she can benefit from it. It's all very new, you know, and there's only so much money in the pot to go around. I suggest you find a cheaper place to live, if you can't afford the one you're in.'

'I don't think they come much cheaper,' Dena said, 'not unless we move in with the rats in the sewers.' This last sharp retort gained her nothing at all, and she quickly found herself once more out in the street, this time with a fistful of indecipherable forms in her hand, feeling utterly helpless and as if she'd been defiled in some way. Even as the woman had thrust the papers at her, she'd bluntly stated that Dena could fill them in, if she was able, but not to hold out any great hope of getting any money out of anyone.

'You aren't the only family to have lost loved ones in recent years. Grit your teeth and bear it, girl, like the rest of us.'

It had been a complete waste of time; yet another fruitless effort.

Now she was late for work, and losing her Saturday job would be just about the last straw. As Dena hurried between the stalls, pushing her way through the crush of people, she could hear the market hall clock chiming ten and her heart sank.

–

First thing Monday morning before even she'd eaten her breakfast the woman was at the door. The heavy, authoritative knock warned of her presence and a peep through Mam's clean lace curtains confirmed her worst fear. Dena groaned. She should have realised that calling in the social was a bad mistake.

'It's that woman from the council offices. She must be here to check up on us.'

'Don't let her in,' Alice warned. 'I don't want no officials snooping round my house.'

'I can't leave her standing on the doorstep making that racket, Mam. All the neighbours will hear. If we don't let her in, Mrs Emmett will for sure.'

Dena took a deep breath and went to open the door, her heart in her boots.

Good manners made it necessary to offer the woman a cup of tea, and Miss Rogers, as she introduced herself, complained about the lack of milk. Dena said nothing. Alice sharply retorted, 'If we could afford milk every day we wouldn't be in this pickle.'

'It's about your situation, that I have called.' She looked closely at Dena. 'How are your bruises? Mending, are they?'

Dena managed a small nod, not even glancing at her mother.

The thin lips beneath the faint shadow of a moustache pursed disapprovingly. 'How do you think she came by that black eye, Mrs Dobson?'

'How would I know? The girl's always up to mischief but on this occasion I reckon it might have had something to do with trying to save her drowning brother.' And Alice went on quietly sipping her tea and chewing on her toast.

Dena, who had been holding her breath without knowing it, let it out in a rush. At least Mam had come up with the same tale, albeit by chance.

Miss Rogers returned her scrutiny to Dena. 'So that we don't disturb your mother while she is enjoying her breakfast, you could show me around.'

Dena looked startled. 'Oh, all right. If that's what you want.'

'I do.'

It didn't take long. There wasn't much to see. Just the one room downstairs where they lived and ate, and one upstairs where they slept. The double bed was made, a clippy rug beside it, the curtains drawn back to let in what little sunshine could be found on a grey winter's day in Barber's Court, and the place neat as a pin, exactly as Alice liked it. Strangely, this seemed to surprise Miss Rogers.

'My word, how very tidy! I can see nothing lying about and the room is really commendably clean.' She ran her finger along the shiny surface of the chest of drawers then lifted a corner of the counterpane to examine the cotton sheets and crochet-trimmed pillow slips. 'Extraordinary!'

Dena bridled. 'Mam doesn't see any excuse for muck and mess just because a person is poor. Soap is cheap, she says.'

'Indeed!' Miss Rogers gave Dena a considering look. 'And there seem to be one or two remarkably fine pieces of furniture in here. That mahogany wardrobe, for instance, and this chest of drawers with the claw feet. They would bring a good price if you were to sell them.'

Dena became alarmed. 'Mam wouldn't hear of it. She's had this furniture since she first got married. They're all the possessions she has in the world. Anyway it would be daft to sell them. What good would that do? We'd have nowhere to put our clothes and the money wouldn't last long, and what then?'

'You seem to be very opinionated, for such a young girl.'

Since Dena hadn't the first idea what she meant by this comment she remained silent, but she was breathing hard, still annoyed and instinctively defensive of the woman's superior attitude.

'I shall call again and hope to see that bruise of yours gone next time. You'll also have found a solution to your current difficulties, your mother back at work, and on the up and up again.'

'She's not fit to work. She hasn't even set foot outside the house yet, not since our Pete... Are you going to let us have some money?' Dena dared to ask.

The woman blinked. 'Dear me, I thought I'd explained all of that. I shall have to keep a close eye on you. One child drowned and the other bruised does not strike me as the mark of a stable home. I shall need to monitor the situation most carefully, make no mistake.'

It sounded very like a threat.

Alice glanced up as they entered the kitchen, a sarcastic sneer on her flushed face. 'Had a good nose round, have you?'

'Thank you, I've seen all I need to.'

Dena showed Miss Rogers to the door then ate her breakfast in silence, ignoring Alice's complaints and questions for once. After that she quickly cleared away and washed up before dashing off to school. But she was troubled by the visit, and by the woman's comments. Her attitude was worrying. Something wasn't right.

Chapter Six

'Have you taken table five's order?' Belle barked, making Dena jump. 'Since you've at least deigned to show up on time this Saturday, you could stop daydreaming and put a bit more effort into your work, girl.'

Dena quickly apologised, bit her lip and dashed off to do her employer's bidding, leaving Belle with a guilty sense of unease.

She did feel sorry for the lass, losing her brother in that terrible accident. Something fishy about that though, in Belle's opinion. The papers had said the boy was a mess when they'd dragged him out, with broken bones and badly decomposed, but the police put the state of the body down to the length of time it had taken them to find it and were not treating the death as suspicious. Belle wasn't convinced so she really shouldn't be too hard on the lass.

'I dare say you're still grieving for your Pete,' she said, the minute Dena returned to the kitchen. 'You must miss him.'

The girl's eyes instantly filled with tears. 'Oh, I do. It's terrible!'

'And your mam not coping too well then?'

Dena shook her head, unable to speak.

Dena herself had likewise been a mass of bruises. Belle had been aware from that first week that she was covering something up because she'd winced whenever a heavy tray pressed on her arm, and she would nurse her ribs whenever she thought no one was looking. Had something occurred on that towpath to cause the boy to fall?

Belle considered asking Carl, or Kenny, to see if they knew anything about this supposed accident but then had taken the view she always took with her sons: the less she knew about their personal affairs, the better.

Belle was no saint herself and always had a few fingers in various pies, which might make her a bob or two. She had her own set of standards that very much put her own needs to the fore. Consequently she judged it wise not to enquire too closely into the rules her boys set for themselves.

They were a close family and she knew how much they loved and protected her. At least, Carl did. Kenny was far too fond of himself to properly understand what caring meant. For this reason, and others of a more personal nature, Belle had never warmed to her younger son as she did to Carl. But that didn't greatly trouble her. Such was life.

The cafe got busier as the morning wore on, customers and stallholders alike popping in for a hot drink or a bite of dinner. Dena waited on them all with a smile, doing her utmost not to be distracted by her troubles.

She felt fortunate to have found Belle in such a benevolent frame of mind when she'd finally got to work last week after speaking to the woman at the social, probably due to the fact that the market superintendent was having his morning coffee at the time.

Belle always liked to promote a good impression of herself when Joe Southworth was around and had accepted Dena's apologies with surprisingly good grace, together with a stern warning not to let it happen again, naturally.

But it didn't pay to take advantage, or to look as if she was neglecting her duties.

Dena set a plate of steaming Lancashire hotpot before a harassed young woman. She didn't seem old enough to be the mother of the young boy beside her, around four or five years of age and happily tossing spoonfuls of mashed potato and bits of chewed sausage on to the floor.

The woman gave his hand a little smack and told him off for being a naughty boy. Dena thought he might wail or cry over the scolding but he looked up at his mum, all big-eyed and smiley and put his hand to his mouth. 'Oops! That means no ice cream now, I suppose.'

The young mother laughed and even Dena stifled a giggle as she hurried back into the kitchen. The boy reminded her so much of Pete at the same age, always into mischief, always testing Mam's patience to the limit. A great lump came into her throat and she instantly wanted to cry. But she refused to allow herself to be sad. The naughty little boy had recalled happy times, of which there'd been plenty once, and that was surely the best way to remember her brother.

'Two pie and peas and one tomato soup for table four,' she told Mrs Garside, and while she waited for this to be served Dena let her mind drift back.

She remembered Mam bathing them both by the fire in the big tin bath, toasting slices of bread on the long toasting fork for supper and then reading them stories while they ate it smothered in dripping, and drank their hot cocoa. They could afford milk in those days.

Alice would read from *Treasure Island* or the *Just William* books to please Pete. All of the *What Katy Did* books and *Little Women* for Dena. And sometimes from her own favourites such as Arnold Bennett or J. B. Priestley. If she came to a romantic scene there would be a long pause and she'd claim that it was a boring bit, quickly turn the page and hurry on to the next exciting part of the story. Her mam was ever the puritan, even in her younger days.

But she'd still had her hopes and dreams then, patience and love for her children, happily waiting for her husband to come home from the war. If she'd smacked them it hadn't been out of temper but because they'd been naughty and deserved it.

But the last few years had seen a change in her. Her grief and disappointment in life had brought out all her worst faults, and she'd turned more and more to the little nips of gin and orange she allowed herself at the end of each day, until she couldn't afford even this little treat.

Dena and her mother had never enjoyed an easy relationship. She somehow didn't come up to her mother's high ideals and

Alice had ever been one to criticise her daughter and point out her mistakes, an attitude that had worsened as she'd grown more lonely and depressed, as her bitterness against life deepened.

Losing Pete was one blow too many. Dena didn't know how to talk to her now. Mam seemed lost inside herself, and the sick feeling Dena carried deep within warned her that the entry of Miss Rogers into their lives was not going to help one little bit.

There'd been menace in the woman's tone when she'd promised to return to 'monitor' their situation, whatever that might mean, and Dena feared the worst. She'd worried about it all week and was now deeply afraid, jumping at every knock on the door, even when it could only be the doctor. Folks round here generally just barged in calling, 'It's only me', so a knock on the door always heralded trouble.

But this woman, poking her nose in where it wasn't wanted, was like a dog with its teeth in a rat. She just wouldn't let go and might well start asking too many questions about what exactly had happened that day down by the canal. As it was, Dena was constantly glancing over her shoulder wherever she went, fearful of being followed, worried that whoever had committed that terrible crime might strike again. And she'd vowed never to venture along the towpath ever again. If this Miss Rogers started stirring up yet more trouble for them, who knew what might happen?

They should have remained invisible after all.

'Dena, you're daydreaming again!' Belle Garside thrust two plates at her and Dena snapped to attention. This wouldn't do at all. She really must pay attention and think about her problems later. She had work to do.

—

At closing time when her employer was putting up the shutters, Dena took her courage in both hands and carefully cleared her throat before making her request. She'd done a great deal of thinking and had come to a decision. Even so her voice sounded squeaky and breathless, the words coming out all in a rush.

'Mrs Garside, I wonder if I could have a word. Mam's not too good at the moment, as you know, and we could do with a bit more money coming in. I wondered if I could work the odd hour after school. We finish at four and I could be here by ten past if I ran all the way.'

Belle Garside cast the girl a sideways glance but didn't rush to answer, considering her query in silence while she rolled down the shutters. It troubled her that Kenny was so smitten when really he could do better, look higher. She was nice enough was the lass, and showed signs of having a brain under that glorious tumble of shiny chestnut curls. And she brought in the punters, as Belle herself used to do once upon a time.

Those were the days, Belle thought with a touch of nostalgia, when chaps would be queuing up for her favours instead of her bacon butties. But her own once voluptuous shape was suffering from too many of Joan's excellent meat and potato pies, and her violet-eyed charm was losing some of its compulsion. She still had her moments, although was more obliged to use other methods to maintain her status in the market these days.

'How old are you now?'

'Fourteen,' Dena lied, crossing her fingers behind her back.

Fourteen and as pretty as a picture. Another two years and she'd be dynamite. Takings always improved on the days Dena was working, during school holidays for instance. Belle could surely control Kenny, and make certain he didn't get too involved. No doubt it was nothing more than a passing fancy and he'd be after some other bit of skirt next week. He'd never stuck with anything for more than five minutes in his entire life had Kenny.

But Belle was playing for higher stakes these days: for power. The market superintendent had a daughter: nice, quiet girl, very biddable, and a link between their two families would be no bad thing, no bad thing at all. It would put her in a very strong position indeed. Dena Dobson might be blessed in the looks' department but she had neither money nor power, both were essential ingredients in Belle's future plans.

She locked the shutters, slipped the keys into her coat pocket and prepared to depart.

'I'd love to help, chuck, but I'm closed by five during the week, sometimes earlier if it's quiet, so what you're offering is no good to me. Why don't you leave school, then you could work full-time? Can't say fairer than that.'

Dena's hopes crashed and she could feel her cheeks start to burn as she confessed the truth. 'I'm sorry Mrs Garside, I'm telling you a fib. I'm really only thirteen, although I will be fourteen in a few weeks at the end of March. I could happen leave school early in the summer, but only if I get a special letter from the social.' It would all be so much easier if she were older.

Belle shrugged, already bored by the discussion. 'Come and see me then, love, after you've left. In the meantime you can carry on with your Saturday job but just remember, you turn up at nine on the dot, not when you feel like it.'

'No, Mrs Garside. I mean, yes Mrs Garside.'

–

Despair hung over Dena like a great grey cloud. It was only escaping to the market every Saturday that kept her cheerful. She loved the sights and sounds of the place, the people popping in and out of the cafe, always with a joke or a witty comment on their lips to lift her spirits.

'What's up, lass?' they'd say if she was looking glum. 'Lost a shilling and found 'apenny? Come on me little sugar butty, give us a smile.' And Dena would find herself laughing, despite the worries heaped on her young shoulders.

But she really didn't have anything much to laugh about. How on earth were they going to manage with not enough money coming in? All her mother's savings had long since been used up and they were now living on tick, a sum that was growing daily at the corner shop on Barber's Court, and how they could ever hope to pay it back Dena couldn't begin to imagine.

She earned only a few shillings at the cafe but sometimes did well with tips. These she was expected to put in a jar to share with Joan and the washer-up in the kitchen. But Mrs Garside also took a share, which Dena didn't think was right at all. She was the proprietor and therefore had already taken her profit from the price of the meal.

In view of her financial difficulties, Joan had suggested a new arrangement whereby if Dena came by an extra-large tip, she wouldn't put that in the jar but quietly share it out later among the kitchen staff.

'Why should Belle benefit from all your smiles?' Joan said, giving the girl an affectionate hug of sympathy. 'And we need it more than she does.'

So when the following Saturday a commercial traveller gave Dena half a crown, she thanked him with a radiant smile, half glanced at the jar set on a table just inside the kitchen door but making no move towards it, slipped the coin quickly into her pocket. She might earn another shilling or two before the day was out, and this would feed them for two days if she was careful, even after she'd shared it with Joan and the washer-up. Dena gave her pocket a little pat of satisfaction.

On her way back into the kitchen carrying a tray of dirty dishes, Carl Garside stepped out in front of her and she realised with a jolt that he had been standing watching her. He must have seen everything. Dena felt her cheeks flush warm with guilt.

But then he often had this effect upon her at the best of times, the way he would hover around watching her, saying little, as if he didn't trust her. And now, sadly, she'd given him proof.

'Got an eye full, have you?' she challenged him, deciding attack was the best method of defence.

'You could say that. What was it you put in your pocket just now?'

Carl Garside was taller than his younger brother, broad-shouldered and with powerful muscles, presumably from all the

44

lifting he did in his job delivering fresh produce to the various Manchester markets. She often saw him bullying Kenny, shoving him around, barking out orders or complaining about something or other that he'd done, or failed to do. She felt sorry for Kenny at times.

But Carl was undoubtedly the better looking of the two, disturbingly so, having an Italian look about him with that smooth Mediterranean olive skin and black, curly hair. He might even have been called handsome, were it not for the insolent twist of his mouth, the flared nostrils, and the fact that his dark blue eyes would so often glare unnervingly at her. As they were doing now.

'It was only my hand, what else would it be?'

'You had something in it, I clearly saw that.'

Guilt made her cheeks fire up all the more but Dena stuck her head in the air and sailed right on past. She'd faced up to bullies before, and had no intention of allowing this one the satisfaction of an explanation.

Chapter Seven

The tall, angular figure of Miss Rogers turned up on their door-step one Sunday in late February when they were least expecting her. It was still bitterly cold with rain and snow sleeting against the windows. Dena quickly closed the door after the social worker to keep out the wind and prevent a puddle from forming on the clean lino.

'I wasn't sure if I'd catch you in. Thought you might be at chapel, or visiting family for your Sunday dinner?'

Dena shook her head and went on with dishing out a warming stew for her mother. It comprised largely of potatoes, carrots and barley with the odd scrap of bacon that Mr Ramsay the butcher had given her to add a bit of flavour. There wasn't really enough for two servings, it being left over from the night before.

Not that it mattered. Strangely, Dena seemed to be losing her appetite although Mam's had not been diminished by her grief, very much the reverse. Sitting about the house all day seemed to provide ample time for her to think about food, and she would enquire when tea would be ready the minute Dena stepped over the threshold.

She'd managed to eat most of the bacon hotpot Dena had made for them last night, not that Dena minded as she herself always got a good dinner every Saturday at the cafe. She looked forward to it all week and yesterday's meal had been excellent: one of Joan's best minced beef pies with a great dollop of mash and buttered carrots. She could still savour the taste of the rich gravy.

Dena now served her mother the largest portion, as usual, then set a plate over the pan to keep the remainder warm while she poured Miss Rogers a cup of milkless tea.

'Still monitoring?' Alice tartly enquired before spooning hot potato into her mouth.

The woman looked at the brown tea, and Alice, with distaste. 'I certainly am.'

'Our Pete was a monitor once but that involved handing out ink pots, not poking his nose into other folk's business. But then he had manners, our Pete, not like some folk I could mention.'

'I'm sorry if my presence disturbs you Mrs Dobson, but I'm concerned about your daughter. It surprises me that you aren't equally worried. Look at her, all skin and bone. Have you so much as got off your backside and cooked a meal for her since I was last here?'

Alice flushed a deep crimson, then slammed her spoon down upon the table. 'Get out! I'll not sit here and be insulted in my own home.'

'Ah, but it isn't your home, is it?' Miss Rogers very reasonably pointed out. 'You only rent it, and although that sum is covered by your late husband's service pension, you would surely starve if it weren't for your daughter. I suspect though that she is half starved and I really don't think that I can allow this situation to go on for very much longer.'

Alice glared across at Dena and opened her mouth as if about to accuse her of bringing this trouble to her door but then closed it again, thinking better of it. 'We manage to get by, as we must, since this fancy new welfare state isn't interested in helping working-class folk like us.'

Miss Rogers was unmoved by the waspish remark. 'You could always go to the labour exchange. I'm sure they would help to find you employment, Mrs Dobson. There are still factories taking on operatives at the moment, though admittedly not too many of them are women. Did you do any factory work during the war? Have you training of any sort?'

Alice glared at the woman. 'I had my children to look after. I worked as a shop assistant, part-time, in some of the better class establishments. But I'll have you know that I've never sunk to working in a dirty mill or factory in my life, and never will. I'm not just some bit of muck carried in on a pair of clogs. I have my standards. My father was a bank clerk, and my mother...'

'Indeed?' Miss Rogers interrupted, perking up. 'And what do they have to say about all of this? Are they willing to help? Would they take Dena for a while till you got back on your feet?'

Alice shifted her gaze and picking up her spoon gave a loud sniff of disdain. 'I haven't asked them. I have my pride.'

Dena hastily butted in. 'We're not sure where they live any more. We haven't heard from them in a long time, d'you see?'

'Yes, I do see.' Miss Rogers thoughtfully replied. She saw a great deal, had years of experience dealing with the misery families heaped upon themselves. She got to her feet. 'I'll leave you to your meal and to think over what I have said but I give you fair warning, Mrs Dobson, that if there is no improvement by the end of the month, I shall have no alternative but to relieve you of your responsibilities.'

'Isn't that what we've been asking for?'

'I mean,' Miss Rogers enunciated carefully, 'that I will be compelled to take Dena into care.'

Dena jerked in terror and looked across at her mother, expecting her to jump to her feet, to spring to life at last and angrily protest that she couldn't possibly bear to be parted from her daughter, not for the world. But she only turned her face away with a dismissive snort and muttered something under her breath.

'What did you say, Mrs Dobson? I didn't catch that?'

'I said do as you please. Damned if I care.'

Dena was shocked to the core. She could hardly believe her own ears. Her mother never swore. Not once in all her life had she ever heard blasphemy come from those lips. Criticisms, complaints, endless moans and groans, but never a single blasphemy. Mam had always claimed she would sooner die than use foul language. This fall from grace only proved how very much she hated her, how she blamed Dena entirely for her son's death. She didn't even care if she was taken away; didn't care what happened to her.

Faced with the evidence of this woman's deeply held resentment towards her own daughter, Miss Rogers was likewise stunned into silence. It had its roots in the loss of the son, if her instincts were correct, and they generally were where family relationships were concerned. She was blaming the girl entirely for the tragedy, but it wasn't, in her opinion, any fault of the daughter's at all.

Turning to Dena, Miss Rogers quietly handed her a card. 'If you should need me, give me a ring. You do know how to use a telephone, I suppose?'

''Course I do!' Even in the depths of her misery Dena felt slightly insulted that the woman should think her so dim she couldn't carry out such a simple task, yet she could find no words to defend herself. She felt too stunned, too startled and dismayed by her mother's reaction. Dena put the card safely in the dresser drawer and instantly forgot all about it.

When Miss Rogers had gone and Dena had quickly shut fast the door against the bad weather, Alice grabbed her by the arm and yanked her about to face her.

'Now Madam, what've you been saying to her? Spinning some yarn about how cruel your mam is to you, is that it?'

Dena's eyes grew round with shock. 'No! How can you even think such a thing? 'Course I haven't. I don't want her poking her nose in any more than you do.'

'I don't believe a word you say. How can I ever trust you again after what you did to my darling boy? Get off to bed with you. No, leave your supper where it is. You don't deserve any tonight. That'll learn you for mouthing off about your own mother. Go on, get off with you, afore you feel the back of my hand.'

Dena went. She ran upstairs and flung herself down on the bed in a flurry of tears. Oh, what a mess! What on earth would happen now?

Life did not improve in the coming weeks. Despite Miss Roger's threats, Alice made no effort to find a job and return to work, nor even to get off her backside and make a cup of tea once in a while for her hard-working daughter.

Most days she sat at home bemoaning her lot, complaining that they didn't have enough food in the house, that they were running out of coal and she was cold, which wasn't surprising considering how much she used each day. Dena was driven to picking over the spoil-heaps like some sort of street urchin to keep her mother's fire blazing.

She had hoped to persuade Alice to pick up her life again, to follow her dream of finding full-time work in Kendals, but she no longer seemed interested in anything.

'What does it matter? I've nothing to live for now,' she would say, whenever Dena suggested it.

'We need the money, Mam, if nothing else. Anyway, it'd do you good to get out of the house for a bit each day and meet new people.'

'Unfeeling hussy! You think I can bury my beloved son and then carry on as if nothing has happened? You might be able to manage that, after what you did to him, but I have finer feelings!'

Then there was the fact that her own family had disowned her. This hadn't bothered Alice for years, now she never stopped going on about how cruel they'd been to her; how uncaring and unfeeling everyone was; that no one could possibly understand the depth of her agony.

'Not so much as a card, or a tear shed for him, their own grandson, never mind a polite enquiry about how I'm coping with this terrible grief.' And yet again she would be overcome by a paroxysm of crying.

Day after day Alice wept for her lost child. Once the period of shock had passed, the tears had started and never properly stopped. The slightest remark would set her off and Dena would rush to put her arms about her mother and try to offer comfort.

'You've got me, Mam. I'm still here.'

'You can leave me alone!' Alice shouted, her voice rising to near hysteria. 'You do nothing but remind me of my loss. If it weren't for you we'd never be in this mess.'

'Mam, don't say such a dreadful thing. It's not true. I tried to save him, I really did.'

Dena put her hands over her eyes as a painful image flashed across her mind. These visions could come to her at any time, day or night, her brain constantly replaying the scene as if from an old black and white film.

Sometimes the picture would vary or she'd almost catch a glimpse of someone, but then it would vanish before she'd grasped it. If only she could get a clear view of their attackers, identify one of them. Surely that would help? But all she could recall was a pair of dark eyes glaring at her from out of a balaclava.

But she mentioned none of this to her mother. How could she? Dena felt helpless in the presence of such profound grief.

—

On her way home one evening Dena stopped off for a mug of tea with Barry, welcoming an opportunity to pour out some of her troubles to a sympathetic listener. She told him about the half crown tip, and how Carl had seen her pocket it.

'He must think I was stealing. What should I do? Ought I to say something?'

'Nay, best to say nothing.'

'I've never dared do it again, and Joan says I'm daft not to. She thinks we deserve better pay anyway. And it's true Belle is mean. Half our wages are supposed to come from the tips, but she takes a cut of them too.'

'I didn't realise things were that bad for you.' Barry at once offered to lend her ten shillings but Dena refused. 'I'll not take charity from me friends. It's the government who should help us, and the navy should pay Mam proper whack, considering they lost me dad in the first place.'

'I won't argue with that one, cherub, but at least take a bag of veg home with you. I'd only be chucking 'em out anyway, as they're past their best, to be honest.'

'Oh, Barry, what would I do without you?'

–

Carl wasn't the only one watching her. Kenny couldn't take his eyes off her. She was so lovely he meant to have her, no matter what it took to get her. He'd seen how Dena mourned for her brother and felt a small nudge of sympathy for her loss, nevertheless he decided it was time to make his move. One evening as Belle pulled down the shutters, he ran a comb through his slicked back Brylcreemed hair, smoothed down the new jacket he'd bought to impress her, and offered to walk her home.

'Thanks, but I'm all right on me own,' she protested.

''Course you are, but you wouldn't object to a bit of company, I hope. You've worked hard today and must be worn out.'

He was so friendly and sympathetic there seemed no harm in accepting his offer. It started to rain and they had to run, drenched to the skin and laughing, to the old bus shelter where they stood for what seemed like hours, chatting happily together about nothing in particular. It wasn't even as if she was waiting for a bus. It was just somewhere to be out of the rain.

Kenny asked how she was coping and if her mother was getting over the tragedy, which irritated Dena a bit as she hated to keep being reminded of it. When she didn't answer he started talking about the cafe, asking if she enjoyed working for his mam, teasing her about how custom dropped off whenever she wasn't there.

Dena relaxed and forgot the time as they started to chat like old friends. But then in a panic she remembered her mam's tea and made a dash for home, Kenny's voice calling after her that he'd see her next week.

The following Saturday he seemed to appear out of nowhere and fell into step beside her as if it were perfectly natural for them to be together. It felt right, and Kenny was fun to be with, entertaining, exciting and easy to talk to. He didn't make her feel uncomfortable, as Carl did.

This time they chatted about the coming celebrations for the coronation, the latest Frankie Lane record and he asked if she'd seen the new film, *High Noon*, which Dena hadn't.

'I'll take you. When would you like to go? Thursday? Friday?'

'It's my birthday next Friday,' Dena said, surprising herself by blurting out this information. 'I'll be fourteen.' She wished she could be older, more sophisticated. Kenny would surely see her as merely a child but his next words disproved that.

'Friday it is then.'

'I haven't said I'll go with you yet.'

'No, but you will,' he said with supreme confidence. 'Why would you refuse? There are dozens of girls begging me to take them to the flicks,' he bragged, flicking back his fair hair.

Dena laughed. 'Then why ask me?'

'Because you're the prettiest, and best girl I know.'

She flushed bright pink. 'All right, I'll come.' Dena didn't know how she'd manage it, but it would be wonderful to escape the house for the evening, and her mother's moans. It was her birthday after all.

–

'Where've you been?' Belle asked the moment Kenny arrived back.

'Out.'

'Up to no good with Chippy and your other namby-pamby friends no doubt.'

Kenny puffed out his chest. 'I was with Dena, as a matter of fact.'

Belle laughed. 'You're wasting your time with that one, lad. She wouldn't look twice at a Mary Ann like you. And what would you do with her, if you caught her?' Flicking the ash from her cigarette on to his shiny shoes, Belle strolled away, laughing delightedly at her own joke.

Glowering, Kenny muttered to himself under his breath. Belle had treated him with this sort of casual contempt for as long as he could remember. Carl she saw as big and tough, a strong man who was going places in the world, while Kenny she belittled at every opportunity, calling him weak, fickle and unreliable, and frequently pointing out his uselessness with girls.

Much as Kenny hated his mother yet he longed to please her, to prove to her his worth. Trouble is, he didn't know how. 'I'll show you I'm no Mary Ann. I'll bloody show you,' he shouted, which only made her laugh all the more.

Chapter Eight

When Friday came round it seemed just like any other day and not her birthday at all. Dena made breakfast as usual, taking porridge and a mug of tea upstairs to her mother in bed, as she said it was too cold in the kitchen yet for her to get up.

Deep inside Dena carried her exciting secret. She hadn't dared to ask yet if she could go to the pictures with Kenny Garside, scared that Mam might say no. Was this the moment? she wondered.

Alice didn't even open her eyes as Dena set the tray by the bed. Later would be a better time, when she was up and dressed.

After Dena had cleared away and washed the dishes, banked up the fire and filled the coal bucket, worrying about the low stock of coal left in the bunker out in the yard, she put on her coat and called upstairs that she was off to school now.

'Is there anything you want before I go?'

Alice did not reply. Dena decided that her mother must have gone back to sleep so there was little point in going up. She'd talk to her this evening about Kenny. As Dena walked to school, she thought that her mother might have a surprise for her at teatime. She can't have forgotten that it's my birthday. She might have slipped out to the corner shop to buy something without telling me.

Once upon a time her mother had used to bake a cake and put candles on the top. They'd sing Happy Birthday and Dena would blow them all out with one breath and make a wish. That had been a long time ago, when she was small.

Tears pricked at the backs of her eyes and she gave them a quick rub, not wanting to disgrace herself as she saw a group of friends ahead, waving to her. She made no mention to them that it was her birthday because they'd ask if she was having a party, or what present her mother had given her that morning. Dena decided it would be best to wait till teatime and see what Alice's surprise might be.

-

There was no surprise. Dena arrived home to find the fire out, no food prepared for any birthday tea, not even a slice of bread spread with marg let alone a cake with candles. And there was no sign of her mother.

'Mam! Where are you?'

A thin wail came from upstairs. 'Where else would I be but in bed? We've run out of coal and I'm starved with cold. You're no use to anyone, girl. And beat those rugs. They're filthy. Useless, dozy numbskull that you are.'

Dena slammed out of the house and, after scavenging in the spoil-heaps and rubbish tips, returned with half a bucketful of coal and an old orange box. Having got the fire going she set about making tea: a fried egg sandwich for herself as a treat. She couldn't remember the last time she'd had an egg. What better way to celebrate her birthday? She licked up every drop of runny yolk, every last crumb and gave a satisfied sigh when it was all gone, knowing she could have easily eaten another.

But Dena was determined to be cheerful and even hummed a little tune as she stood in the yard beating the clippy rugs with the carpet beater. But then she still had the evening to look forward to.

When she went upstairs to ask if Alice would like a boiled egg for her tea she always enjoyed, she found her mother fast asleep.

Dena stood in the bedroom doorway and felt once more plunged into helplessness and despair. Why did she sleep all the time? She must have been up for some hours today though, as she'd used up all the coal, but why go back to bed in the middle of the afternoon? Dena pulled open the little drawer where she'd hidden the sleeping tablets and counted them out. She could have sworn there should have been ten but there were only eight. Mam must have taken a couple this afternoon and was now snoring like a banshee, loud enough to wake all the neighbours.

She couldn't be bothered to stay awake long enough to make her a surprise tea, buy her own daughter a birthday present, or even to wish her a happy birthday.

Well, what of it! If she was determined to stay in bed and be miserable, let her. Dena meant to enjoy her birthday in her own way without any help from her mam.

Her mother being asleep, deprived Dena of any chance to ask if she could go to the pictures with Kenny, as she'd intended, but surely she couldn't blame her for that? Mam was forever slagging her off over some supposed fault, or else fast asleep and snoring her head off. She wasn't interested in anything Dena did or said, so what did it matter?

Half an hour later Dena set a tray of sandwiches and flask of tea on the bedside table, then crept silently out of the house without waking her.

Kenny was waiting, as promised, on Slate Wharf. They walked along by the canal basin, much quieter now that the day's work was done and most of the tugs and barges had been tied up for the night. Neither of them spoke, Dena simply thrilled to be out of the house. Free at last.

Castlefield had once been a thriving industrial area, the heart of Manchester's wealth. Now it looked half derelict and carried an air of sadness with its bombed-out sites and flattened warehouses. Children played among the rubble and people hurried by with their collars turned up against the wind, unseeing of the desolation around them.

When they reached the place where the Manchester Ship Canal merged with the Rochdale and Bridgewater Canals, Kenny said, 'This is the last lock on the Rochdale Canal, once owned by the Duke of Bridgewater. There are nine more locks between here and Dale Street Basin, along what they call the Castlefield Flight, allowing the canal to rise sixty-three feet. Amazing piece of engineering that, eh?'

How he loved to show off, Dena thought, not really listening. She was still worrying about her mam in the house alone, about the missing tablets and the constant criticism of everything she did. Would Alice never forgive her for not protecting Pete that day? Would she never recover from her grief? Dena longed for her to be as she once had been, at least interested in what her daughter did, even if she wasn't the most loving mother in the world.

If only there was someone she could talk to properly about her problem. But how could she without giving away the whole story of what had happened that day by the canal? Dena was convinced that whoever had been bullying her brother were the ones responsible for his death. Yet even if she could find out who the culprits were, what could she do about it? Nothing! She couldn't even bear to think about them.

'Hello, are you still with me?' Kenny's voice was in her ear.

'Oh, sorry, I was miles away.'

'Shows how fascinating I must be. Penny for 'em.'

Dena shook her head, finding her cheeks growing warm at his comment. Was he being sarcastic or just teasing her? She couldn't be sure.

They were now walking past Giant's Basin, a great curving overflow sluice that took surplus water from the canal down into the river Medlock, which reminded her of what he'd been trying to tell her. 'You were saying something about the canal, some engineering thing.'

Kenny gave a cocky grin. 'I like being with you, Dena. You're so appreciative of what I have to say, unlike other people I know.' And then began to bore her rigid by talking about his new job at the engineering works, how he was serving an apprenticeship for which he was very badly paid. 'I deserve more,' he said, with his characteristic swagger. 'I'm good at me job. One of the best.'

Dena hid a smile. 'You can hardly have been there any time at all.'

'So? One day I'll be a fully fledged mechanic. That's something, isn't it?'

'That would be grand,' Dena agreed.

'Then I'll make a load of brass, buy myself a big house. Maybe invent something important what everyone'll pay a fortune for. I mean it you know. I have big plans, me.'

'Good for you! But why do you always have to be showing off? It's so unnecessary. Why not just be yourself.'

Kenny looked startled, as if such a consideration had never entered his head. True, he had been trying to impress her, but wasn't that what a lad was supposed to do with a lass? 'I don't know what you mean.'

'Yes, you do. You know exactly what I mean. Playing the big man all the time. Look at you now, combing your hair, preening yourself.' She wondered if she was being unkind, if he might be nervous so couldn't stop himself from fidgeting. 'You think far too much of yourself, Kenny Garside.'

'What's wrong with a person taking a pride in their appearance?' Kenny protested, but slid the comb back in his pocket and stuffed his hands in too, as if he didn't know what to do with them when he wasn't using them for the purposes of grooming.

Dena did admit that he wasn't bad looking. The quiff of blond hair seemed to be causing him so much trouble, flopped enticingly over his forehead and his eyes were a clear light blue, as if the sun was shining behind them. He had a nice face with a sort of boyish innocence about it, not nearly so surly as Carl's. He wasn't as tall as Carl either, but loose-limbed and with a sexy swagger to his walk. It was no wonder all the girls fancied the Garside brothers. Dena was happy to be seen out with Kenny and it felt perfectly natural to slip her arm into his as they walked along, sharing a moment of complete contentment.

–

They caught a bus at the end of Liverpool Road, which would take them into the city centre. Kenny insisted on paying, as it was his treat. Yet he made no mention of it being her birthday and Dena wondered if he'd forgotten. After all, why should he remember if her mother couldn't?

They went up on the top deck and it felt good to be sitting with him in the warm fug of the bus. 'Tell me about your brother, about Carl. Is he still doing the driving?'

Kenny's face clouded. 'Aye, for Catlow's warehouse taking stuff back and forth from the dock all the time. Bore me to tears that would, but he seems to like it. He's a brainless idiot is my brother, not like me at all.'

'I'm sure he isn't.' Again there was that touch of amusement in her voice, which Kenny picked up on.

'He is, far too solemn and serious for his own good. I do at least know how to have a bit of fun in life…'

'As well as being more handsome and intelligent,' Dena teased.

'That's right,' Kenny agreed, taking her seriously. 'He has none at all.'

'Oh, Kenny, do stop bragging. I'm sure he says the same about you.'

'No, he doesn't. How could he? You watch out, Dena. He's a shocking flirt, and he's not one to cross, isn't our Carl. Not that he can do any wrong in Mam's eyes. Makes me furious at times the way she lets him get away with stuff. He orders me about all the time, then sits back expecting her to wait on him hand, foot and finger, and she does, soft cow. But she won't do anything for me, quite the reverse. Kenny do this. Kenny do that! Kenny will you fetch that? An order, not a request, like I'm some sort of slave.'

Dena gave a bitter little laugh. 'Oh, I know about that feeling right enough. My mam's just as bad. She never gets out of bed unless she has to, so I have to do everything.'

'Oh no, Mam isn't lazy. She's at the cafe from cock-crow.'

'Yes, I know that. I wasn't meaning to imply otherwise. She's a worker your mam and expects us girls to be too. She makes sure we earn our wages for all she takes a share of our tips.'

Dena had tried to sound light-hearted but she'd clearly touched a nerve as Kenny bridled. 'Mam's had it tough. It's not meanness what makes her hard on you girls, it's because she needs to be. If you must know, her mother was a prossy and Mam spent time in a children's home when she was young, so everything she has she's had to earn for herself. And she's beautiful, you must admit.'

'Oh, yes, she is indeed. Belle is very attractive, almost as glamorous as Elizabeth Taylor with those lovely violet eyes of hers.'

'And I don't believe she does pinch your tips.'

Dena decided not to dispute that one. 'I wasn't really criticising her, Kenny, just sympathising. She's a good employer and she's been kind to me, letting me have time off and such.'

He appeared slightly mollified. 'Aye, well, a woman has to watch out for herself in this world, eh? Mam has a job holding off the men, her being so good-looking. Like vultures some of them.'

'I can imagine.' There was an awkward pause and Dena was careful to make no mention of Belle's reputation for being flighty. Kenny might seem friendly enough on the surface but he was clearly a bit prickly underneath.

She frantically sought for something else to say, anxious to rectify her blunder and return to that feeling of mutual accord they'd enjoyed only moments earlier. 'I just meant that I understand about mothers having favourites. Mine thought the sun shone out of our Pete's backside, still does, even though he's dead.'

Kenny said nothing to this as he counted out pennies for the bus fare.

When the conductor had handed over their tickets and moved on, Dena continued in a quieter voice. 'I loved him though, our Pete. He were a right little monkey but he was my brother, you know?'

Kenny put a hand on her arm and gave it a little squeeze. 'It must be hard for you.'

'It is.'

'What I don't understand is how he came to fall in the canal in the first place. Was he larking about and acting daft?'

'Something like that I don't like to talk about, if you don't mind. Look, let's agree not to talk about our families any more, shall we? Let's just enjoy ourselves.'

'Right, you're on. It's your birthday and I want you to have a good time.'

Dena was so thrilled that he hadn't forgotten after all, that she rewarded him with one of her famous smiles. Kenny thought his heart might stop there and then, she was so lovely.

–

They sat on the back row and first of all he held her hand, then slid his arm along the back of the seat and before she knew what was happening, somehow the arm was round her shoulders. He didn't try anything on although he sat very close. Dena was so entranced by the warmth of his body pressed against her own that she almost wished he would.

Sometimes he would whisper some comment about the film in her ear, making her laugh with one of his jokes and tickling her cheek with his warm breath. She felt safe and protected, as if he really cared for her. She couldn't remember ever feeling that way before. It was all so exciting!

In the interval Kenny bought her an ice cream and later as they walked back from the bus stop along Liverpool Road, he stopped under a lamp post and pulled something out of his pocket.

'This is for you, Dena, for your birthday.' It was a locket with a silver heart, which opened. She could see it glinting in the lamplight as he laid it gently on her palm. 'I wanted to give you something special because I'd like you to be my girl. I hope you'll say yes, Dena. I like you a lot, I really do.' For the first time she could remember, he dropped the cocky tone and sounded really unsure of himself.

'Oh, Kenny, it's lovely. It's the most wonderful birthday present any girl could have.' She let him fasten it around her neck, then impulsively reached up and kissed him on the cheek. They were both surprised by the gesture and looked into each other's eyes, transfixed by the intimacy of the moment.

Dena might well have panicked and turned and run away but Kenny took her by the shoulders and kissed her again, properly this time, full on the mouth. It was a very gentle sort of kiss, quite chaste and proper but as she leaned against him, savouring every second, Dena knew that nothing would ever be the same again.

After she'd waved goodbye and run off down the street, Kenny smiled wryly to himself. 'Got her,' he thought. 'All it took was a bit of charm.'

Chapter Nine

After that, they couldn't bear to be apart. Dena saw Kenny night after night and although she meant to tell Alice what was going on, she never got around to it. Each Saturday he would walk her home from the market and sometimes he would take her up a back street.

'You're all mine, aren't you Dena?' he would murmur between long drawn-out kisses that made her gasp for breath. 'I'm so lucky to have a girl like you.'

He kissed her till she was rosy with his kisses and her chin sore from rubbing against his. Dena found that she liked being kissed, needed this closeness and would not have objected if he'd tried to go a bit further, but to her surprise and pleasure he behaved like the perfect gentleman. It was almost as if he was afraid to touch her, for fear of offending her.

Heaven knows what her mother would say if she ever discovered that she was walking out with Kenny Garside. To her shame, Dena made no attempt to stop her from taking the sleeping tablets that she relied upon so heavily. She didn't actively encourage her to take them, nor did she object when the doctor prescribed more. And while Alice slept, Dena was free to slip out to meet Kenny round the backstreet, or down by the canal under the bridge.

He was exciting and Dena was desperate for a bit of fun in her life. Though he was still a show off.

'Watch me, Dena,' he called to her one night, and she looked up to find him walking on the parapet of the bridge high above the canal.

'Stop that! Come down this minute. You'll fall in and drown.'

An image of dark eyes hidden behind a balaclava rushed into her mind, of her young brother's thrashing limbs, and that terrible, deathly silence when the sound of Pete's cries had stopped and the pounding feet had gone. 'Stop it, Kenny, it's not funny!' and she began to cry.

He came rushing back to hold her in his arms and kiss the tears away, instantly contrite. It made him feel big and powerful to see her distress, as if he were a real man. One kiss led to another, all to the good, he supposed, a step nearer to his goal. But all of this kissy-kissy stuff did nothing for him at all. He tried not to let this trouble him but it was true that she awakened urges in him he'd experienced with no one else. Just the thought of what he might do to her got him all excited, and his patience was being stretched to the limit. All he wanted was to get on with it and take her, make her his for good and all.

But Kenny was growing increasingly confused, not sure how to take things further. One minute he would think that he was on to a sure thing, the next she would shy away and he'd be right back where he started.

Girls were such a mystery. If she fancied him, why couldn't she just open her legs and have done with it instead of all this messing about.

On Dena's part she wondered how long she could hope to keep their friendship a secret. Kenny was getting serious, and she could tell this must mean he liked her? It was becoming much more difficult to control their feelings when they indulged in this kind of kissing and heavy petting. She just seemed to lose herself in the moment.

One evening, her head spinning from his kisses, she heard a clock start to chime and pushed him away. 'Oh Lord, what time is it? I must go. I was late home the other night and got into terrible trouble. Mam's still not well and might wake up and need me.'

Kenny put out a hand to stop her as she turned to run. 'Just one more, Dena.' And she simply couldn't resist him, melting back in to his arms at once.

Before she knew it his hand was sneaking up inside her blouse, squeezing her breasts. It was the first time he'd done this so that's probably why it felt painful and uncomfortable, because he was awkward and shy.

Kenny felt a kick of excitement. She wasn't even wearing a bra. Her breasts were bare and firm and velvety, the nipples rapidly hardening beneath his fingers. He'd never touched a woman so intimately before and it wasn't nearly as unpleasant as he'd imagined it would be. He might try this again when they had more time. But the question was, did it make her want it?

'Oh, Dena, I want you so much. Let me do it quickly, right now.'

'Kenny Garside, don't talk so daft!' Somehow Dena managed to break free, laughing as she escaped his grasping fingers and pretended to be cross with him, while secretly she was flattered that he wanted her so badly.

She was halfway down the road, a good couple of hundred yards away, when he called after her, 'You're still my girl then?'

Dena whirled about and called right back to him. 'Course I am, you daft 'apporth. I don't let just anyone do that, you know.'

He was still standing grinning in the middle of the road when she turned the corner and ran all the way down Water Street. But as she pushed open her front door and crept quietly inside, she was greeted by a familiar voice. 'And where might you have you been till this time, madam?'

—

It was dreadful. Dena couldn't ever remember seeing her mother this angry. She wasn't sitting huddled in the chair feeling sorry for herself now. She was standing, feet astride, arms folded and with a face like thunder, although not for long. The minute Dena stepped over the threshold she pounced, grabbed her by one ear and shook her like a rabbit before dragging her over to a kitchen chair and pushing her into it.

'You sly little madam! I would never have known if Mrs Emmett hadn't poked her head round the door and happened to mention that she'd seen you walking out with your young man.'

Dena felt suddenly sick, as if she might throw up, and then came a great surge of anger. She seemed to have spent so much of her life running round looking after her mother, particularly in recent weeks, and what thanks had she ever got? Didn't she deserve a bit of fun now and again? Her resentment produced a burst of rebellion. 'Sneeze round here and half the town hears about it. Lot of fusty old gossips.'

'Are you denying it then?'

Dena shook her head, 'No, I'm not denying it.'

'How long has it been going on then?'

'Since my birthday if you must know! Not that you did anything for me on that day, so why should you care?'

The slap came hard and fast, sending her flying out of the chair, sprawling on to the hard flagged floor. On the way down she knocked her head on the corner of the table, which made Dena see double for a moment and the room to spin around her. Alice grabbed her daughter's arm and yanked her to her feet, only to fling her back into the chair.

'Now shut your whimpering and listen to me, you little whore! I'll not have no boys pawing over you. You might be fourteen but you're still a child not a woman, and far too young for such dirty goings-on. If you bring trouble to my door – and you know what I'm talking about – I'll whip the hide off you. Do you hear me, girl?'

Dena thought the entire neighbourhood could probably hear. She expected Mrs Emmett to appear at the door any second. 'We didn't do nothing. He never touched me! Not like that. I'm not stupid!' Dena flushed with guilt, but it was only a small white lie, wasn't it?

'That's a matter of opinion, and I've only your word for that. What's his name? Who is he this boy?'

'Aren't I allowed to even have any friends now?'

'I'm your mother! I'll decide which friends you have. And you should ask permission before you go out anywhere.'

Dena hung her head in shame, knowing this to be true and perfectly reasonable. 'I'm sorry, Mam, but you always seem to be asleep, or else tired out and in a bad mood. I accepted that first date because I needed a break and...'

'You needed a break? What about me? I can't run away from this terrible tragedy you've inflicted on us. No wonder I'm always tired and in a bad mood after what you've done.'

'But I didn't...'

'My father would have skinned me alive if I'd sneaked off, without telling him, to cavort with the opposite sex.' That was how she'd very nearly missed the boat altogether, never being allowed the chance to get to know any boys. But he was surely right. What good would it have done for her to make herself look cheap? None at all.

'I've said I'm sorry.'

Alice glared at her daughter. 'Being sorry isn't good enough. Your own father was a saint, God rest his soul. He'll be turning in his grave at such disgusting carryings-on.'

'Oh, Mam, please don't say that.'

'I'll not have you ruin your reputation with such scandalous behaviour, nor mine neither. I'll let you know when you're old enough to start courting, and even then it will be with a good, respectable man, not some ne'er do well. Who was he then, some bloke you picked up?'

'No! I didn't pick up some bloke. It was only Kenny – Kenny Garside. He's walked me home from the market once or twice, and when he heard it was my birthday, offered to take me to the flicks. We saw *High Noon* and it was lovely and since then we've seen each other a few times and...'

'Kenny Garside?' The tone of voice implied he might be the devil himself. 'Right, that does it. You'll have no more to do with that family. I always said they were rubbish. That Belle Garside is no better than she should be, a common little fancy piece. Always was, and her mother, well, we won't go into that history. Didn't I say I never wanted you to work in the market cafe in the first place? You should've listened to me and gone for a Saturday job at Kendals. But oh no, you must do as you think best. When did you ever listen to me, your mam?'

'But I like the market and...'

'I'm at my wits' end over how to cope with you, girl. You're growing increasingly wayward. You took no notice when I asked you to mind our Pete, did you? This house is like a pigsty with nothing as clean as it should be, and now you're opening your legs for every Tom, Dick and Harry.'

'I'm not, I'm not!' Dena's sobs of protest were entirely ignored.

'Get to bed! It shames me just to look at you.'

–

Dena was devastated. If she slept that night she had no recollection of it. Her head ached from where she'd banged it against the table, and she sobbed until her throat was raw, her eyes hot and scratchy and there were no more tears left to shed.

It was all her fault. She ought to have owned up to what was happening, like Mam said, and asked her permission for that first date. If she were honest with herself, she'd avoided doing so because she'd been afraid of Alice's reaction. Her mother had always been puritanical about love and stuff. How she'd ever got pregnant with two children was a mystery to Dena.

But then sex generally was a bit of a mystery to Dena. Mam had never got around to explaining the facts of life, probably never would, so her knowledge was pretty sketchy. She'd once asked for a book about it at the library when she'd found blood in her knickers, and even the librarian had been shocked. 'Go home and talk to your mother, girl,' had been her brisk advice.

But Dena had never plucked up the courage.

She'd managed to discover the basic essentials for herself, procured largely from scraps of information told by friends, so knew she wasn't in any danger. Kenny hadn't put his tongue in her mouth, nor would she allow him to, so she couldn't start a baby, could she?

But would Mam stick by her threat and stop her from seeing him? She could only do that by making her give up her job at the market cafe she'd threatened to do. Oh, but that would be awful! Dena knew she would miss it so much. And not seeing Kenny again didn't even bear thinking about.

Dena had never paid him much attention until now, always having dismissed him as a big show off who liked to brag about all the girls lusting after him, far too full of himself. She'd always been aware of him watching her, having embarrassed and annoyed her at one time. But now after their heart-to-heart chats, their many evenings out, and his lovely kisses, she wasn't embarrassed or annoyed any more. He was her friend and she liked him a lot! She didn't get the chance to have many friends with Mam being so demanding but Kenny Garside was exciting, dangerous even, and Dena desperately wanted to be his girl.

Yet in a way Mam was right. She must be careful. She was only fourteen. Far too young to be having such feelings, even if it did seem right and perfectly innocent when she was with him.

Dena felt suddenly ashamed: overwhelmed by a sense of selfishness because there were surely far more important matters to consider than losing her first boyfriend. Setting her own disappointment to one side for a moment, how on earth would they manage if she did have to give up her job at the market? They'd have no money for food. None at all. That was much more serious than losing Kenny.

Dena finally fell asleep just as dawn was breaking, her last thought being that her mam would have calmed down by morning, then she could again apologise and everything would return to normal.

It was a forlorn hope.

If she thought the lecture the night before had been bad, there was worse waiting for her when she came downstairs the following morning.

Seated at the kitchen table was the angular figure of Miss Rogers, her long narrow face pinched into lines of disapproval, and at the open front door stood a large black car and a very official looking driver.

'What's going on? Mam, what's happening?'

It was Miss Rogers who answered while Alice just sat there, saying nothing. 'Your poor mother can no longer cope with your waywardness, Dena. We're taking you into care.'

–

Dena felt as if she'd slipped into a nightmare. The social worker instructed her to eat up her breakfast then pack one small bag with the barest essentials and one or two of her favourite books. Everything else, she assured her, would be provided.

Hunger deserting her upon the instant, Dena demanded an explanation. 'I don't understand. Where am I going? Where are you taking me? I've done nothing. Mam, tell them I've done nothing wrong. I'm not wayward, am I?'

'Your mother isn't well enough to bring you up properly. She's sick, so we will take her place from now on. You will be raised by the state.'

Dena did not understand a word the woman was saying but it soon became clear that after months of never having set foot outside her own home, Alice had taken the slip of paper with Miss Roger's telephone number on it from the dresser drawer, gone to the telephone box on the corner and called her.

It felt like a betrayal.

Dena was near to tears but determined not to cry. She was worn out with crying. 'I won't go! You're not taking me nowhere and I can raise myself, ta very much.'

'No, indeed you can't.'

'I've been managing well enough up to now,' Dena protested.

Miss Rogers cast her a sad look. 'No you haven't, Dena. You haven't been managing very well at all. Look at you, thin and pasty-faced, and exhausted. And that's another bruise on your face, isn't it? Looks nasty. It's all right, don't worry. You'll like this place and will get plenty of good food, put some flesh on those skinny bones of yours, and they'll provide you with an excellent education. After that, they'll even help to find you employment. What more could you ask for?'

Dena stared at the social worker in stunned disbelief. What more could she ask for, her own home, her mam, friends and Kenny? Were all of these to be taken away from her? She ran to her mother and fell to her knees before her. 'Is this because of last night? Oh, I'm sorry Mam, I am really. It won't happen again, I swear it! Don't send me away. Please!'

Alice turned her face away to stare blankly into the fire.

Dena could feel panic rising inside of her. Her mother was not the demonstrative sort, never had been much of a one for cuddles or kisses, not at all the warm, loving parent of story books, but she was still her mam. Even if Pete had been her favourite, Dena had always been convinced that Alice cared about her, in her own rough and ready way. Surely her criticisms and constant scolding were only Mam's way of showing that her only daughter was important to her. It couldn't simply be that her own standards were all that mattered, could it?

'Look at me Mam, please, look at me. Tell them it's all right, that we have these little spats but then get over them. I'm your daughter!'

Alice did look at her then and her lips curled with distaste as she spat out the words. 'Not any more you're not!'

They had to drag her sobbing from her mother's knee and push her into the car. Dena's last view of Barber's Court as they drove away was of old Mrs Emmett standing at her front door with one hand clapped over her mouth in shock. They hadn't even remembered to pack her a bag, or collect up any of her favourite things. Dena felt in that moment entirely abandoned and bereft, as if she possessed nothing but the clothes on her back, and not a soul in the world cared about her. Not even her own mother.

Chapter Ten

They took Dena to a large Victorian mansion set in the depths of the country where she could smell cows and green grass. Miss Rogers informed her that it was called Ivy Bank and was run by Wesleyan Methodists so she must be on her best behaviour at all times. Right from the start Dena knew that she would hate it.

Even the smell of the place was dreadful: stale cabbage and vomit mixed with pig muck. Dena preferred traffic fumes and the noise of the city.

And that was another thing. She hated the silence, but then again the raucous sound of the rooks cawing in the trees that overhung the yard seemed somehow sinister and kept her awake that first night, and for several nights following.

At first she was put in something like a cow shed they called the sanatorium, for two whole weeks. A very fierce looking woman in a starched grey long-sleeved dress and cap, who insisted she be addressed as Matron, explained that Dena was now in quarantine to make sure that she had no infectious diseases.

There was nothing to do in the sanatorium, no entertainment save for a few worthy books. Dena endured it in silence, and largely alone as Matron apparently had far more important matters to deal with.

But Dena had come to a decision that enough was enough. There would be no more tears, not a single drop. A vain hope at Ivy Bank, but from now on no matter what life threw at her she was determined to cope, and never again expect help from anyone.

Who could she trust, after all, if not her own mother? If Alice could not be relied upon to support her, then there was no one.

When Saturday came round and Dena did not appear, Belle was at first annoyed and then curious. The girl had sometimes been late but never shied off work altogether. She needed the money too much. Belle decided to ask around. No doubt Winnie would have heard something. Several days later Barry Holmes was carefully stacking his best oranges to the front of his stall when Belle Garside accosted him.

'Have you seen Dena Dobson lately? She didn't turn up for work last Saturday.'

Barry shook his head. 'How would I know?'

'You always seem friendly enough with her, as you were with that brother of hers, young Pete. He was one of your boys, wasn't he?' Belle's tone was light although there was an edge to her sweetness. 'I assumed you still took an interest.'

'Aye, I do, as a matter of fact.'

'Rumour has it that she's been taken into care and I wondered if it were true.'

Barry looked concerned as he moved a slightly scarred orange to the back of the pile. 'I hadn't heard but I'll see what I can find out.'

'I'd appreciate it. Nobody ever tells me anything.' Belle turned to go then hesitated, as if she'd just had a thought. Picking up the orange she began rolling it in the palm of her hand. 'I don't suppose you'd consider proposing me for the new committee at the next AGM?'

Barry looked at her. 'I don't suppose I would.'

Belle smiled at him, and there was little humour in it. 'No, I didn't think you would.' And she dropped the orange onto the floor. A puff of green powder came out. 'Dear me, not so fresh as it should be?'

It was indeed Winnie Watkins who finally confirmed that the dreadful news was true, telling Belle that she'd got this information directly from Alice only this morning when she came into the market hall to buy thread.

'Not that it's any of my business, but would you believe that woman hasn't set foot outside the door since their Pete was drowned. Now that she no longer has Dena to wait on her hand, foot and finger, she's out and about every day all dolled up like a dog's dinner.'

Belle shook her head in disbelief. 'Selfish cow!'

'It's that young lass I feel sorry for. Sweet on your Kenny, apparently, and Alice didn't approve of them walking out together, so she called in the social, claiming her daughter was beyond parental control.' Nor did Winnie approve of Kenny Garside. She was very fond of Dena and privately considered Kenny nowhere near good enough for her, so she revelled in this opportunity to put some of the blame for the tragedy on Belle's lap. 'What sort of a world is it when a mother gives her own child away rather than take responsibility for her behaviour?'

Belle bristled. 'I'm sure it's nothing our Kenny's done, so you can take that disapproving look off your face, Winnie Watkins.'

'I never said it was,' said Winnie primly, her face now carefully devoid of expression. It was none of her business after all.

–

Belle went straight to her son where he was sulkily stacking plates in the kitchen, having lost his job at the engineering plant just because he turned up late for work one morning. A poor show in Kenny's opinion that they made no allowance for youth or a hangover. 'What you been doing to the Dobson girl?'

Kenny jerked as if shot. 'Nowt!'

She clipped him round the ear. 'Don't lie to me, son. I'll find out, so help me. If you've been interfering with that young lass…'

'Mam, I haven't, I swear it. I haven't touched her, not much anyway. Why would I?' Kenny whined, smearing his face with soap suds as he held his burning hot ear.

'Aye, why would you, great soft lump that you are? You wouldn't know what to do with the girl, not even if she drew you a picture. I said as much to Winnie only this morning.'

'I wouldn't go that far,' Kenny protested, feeling his manhood was being challenged.

'Young stud are you now?'

'Let it go, Mam,' Carl warned. 'She's no great loss.'

Belle drew in a calming breath as she contemplated her two boys, then overcome with a burst of maternal emotion, clasped Kenny to her breast as if he were five years old and not fifteen. 'I'm sorry for landing you one, love, only that Winnie Watkins got me proper narked. 'Course, you've more sense than to do anything to harm the silly lass, so you can stop looking sorry for yourself. It's that poor girl you should pity. She's been taken away, shopped by that hysterical mother of hers.' Belle gently patted her son's soapy cheek. 'I knew you'd never lift a finger to hurt anyone, would you Kenny love?'

Kenny glowed beneath this uncharacteristic show of approbation, might well have tried to take advantage of it but was so stunned by the news that he stopped thinking about himself for several long seconds. Dena taken into care, this was awful! Dreadful! Not what he'd planned at all. Only when Carl kicked his ankle did he answer his mother's question. 'No, Mam, I wouldn't. I'd never hurt a living soul.'

Belle sashayed off to flirt with Sam Beckett, who'd come in search of his usual sausage sandwich, and Kenny turned on his brother, venom hissing out on a blast of beer tainted breath. 'This is your fault that you've done this. You must have told on us. How would she have known about us otherwise?'

Carl let out a snort of amusement. 'I reckon all the market knew, if not half the city of Manchester, that you were having it off with her.'

'I wasn't having it off.'

Carl chortled all the more, pleased to have riled his younger brother. 'Whether or not you've got your leg over yet, you're hot gossip round here. And she isn't so innocent and lily-white either.'

Without pausing for thought, Kenny took a swing at him, spitting with fury. 'Don't you insult my girl. She isn't like that!'

Caught off balance, Carl's head jerked back as he took the full force of the blow. 'Oh, but she is. And she's also a little thief.'

'She is not!'

Kenny would have shoved him aside, but, more prepared this time, Carl easily prevented his escape by pushing him up against the greasy kitchen wall, pinning him there like a fly on sticky paper.

There was a long drawn-out moment of silence while both brothers breathed hard and considered their options, Kenny inwardly shaking with fear at what Carl might do next. His brother could easily break his neck with one flick of that powerful wrist. When it seemed as if this part of his anatomy was to remain safe, for now at least, he said on a note of bravado, 'We'll settle this on Friday night at the club, right? Once and for all! I'll not have you insult Dena. She's my girl.'

Carl's smile chilled him to his very soul. 'You're on. I'll take great pleasure in cutting you down to size, little brother. As you say, once and for all.'

–

When the quarantine was over, Dena was moved to the main house and put in a cavernous freezing cold room, called a dormitory, with eleven other girls, in the charge of a housemother.

She was a huge woman built like a tank, or a female version of Desperate Dan from *The Beano* comic. The advantage of this was that the girls could hear her approach from some distance away, thumping along the corridor or blundering up the stairs. Her real name was Dorothy Carter but was known to the girls as Carthorse.

'This is where you keep all your possessions, Dena Dobson, in your own personal locker. And see that you keep it tidy.'

This amused Dena since she had nothing to put in the locker save for the clothes they'd given her. She'd already tried explaining to Matron that she'd been given no chance to bring any of her own things with her, and had asked if they could perhaps be sent on.

Matron had merely sniffed disapprovingly and told her she would have no further need of such trifles and a full uniform would be provided. Now Dena was being taken up to a huge room lined with cupboards that were packed with piles of clothing. The faint musty smell that emanated from them, when the cupboard doors were opened, clearly indicated that these were other folks' cast-offs. Since Dena had never owned anything new in her entire life, this didn't trouble her in the slightest.

She was presented with two pale blue blouses, a darker blue gymslip made out of stiff calico, black tie shoes and short white socks, also an overall for rough work, and an apron for cooking. The undergarments were the strangest of all with two pairs of flannel knickers in a washed out blue that came nearly to her knees; two vests and a liberty bodice with suspenders that buttoned on to long black woollen stockings. The only touch of colourful frivolity was a pink flannel petticoat decorated with cross-stitch in a pale blue thread.

Dena learned later that the clothes were made in the sewing room by the girls themselves, although you'd be very fortunate indeed to be given anything new. These were reserved for the prefects and the most favoured. Dena looked forward to discovering who had been daring enough to embroider the hem with cross-stitch.

She was also provided with a wash bag in which was placed a toothbrush and toothpaste, tablet of soap, comb and a face cloth. This had to be hung on a special hook by her locker. Last of all came two nightdresses, also in warm pink flannel, a dressing gown, slippers, and a pair of wellingtons for working in the garden.

The only item she possessed in all the world that was entirely hers, was the locket that Kenny had given her. To keep it safe and out of sight of the other girls she slipped it inside the bible that Carthorse presented her with, and stowed it away in her locker. Surely it would be safe there. Oh, Kenny, she thought. I'm missing you so much already.

Carl presaged the fight by taking great pleasure in telling Kenny all about the little tricks with the tips the wonderful Dena got up to when she thought folk weren't watching. 'Except that I was watching, and saw it all.'

Kenny refused to believe a word of it. She was, in his eyes, an angel from heaven who could do no wrong, incapable of stealing from anyone least of all her employer. 'I'll kill you if you say anything different,' he roared.

Carl snorted his derision. 'I'd like to see you try.'

Barry Holmes's job was to ensure that the fight was carried out strictly according to Queensbury rules. 'Right lads, we'll have a fair fight, no hitting below the belt and you stop when I say so.'

Despite his challenge Carl was wary of hurting his brother and the fight began slowly with the pair of them dancing about the ring, neither making any move to be the first to come in. Then Kenny sprang forward, leading from the shoulder with a good straight jab right in the ribs, finding his range nicely. After two or three more accurately aimed punches, Carl realised that if this was going to be a serious fight, he'd better tighten up and take it seriously.

Kenny, ever light on his feet, managed to avoid most of Carl's jabs in the first round, and even got in a few more of his own. In the second he began to tire and Carl got in with one or two cross punches, with Kenny only managing to land one right hook that had little power in it. Then before Kenny could get into his stride in the third, Carl seemed to grow bored with the whole idea, brought in a left uppercut and knocked him out cold.

He stood back to allow Barry to dash over and fuss about with bucket and sponge, worrying that he might have been a bit hard on him. He was his brother after all. Kenny had a cut over one eye and a split lip but he was starting to come round already, so not too badly hurt.

Carl watched impassively as Barry bore Kenny off to his own house for more treatment before taking him on home. For all he'd been reluctant to hurt the lad, he felt a deep sadness that it should come to this, the pair of them fighting instead of just enjoying a bit of sparring, as they'd used to.

Kenny had been a good kid when he was young, always cheerful and happy, but then for no reason anyone could explain, he'd changed. Almost overnight he'd become very much a troublemaker as young Pete Dobson, whom he claimed to despise for that very reason.

There'd been a lot going on around that time, yet another man walking out on their mam, but from the age of about nine Kenny was either always up to mischief or else moody and uncooperative. He would throw tantrums, get into fights, tried his hand at shoplifting from Woolworths, or would simply sit for hours with his hands over his head refusing to speak to anyone. His mam had been at her wit's end at times over his behaviour.

And Carl, at eleven years old and the man of the house, had felt duty-bound to do what he could to help. Not that any of his lectures had ever penetrated an inch into his brother's thick skull. Not then, and not now. He listened to no one, heard nothing but the crazy ideas that racketed about in his own stupid head.

But then why should he listen to Carl when there was only a couple of years between them? Having a father around instead of a nagging brother would have done him a great deal of good. Trouble was, men didn't ever seem to stick around very long in Belle's life.

Now, even at fifteen, he remained as stubborn as ever and just as unpredictable, but if he wanted Dena Dobson then Carl didn't doubt that he would get her, in the end. Once he'd set his heart on something, Kenny wasn't one to give up.

And if he was honest, Carl too had thought the girl was different, a bit better than most: pretty and cheerful, out-going and really nice, having a hard time of it with that moaning Minnie of a mother. While all the time she was a right little minx, as bad as all the rest of her sex. Out for what she could get and nothing more.

Carl went off to treat himself to a pint, feeling in sore need of one. Kenny still hadn't emerged from Barry's house by the time he'd finished it, and he wondered if he'd punched him over-hard after all, but the lad had been spoiling for a fight so had it coming to him. Maybe this would teach him to choose his girls more carefully in future.

Chapter Eleven

Dena seemed to hit trouble from the very first day. A handbell was rung to mark the start of every activity, whether it be bed making, baths or breakfast. No one told her this, nor that talking while such activities were carried out was entirely forbidden. Thus Carthorse found her still fast asleep when all the other girls had gone down to breakfast.

'Didn't you hear the bell? Get along with you, girl. And make your bed for goodness sake. There's nobody to wait on you here, you know.' Just as if she'd had three servants to do her every bidding back home in Barber's Court.

A person less motherly would be hard to find, in Dena's opinion, apart from her own. It was constantly drummed into the girls how very worthless they were, how they were inferior to 'real' people who lived outside. 'No wonder your mother doesn't want you any more,' the woman would say at the slightest transgression that left Dena feeling even more rejected.

That first week in the main school seemed bewildering with so much to learn. A strict routine of early morning chores, breakfast and prayers, the latter often accompanied by a long sermon, seemed to go on interminably. Dena had never been particularly religious so had breathed a sigh of relief when Miss Rogers hadn't placed her with the nuns. Now she was beginning to wonder.

Bath time was another nightmare with girls having to queue naked along the corridor, cold and embarrassed. Dressing gowns, apparently, were not allowed as they might get wet.

Apart from Matron and three housemothers responsible for over a hundred girls, plus a handful of teachers who came in for a few hours each day, there was one cook and a skivvy in the kitchen. The girls themselves, under strict supervision, carried out all domestic duties, like cooking and cleaning, washing and ironing. This was considered to be useful training for their future, either in marriage – if they were fortunate enough to find a man willing to take them on, or in domestic service. Though as such positions were harder to come by since the war, Dena couldn't see the point. Learning to read, which many of the girls couldn't do, would surely have done them much more good.

Her allotted task on that first day was to slice dozens of loaves of bread and spread them with margarine and a thin layer of jam, to make sandwiches for tea.

The food was wholesome and plain, although not particularly substantial. And having milk in one's tea was not so wonderful, Dena discovered, as more often than not it had gone sour in the heat of the kitchen. Breakfast had been porridge, which she'd missed this morning, as she'd been late making her bed, and for dinner mutton stew followed by tapioca pudding. Dena seemed to be perpetually hungry, so when no one was looking she sneaked a small piece of bread and jam. She was still chewing this when cook asked her to fetch a pitcher of milk from the dairy and unfortunately noticed a betraying scrap of jam at the corner of Dena's mouth.

'Are you eating, girl? Empty your mouth this instant.'

Desperately, Dena swallowed the evidence in one gulp. 'No, Cook!' She could tell by the hard glare the woman was giving her that she didn't believe her. 'I'll go and fetch the milk, shall I?' Only too happy to escape her eagle eye.

Unfortunately, on her way back from the dairy, Dena encountered the geese. She'd heard them cackling but this was the closest she'd ever come to the vicious creatures. Most girls had learned to take a few crusts with them to use as a bribe and lure the birds out of the way. Unaware of this, and never having seen geese before, Dena was startled and then frightened when they crowded around her, cackling and gabbling.

She flapped at them with her free hand. 'Go away!' This annoyed them more than ever.

Her alarm turned to fear when they reached up their long necks and started pecking at the milk jug clasped in her other hand. Dena panicked and fled for her life. Unfortunately the flag stones in the yard were uneven, the geese were pecking at her backside by this time and in her terror Dena tripped and fell, spilling milk everywhere.

Cook came storming out wielding a brush to chase the creatures off. Dena expected the dreadful woman to batter her with it too, but fortunately she managed to control herself and just yelled at her instead.

'What do you think you're doing, girl? Get up, have you no sense at all? Can't you deal with a few geese?'

Dena had so wanted to impress but her efforts were a complete disaster.

She was set to scrubbing the outside steps by way of punishment for lying, and stealing and wasting food. It was not a propitious start. And because there were so many steps, pinching the jam butty did her no good at all as she now missed out on tea as well.

Nor was she allowed to go to the playground with the other girls before supper. Instead she was sent to the quiet room beside the chapel and instructed to write out several verses from the gospel of Saint Matthew, ready to recite them off by heart to Matron the following morning.

Despite her vow not to, Dena did a lot of weeping in those first few days and nights, stuffing the sheet into her mouth so that there would be no sound. Though who she was crying for she couldn't rightly have said. Not her mother, that was for sure. Kenny, Pete, or simply herself.

She would slip the locket over her head and wear it in bed where nobody could see it. It gave her great comfort to feel the smoothness of the silver heart between her fingers, and helped her to remember those few magical moments when Kenny had kissed her.

Dena thought she wasn't alone in her misery as sometimes she heard other sniffs and sobs in the still darkness, but not a word was ever spoken, most of the girls being too fearful of Matron, which Dena didn't wonder at.

Others, however, were not so timid.

On the third night she was dozing nicely, just slipping into sleep when the blankets were ripped from her and a dozen pairs of hands lifted her from the bed. They laid her on one of the scratchy brown blankets then lifted it up and tossed her high in the air. It was pitch dark, Dena couldn't work out where she was or how high they were tossing her, and was absolutely terrified. Even more so when something hit her hard on the head. Had they sent her right up to the ceiling? Surely not, it must be too high!

She squealed and begged them to stop but that only brought a harder battering to her head.

'Don't make a sound or you'll get far worse.' This from Norah Talbot who fervently believed that she ruled the roost in this dormitory.

Dena bit down hard on her lip and remained silent even though she was terrified that at any moment they'd toss her out of the blanket and she'd crash on to the hard wooden floor. They were only hitting her head with a book, a large atlas kept specifically for the purpose, and afterwards Dena felt something of a fool to have been so worried.

Another night came the "ghost": a white figure appearing at her bedside emitting a stomach-churning wail. Dena was so petrified that she leapt screaming from her bed, and only when she heard the soft giggles all around her did she realise that she'd been tricked yet again.

So many rules to learn and be wary of!

And she was starting to feel so homesick, though why she couldn't imagine. For Kenny at least. She missed him so much! Talking about home, particularly in bed, was generally discouraged as it was believed that this hindered the girls from settling, although some did indulge in a few reminiscences on occasion. Dena was happy to comply with this rule, at least. She had no wish to reveal the fact that her own mother had voluntarily handed her into care, like a dog she was tired of and couldn't be bothered to look after any more.

But it didn't stop the questions from going round and round in her own head. Why didn't Mam want her? Why did she no longer love her? And what if she never came back for her? It didn't bear thinking about.

–

Kenny was feeling deeply dissatisfied with his lot. He was really missing Dena, not broken-hearted exactly but definitely regretting her hasty departure. And just when he'd been getting somewhere at last.

He glanced sideways at the girl sitting beside him in the cinema and couldn't, for a moment, remember her name. Gladys? Glenda? Jeannie: that was it. Then again, it might be Jenny.

At least the film had been good. Alan Ladd in *Shane*. The only disappointment was that although the gunman was a fast enough draw with his six-shooter, he was never keen to use it. He beat the cattle farmers in the end, but Kenny felt that he would have had them begging for mercy much sooner. Still, it was a good film, better than that soppy *Call Me Madam* Jenny had insisted they see last week. She didn't seem to have enjoyed this one much, judging by the way she'd hardly kept her eyes on the screen for more than five minutes.

This wasn't a problem when she'd been all over him earlier, till he'd got bored and told her to stop, admitting to himself that he was actually more interested in the film. His rebuff hadn't seemed to shut her up though. Never stopped talking the whole way through, and why should he bother to put up with her endless prattling when there were plenty of other girls ready and willing to take her place?

Hell, he liked girls, never seemed to have any trouble in attracting them. They admired his boyish charms, liked to run their fingers through his soft fair locks, and it felt good to have an attractive bird on his arm. Made him look important, a sort of man-about-town. But why was it that they were all so dead boring?

Kenny walked her to the bus stop, making some excuse about having to be home at a decent hour as he was on earlies the next day. That was another thing: his job. He'd managed to get taken on in a warehouse by Salford docks, but he wasn't getting on with his new boss one bit. The man was always complaining he wasn't working hard enough. He kept saying boxes had to be loaded, not used to park your bum on for a smoke. Nag, nag, nag, the whole bleeding time.

'You're not going to walk me home then, Kenny, the long way?' She was fluttering her eyelashes suggestively at him, and wiggling her skinny hips.

'Not tonight Jenny love.'

'Josie. Me name's Josie.' She sounded very slightly put out.

'Sorry. Anyway, got to run. See you.'

He heard her call after him, asking if he wanted to see her again, something about having a free evening next Wednesday. She worked in the tobacconists on Castle Street where he'd met her. She'd looked sexy behind the counter when reaching for a packet of Gold Flake, then leaning over the counter so he could see right down her blouse. Now he pretended not to hear her.

Jenny, Josie, whatever her flaming name was, her head was as empty as a tin bucket.

Sometimes he felt a nudge of guilt cheating on Dena like this. Not that she'd know, locked up in that home. The point was, who knew how long she'd be in that place and he had things to prove, didn't he? He was fifteen already and still hadn't plucked up the courage to go all the way with any of these floosies he picked up, ready and willing though some of them may be.

Trouble was, he couldn't seem to get the right sort of urges, and he blamed that entirely on Dena's untimely departure.

As the days and weeks slipped by Dena grew accustomed to the tricks and practical jokes, the rules and taboos, and even the joys and treats of life at Ivy Bank. There was always time allowed for games after dinner and then again in the evening: netball and rounders being among the favourites. There was a library with books she could borrow, all rather dreary and worthy but better than nothing. Best of all there was a common room with a table tennis table, together with a selection of board games, which they were allowed to use for an hour each evening. Or sometimes the girls would just sit by the fire and chat, dreaming of a future far away from Ivy Bank.

Most of all, Dena found that she thoroughly enjoyed the time they spent in lessons. This included such subjects as biology, geography and history, as well as the usual mathematics and English. And the staff were friendly, apart from fat Mrs Wallace, the French teacher, who took a caustic pleasure in catching them out in a mistake and would then beat them over the head with a ruler. She also took them for mathematics, so it was no wonder that Dena hated both subjects and felt the sting of that weapon on numerous occasions.

Dena particularly liked Miss Stanford, who took needlework. She was a small, neat woman with a kind smile who seemed to take a genuine interest in the girls.

One full morning a week was devoted to needlework and Dena found that she had a natural skill for sewing, although it was rarely anything more exciting than an apron or a peg bag. She was even permitted to use a treadle sewing machine, so much faster than stitching it by hand, and after a few weeks of hemming tea towels and dusters, she began to grow more ambitious.

Many of the girls liked to continue with their knitting and sewing of an evening and Dena would join in this little circle. One night she dared to make a suggestion.

'Do you think Miss Stanford might allow us to make ourselves a proper dress each for the summer. One that's a bit more fashionable than this dreadful gymslip?' The other girls looked at her as if she'd gone wrong in the head.

A welsh girl called Gwen said, 'Miss Stanford might agree but I should think Matron would consider it to be an unnecessary vanity and therefore a complete waste of money, no doubt would be better sent to the starving babies in Africa.'

'I could ask.'

'You could jump out of an aeroplane without a parachute but she would never allow it. She simply wouldn't provide the material.'

'We could buy remnants of cotton quite cheap at the indoor market on Champion Street. I know a really good stall.'

But Gwen was proved to be entirely correct. When Dena dared to broach the subject to Miss Stanford, she looked flustered by the very idea. 'Oh dear, I don't think so Dena. That would not be allowed at all.'

'Why not? We could all make ourselves a party dress for the coronation. What do you think?'

'Well!' Miss Stanford looked thoughtful, clearly tempted by this notion. Plans for the celebration, in just a few weeks, were well advanced but no one had given any thought to what the girls were meant to wear for the party.

'Couldn't you at least ask? She can only say no.'

The teacher gave a tired smile. 'Dear me, Dena, she can do a great deal more than that. She could dismiss me for impertinence and I have no wish to lose my job.'

Dena giggled. 'Then I'll ask her. She's welcome to dismiss me if she wants.'

Matron was appalled by the very idea. More dangerously, she issued a stern warning. 'You've only been with us a few short weeks, Dena Dobson, but I'd take care not to step out of line, if I were you. You're making yourself overly conspicuous if you go on trying to find ways to bend the rules. We like people to blend in at Ivy Bank, not make an exhibition of themselves.'

Dena was more disappointed than seemed quite justified in the circumstances. She did admit to herself that it wasn't so much that she'd wanted a new dress, as she'd been hoping for an excuse to visit Champion Street Market again to buy the fabric.

Wouldn't she just love to have a natter with her friend, Winnie Watkins?

Chapter Twelve

April and May passed by in a blur but at last June arrived. With it came the excitement of the coronation, and even more thrilling on the day before, a letter came for Dena, the first one she'd received since she arrived at Ivy Bank. She knew at once that it must be from Kenny. Who else would write to her? She hadn't received so much as a postcard from her mother. Now here was a long letter for her to enjoy. Dena was filled with excitement and couldn't wait for night to come so that she could read it under the bed covers in private. In the meantime, Dena hid it away in her bible with the locket.

The day seemed endless, but when bedtime came at last she borrowed a small electric torch from Gwen, pulled the covers right over her head and began to read the message Kenny had sent her. She'd expected him to have forgotten all about her, yet he was promising to wait for her; saying how he couldn't even look at another girl, he was missing her that much. His first words were to tell her that he still loved her and Dena's heart gave a fierce beat of delight.

> *They can't keep you in that home forever. Once you're sixteen we can get engaged, and marry as soon as you turn eighteen. We just need your mother to give her permission, and why would she refuse? It would free her of all duty towards you. You'd be my responsibility after that, and I could look after you. Till then you can come and live with us, and work full-time on the market. Mam won't mind.*

Responsibility! Duty! Dena experienced the slightest stirring of unease. Having her life so blatantly planned out for her by Kenny Garside didn't seem right. She'd make up her own mind where she lived, let alone who and when she married, thank you very much. Dena decided she would write back and tell him not to be so presumptuous. Cheeky monkey!

Oh, but she would also tell him how pleased she was that she was still his girl. It made her feel that someone cared for her. Kenny, at least, had not let her down.

When she had read the letter through three more times and caught up on all the news from the market, she began to feel sleepy. Dena slipped the letter carefully back between the pages of her bible, hung her precious locket around her neck and went blissfully to sleep.

–

More than a hundred girls crowded into the common room the next day where two television sets were set up, one at each end of the room, as they were to be allowed to watch the crowning of Queen Elizabeth.

Not that it was possible to see much over so many heads, the screen of the television sets being dreadfully small. Nor could they see the colour of her velvet robe or the true magnificence of her golden coach since it was all in black and white, yet it was so exciting to witness this awesome spectacle. They watched transfixed as the young Elizabeth in her plain white gown, looking so pale and serene, was dressed in her finery little by little till she became a true Queen with crown, orb and sceptre.

And when the long ceremony was finally over, they had the best part still to come. The party! And that was even more exciting, even if they were all still dressed in their boring gymslips.

There was egg, and salmon paste sandwiches, jelly and ice cream, iced buns, and Tizer to drink. An unheard of treat! Everyone was given a balloon and paper hat to wear, and after the tea party a magician was brought in to entertain them. He made rabbits disappear and pulled coins from behind their ears. He even pretended to pour water over Matron's head, making all the girls scream in horror. Fortunately no water came out and they could all breathe again.

Later there were three-legged-races, 'Hunt the Thimble' and 'Pin the Tail on the Donkey', with prizes for the winners. Dena came first in the sack race and won a pocket diary, which pleased her enormously. It represented something to add to her small collection of treasured possessions.

That evening as they all sat around in their dressing gowns drinking their cocoa, even stuck-up Nora Talbot conceded that it had been a wonderful day. And then Miss Stanford came in and got everyone excited again by announcing that she had an extra little treat for them.

She was carrying a large brown paper bag and, dipping in her hand came up with a fistful of sweets, which she began tossing up in the air. There was a mad scramble as everyone dived to catch one. Sweets still being on ration they were a rare treat. Dena managed to catch a stick of coltsfoot rock but Norah Talbot pushed her over and snatched it out of her hand.

'You nasty piece of work, give that back.' Dena tried to grab her but Norah held it too high for her to reach, so she was forced to return to the fray and try and catch another sweet instead. Unfortunately she was too late and they were all gone, Miss Stanford too. Dena was bitterly disappointed and felt a betraying prick of tears at the back of her eyes.

'Aw, diddums, not going to cry are you? Did the poor little new girl not get a toffee then? What a shame!'

Dena turned on Norah with a hiss. 'Don't think you can bully me. I know all about bullies and I'll not put up with it.'

Norah laughed. 'You'll not have this coltsfoot rock neither. Not unless you can give me something in return for it. What all new girls have to learn,' she continued, clearly enjoying herself, 'is that we do swaps here. We don't mind what it is, nice new hanky, bar of soap, sweeties sent from home, but if you want any peace and to be left alone, it'll cost you. Understand?'

Dena was silent. She understood well enough what Norah was telling her, and didn't like the sound of it one little bit.

'And what if I don't have anything to swap?'

'Everyone has something, like that new diary for instance.'

'I won that fair and square.'

'Show her how it's done, Katy,' Norah said, folding her arms in that self-important manner she had.

The quiet, obedient Katy held out a tatty copy of *The Beano* and began to walk around the common room chanting, 'Who'll swap something for this?'

Another girl stepped forward. 'I'll swap you this school friend.' And so the deal was done. Then Norah broke off a tiny piece of the rock and offered it to Katy in exchange for the new comic. Katy reluctantly agreed. Although she hadn't been allowed the chance to even read it yet and really didn't care for coltsfoot rock, she knew better than to argue with Norah. The rest of the girls sat sucking their sweets, thankful that this little contest of wills didn't involve them.

'There you are,' said Norah, 'that wasn't too painful, was it? So now, what have you got in exchange for the rest of this stick of coltsfoot rock?'

Dena would have loved to say that she did have something to swap, not only for the rock but to trade for a new comic instead of the dreary religious tomes that filled the library shelves. But not for the world would she hand over the diary. She pointedly slipped it in her dressing gown pocket. 'I told you, I've nothing.'

'That's a bare-faced lie. I know for a fact that you do, something far more valuable than a diary.' Norah pulled something from her own pocket then dangled the silver heart locket that Kenny had given her, right before Dena's eyes.

Dena was appalled. Shock rippled through her and she began to shake with fury. 'You've been in my locker! You thief!' She flew at the other girl, made a grab for the locket but missed entirely as Norah swung it out of reach. Seconds later the two girls were grappling with each other on the floor and all the rest were cheering them on. Norah spat in her face, peevishly pinched the skin on her arm, then kneed her in the stomach. Dena doubled up in agony for a moment before lurching forward and grabbing a fistful of Norah's hair, and made the other girl scream at the top of her voice.

Unfortunately the sound alerted Carthorse who came galloping into the room snorting with fury. 'What on earth is going on here!'

Fighting was forbidden at Ivy Bank and they were both severely punished by being made to scrub the bathroom floors and clean the lavatories for a whole week.

The party was most definitely over, but the feud between the two girls had only just begun.

–

Belle too was missing Dena, far more than she'd expected. Not only had the girl been a good worker, but trade had fallen off considerably since she left. It was astonishing how many people no longer visited the cafe now that the girl was no longer there to serve them. Infuriating! If Belle wasn't so dependent upon the cafe for her profits, then it really wouldn't matter. The way this market operated at present was, in Belle's humble opinion, a complete shambles.

There was so much needing to be done, and she was the one to do it. She'd be much more effective than Joe Southworth. A real loser he was! Soft-hearted and henpecked, and terrified of stepping on anyone's toes, that was Joe's problem. Though he did have a few hidden charms.

She glanced fondly across at the head lying beside her on the pillow and smiled to herself. What was she worrying about? She still had plenty of charms of her own, despite the passing of the years, and Joe was putty in her hands, just like all the other losers.

Leaning closer she kissed his shoulder, then his cheek, rough with stubble. Then she tickled his ear. 'Joe, isn't it time you weren't here? Won't Irma be wondering where you've got to?'

He was out of bed like a pellet fired from a gun, and Belle burst out laughing. 'Don't panic, it isn't morning yet. You can tell her that you had some late business to attend to, eh?'

He was busily trying to squeeze his fat buttocks into his trousers. 'I've told her that tale so many times she's beginning to grow suspicious.'

Belle pushed back the sheets a little, allowing them to drape provocatively over the rise of her full breasts as she smiled up at him, violet eyes issuing a challenge as she licked her rosebud lips. 'Not regretting our little tumble are you, Joey dear?' and laughed all the more as she saw the movement in his trousers. 'Apparently not.'

The hunger in his eyes was most gratifying and Belle pulled back the sheet to allow a better view of her still fascinating figure. He gulped, giving a little groan deep in his throat.

Belle's expert fingers swiftly unbuttoned the flies he'd so carefully done up before he realised what was happening, fondling his penis as if it were an old friend, as indeed it was. 'Joey,' she purred. 'One for the road, eh?'

She had his trousers off in no time and was soon homing her old friend back into familiar territory. Joe liked it a bit rough and Belle was always happy to oblige with any little peccadilloes her men-friends might have. Like all her previous lovers, he adored the fact that she took control, and that she was a noisy and enthusiastic mistress.

But then Belle enjoyed sex. It was her favourite pastime. And the second time in a night was always better than the first.

She gasped out loud and arched her back, a spasm running through her. 'Oh God, Joe, that's so good. No, no, let me just…'

She was on top of him now, riding him hard, watching the sweat roll down his flabby face as his excitement mounted. On and on she rode, impatient to reach that perfect pitch of pleasure, and achieving it long before he did. She slumped in triumph when he finally climaxed.

Was this the moment to ask?

But then she heard a resonant snore and chuckled softly to herself.

It was almost an hour later before he woke and reluctantly climbed out of bed once more. 'Dammit, it's no good, Belle, I'll have to go.'

She sat up, leaning casually back against the mound of soft, silky pillows. Belle might have come up from the gutter but she had impeccable taste, knew how to provide comfort, and how to satisfy a man's every need, that his wife wouldn't ever have heard of.

She judged the moment to be opportune. 'I was wondering if you'd given any further thought to what I mentioned the other day about a change in the regulations? You know, the sale of goodwill and licences, fines over market discipline and such. And really, the place looks untidy at times with cabbage leaves and litter everywhere. Some of these new stallholders don't show the same sense of responsibility as we old-timers. They should pay more for the privilege then they might appreciate what they have. Don't you think so?'

Joe had fought his way into his shirt and waistcoat by this time and wasn't really listening. 'I can't talk about this just now, Belle. It's not the right time, I have to go.'

The smile vanished in an instant. 'So when is the right time? If I mention it in the office, you're too busy with your normal day's routine. If we're in the pub you want to relax, and now that you have relaxed, you still haven't time. Champion Street Market needs expanding and bringing up to date. We could build some covered stalls outside, for instance. Perhaps increase the size of the fish market. There's a great deal could be done, and I'd be willing to help, draw up a few plans?'

Joe shrugged on his jacket and was already halfway to the door but he paused momentarily to heave a gentle sigh. 'Not now, Belle love! Anyway, I can see no reason for any changes. We're a small friendly market, let's leave it at that. Things are fine as they are. Anyway, we've no money.'

'You could put up the fees, charge extra for disposing of rubbish or for having the best pitch such as being on the front line.'

'Folk would object. They can't afford to pay any more, not with trade going downhill as it is, and I'd have to consult the council. They'd need to have their say and they might not approve. They can be very difficult.'

'Don't be so defeatist, Joe. The council might like the idea of a bigger and better market and offer us a grant. If you put me on the committee, I'd be happy to discuss it with them. A few grumpy old councillors don't worry me.' Anyway, she'd slept with a few of them, Belle thought with a soft smile of nostalgia.

'Nay, Irma would really smell a rat if I put you on the market committee.'

'Why would she? I've stood this market for twenty years, and owned the cafe for nearly ten. I surely deserve some say.'

'It would be best if you got someone else to propose you, Belle love, anyone but me. I'll have a quiet word with some of the new stallholders, point out they need to mend their ways and be a bit tidier, but I'm not inclined to change any of the rules at this juncture, or try anything new at the present time.'

'Pompous twit!' Belle muttered as the door closed behind him. If she were market superintendent it would all be very different. But she couldn't even get herself elected on to the committee.

Well, there were more ways than one of skinning a rabbit. She'd get her own way in this, if she had to strangle the little bleeder with her own fair hands.

Chapter Thirteen

Carl was sitting in the kitchen when Belle sauntered downstairs half an hour later in her jazzy pink dressing gown. She could tell by the way he glared at her that he'd seen Joe sneaking off, and didn't approve. She adored this elder son of hers but he seemed to find the fact that his mother was still capable of having sex, as an embarrassment.

Belle went to put on the kettle. 'Go on, get it off your chest. Say what you have to say.'

'What game are you up to this time? Where is all this leading? Joe Southworth isn't your type. He's a happily married man with two kids and you promised me faithfully you'd leave the married ones alone in future, after that trouble you had the last time.'

Belle shrugged and lit up a Capstan Full Strength. 'I'm making an exception in Joe's case. He's worth the effort. Anyway, that Irma's a right little cow. He deserves better.'

'You're up to something. I know you.' Carl got up from the kitchen table and went to stand beside his mother, watching with some impatience while she spooned tea in the pot and poured boiling water over it. 'Well, are you going to tell me, or what?'

Belle looked at him with fond affection. Carl had always been over-protective of her, ever since he was a small boy. He loved his mam, and why shouldn't he? Strictly speaking he and Kenny were only half-brothers, and Carl's olive skin gave some hint of his Italian ancestry. Not that Belle was saying who his father was. That was her secret, one she'd take with her to the grave if necessary.

Fortunately, the boy had never shown any inclination to find out, probably assuming she didn't even know for certain. Belle drew on her cigarette, smiling at him through the curl of smoke. He might be right there, but there was always room for doubt.

'Joe and me go a long way back, and he's been having a hard time of it lately. If I can bring him a bit of comfort, so what?' Her silk dressing gown slid off one shoulder as she shrugged and Carl pushed it back into place.

His life seemed to be full of problems at the moment. As if he didn't have enough to worry about with Kenny, now his mother seemed hell-bent on making a complete fool of herself over the market superintendent.

His brother was behaving like a proper prat over that young lass, writing letters to her, mooning about how he missed her and couldn't live without her. What had got into the lad Carl simply couldn't understand. Dena Dobson was just a silly young girl, no different from a thousand others, and more light-fingered than some. Nowhere near as innocent as she made out.

Yet this calf love of Kenny's didn't seem to stop him playing the field, judging by the number of girls he'd taken out lately, there wasn't too much to worry about.

'So what's in it for you?' he asked Belle, accepting the mug of tea she handed to him. 'No one can accuse Joe Southworth of being the most handsome creature on God's earth.'

'Depends who's looking.' Belle sat down at the table and crossed one leg over the other, making sure she carefully covered her knee with her dressing gown. Carl was a bit of a prude, always concerned about what was right and proper, reputation and such like, and very strong on family. Now that was another thing he got from his father. 'All right, I agree, Joe is no James Mason. Doesn't have much in the upstairs department either, although downstairs seems to be in full working order.'

'Mam!'

'Sorry, love! Fact is, I think he's pretty useless as a market super-intendent, if you want my opinion. Right piece of wet lettuce, and as a result folk run rings round him. They take advantage all the time. Champion Street Market is going downhill fast and customers are voting with their feet and going to other markets instead. It won't do. The stallholders are complaining, and is it any wonder? This is our livelihood we're talking about here.'

'So what's the answer?' She'd captured his attention now and Carl sat down at the table opposite her, interested to hear her solution.

'I could do a much better job, you know I could. The only problem is, I can't seem to get myself voted on to the committee, so how can I hope to take over, or squeeze him out? And I'm quite sure he's the one blocking me, so I thought why not try a little gentle persuasion. It's worth a try.'

'OK, I get the picture.' It was no wonder she attracted men like flies round a jam pot. For all she was over forty her figure was still good, her brunette hair thick and vibrant, and her heart-shaped face and full pouting lips a strange mix of innocence and beguiling allure. But Joe Southworth should know better.

'So what's sparked off your interest? You've never shown any inclination in getting involved with the committee before. Don't tell me that you're learning a bit of responsibility in your old age? Although I must say I admire your concern over the other stallholders, Mam, even if it does take a bit of swallowing.'

She looked at him as if he'd run mad. 'I don't give a shit about the other stallholders, pardon my French. It's me own profits I'm thinking of, and they're going downhill fast, chuck. Not a good direction to be moving in, and I blame useless old Joe Southworth for that, bless his cotton socks.'

Carl sighed. 'I should've known. You haven't considered the possibility that the drop in profits at the cafe might have some other cause, I don't suppose?'

'No, I haven't!'

'Like pretty little Dena has left, service is slow and Joan isn't pulling her weight like she used to? That steak pie she made the other day was tough as old boots. Where did you buy the meat?'

'It was a bargain offer.' Belle drew heavily on the cigarette then impatiently docked it out. 'Like I told you, profits are down. I have to make savings where I can. Look, if you're only going to criticise, you can shut your face!'

'It's you I'm thinking of, Mam. I worry about you.'

Her gaze softened, and she smiled lovingly at him. 'I know, love. You're a good lad, but don't you see, it's you and our Kenny I'm thinking of. Working the market is a fool's game, one I seem to be stuck with so must make the most of. Then happen I can afford to get something better for my boys, for you both. A business you can be proud of.'

'I can look after myself, thanks.'

'Happen you can. I'm not so sure about our Kenny though.' She frowned, looking troubled for a moment, then pushed back her rumpled brunette curls in a characteristically erotic gesture. 'Think yourself lucky you have a nice safe job and only need to worry about collecting your wages at the end of the week. That'll do you nicely for now, chuck, till you go into business on your own account. Once we've got a bit of capital put by, you could maybe own your transport company one day, eh?'

Carl sighed, having heard this all before. 'I've no plans in that direction, Mam.'

''Course you haven't, you're young yet, but I have great hopes for you, love. Great hopes! So don't you let me down.' She wagged a scarlet tipped fingernail at him. 'In the meantime, I mean to get on that flaming committee and start to make some improvements round here. You can take my word for it. So, unless you've any better suggestions, I'll carry on softening Joe up. Now I'm going to take a nice, leisurely bath. Ta-ra, chuck.'

As she reached the door, he got up and went after her to rest one long brown hand on her shoulder. 'Mam, I love you, right? We don't have to make a fortune to be happy, so stop making yourself look cheap in this way. I don't like it.'

She patted his cheek with genuine affection, tears shining like jewels in her violet eyes. 'I know you don't, lovey, but needs must when the devil drives, eh? Like Mae West used to say, "I've been rich and I've been poor. Rich is better."'

Barry Holmes, having lost Pete's willing assistance, found himself a new Saturday lad. Like all his predecessors, the boy attended the club for a spot of coaching every Friday evening, regular as clockwork. He was tall and skinny, all legs and arms with a top-knot of wild red hair, frayed grey trousers down to his knees, National Health specs and a snotty nose, and went by the name of Spider.

On this particular night Barry had him doing circuit training, a workout on the weights, then the expander. After that it was on the mat for some ground exercises and a spot of wrestling to tone up the muscles, a bit of leg-work on his favourite exercise, the skipping rope. Nothing like it for toning up those heart muscles!

It was while he was putting the boy through his paces that Carl walked in, took one look and said, 'Poor lad. You're a hard taskmaster Barry. At least give him time to wipe his nose.'

Barry grinned good-naturedly, not taking offence. 'Hey up, where's your Kenny then? Haven't seen him since that little contest of yours.'

'He's busy chasing a bit of skirt. Generally a different one each week.'

'I thought he were sweet on our lovely Dena, that she was his one and only?'

'Not so's you'd notice.'

Barry frowned. 'Growing up fast then, is he? Go on lad, ten more push ups. 'Course you can do it. One, two, three...'

'He thinks so, at least he's doing his best to flex some different muscles, shall we say? Whether he's managed it or not, I wouldn't care to hazard a guess.' Carl shook his head on a snort of laughter, then quickly changed into his warm-up gear and headed off to the punchbag. Barry followed him.

'Tell Kenny I'd still like him to pop in here from time to time. It's important he keeps up with his training and maintains his level of fitness. We don't want him running to flab. Anyway, there's that under eighteen's competition he was interested in entering coming up soon.'

'I'll mention it,' Carl agreed.

'Can I go home now?' Spider asked, butting in. 'Mam says I've to be in by eight.'

'I thought you'd want to go a couple of rounds?'

The boys eyes lit up. 'What now? Right y'are mister.'

Barry loved coaching but was never soft with his boys. As a lad himself he was worked hard by his own father in a strongman act touring the music halls, and would be tossed around like a shuttlecock, or made to do hand-to-hand balancing. This would always start off the act before his father moved on to lifting the heavy weights.

His father would then bend inch-thick steel bars, hammer six inch nails through a plank with his bare fists and, for a finale, would call on a few men from out of the audience. He'd have a couple hanging around his neck down his back and one tucked under each arm, then Barry would climb up to stand on his shoulders, and he'd lift the whole lot of them. He had grown into a replica of his father, being equally short and stocky, but did not possess anywhere near his physical strength. His father hadn't been a particularly gentle or soft parent, but Barry had survived, learning to look after himself. He had similar characteristics: a strange mix of tender heart and physical toughness. The only way, in his opinion, to win through.

And Barry certainly liked to win.

He tried to deal with his boys at the club fairly. But if sometimes they complained that they were tired, or saw him as something of a martinet because of the tough routines he put them through, he took absolutely no notice. Surely it was better that he keep these local tearaways fully occupied in his lad's club, guiding them along the right lines to become prize fighters, rather than have them hanging around street corners?

The new lad, gangly and a bit uncontrolled though his long limbs might be, proved to be quick and light on his feet, showing considerable potential. 'Keep your eyes on your opponent's gloves, not on the floor,' Barry instructed. Then he wiped his grimy face and sent him in for the second round. He was up against one of Barry's star pupils and not disgracing himself.

Barry stopped the fight early on before the pair could do too much damage to each other. 'Right, lads, that'll do. You can get off to your mam now, Spider. Only don't forget to shower first. We can't have you going home stinking of sweat and sawdust, so see you get clean. I'll be in later to check you've washed behind your ears.'

The boy grinned. 'I'll wash 'em right good, Mr Holmes. I promise.'

''Course you will, son.' So keen and eager, Barry thought, just like young Pete, and Kenny too in his day. How he missed them both.

This particular lad though was showing willing. Barry thought he would do very well indeed, might even make a champion one day, as Pete would have, if only things hadn't gone terribly wrong for the poor little tyke.

–

On his way home Barry ran into Winnie Watkins. 'Have you heard that Belle is after getting herself elected on to the committee?' Winnie asked him.

'May the Lord preserve us. She'd be queening it over all of us if she ever succeeded.'

'Exactly. There's a few of us getting together in my front room, my Donald having gone to bed early with a bad head, so I wondered if you'd care to join us.'

They were all there, Marco Bertalone and his pretty wife Carlotta, the Higginson sisters all neat and proper, each wearing this season's hat; big Molly Poulson, and Alec Hall in his familiar pink bow tie together with a smart velvet jacket. He was evidently on his way to an orchestral concert, which he was so fond of doing once he'd closed his music stall for the day. Sam Beckett was there too, as well as Jimmy Ramsay ruddy cheeked, as you would expect a butcher to be, along with several others.

It was Jimmy who got the proceedings under way, pointing out to all present why they'd decided to meet; that he'd nothing against Belle Garside personally, so long as she didn't try telling him how to run his business.

'Or the market,' put in Winnie, who was less of a fan.

'I think we are all agreed that it would not be a good idea for Belle to be put on the committee as she'd be sure to try and take over, and we're really quite happy with Joe.'

There were gentle murmurs of agreement.

'How to stop it happening, that is the point,' said Winnie. 'Make no mistake she has her sights set on power and glory.'

Annie Higginson cleared her throat before politely asking, 'Wouldn't Mr Southworth object? I mean, no one is due to stand down from the committee, are they?'

Alec Hall gave a little snort of derision. 'True, the next AGM is some months off but Belle is sorely miffed that she didn't get on this round, so she's going to use some strong persuasion tactics. We can't rely too much on Joe Southworth, and who knows what side he thinks his bread is buttered? Depends on events.'

Eyes shifted and there were a few embarrassed little coughs as his meaning sank in, then Barry Holmes said, 'To be fair, Belle has some good ideas, and she might be able to do something about security. I've had money stolen from my lock-up recently. Has anyone else had problems?'

No one said they had and so Sam Beckett chimed in with, 'I don't think there's any real cause for concern. Like Miss Higginson says, nothing's going to happen in a hurry, and Barry's right, Belle isn't all bad, just a bit too full of herself.'

Winnie was anxious to press her case. 'But we should all be aware of what she has in her sight, complete control of the market, not necessarily for our benefit, but hers. Therefore, we need to be diligent, that's all I'm saying.'

A small silence as heads nodded and frowns puckered on thoughtful brows. Finally, Molly Poulson slapped her hands down on her big fat knees, calling them all to attention. 'The important thing to come out of this meeting must be that we agree we don't want Belle elected, and if we stick together on this she's wasting her time, no matter how hard she campaigns. What can she do, anyway? She can't force us to vote for her?'

'She has two sons,' said Winnie quietly. 'Carl might be all right and a hard worker, but Kenny would shoot his own grandmother if Belle asked him to. He's a wild card that lad, always was, ready to do anything for a bit of attention.'

The silence this time was more troubled, broken by Barry Holmes. 'I agree the lad is a bit disturbed, churned up with jealousy over his more popular brother, and happen feeling a bit neglected by his mam, but that doesn't mean he's entirely without morals.'

Jimmy Ramsay made a few tutting noises. 'Let's not overreact, as we are all aware of the situation, and in agreement that we will remain vigilant.' The meeting was brought to a close.

Chapter Fourteen

Following the fight, Norah was consigned to kitchen duties and Dena was put in the laundry where she worked for five hours each day, thereby missing many of her favourite lessons. She'd been working there for months now and it was heartbreaking! For this she was paid two shillings and sixpence a week, a paltry sum that in no way compensated for the loss of her education, but did at least give her a little money to spend on writing paper, toothpaste and soap.

The job was not only boring, but exhausting. First she had to collect the dirty laundry from each dormitory, bundling it up in a sheet and lugging it down to the big, steamy laundry room. Here were set three great coppers of boiling water which were kept going all day long.

After the dirty washing had been sorted into their appropriate piles: sheets and towels and mountains of handkerchiefs in one, underwear in another, and the girls' socks, blouses and other garments sorted according to colour and fabric; woe betide Dena if she got it wrong, then the process began again.

There was the scrubbing and the bleaching, the pounding and the boiling. Next came the part Dena hated most, pushing the sopping wet sheets through the wringers. These were huge wooden rollers and turning them with the big wheel took every ounce of her strength. Even then she would have to push the thick fabric through till it caught on the rollers, very nearly trapping her fingers as she did so.

Last of all, the clean wet laundry had to be folded and carried outside to be pegged out on clothes lines, and on hot days she'd be dripping with sweat after the exertion. In less clement weather, cold water would run down her arms and her fingers would be numb by the time she was finished.

And when the ironing was done, it was time to begin the entire process all over again. What she wouldn't give to be back in the cafe.

Sundays at Ivy Bank should have been a pleasure since it was the only day of the week when there were no domestic duties, no chores of any kind beyond being required to neatly make their beds, as usual. Matron, being a strict Methodist was adamant on this score. Sunday must be a day of complete rest and recuperation, and also one of peaceful contemplation. There were times when even the laundry would have been an improvement.

Following chapel, enlivened by a few jolly hymns that did little to offset the boredom of the interminable sermon, would come endless classes. In these the girls were expected to recite texts they had been given to learn from the previous Sunday, and discuss their meaning, also display evidence of good works they had carried out during the previous week before settling to some worthy activity such as plain sewing or reading the bible.

They were constantly reminded how they would still be out on the streets if it weren't for the charity shown to them by the Methodist Church, and duly instructed to be grateful for the care they received at Ivy Bank. No one else had wanted them so they must be good girls and fear God, or even He might reject them.

Dena couldn't help thinking that this was a sad indictment on the Almighty. Would he really be so cruel as to punish her because she didn't have sufficient time to learn all these bible verses, now that her evenings were spent largely copying up notes she'd missed from lessons? Somehow she didn't think so.

Sunday lunch was always special with some sort of roast and a hearty fruit crumble with custard. The girls would look forward to it all week. And Sunday afternoons were more special for those with visits from family to look forward to.

Very few of the girls were orphans, most having families who were simply unable to care for them either through illness or death of a parent, poverty, or in some cases because the girl was illegitimate or the mother had married again, and her second husband refused to accept the children of her first marriage. Some, like herself, had been largely abandoned but there were a surprising number who did have family members who came to visit, and would often bring treats and presents from home.

No one ever came to see Dena, which added to her sense of isolation. But then since she was this dreadful person who had failed to protect her own brother while he was beaten up and drowned, was it any wonder if nobody cared about her? While the other girls sat and chatted with their families, Dena would hide away in her room reading, preferring to be alone, and trying not to think of Pete's cheerful face or her mother's anger.

So it was that when the housemother came charging into the dormitory in her blundering way, Dena could hardly believe her ears to find herself ordered to run along to the common room as she too had a visitor today. Who could it possibly be? Kenny? Surely he wouldn't dare? Dena ran all the way along the landing and down the stairs against the rules.

–

She found Miss Rogers waiting for her in the common room and was surprisingly pleased to see the familiar, tall, angular figure of the social worker. The woman suddenly seemed like a friend in this world of strangers. Even her be-whiskered chin and tightly pursed mouth didn't seem half so threatening as they once had. Dena rushed to her on a burst of enthusiasm.

'Miss Rogers, how lovely to see you.' She was wearing a severe grey coat and matching felt hat, black gloves and handbag, as if it were November instead of August.

Looking slightly taken aback by the welcome the woman managed a thin smile. 'I trust you are well, Dena. I deliberately left it a few months before I came, so as not to unsettle you.'

Dena agreed that she was very well, thank you, as this seemed to be the required response. Miss Rogers then informed her that she was looking much better, and appeared to have put on weight. 'You have round pink cheeks at last. Clearly the good food, fresh air and excellent care you are receiving here is proving to be entirely beneficial. Splendid!'

'I eat everything they put before me,' Dena agreed, and sometimes what they don't, she thought, wisely making no reference to the jam butty she'd stolen in those first few frightening days.

They sat in a corner of the common room and Dena gave a carefully edited version of life at Ivy Bank, judiciously making no mention either of being punished for spilling milk when she was chased by the geese, nor the fight with Norah Talbot.

She did tell her all about the party they'd recently enjoyed to celebrate the coronation. 'I expect they all had street parties back home, didn't they?'

'Oh yes,' Miss Rogers agreed. 'They did and your beloved market was royally trimmed up with bunting and Union flags.'

A lump came into Dena's throat. 'I think of them all at Champion Street Market every single day. I do miss them! My friend Winnie on the fabric stall in particular, and Mrs Poulson's pies, and jolly Mr Ramsay and his lovely pork sausages. He always gave me an extra one when I bought a few for Mam and me.'

There followed a small silence, then, 'How is Mam? Have you seen her?'

Miss Rogers cleared her throat. 'I did call in on her, after I'd returned from bringing you here. But she was out.'

'What? I heard what you said, Miss Rogers, but until the day she went to phone you, she'd never set foot outside the door, not since our Pete was drowned.'

'I expect she'd only gone to the corner shop to do some buying in. Remember she no longer has you to do all of that for her now.'

It seemed so unfair, somehow, that her mother could achieve such a rapid recovery, and only because Dena was no longer there to look after her.

'I also called on her a few days ago, to tell her that I was coming to see you today, and ask if she would care to accompany me.'

'Obviously she said no, since there's no sign of her,' said Dena, a bitter edge to her tone.

Again Miss Rogers seemed troubled by a cough. 'Actually, she was packing when I called. Clearing out the house and preparing to leave.'

'Clearing out the house? Why? Where could she go?' Dena felt bemused by her mother's odd behaviour. It was all very puzzling. 'She hasn't been evicted, has she, for not paying rent?'

'No, nothing like that! Alice told me that she was moving in with her brother. It seems that he called one afternoon and they talked, for the first time in years apparently. Her parents – your grandparents – have both passed away and he – your uncle – is all alone in the world now. He has invited your mother to join him at the family home. She seemed pleased to be returning to the bosom of her family, as it were, and it will be much better for her.'

Dena had been listening to all of this in astonishment, eyes shining with new hope. 'So you've come to take me home, haven't you, Miss? I can go and live with me uncle now.'

The silence that followed this heartfelt plea was long and heavy, and the pain of the woman's next words would live with Dena forever. 'Sadly, your mother still does not feel able to cope with you, Dena, and was most adamant that you were not included in the invitation. You must stay here, at Ivy Bank.'

Dena blinked at her in blank incomprehension. 'You mean me mam doesn't want me to go back home and live with her in the family house? Me uncle neither?'

'No,' murmured the social worker, pity husking her voice. 'I'm afraid not.'

–

To be rejected once by her mother had been bad enough, twice left Dena stunned, paralysed with shock. For the rest of that day she didn't utter a single word. Dena chose to withdraw from the noise and excitement of the other girls' reaction to their visitors and sit alone in a corner, asking herself what she had done to deserve such treatment. She knew the answer: her mother still blamed her for Pete's death. No matter how fiercely Dena might protest that she had done all she could to protect her little brother, Mam would never believe it. She was condemned to carry the blame of it for the rest of her life. Never to be forgiven.

But how could she be so unfeeling, so unkind, so cruel? And this brother of hers, Dena's uncle apparently, was obviously just as bad. Well, they deserved each other. Dena resolved not to allow them, or anyone else for that matter, to ever be made aware of the terrible pain they'd caused her, or of the scars their rejection had left.

She'd survive on her own, without any help from anyone, she decided, a healthy anger firing up inside.

When she got ready for bed that night, Dena read Kenny's letter again, trying to assuage the heat of her resentment by finding evidence of love written within its pages, but the pain was too strong, too deeply ingrained, and even his loving words could offer no comfort. Nor, for once, did she put on her precious locket but left it tucked inside her bible with the letter.

Dena lay wide-eyed in the darkness, unable to sleep. Nor was she able to shut out the image of Pete's cheeky grin. She felt too wretched, the rejection by her mother simply too much to bear.

Her one consolation was that at least she didn't shed a single tear. She felt strangely calm inside, as if a steel door had come down and shut away all feeling. Miss Rogers had kindly brought Dena two tablets of soap and a tin of talcum powder, which she'd stowed carefully away in her locker, grateful for the woman's thoughtfulness. The social worker had also brought a small square of ginger cake, and Dena had smuggled this too into the dormitory, against the rules.

Later that night, hearing the other girls around her doing the same, she brought out the cake and shared it with her friend, Gwen. Between them they gobbled it all up. And although eating illicit cake at midnight was no compensation for being rejected by her mother, it was nevertheless delicious and preferable to sobbing her heart out.

And they were not alone. There were muted giggles all around, a bubbling excitement and happiness in the dormitory, for once, from those girls fortunate enough to be brought sweets or treats by their family.

For those who had spent the day alone, without visitors, and had nothing to nibble in bed, it was a miserable time, dependant upon the generosity of others. Dena was usually one of their number, so for once revelled in the thrill of being in possession of being able to share it with her friend. She didn't even care if Matron came in and caught them. They were just finishing off the last crumbs when a torch flashed and both dived under the covers.

A familiar voice came out of the darkness. 'I know you two are eating. I can hear you munching and giggling. Give me a piece or I'll tell.'

'Get lost, Norah! There's none left, anyway.'

'Give me something else then.'

Dena turned her back on the girl and pulled the covers over her head. 'Why should I? Do your worst, what do I care?'

Chapter Fifteen

Norah did indeed do her worst. First thing the following morning when Carthorse came lumbering into the dormitory on the dot of seven, issuing orders and ringing her beloved handbell, she instantly went up to the housemother and reported Dena for breaking the rules by eating in bed. Everyone else, equally guilty, listened in stunned silence as Norah betrayed Dena in her sing-song catty voice. Yet not a soul dared argue or attempt to defend her against the accusation, in case they implicated themselves.

'If you look in her locker you'll find the paper it was wrapped in. It was a huge cake and we all told her that she must hand it in to cook so it could be shared amongst us all at teatime, but she wouldn't listen.'

Dena's locker was indeed searched, the incriminating paper covered with sticky ginger crumbs was found, and the soap and talcum powder confiscated. The deprivation of these gifts was clearly intended to teach her a lesson for the sin of greed.

Dena fiercely protested, declaring that no one had any right to take her possessions. Didn't she have little enough to call her own?

'You should have thought about that before you broke the rules, Dena Dobson. You don't seem to be very good at fitting in, do you? Well, you'll think twice next time.'

Dena steamed with inner rage against her rival, yet managed to remain silent, knowing when she was beaten.

It proved to be a long unhappy day but worse was to come.

That evening when Dena reached for her precious locket to wear beneath her nightie as she so liked to do, she found, to her horror, that it was gone, along with her letter from Kenny. They were both missing.

'Have you seen my locket?' she asked Gwen, desperation in her tone. But the other girl shook her head.

'It's all I have left in the world to call my own. I'll kill whoever's taken it.'

Carthorse appeared. 'Lights out, girls. Dena Dobson, in bed this minute.'

She'd have to wait to deal with the matter first thing in the morning, but she knew who to blame.

–

Dena pushed her way through the line of naked girls all desperately trying to cover their modesty with one inadequate towel as they waited their turn for the bathroom, and caught up with Norah just as she stepped out of the bath. Norah Talbot always made sure that she was first in line to enjoy the privilege of the hottest, freshest water.

Without pause for thought Dena leapt forward and gave the girl a hefty punch in the shoulder. 'Where is it? What have you done with my locket?' She pushed her again, harder this time to emphasise her words.

Norah's feet suddenly went from under her on the wet slippy floor and she fell backwards, cracking her head on the tiles. A gasp went up from the horrified audience, and then a sigh of relief as they realised that she hadn't been knocked unconscious by the fall but was lying on the floor laughing up at Dena.

'And you're a liar, telling me you had nothing to swap. Well, your precious locket is mine now, so take your hands off me. I have your love letter too, and might even write to that soppy boyfriend of yours.'

Dena lost control. All the anger stored up inside her as a result of the dreadful news brought to her yesterday by Miss Rogers, of her mother's further rejection, and the guilt she felt over her brother's death, seemed to explode inside, bursting out in a white hot rage.

She tore at Norah's hair, slapped her about the face, kicked and thumped her with bare feet and fists, heedless of the screams of the other girls, or of the clatter of boots pounding down the corridor. She didn't even stop fighting when hands lifted her bodily from the now still figure of Norah Talbot and carried her bodily away.

–

Dena stood before Matron in her stark, gloomy office and endured a merciless lecture that seemed to go on for hours, hearing how this kind of dreadful behaviour would no longer be tolerated.

'I really am growing tired of this habit you have of stirring up trouble, Dobson. Either you calm down and conform to the rules set down for your own good, or you will be sent to a reformatory where you will soon learn the error of your ways. The choice is yours, girl. Get yourself under control or you'll find the cost of your wilfulness greater than you ever imagined. Never, in all my days have I witnessed such appalling behaviour! Poor Norah is now in the sanatorium with all manner of cuts and bruises, as well as a most dreadful headache.'

Good, Dena thought, although was sensible enough not to express this remark out loud.

'Can you offer any explanation at all for attacking her?' Matron's stern gaze seemed to penetrate to the core of her being. 'I am giving you one last chance to tell the truth. Speak up, girl!'

Dena remained silent. Would it help if she accused Norah of stealing? Should she tell Matron that the girl was a bully who terrorised the younger girls? She rather thought not. Norah might go in for snitching on others, Dena never would. It might only create further problems in the form of retaliation, on others as well as herself. An endless, self-perpetuating vendetta! She fully intended to retrieve her beloved locket, and deal with Norah in her own time, and in her own way.

She looked Matron in the face, a hardness in her own that shocked the older woman, inured as she was to rebellious young girls. 'No, Matron! I have no explanation at all.'

'And for no reason whatsoever, you hit her? This was a completely unprovoked attack?'

Silence.

'I'm waiting.'

'Yes,' Dena hissed under her breath.

'What did you say?'

'I said, yes! We don't get on. I hate the little piece of shit.'

For the heinous crime of fighting, made worse by using profane language, Dena was locked in an empty room with nothing but a mat to sleep on and bread and water to drink. She was left there for three long days, with the stink of her own urine and excrement coming from a chamber pot standing in one corner.

It felt like a living hell. Nevertheless, Dena endured the punishment without a word of complaint, nor shedding a single tear. She no longer cared what they did to her any more. She was beyond emotion. Her heart had solidified into a hard, unfeeling ball of ice and Dena very much doubted she would ever feel warm or happy again.

–

Kenny arrived at the club late, having stopped off to buy himself some fish and chips then inadvertently found himself embroiled in a bit of a fracas with some of the bigger lads. 'Look out, it's Mary Ann,' one called out. 'Went out with Sandra Phillips, who's anybody's for threepence, and couldn't get it up.'

He'd kill that Sandra next time he saw her.

Kenny laughed, put on his most convincing swagger, curling his lip and sneering, doing his best to look tough and disguise the fear and shame churning inside. 'I didn't even bother to try. I like 'em young and fresh not well used.' Since Kenny was still a virgin himself this wasn't strictly true but he had to save face somehow.

Kenny liked girls, particularly Dena who was special, but he found it easier to keep them at a distance. He really didn't like to be touched. He didn't even care to touch a girl's private parts. It felt like an invasion, as if she might not like it, as if it would be wrong if she did like it. And he'd tried hard enough, had taken out any number. He would get all excited but then be repelled by the very thought of actually doing it!

What was wrong with him?

He preferred to simply admire their feminine prettiness, to have them flirt with him, but taking it any further, actually getting down to the messy business of making love was a different matter altogether. He really wasn't sure he could manage that.

This particular gang was one of the worst in the neighbourhood. They were all wielding coshes and knuckle-dusters, and looking very dangerous indeed. Kenny thought it would be no bad thing if he were similarly armed himself. For now, though, he decided that caution was his best option and took to his heels and ran, trying not to listen to the raucous laughter that echoed the length of the street behind him.

Once at the club he took out his pent-up frustration by pummelling young Spider to within an inch of his puny life. He gave him such a beating that Barry stopped the fight in the third round.

'That's enough, lad. Enough, I say!'

Blood was pouring out of Spider's nose and there were cuts above his eyes and on his lips. Barry reached for the sponge to start mopping him up, fuming quietly inside.

'What's got you in a paddy tonight? Whatever it is, there's no reason to take it out on poor Spider. We can't send you home looking like this, lad. Your mam'll have a fit. We'll have to get you seen by the doc tomorrow. You're my best chance for the under-eighteens' trophy.'

Kenny knocked the sponge out of Barry's hands. 'Don't push him so flippin' hard. Leave the poor lad alone.'

Barry's eyes glittered. 'Jealous are you, Kenny?'

'No, I'm flaming not.'

'You could be winning prizes too, Kenny, if you put the training in. Trouble is, you don't have the control or the discipline. Why not come round to mine and we'll talk things through, eh? I've got plenty of beer in.'

'No thanks,' Kenny muttered, half under his breath. 'I've places to go, things to do.'

'Suit yourself. You know you're always welcome. You come along with me, Spider lad, while I find some antiseptic. And we need to talk about next week's competition, about how best you should play it.'

Kenny swung away from them and set off home alone, hands thrust deep in his pockets, kicking moodily through puddles, unheeding of the soaking his trousers were getting as bubbles of rain bounced off the pavements. The house would be empty, his mam no doubt out with some geyser or other, and he really didn't feel up to coping with another lecture from Carl. He didn't have a date tonight and he suddenly felt overwhelmed by loneliness, by the feeling that nobody cared about him. Feeling decidedly sorry for himself he called in at the off-licence and bought himself a few beers. It was possible to get anything, even if you were underage. It just took the right sort of tactics.

–

When Dena finally arrived back in the dormitory, all the girls gathered round, eager to show sympathy and support for the punishment she'd endured in her solitary cell. It was a strangely moving moment. No one had ever shown the slightest compassion towards her before. Other than her friend Barry, but that had been so long ago she could scarcely remember. The other girls too were fed up of Norah's bullying tactics, and admired the fact that Dena had been brave enough to stand up to her.

Norah Talbot returned a few days later, none the worse for her spell in the sanatorium. In fact, crowing with satisfaction over her apparent triumph over Dena, and bragging about how she'd been spoiled by Matron who'd allowed her special treats of cakes and chocolate and grapes to eat.

As if by common consent a plan was hatched, and this time it was Norah herself who became the victim.

That night the girls crept up to her bed and slid their dressing cords over Norah as she slept, tying her to the bedpost. Just as she awoke and opened her mouth to call out, Dena shoved in a scarf and gagged her.

'Now listen very carefully,' Dena whispered. 'When I remove this scarf from your big fat mouth, you're going to tell me where you have put my locket, and quietly return it to me. You're also going to return Gwen's Five Boys chocolate, Phyllis's book and Katy's new handkerchief, plus any other treasures your greedy little magpie fingers might have nicked. If you don't, then we are going to pour these two jugs of icy cold water all over you and your bed, and soak you right through. Understand? Got that?'

She gave a small nod.

'Good, because that would be just a beginning. We could think of any number of other little tricks to play on you, if we put our mind to it.'

Dena slowly unfastened the scarf while every girl in the room held her breath. They all knew it would take only one loud yell from Norah to bring the wrath of the dreaded Carthorse – or worse, Matron herself – down upon them. Then the fat really would be in the fire. Every last one of them would be severely punished. It really didn't bear thinking about.

But, for once, Norah was genuinely frightened. It was all too easy to bully one girl, but not so comfortable to attempt the same trick on a whole group.

The locket, along with many other items of value, was recovered and an uneasy peace ensued. Although Dena remained wary of Norah Talbot, not trusting the girl as far as she could throw her, the incident so far as she was concerned, was closed.

Chapter Sixteen

Life continued at Ivy Bank much as normal, even though the days seemed longer than ever as Dena waited impatiently for release. The second year of her stay seemed to go by much quicker than the first, and in no time at all Christmas was almost upon them once more. She was well used to the routine and had plenty of friends now: Gwen, Phyllis, and even Katy who had once been hand in glove with Norah, and although there was still animosity between herself and the erstwhile bully, Dena managed to keep her distance.

But she was lonely for the market, longed for her freedom and to have someone who really cared about her. She lived for Kenny's weekly letter, generally short and with nowhere near as much news of her friends on the market as she would have liked, but always full of his love for her.

One day, quite out of the blue, he announced that he intended coming to see her just before Christmas, and Dena was filled with excitement. Boyfriends were not allowed at Ivy Bank but she wouldn't let that stop her. What did she have to lose? Nothing!

Kenny was the only person in the entire world who cared a jot about her. She hated the home, the staff, Carthorse the housemother, Matron, everyone. Dena hated the entire world that held her prisoner and wanted to rebel against it, if only to prove that she was her own person and needed no one. She wanted to make it plain to everyone that she absolutely refused to be bullied and would do exactly as she pleased.

Most of all, she hated Alice, her so-called mother.

In the twelve long months since the fight and incarceration in that terrible windowless room, Dena had managed to avoid

Norah Talbot, largely by keeping herself to herself. She'd obeyed all the rules, done exactly as she was told and concentrated entirely on serving her time, rather like a prison sentence.

But she felt as if her young life was passing her by.

Dena had read in the papers that boys were creating a scandal by wearing Edwardian style suits and having their hair frizzed, and girls were wearing fashionable A-line dresses while she was still stuck with this dreadful old gymslip. Sweet rationing had finally ended and there were enticing posters advertising Wall's ice cream everywhere you looked, which they weren't allowed to eat at Ivy Bank. Roger Bannister had broken the four-minute mile, and *The Grove Family* had started on television. Not that they were ever allowed to watch it. And a singer called Elvis Presley had made a record called 'That's All Right, Mama', which all the girls wanted to listen to whenever it came on the wireless.

In just a few short months, and she was counting the days, she would turn sixteen and then she would kick the dust of this uncaring place off her heels for good.

Dena already knew that she intended to return to Champion Street Market. She would ask Belle for her old job back, and if that wasn't possible, she was certain that one of the other stallholders would offer her work. Where she would live and whether she could afford to support herself on such low wages she wasn't sure, but that was no reason not to try.

She meant also to have a good time: to buy lovely fashionable clothes, to go to dances and buy records as other girls did. Dena meant to live life to the full, and nothing and no one would stand in her way.

In the meantime, the prospect of seeing Kenny was like a miracle, a wonderful treat to look forward to. To once more feel his arms around her, his lips on hers, was something she dreamed of night after night. Dena was willing to take any risk to turn that dream into reality.

She began to make plans.

Girls often bunked off, slipping down the fire escape and trying to catch a bus or train that would take them miles away from Ivy

Bank, back to their families. Generally speaking they were soon found and returned to Matron's tender care, sometimes before they'd got a mile from the door.

Dena meant to be much cleverer than that. She had no intention of absconding, therefore would be in no danger of being spotted by some eagle-eyed bus conductor or railway porter.

She felt jittery with excitement. A romantic tryst in the woods with Kenny Garside was even better than her wildest dreams. Worth being locked away for a whole week on bread and water, worth any punishment Matron could dream up. Not that she had any intention of getting caught. Nor would she be, so long as none of the girls heard her leave, or no one inadvertently locked the fire escape while she was out.

Dena wrote back to Kenny straightaway, mentioning a spot in a nearby wood where the girls were often taken for a healthy walk. But no one would be going on nature rambles at midnight, so they'd be perfectly safe to meet there.

–

Carl told himself countless times that he really shouldn't be troubling his head about his stupid brother, or his mother either for that matter. If she wanted to behave like a whore, that was her business. He just hoped she didn't bring shame down upon them all. Her latest beau seemed to be Sam Beckett from the neighbouring ironmongery stall, though Carl was quite convinced she was also still seeing Joe Southworth, despite her protests of innocence in this regard.

Sam wasn't a typical Belle victim. For one thing, unlike Joe Southworth, he didn't have a wife, and being a stubborn sort of bloke he didn't like to be pushed around. In his mid thirties he was younger than Belle and had spent much of the latter years of the war as a POW. He'd had a hard time getting over that so she wouldn't find him quite so easy to handle. They'd already had a bit of a barney when Belle had asked him to put her forward for the market committee and he'd laughed his head off.

'And what would you use for brains, Belle?'

'At least mine aren't in my trousers,' she'd shouted back, but the row that ensued got her nowhere. Nor would it. Sam had a mind of his own and Carl understood perfectly why he was keen not to allow Belle on to that dratted committee, as was everyone.

She'd take it over completely, order everyone around and think herself Queen of the market. She would start demanding all kinds of changes because she was fiercely ambitious and not a little greedy, and would be eager to make some sort of impact to prove herself, while most of the other stallholders would prefer things to stay exactly as they were.

As for Kenny, he too seemed hell-bent on creating problems. Today Carl had arrived home from work to find him dressed up like something out of a western. Long jacket complete with velvet collar, tight drainpipe trousers, even a bootlace tie. There he stood in front of the hall mirror admiring himself as if he were a girl.

Carl burst out laughing. 'What's all this about? Are you off to a fancy dress party?'

Kenny stuck out his lower lip in that moody way he had, a bitter look in his eyes as he turned on his brother. 'This is the latest fashion I'll have you know. Not everyone wants to look like they've picked their clothes out of a rag-bag.'

Carl glanced ruefully down at his dusty blue overalls bearing the Catlow's motif on the breast pocket, and with a careless shrug went to the kitchen sink to rinse his hands and face in cold water. 'Who are you out with tonight? Jenny, Josie or Jeannie? It must get confusing. You could start working your way through the Ks next.'

'I'll go out with who I bleeding want.'

'Does this mean you're over Dena Dobson at last?' Carl asked as he rubbed his face dry on a rough towel, amusement rich in his tone. 'Thank the Lord for that, at least.'

'No, it doesn't. These dates don't mean a thing. They just help to pass the time. Dena is still my girl. She's the one for me.'

Carl reached for the frying pan and took four large pork sausages from the new green and cream refrigerator standing in the corner. 'They might mean something to her, if she ever finds out you're two-timing her.'

'You mind your own business, you. I thought we'd settled this once and for all, that you should keep your nose out of how I feel about Dena.'

'Aye, but I seem to recall that I won that particular contest, so I reckon I can keep on asking.' Carl jabbed at the sausages as they began to sizzle.

Kenny was dabbing Clearasil on a few spots he'd discovered on his chin. 'Well, I say you can't. I had enough problems with that brother of hers forever turning up at the wrong moment, just when I was trying to chat Dena up, so don't you start.'

Carl hadn't cared much for the little squirt either, right little troublemaker he was, always in trouble and ready to put folks' noses out of joint. It was no surprise to him that he'd come a cropper.

Kenny frowned at the spotted image of himself in the mirror, hoping the ointment would soon soak in. 'Matter of fact, I were thinking of going to see her in that home they've got her in. I don't suppose her mam bothers to go and see her and she must get fed up with having no visitors. Besides, she needs to know that she's still my girl. They'll be letting her out in just a few months and it's happen time we got engaged.'

Carl was shocked into silence by this surprising statement and stood, frying pan in hand, watching in astonishment as Kenny blithely applied yet more Brylcreem to his hair. He'd let it grow right down to his collar, with long sideburns, flicking back the front part into a quiff. Having satisfied himself that it was exactly how he liked it, Kenny smoothed down his jacket like a bird of paradise might groom his ruffled feathers.

Carl piled his cooked sausages on to a plate, along with two thick slices of buttered bread. 'Don't talk so daft! You're far too young to be getting serious.'

'Sez who?'

'Me! I say so.'

Kenny's response was to swagger out of the house, slamming the door behind him. Carl watched him go on a sigh of despair.

-

Carl spent a quiet evening in alone with the new Bush television set he'd bought for them, and thought maybe he must be getting old to be staying in on a Friday night, not even going down to the club for a workout. But somehow he felt in need of time on his own to think. He drank a few beers, watched Gilbert Harding, and wondered what the hell he was doing with his life. He told himself that it was time he stopped worrying about his flaming family, stopped watching and fretting over Kenny and left him to sort his own life out, the same with Belle. Long past time he gave more attention to his own future. And while he sat there watching the swan floating on the river in the programme interlude, it occurred to him that he was doing the same thing. Drifting along, getting nowhere, doing nothing.

Carl came to a decision. He would give up the driving. It was a dead-end job going nowhere anyway, and he wanted something better. He enjoyed driving his wagon to and from Manchester's many markets, loved the hustle and bustle, the urgency to deliver food early while it was still fresh and new. He'd lived and breathed the market all his life. This was where he belonged and wanted to be.

But his mam was right in one respect at least. He did want to be his own boss, and build up a business for himself, although not in transport.

She would not be pleased, given these grand ideas she nursed for 'her boys', but that was her problem. Belle had spoiled him rotten all his life, right from when he was little, for some reason always favouring him over Kenny. Perhaps it had more to do with who had fathered them than anything else. Whatever the reason, her attitude hadn't helped Kenny one bit, nor Carl himself for that matter. But he wasn't a silly kid any more. He was a grown man and he'd please himself what he did with his own life.

Nevertheless Carl had no wish to blunder into something without first getting all the facts. He needed much more information before he put the proposition to her. It would never do to alienate her from the start. Best to make sure that his idea could work, then he'd tell her.

What he needed was a bit of advice from a mate. He glanced at his watch. Not too late to nip down to the club for a beer, he decided, and reached for his coat.

Barry, he was told when he got there, had left minutes before. 'He's seeing some of his lads home. You'll probably catch up with them if you hurry,' the barman said, but Carl had a pint in front of him by this time and decided it could wait. After all, there really wasn't any rush. He couldn't pack in his job right now, not with Christmas just around the corner. He'd catch up with Barry another time.

-

On the way home from the club Kenny passed under the railway arches, the canal water glinting like ink in the light from a pale moon. He quickened his pace, as it was after closing time and there were a few rabble-rousers about very much the worse for booze. He'd had a few drinks himself, for all he was underage, and no doubt some of his mates would still be knocking it back, if they got half a chance.

For once Chippy wasn't with him, which was a relief.

Kenny enjoyed having a gang of lads around him, looking up to him as leader, doing his bidding, but tonight he was thankful to be on his own as he had a plan in mind. He was sixteen years old, not far off seventeen and still a virgin. And this problem he had with girls and sex was worrying him badly. How could he be a proper husband to Dena, if he couldn't get himself worked up to do what was required of him? Kenny had thought long and hard about this and believed he had found a solution.

He walked and walked and eventually came to the spot where he knew the prossies hung out. He took a moment or two to weigh them up, anxious to choose the right one. Most of them were young girls, experienced in the game he had little doubt, but not necessarily the best choice for him. They'd be sure to guess that it was his first time and could easily make him look a complete fool. Not that it would help at all.

And then he spotted her.

She was tall, rather graceful in stature, not so flashily dressed as the others and she had a pleasant smile on her face. Most important of all, she was older than the rest by a good ten years.

The woman saw him looking at her, seemed to recognise his shy hesitation yet obvious interest and sauntered over to talk to him. 'Hiya, chuck, my name's Maureen and I'm looking for a good time.'

He was searching for an education, for Maureen to solve this terrible problem he had, but he didn't say as much. Kenny just nodded, feeling suddenly tongue-tied. She smiled at him but didn't laugh, much to his relief; then she linked her arm in his in a friendly way and led him away into the darkness.

Chapter Seventeen

When the day of Kenny's visit finally arrived, Dena felt sick with anticipation and excitement at the prospect of seeing him again, as well as a secret joy over this private bit of rebellion. It proved that she was still a person in her own right, with a mind of her own who could do exactly as she pleased, even if she was incarcerated in this dreadful place. She waited until everyone was asleep and then put her plan into action. Slipping down the fire escape proved to be much easier than she'd expected. As soon as Dena reached the bottom she pulled out the bundle of clothing she'd hidden earlier beneath a laurel bush, and quickly pulled on a skirt and jumper over her nightie. Because it was such a cold night, she then put her raincoat on top.

After that it was simply a matter of tiptoeing across the lawn, climbing over the garden wall and ducking quickly into the undergrowth of hazel that grew beneath the taller ash and birch trees in the wood.

It was a clear night in early December, her way lit by a bright, full moon so that Dena reached the ancient oak in the heart of the woodland in no time at all. He was already there, waiting for her, and the moment he saw her Kenny ran to her and crushed her tightly in his arms. 'Dena, you don't know how much I've missed you! I've ached for you. Have you missed me?'

Dena was so thrilled she could hardly breathe. 'Oh, Kenny, you wouldn't believe how much.'

He seemed so pleased to see her, but then this was her Kenny, the only friend she had in all the world. Even so, he looked different from the Kenny Garside she remembered. Older, but then she too had changed, had filled out somewhat. Then it came to her that he was wearing one of those Teddy boy suits, had grown his hair and developed – what were they called – sideburns? He looked dashing, so fashionable and yet so dangerous. Nobody would push Kenny Garside around, not dressed like that.

And when he kissed her she felt overwhelmed by emotion, not wanting the magic ever to stop. So bewitched was she by his loyalty and love, Dena would have done anything for him, anything at all. She wanted, needed, longed for him to love her.

He pushed his tongue into her mouth and she welcomed that too, but then she'd learned a good deal from the other girls since she'd come to Ivy Bank, and understood now that this sort of kissing, French, they called it, would not get her pregnant. The tongue darted, circling her own and Dena felt a tightening in her belly.

His urgency thrilled her and she helped him spread out his raincoat so that they could sit together under the tree, holding each other close. 'It's so lovely that you haven't forgotten me after all this time, and that you came to see me. I never expected you to.'

'I wanted you to know that you're still my girl. I want you to come back to the market when you leave here.'

'I mean to. With luck I'll be there by Easter. I hoped that maybe your mam would let me have my old job back?'

''Course she will, and you must live with us. She won't mind. We have to put up with her boyfriends often enough,' Kenny said, his voice turning cold for a second. 'We'll get married as soon as you turn eighteen, if your mam will let you.'

Dena gave a bitter little laugh. 'My mam doesn't care what I do, but I'm not sure I'm ready for marriage yet, Kenny, or all that domestic, housewife stuff. There's no rush, is there? I mean, you don't have to marry me just because I've nowhere to live.'

'I love you, don't I? And I'll show you just how much.' He pushed her down and Dena thought that he was going to kiss her some more, but her school raincoat fell open and he noticed that she hadn't bothered to remove her nightie, seeing it drooping down below her skirt.

'Hecky-thump, you're a one. You came ready prepared, then?' He chuckled deep in his throat, and then he was fiddling with the button at the waistband of her skirt and peeled it off in no time, leaving her clad only in the flannel nightie. Only then did Dena remember that she was wearing no undergarments, no bra, not even her knickers, and felt herself blush with shame even as her heart quickened with desire. She'd given entirely the wrong impression. What would he think of her?

Kenny lifted the nightdress as far as her breasts so that he could see her naked body in the moonlight, and she could tell by the stunned admiration in his glinting eyes that he thought her beautiful. She expected him to touch her, to stroke her breasts, to caress her and tell her how pretty she was. But he seemed content simply to drink in the sight of her, which was a little disappointing and made her feel most desperately shy and embarrassed.

'Don't,' she murmured. 'We shouldn't be doing this.'

'Why shouldn't we?'

She tried to tell him why but he didn't seem to be listening. He was making peculiar little gasping noises, and was busy with the buttons of his trousers. The other girls had said that boys liked to be touched and caressed too, just as they did. That it really turned them on and helped to ease things along, as it were. Dena thought that might be what he wanted from her but when she made a move and attempted to take hold of his penis, he shoved her hand away. 'No, don't do that. I can manage.'

The next instant he was on top of her and Dena gave a little squeal of surprise. 'Hey, what's the rush. Just remember I'm your girlfriend, not some cheap prossy on the make.'

'So why don't we get on with it? Who are you saving yourself for if not me? You want it, don't you? You aren't going to let that lot in there tell you what to do, are you?'

The rebellious streak again leapt to the fore. ''Course I'm not. But if we do it, you won't respect me any more.'

'I love you, don't I? We're going to be wed.'

'We haven't decided that yet, Kenny. Anyway, I don't want you to think I'm easy.'

'Don't you want me to make love to you then?'

'I want you to kiss me first. Lots and lots of kisses. There's plenty of time, after all. No one knows I'm here and we won't be disturbed. I want you to touch me and stroke my breasts. Go on, I don't mind. Oh, I want you so much, Kenny.'

He said nothing. Just stared at her. Dena noticed a tic just below his left eye and thought he must be as shy and anxious as she was. They were both so young, after all. But he loved her, so it couldn't be wrong, could it?

'Shall I touch you? It's all right, I don't mind. I like the feel of it, all smooth and velvety. Why don't I help you take your clothes off too?'

But he didn't react at all as the other girls had suggested and again pushed her hand away, as if he was annoyed with her. 'I should be the one to tell you what to do. Girls aren't supposed to know about such things, not if they're a virgin. You just do what I say.'

'Don't be daft. We talk about sex all the time in the home. I'm not stupid, nor so ignorant as I once was, Kenny. One of the girls has a book, and tells how a woman can be a good lover. I'm only trying to help and make it good for us both.'

Dena was more than ready to take a full part in this experiment. Why not? To have someone touch, caress and kiss her was blissful. Week after week, month after month, no one ever did touch her, not even to give her a hug. She felt starved of affection. She could feel her breasts start to tingle, a yearning deep inside. Oh, she wanted him to love her so much. She began to unbutton his shirt.

Kenny was staring at her in astonishment. 'Women aren't supposed to enjoy it.'

'Why not? I intend to.'

'You *are* a virgin, right?'

'Kenny Garside, what a thing to say! 'Course I am, what chance have I to be anything else, living in this place?'

He grinned at her, his anxiety seeming to fall away. 'Well, I don't know, do I? You've managed to get out to see me.'

She chuckled. 'I think you're jealous. Well, let me tell you Kenny love, there's no one to be jealous of. I just want to please you, that's all. I want us to be good lovers, like it says in that book.'

To bring about this happy state of affairs, Dena took the initiative and started kissing him, long and hard, pressing herself against him while all her inhibitions seemed to fall away.

She reached for his hands and put them to her breasts. 'Touch me here, no here on my nipples. Press them, squeeze them. Oh!' She was astonished by the sensation this instilled in her. She couldn't remember anything feeling so good. Dena instinctively arched her back, pushing herself closer. 'Oh, please, do it some more, Kenny.'

To her shame, she wanted him to do all kinds of things to her and didn't know where this need, these dreadfully wicked ideas were coming from. Had they all come from that book? She really didn't think so. They seemed to emerge naturally from some sinful inner part of herself, a wanton need that had to be sated. Mam was right: she was wayward.

Kenny suddenly stopped touching her, stopped kissing her even, and was breathing hard as if he'd been running a race. He pushed his knee between her legs. 'Stop talking Dena, will you, and keep still. Don't move. It's all right, I won't hurt you. You'll like it. It'll be good.'

When he slid into her she was not unresistant. She wanted him as much as he needed her. His passion stirred something in her, eased the rawness of that painful rejection.

He was thrusting inside her, pushing as hard as he could and Dena's head knocked against a root of the tree, bringing a start of tears to her eyes. She wanted to tell him to hang on a minute till she'd moved out of the way of it, but he didn't seem to notice as his hands kneaded her buttocks. It hurt more than she'd expected but even as she tried to relax, it seemed to be all over. He gave a strange sort of shudder and collapsed on top of her.

She felt very slightly cheated.

Shouldn't there be a bit more to it? Dena lay quietly beneath him as his skin, slick with sweat, rapidly turned cold in the night air. Was this what her friends had been talking about with such feverish excitement night after night in the common room? Was this the glory of sex?

But then she thought, okay, they were both young and inexperienced but I've done it! I'm a woman now. And she felt suddenly jubilant, triumphant in her act of rebellion. That would show them! She'd wanted to defy Carthorse, Matron and the rest, to hurt someone, most of all herself, for didn't she deserve to suffer? Wasn't she to blame for the whole sorry mess of losing her brother? If Kenny hadn't caressed and touched her as much as she would have liked, that was surely only because he'd been shy and nervous too.

She'd longed to have something good happen to her, instead of all bad. And next time it would be even better. Dena had wanted someone in her life, someone of her own. And she'd achieved that tonight at least, hadn't she?

–

She must have fallen asleep because she was woken by streaks of sunlight slanting through the branches and leapt to her feet. 'What time is it?'

Kenny glanced sleepily at his watch. 'Christ, it's half past six!'

Dena ran all the way back, crashing through the woods and blundering through the bushes, not caring about brambles scratching her or snagging her clothes. There hadn't even been time for a proper goodbye. Nor had they made any arrangements to meet again. Kenny had just yelled that he would write, claimed that he loved her, and they were united.

She didn't waste a moment as she leapt up the fire escape two steps at a time, only to find the door locked. Damn! Did someone know that she was out? Had she been discovered? Surely not. Maybe the catch had stuck. Her heart beating with fear she turned and ran back down again, nearly tripping on the metal stairs in her anxiety to hurry, and without pausing to catch her breath headed for the old pantry, she ran round to the back of the house. This was where cook stored the meat and milk, the theory being that it was cold in this old larder to keep the food fresh, although that never seemed to be the case.

The catch on this window was broken, and it creaked open easily when she pushed it. Unfortunately, the gap looked smaller than Dena remembered it. Surely far too small now that she'd filled out a little, and even got breasts?

Hitching up her skirts, she put one foot on a nearby tree root and hoisted herself up the wall. She just about managed to squeeze head first through the narrow opening, only to fall on to a marble shelf and put her knee in a blancmange, squashing it flat. So much for Monday's pudding! If she left the door of the pantry open, cook would think that the cat had got in?

Dena rubbed the sticky pink blancmange off her leg as best she could then quietly tugged open the pantry door. She was holding her breath tight in her chest, since cook was known for being an early riser and often in the kitchen stirring porridge by six.

She was lucky this morning, the kitchen was empty and Dena let out a huge sigh of relief. Swiftly and silently she crept across the big old Victorian kitchen, along the back passage then up the back stairs. By the time she reached her bed, heart thumping, she just managed to slide beneath the covers as the rising bell rang. No one had seen her. At least she hoped not.

Chapter Eighteen

Champion Street Market started life way back in the early fourteenth century when a charter was granted to the burgesses of Manchester to allow them to hold a market in return for paying the Duke of Lancaster a fixed rent for the privilege. It could trace its history to a two-day annual fair dating right back to William the Conqueror when farmer's wives would come along to sell their wares. But it wasn't until late in the nineteenth century that the market hall had been built: a large, glazed building with a cast-iron frame.

There are other markets in Manchester: Smithfield, Shude-hill, Campfield, Grey Mare Lane, and the Victoria meat market amongst others, selling everything from fruit and veg, fish and meat, to fresh flowers and plants. Carl drove his wagon to each and every one of them. This morning it was laden with crates of lettuces, mushrooms and potatoes, as well as a load of Christmas trees for the coming season.

Lorries arrived from market gardens all over Britain and even overseas: potatoes from Norfolk, apples from Kent, oranges and lemons from Spain. At the right season, tulips would be flown in from Holland, and daffodils from the Scillies and Channel Isles. All of this in addition to the local produce, to the cabbages and leeks, peas and carrots brought in from farms across Cheshire and Lancashire, as well as fish from Grimsby and Whitby.

It was still the small hours of the morning but getting up early didn't trouble him. Carl was used to working odd hours, and, unlike his younger brother, didn't spend half the night racketing about the streets with his tearaway friends.

The other Friday night Kenny had come home after midnight, singing at the top of his voice and clearly very much the worse for drink. He'd woken Carl up, which didn't help him to feel benevolent; their mother was evident by her absence. Carl had stood on the landing in his vest and pyjama trousers shouting at Kenny for getting into such a state, not to mention drinking under age. Then he'd held his head while he was sick, just as he'd done when he was a kid. Daft idiot!

On Saturday he'd been later still and the following Sunday had stayed out all night. Carl couldn't begin to guess where he'd been but Kenny had reacted badly when he'd tackled him on the subject, screaming at Carl to mind his own flaming business.

He seemed to be in a state of high nervous energy, and finally the truth all came rushing out. 'All right, I saw her. I told you I would. She's still my girl and come Easter she'll be home again. She's going to work on the market and we're going to get married.'

Carl didn't need to ask who he'd seen but was shocked nonetheless. 'Don't talk so daft. How can you afford to keep a wife? You're far too young and you haven't even a decent job. Every job I find for you, you screw up and get fired. Engineering, warehousing, loading at the docks, labouring. You haven't got it in you to stick at anything for more than five minutes. Can't even look after yourself properly let alone be responsible for a wife.'

'Aw, spare me the lecture. I've heard it all before a million times.'

'What if she starts having babies? Women do, you know. Itching to dangle a babby on their knee from the minute they catch a fella.'

'Dena isn't like that. She has ambition and isn't in a hurry to start a family.'

'Oh, you've talked about it with her then?'

'Not exactly, but I did ask her to marry me.'

'And what did she say?'

Kenny looked uncomfortable. 'Well, she said that she wasn't yet ready for all that domestic, housewife stuff.'

'Sensible girl! She's gone up a notch in my estimation. However, I wouldn't bank on that attitude lasting. Once you start – you know – a bit of how's-your-father, you might not have any choice in the matter. Then she'll have you down that aisle faster than greased lightening. They're all the same.' Carl looked at his brother more keenly. 'I take it you were careful. You didn't go that far?'

Kenny's face told all. It was riddled with guilt and a sort of self-satisfied triumph.

'Oh no, you haven't! Is that the real reason you went down there, to have it away with her? Don't they keep any control over girls in that home?'

'They didn't even know I was there. She sneaked out to see me at night. It was right good, I don't mind telling you. Better than I'd expected, actually. At least I proved I could do it, proved I'm a real man.'

Carl looked at him. His brother said the oddest things at times, never giving the reaction you'd expect. 'Why wouldn't you be able to do it?'

'No reason.' Kenny shrugged his shoulders, thrust his hands in his pockets and half turned away, although not before Carl had seen a telltale crimson flush start to creep up his neck. Had he been as shy and awkward at that age? Carl wondered.

Once again he sensed that something wasn't right with his younger brother, as if he had a more serious problem troubling him.

'Kenny, is there anything else bothering you? Something on your mind that you'd like to share?'

Kenny laughed, adopting that famous devil-may-care attitude of his. 'Why would there be? I'm on top of the world.' Then he was gone, leaving Carl still nursing a nudge of concern.

It was a few days later when he spotted him going into the Odeon cinema with another girl on his arm. Nothing to worry about after all then.

But it was on that particular evening after his brother had gone to bed that Carl discovered the bicycle chain. He'd seen the bulge in the inside pocket of his jacket as it hung behind the door, investigated and realised it was obviously meant as an offensive weapon.

Now that did worry him. So much so that he put it back exactly where he found it, resolving to speak to his mother about it before tackling Kenny. He'd maybe take a telling-off from Belle better than from his elder brother.

Naturally, such a difficult conversation would have to wait until she stayed in the house long enough for her to listen to the tale.

In the meantime, Carl intended to put his stupid brother, his rabble-rousing and his nonsensical romantic dreams, out of his mind and concentrate on himself for a change. He still hadn't spoken to Barry Holmes, which he meant to do first thing.

–

Carl found Barry working on his allotment, digging up long rows of carrots, his bowler hat still in place although he was clad only in shirtsleeves, waistcoat and old gardening trousers. His tweed jacket was draped over the handle of the wheelbarrow, for once without the usual trademark carnation stuck in the buttonhole. Barry's round face was flushed by the exertion of his efforts and when he saw Carl approach he took off the hat to wipe the sweat off his brow with a blue spotted handkerchief.

'Hey up, Carl, me old son. How are you on this fine crisp morning?'

'I was wanting a word.'

'Anything in particular?'

'I'd like to sound out an idea I've got. I could do with a bit of advice.'

'Oh, right?' Barry agreed. 'Just let me pack these carrots and finish loading the van, then I'm your man, never can resist poking me nose into other folks' affairs, so long as they leave mine well alone, you understand?' He chuckled, put away his tools, locked the doors of his shed and pocketed the key.

Minutes later they were sitting in Belle's cafe eating sausage and bacon on a bap, a mug of tea set before each of them. Barry took a huge bite, and, as he chewed, said, 'Eeh, I were ready for this. It does my old back no good at all digging and humping vegetables about. They don't get any lighter don't them boxes of spuds, do they? Not that they'd be a problem for a great brawny lad like you. Always were fit, I seem to recall.'

'I never beat you in the ring though, Barry.'

Barry's eyes glistened with pride. 'Few can. So, what's this idea you've had then?'

'I'm fed up with the driving and was wondering about setting up with a stall of my own on the market.'

'What sort of stall?'

'This and that. Household goods mostly. Soap, washing lines, mops and buckets, brushes and dusters, you know the sort of thing. And I thought I could also do pans and electric kettles, kitchen gadgets and the like. They're all the rage now that folk have so much more money to spend. We don't have such a stall on the outside market, let alone in the market hall. Do you think it'd do well?'

'Sounds a good notion. I reckon you'd make a bomb. What does your mam say?' Barry jerked his head in the direction of the counter where Belle was gossiping with Sam Becket. 'She's the one with the ear of the market superintendent. If anyone knows whether a stall is due to fall vacant, it's Belle.'

Carl fidgeted and chewed on his sandwich for a bit. 'I haven't mentioned the idea to Mam yet. I thought she might raise all sorts of objections and I just wanted to talk it through with a mate first.'

'I'm flattered, but why do you reckon she'd object?'

'She has grand ideas for Kenny and me. Says she hasn't slaved away on the market all her life for us to follow suit. I think she imagines that we should turn into prosperous businessmen, almost overnight, that's assuming we don't actually stand for parliament and run the country. You know how mothers are.' Carl pulled a wry face.

Barry grinned. 'Mine was just as bad. Always telling me off for something or other, but fierce as a terrier if anyone else said a word against me. Nay, I wouldn't hang about. There's plenty of room for another stall on the outside market, even if you might have to wait a year or two to move indoors, till somebody pops their clogs. I wouldn't mind moving into the warm myself, but I'm still waiting.'

Carl felt decidedly perky having sounded out his idea. It suddenly seemed feasible, and his doubts vanished. Barry was a bit of an old woman himself but had a sound business head on his shoulders.

'Before I tell her, I need to have costed it out as a business proposition. Trouble is, Mam plays her cards close to her chest, so I haven't been able to gather all the facts, not properly. I don't know all the regulations, for instance, nor do I want to go and see Joe Southworth until I'm ready to come clean with Mam. I know what the rents are, insurance, cost of running a van. What else do you reckon I should take into account? I'll be eighteen next month, would I be allowed to have a stall? And how many days a week would I be likely to get?'

The two men quietly talked business for a good hour, Barry helping as best he could to answer Carl's questions. Occasionally Belle would glance over in their direction but she never came near. Barry wasn't her favourite person, but he was accommodating and helpful. They had a good enough working relationship.

Barry said, 'I like to see a young man making his way in the world. Who knows, you could be a millionaire by the time you're thirty.'

Carl laughed. 'I very much doubt it, but I am keen to work for myself.' He got up to leave. 'I'd best be off. I'll be in dead lumber with my boss for taking so much time out, but I mean to hand in me notice straight after Christmas. As you say, no point in hanging about. Then I can give this plan my full attention. The world is changing, folk are wanting nice things to put in their houses, and I mean to take advantage of that fact.'

'Good for you! Well, you know where I am if you want another chat, lad. You'll happen be down at the club on Friday, eh?'

'Aye, I reckon so. See you there. I'll let you know how I'm getting on.'

'And if you don't show up,' Barry laughed. 'I'll know that Belle has killed you and chucked you in the cut.'

'Don't even joke about it.' Carl shuddered. He had the chilling feeling that some person or persons unknown had done that once already.

—

Belle's reaction to Carl's plan was exactly as her son predicted. She was furious. After weeks of making careful plans he thought he'd chosen a good moment. It was the following Sunday morning and she was happily frying bacon and eggs for their usual family breakfast, loudly singing 'Love Is a Many Splendoured Thing' in tune to the wireless when he announced his decision. Carl thought for a moment that she might actually hit him over the head with the frying pan.

She looked at him aghast. 'You've what?'

'I've decided to leave the transport. Christmas Eve will be my last day. I'll collect me wage packet and that'll be that. Job done!'

There was a long and terrible silence. 'How dare you hand in your notice without even telling me! What the hell are you going to do now without a job?'

Carl told her that too and stood back to await the fireworks.

Belle went dangerously quiet, always a bad sign where she was concerned. Carl found her much easier to deal with when she was screaming at him.

'I don't believe I'm hearing this. Well, you can think again. Go back this minute and tell Catlow's that you made a mistake and you've changed your mind. Tell 'em you want your job back.'

'No, Mam, I'm not going to do any such thing. I don't want me old job back. I've talked to Barry, got some tips, and I've been to see Joe. He's agreed for me to have a stall. It's not in a particularly good position, being right at the back but he's promised to let me know if a better pitch comes vacant. I've even looked out a few suppliers.'

Belle sank slowly into a chair, her knees unable to hold her any longer, the frying pan still in her hand. 'You've got it all worked out, haven't you?'

'First thing Monday morning I'm expecting deliveries to start arriving. Barry has offered me some space in his lock-up for the time being, till I can find something of me own.'

'You knew how I'd feel about this. That's why you didn't tell me, isn't it?'

Carl looked uncomfortable for a moment, taking refuge in filling the kettle. 'Look, don't get upset, Mam. It's my life and I should decide what I want to do with it. Tea or coffee?'

'I don't want no coffee; I want you to come to your flaming senses. All my life I've worked hard, scrimped and saved, done my best to build a better future for both you two lads, and this is the thanks I get!'

She suddenly leapt out of the chair and slapped him across the head with the back of her hand. 'You great lummock, you've ruined everything. I'll never forgive you for this. Never! I meant for you to get out of this place, not struggle all your life as I have done.

'And as for Casanova here…' She turned on Kenny, who'd been quietly eating his cornflakes, oblivious of the row. 'You were going to be a famous engineer yet gave up on that after only a few months. What have you achieved since? Nowt, just mooching about going from one job to another, great lazy lump that you are!'

Kenny pouted. 'I earn a bit of brass here and there.'

'I'll bet you do, but is it honestly earned or one of your scams, or else a lucky bet on the gee-gees?'

Kenny had a sudden brainwave, meant to mollify her. 'Hey, I might pop over to Catlow's and ask for our Carl's old job on the driving. How would that be?'

'How would that be? Illegal, that's what it would be. You're too young to take the test yet.'

Kenny looked deflated and slightly peeved, clearly viewing such a regulation as an irritating nuisance. 'Well, I haven't decided what I'll do yet, not long term. Happen I'll stand the market an' all. Happen I won't. Anyway, I mean to find myself a job one day, all in good time, don't you fret about that. I need to have some money for when Dena gets out. They'll have to let her out of that place soon, when she turns sixteen.'

Belle looked astounded. 'You're not still soft on that lass? If you bring any trouble to my door, you'll be sorry. Do you hear?'

Kenny looked at his mother with a cold expression in his light blue eyes, annoyed by her reaction to this great love of his life he believed in completely. 'That's a bit rich coming from a woman who's had two children from different fathers, a couple of abortions and more men than I've had hot dinners.'

Belle knocked the dish of cornflakes off the table, flung the pan of half-fried bacon in the sink and stormed out of the house.

Chapter Nineteen

Norah crept up behind Dena when she was standing in line for her morning porridge to whisper in her ear, 'I saw you go out, and I heard you come back.'

Dena's heart skipped a beat. 'I don't know what you're talking about.'

'Aye, you do. I just want you to know that you were seen. Where did you go?'

Dena's mind was racing but decided there was little point in denying it since the girl seemed to know so much already. 'For a breath of fresh air I couldn't sleep. What's it to you?'

'Nothing. Just remember I saw you, that's all. Tread carefully, Dena Dobson.'

'Is that some sort of threat?'

'You must make up your own mind about that.' And with a sarcastic little chuckle, Norah picked up her dish of porridge and sauntered off, a smile of pure triumph on her nasty face.

Dena understood perfectly. It meant that she must tread very carefully indeed, that Norah could hold this knowledge over her, and were she to offend the girl, would not hesitate to use it. Despite this simmering animosity between the pair of them Dena began almost to enjoy life. They were having great fun that winter sledging and even skating on the duck pond, making snowmen and throwing snowballs at each other.

On Christmas Eve they were all given hot chocolate and a sticky iced bun for supper, and in the morning the usual bag of treats: a book or game, orange or apple and a small bag of sweets. No more tossing them in the air for the fittest and fastest to catch.

Christmas dinner was festive with paper hats and crackers, and a choice of roast chicken or turkey. Afterwards they played charades and other silly games, and then sang carols around tree. The tea table positively groaned with cakes and jellies, grapes, nuts and raisins, and then best of all they were all allowed to watch *I Love Lucy* on the television, and a special edition of *What's My Line*.

January saw the usual outbreak of coughs and colds, Dena herself spending a few days in the sanatorium with flu. By February she was permitted to leave the laundry and start work in the garden and Dena happily sowed seeds in the old Victorian glasshouses ready for planting out when spring came to warm the land. It pleased her to think that by the time they were fully grown, she wouldn't even be here.

When she wasn't thus engaged, Dena spent a great deal of time in the needlework room happily sewing, and so, by and large, life had grown pleasant. She felt much calmer and more relaxed, and, to her surprise, Dena even discovered that her anger and rebellion seemed to have burned out.

For the first time in years she felt content.

Somehow, without even realising it, she'd managed to put the tragedy of her little brother behind her. That wasn't to say she didn't still think of him a great deal. A part of her would always ache for him but she was young still, with all her life before her, and, give or take a few worries about her mam and what the future might hold, she felt pretty good.

Best of all, by April she would be packing her bags and leaving Ivy Bank for good. In preparation for this great day most of the girls in Dena's dormitory would likewise be leaving at Easter. They were permitted to choose the fabric for a new dress made up for them over the winter in the needlework room. Dena had chosen a pretty pink floral cotton for herself.

The first week of March was set aside to make plans for leaving. Time was allowed for important decisions to be made and extra training and lectures given. They were taught how to manage their money and organise a bank account; how they must behave towards an employer or mistress, and how they must always behave with decorum, dignity and absolute honesty as they had been taught to do at Ivy Bank.

One day a very embarrassed biology teacher explained to them the facts of life, with the girls sitting listening in silence, their faces bright red and simply bursting to giggle. It fleetingly crossed Dena's mind to ask if a dose of flu always caused periods to be late, but couldn't pluck up the courage to do so. Besides there was so much going on, and she was so excited about leaving, that the instant the lesson was over, she forgot all about it.

Each of the leavers were called in turn to Matron's office where they were grilled on their plans, or lack of them, for the future. She was far from impressed by Dena's decision to go back to working on the market.

'Isn't that how you got into trouble in the first place?'

'I was never in trouble. My mother was ill, that's why I was sent here.'

Matron gave one of her disapproving sniffs. 'Misbehaving with some young man, that's what I was told.'

'Then you were told wrong.' Dena didn't know what had come over her. She really shouldn't be arguing with Matron, not at this late stage. She tried to soften her words with a smile. 'Sorry, but I feel I belong on that market, Matron, d'you see? I've worked there for years as a Saturday girl, and now I've got promise of a full-time job back at the cafe with Mrs Garside. She'll keep an eye on me.'

'Indeed I hope she does. This will all have to be checked out, you understand? Someone from the council offices will need to go and see this Mrs Garside and make sure that she is prepared to have you back. Is she also willing to offer you accommodation?'

'I believe so.'

'That will need to be checked too. She must be made fully aware of what she is taking on.'

Dena nodded. 'I'm sure it will be all right.' She prudently decided to make no mention of Kenny and his hopes for them to

148

wed. Dena thought that Matron would not approve of that bit, and might start asking even more awkward questions. As it was, Dena considered that she'd got off lightly.

Some of the girls attended interviews at local shops, offices and factories, or were taken into Manchester for this purpose. Others were to be placed in domestic service, and one or two were to go into nursing.

This was all thrilling enough but then a hairdresser was brought in to give their untidy locks a neat trim. The girls were abuzz with excitement, eagerly deciding what style they would like.

Dena opted to have her long hair cut very short into the kind of urchin style currently favoured by Audrey Hepburn. She'd seen pictures of her in the magazines that some of the girls' families brought in.

'Gosh, it suits you,' Gwen said, awe in her voice. 'You look so different. Really sophisticated. I wish I was as thin as you. Look at my boobs, an absolute sight.'

Dena laughed. She'd grown since she came to Ivy Bank, but although she'd filled out somewhat, she was still slender and always would be as she never seemed to put on weight like the other girls. Dena thought this might be because of too much hunger when she was young but her breasts had plumped up nicely in recent months. Beneath the plain school uniform was emerging a sophisticated young woman. In two weeks' time she would be sixteen years old and no longer a schoolgirl.

Phyllis was saying, '…with the right clothes, and this new hairstyle, you could easily be taken for one of those mannequins at dress shows.'

'Ooh, yes Dena, you could. You look lovely,' added Katy, not wanting to be left out.

Dena caught sight of Norah glowering across at them. How she hated it when the other girls said nice things about her. Norah Talbot no longer wielded the power she once had, and she blamed Dena entirely for that. Dena was all too aware that the resentment that still burned fierce in her old enemy's heart was really very silly.

Feeling good about herself now, she turned to Norah with a generous smile. 'Why don't you have yours cut short too? It would suit you.'

The other girl shook her head, tossing back her long fair curls. 'Why would I want to look like you, Dena Dobson? Anyway, I've always found that boys prefer long hair, and a curvaceous figure. They don't want to go out with someone who looks very like themselves.'

Dena felt strangely put down by this comment but tried not to let her insecurity show. Would Kenny like her new hair cut? Would he still love her?

Her lack of confidence overriding common sense yet again, she decided to write and ask him to come down to see her one more time before she left, if only to celebrate her sixteenth birthday. A last romantic tryst beneath the old oak would be lovely, and surely safe now that she was leaving?

-

Belle was taken aback to receive a visit from a social worker at eight-thirty in the morning, particularly one as nosy as this one. Breakfast was always her busy time and she was busy frying eggs when the woman suddenly appeared at her elbow. Not that this stopped her. She briefly introduced herself as one Miss Rogers who had in the past been responsible for Dena Dobson, then began firing questions at Belle with bewildering speed.

Was she willing to take Dena back as an employee in the cafe? Would she undertake to keep a proper eye on the girl? In addition, was she willing to offer her accommodation, and could she please make an appointment to inspect her room just to make sure that it was suitable? Miss Rogers also wanted to know what Dena's wages would be and how much she'd be charged for her keep?

Belle yelled out, 'Two full English,' shoved the plates into the hands of her new young waitress and turned back to Miss Rogers with barely concealed impatience. 'I think you'd better start again. What exactly is it I'm supposed to be offering her?'

'Surely you know.'

Belle looked at the tall-framed woman with the sprouting whiskers on her pointed chin and then swung about and called into the back kitchen. 'Kenny! Get yourself out here this minute, I want a word with you.'

Kenny came, trembling in every limb. He could tell by the tone in his mother's voice that this meant trouble and would much rather stay where he was in the back, even though he hated washing up.

One glance at the tall, sour-faced woman and he guessed she must be the social worker who had something to do with Dena. Had his mam found out that he went to visit her before Christmas, or what they'd got up to under that old oak tree? He sincerely hoped not.

Belle said, 'I understand that Dena wants to come back here and work on the market, and seems to think we'll put her up an' all. Has this anything to do with you, by any chance?'

'You don't mind, do you, Mam, as you always liked her?'

'Did I?' Belle rolled her beautiful violet eyes in despair, then folded her arms and pressed fuchsia-painted lips together while she considered how best to deal with this unexpected turn of events. It seemed the lad still hadn't got over his crush on the girl. If Miss Moustache hadn't been here, she'd have clipped him round the ear for dropping this on her without so much as a by-your-leave.

Miss Rogers interrupted her thoughts with a question of her own, 'Am I correct in assuming that there is some sort of understanding between yourself and Dena, young man?'

Kenny didn't entirely follow the woman's old-fashioned way of speaking but he caught the general drift and puffed out his chest. It was such a relief that his visit to the home hadn't actually been discovered that he didn't object to being interrogated in the slightest. He willingly agreed that he had been in touch with Dena, although was careful not to give specific details, letting both women assume it had simply been by letter. 'Me and Dena have been going out since she were fourteen,' he agreed. 'And one day we mean to wed,' just so there was no mistake about his intentions.

'Good heavens, you must be the very young man that she was cavorting with when her mother was forced to have her taken into care! Oh deary me, no! This will not do at all. She cannot possibly stay in your house, Mrs Garside. I'm sorry but I even have my doubts about allowing her to work in the cafe under the circumstances, but that may still prove to be feasible so long as you undertake to keep a careful eye on her. At sixteen she is still a young and vulnerable girl, and with little experience of the outside world after her long stay at Ivy bank.'

'Hold on a minute, I'm not her mother. Why should I be responsible for the lass? Why can't she go back home?'

'Ah, well now that is the problem. The mother has moved back into the family home to live with her brother, and Dena has not been included in the arrangement.'

Kenny was feeling a bit left out of this conversation and had taken great exception to Miss Roger's condescending tone regarding his own honourable intentions. 'Hey, listen to me a minute, you silly old faggot. We weren't cavorting, we are in love. Still are. Do you understand what that means you miserable old cow? I mean to marry her and make her my wife, so I'll be the one what keeps an eye on her, thank you very much, not me mam.'

The sound of the kitchen door closing brought customer's heads swivelling and gossip humming around the cafe.

'Well,' said Belle, 'you seem to have sorted that little problem out nicely, Kenny. Good lad!'

Chapter Twenty

It was late in the afternoon that Belle Garside sauntered by Winnie Watkin's stall, hips undulating in her famously provocative walk. She was carrying a wad of posters in her arms, smiled sweetly at Winnie and asked if she minded putting one up next to her stall.

Winnie had just happened to be standing out in the aisle rather than tucked behind her rolls of fabric, as she usually was, when she'd spotted the masculine-looking woman approach Belle's cafe earlier. She could recognise a council official a mile off so had hung around to see what it was all about.

Unfortunately, she hadn't been able to get near enough to hear what was going on inside the cafe, although she'd learned a good deal more as the day progressed. Several of Belle's customers had witnessed the fracas.

Winnie had also witnessed the council official's hasty departure; a telling moment. Now she peered short-sightedly at the large print on the poster, pretending not to understand. 'Somebody standing for the market committee? Now who could that be, I wonder?'

Belle ground her teeth together but managed to hold on to her patience. 'I hope that I can depend upon your vote, Winnie. After all, we've been neighbours for many a long year.'

'Aye,' Winnie agreed. 'Some might say too long. Not that it's any of my business but rumour has it you had a visitor from the social about our little Dena this morning. Are they letting her out, then?'

'She isn't in prison,' Belle snapped, annoyed by the change of subject.

'Might as well be, from what I've heard about them places. Is she still thick with your Kenny? We'll be hearing wedding bells before we're done I expect.'

'You were right,' Belle said sharply as she made to walk on by, 'it is none of your business.'

Winnie Watkin's next words stopped her in her tracks. Arms folded, the plump little woman raised her voice so that it carried well in the echoing chamber of the market hall, it being fairly empty at this time of the day. 'I must say I'm surprised. Everyone knows how your Kenny loathed her little brother, and I'm not the only one wondering if he didn't have something to do with the poor lad falling in the canal that day. Lucky the police didn't question him on the subject, eh?'

Belle swung about and rushed back to Winnie, violet eyes now a dark, simmering purple, pointed chin jutting forward in fury. 'You'd do well to keep that loose tongue of yours in check, and that famous long nose of yours out of matters that don't concern you.'

'You can't fool me. I'm all there with me mint drops, I am, and I'll go on poking me long nose into anything I fancy, particularly if it concerns that lass. I'm very fond of Dena and somebody has to keep a lookout for her.'

'Perhaps you should offer her a job, then put her up in your front room, and have the social on your back. Much better they interfere in your life, not our Kenny's.'

Winnie chuckled, her usual good nature restored when she saw how she'd touched a raw nerve. 'So Dena's looking for work is she, and somewhere to stay? I might have considered taking her in only my Donald needs a quiet life. He much prefers us to be on our own.'

A wry smile of disbelief twisted Belle's full lips. 'Would he indeed? Are you sure it isn't you who would object to having a young intruder in your home, one who can poke her little nose into all your private business?'

'If you're suggesting that I'm worried my lovely husband might stray, you couldn't be more wrong, not after all these years. My

Donald would much rather listen to United play footie on the wireless than play footsie with a young lass, but at least she'd be safe with me, unlike what might happen to her at yours.'

'Oh, for goodness sake, we all know about your Donald, Winnie, so stop talking rubbish.'

Winnie's expression darkened and animosity between the two women simmered, as it always did but she quickly rallied and swung back into attack. 'Your Kenny's out of control, in my opinion. He thinks he's that James Dean, or else Wyatt Earp. He's nothing but trouble.'

Belle turned on her heel and flounced away but not before Winnie delivered her parting shot. 'So you don't want me to put up one of them posters then? Just as well. If you think I'd vote for you to go on the market committee, you must think I've a screw loose. I'd sooner take a long jump off a short pier.'

-

The very week Dena decided to write to Kenny, she received a letter from him saying that he needed to see her. She read the words through twice, to be sure she'd got them right the first time, but yes, he was actually saying that he needed her! Oh, music to her ears. He even went on to apologise for leaving it so long, and not having come to see her since Christmas. He'd been afraid of taking the risk in case someone should find out about their meeting and get Dena into trouble.

His consideration and love brought tears to her eyes.

He'd be there on Sunday night, same time, same place, he promised. And he couldn't wait to see her and kiss her all over. He hinted that he might even have a little birthday surprise for her.

Dena could hardly wait either. Memories of their last meeting rose temptingly in her mind. Would they do it again? Not feeling ready to tie herself down yet, Dena thought that she should behave more sensibly this time. Kenny was good-looking and she liked him a lot, but was she ready for marriage and all that stuff?

She really didn't think so. Oh, but she was longing to see him again, and wouldn't object to a few more of those exciting kisses.

Dena went through the same meticulously careful planning, and when the day came, hid a bundle of clothes out of sight under a large laurel bush, exactly as she had done before. That night she was one of the first to switch off her light and settle down to sleep, or at least feign it. She could only guess the correct time as she had no watch, and no means of knowing beyond listening for the church clock chiming over in the village. She could only hear it properly if the wind was in a certain direction, so it wasn't a reliable way of telling the time.

And somehow time seemed to move much slower than usual. Dena counted nine o'clock, then after what seemed like three hours, she counted out ten strokes, then eleven. She must have dozed off for a while after that because she suddenly woke to hear it striking the half hour.

Half past eleven, at last! Or was it half past twelve? Panicking, she slipped silently out of bed and with shoes in hand tiptoed across the room. The creak of the door handle turning made her heart go pit-pat, exactly as it had done last time. But in an instant she was speeding barefoot along the landing.

As always the fire door was not locked but simply bolted on the inside. They hadn't had a fire drill for a week or two and Dena was worried that it might prove difficult to shift. In fact it proved to be well oiled and slid back easily beneath her hand.

She pushed open the fire door and had just placed her foot on the top step when she heard a sound. Dena half turned, about to swing round to check who might be following her when something struck the back of her head. It took her by surprise. She scarcely had time to wonder if the door had blown open and accidentally hit her, or whether someone had indeed followed her when a pair of hands pushed at her shoulders, she lost her balance completely and tumbled down the stairs.

–

Kenny wasn't pleased to be kept waiting. He'd smoked five of his Gold Flake cigarettes and kept himself amused by blowing smoke rings, as he'd recently learned to do. Now he stood under the ancient oak listening to the village clock strike one o'clock and finally admitted that she wasn't coming. It wasn't a good feeling. Kenny didn't care to have women stand him up. It was fine the other way round since girls were two a penny, but he was a man and had his pride.

He tried to give her the benefit of the doubt, thinking that Dena had found it impossible to escape, but that didn't help to soothe his wounded pride. She surely could have tried harder. He felt let down, hurt and offended, and rather sorry for himself.

He'd bought himself some wheels the day he turned seventeen: a Triumph motorbike, which he was extremely proud of. He'd got it cheap from a mate of his in return for a few favours and it made him feel as if he was somebody. He'd even bought himself a leather jacket and helmet off Abe Johnson's second-hand stall so he looked the part, and had intended taking Dena for a spin down the quiet back roads. Now she'd just have to wait for some other occasion.

He got home at around three in the morning and since he was due to start washing-up duties at seven-thirty, it didn't seem worth going to bed. It was unfortunate his mother had changed her mind about never letting him work in the cafe and had set him on kitchen duties, no doubt to teach him a lesson. It looked as though he might have to find himself a proper job after all. He made a bob or two on the ponies, and had one or two other irons in the fire, which he hadn't told his mother about. But he was in no hurry to make any further decisions about his future. Something would turn up, he was sure of it.

Kenny parked his bike round the back of a row of houses, climbed over a backyard wall then flung some gravel up at the back bedroom window. Minutes later the sash window slid open and a woman's face appeared. She rubbed sleep from her eyes then ran her fingers through tousled hair.

'Is that you, Kenny?'

'Who else, Maureen love?'

'Hang on, I'll come down and let you in. I'll not be a jiffy.'

Minutes later he was in her warm bed, thrusting furiously for all he was worth. But then Maureen was a mature woman, not interested in soft words and teasing kisses. Nor did she need to be caressed or cuddled. She was happy just to get on with the job, as he was. He blessed the day he'd met her, and she helped to sooth his disappointment over Dena letting him down so badly. What better way of spending his money?

Chapter Twenty-One

Dena was taken straight to hospital by ambulance. Apparently one of the girls had heard her scream and alerted Carthorse, who rang the emergency services immediately. Dena had been knocked unconscious and when she came round, didn't have the least idea where she was or what was going on. She could tell though that she was in hospital because there was the housemother sitting at the bottom of her bed reading *The Sunday Post* and, in a flash it all came back to her: the sound from behind, her turning to see who might be following, and then the blow. And something more that Dena could now clearly remember: the face of her attacker.

Who else but Norah Talbot?

Her head was aching abominably, and, hearing her groan, a young nurse bustled over to the bed. 'Good for you, you're awake.' She gave Dena a sip of water and made her take a couple of aspirin to ease the headache.

Apparently she'd fallen awkwardly and broken her right ankle, but apart from that, and the concussion, the nurse thought she'd got off lightly. 'Considering you fell a fair distance, the full length of the fire escape.'

Dena agreed that she probably had.

'But don't fret,' the kindly nurse told her. 'You'll live, and the baby is safe.'

'Baby?'

She smiled ruefully at Dena, then, glancing across at the housemother still engrossed in her newspaper, the young nurse leaned closer so that she could whisper. 'You did know that you were pregnant, didn't you love? About three months the doctor says.'

Dena's first visitor was her mother, of all people. She didn't come alone but with Miss Rogers, who had no doubt dragged her along by force. Alice was looking even more disapproving than usual, all tight-lipped and with a closed expression on her face. She was wearing a new coat and hat, Dena noticed; looking considerably smarter than the last time she'd seen her on the day she'd allowed her daughter to be taken into care nearly two years ago.

She didn't expect a kiss or any sort of warm greeting from her mother, nor did she get one. Nevertheless, Dena sat up in bed and felt ridiculously pleased to see her.

'So what have you done now?' were Alice's first words.

'It wasn't my fault. I tripped, that's all.' There seemed little point in saying that she was pushed. That would demand too long an explanation and result in all manner of repercussions. Besides which, Dena's life-long policy of striving to be invisible automatically came into play.

'And what were you doing on the fire escape at that time of night?'

'Star gazing.'

Miss Rogers interrupted. 'It does you no good to lie, Dena. A proper explanation will serve you much better in the end.'

'I leave Ivy Bank in a few weeks, so what does it matter? I wasn't sleepy and wanted a breath of fresh air. I wasn't intending to do a runner, if that's what's bothering you. What would be the point?'

'Then nothing – untoward – occurred?'

Dena looked at the woman in silence for a moment. 'No, nothing at all. It was an accident.'

She hoped that the social worker might accept this and leave, but she should have known better. Miss Rogers gave a heavy sigh and, pulling up a chair, sat down. For some reason her plain face looked infinitely less forbidding than her own mother's, gazing at her with something like sympathy in the grey eyes. 'Dena, we know about the baby. Is that what you were doing that night, going to meet your boyfriend?'

Dena started. She was still reeling from the news herself, felt too stunned to take it in properly. She preferred to deny that it could be true, determined to believe that the nurse, or the doctor, had made a mistake. How could she be pregnant? They'd only made love the one time, and it had been so quick, nothing at all really, surely not long enough to make a baby?

But if it was common knowledge and all and sundry knew about it, then maybe it was true after all, and she'd have to accept it as fact.

Dena glanced sideways at her mother seated beside the social worker, handbag clasped in her gloved hands on her knee, a tight frizz of hair escaping from beneath the blue felt hat, indicating a recent perm; her mouth barely visible so tightly pressed were her lips.

Sex, to Alice, was still a dirty word. Never to be discussed or mentioned, even in private, let alone in a public hospital ward. She would never forgive her for this. Never! To bring such shame upon the family was the worst thing she could possibly have done.

Miss Roger's voice again, quiet and soothingly encouraging. 'Dena, answer me please. You can tell me the truth. Were you going to meet Kenny that night?'

Weariness washed over her as Dena realised that the woman even knew his name. What did it matter what they thought? She was the one up the spout, the one who would have to live with the consequences of one night of foolish rebellion. 'All right, yes I was. But I didn't know then about – about the baby. Not till the nurse told me today. I can't think how it happened.'

'The same way it usually happens, Dena. Kenny has been to see you before, I take it?'

'What is this? Am I on trial or something? All right, so we went a bit too far but Kenny loves me and...'

Miss Rogers interrupted. 'Dena, we cannot possibly allow you to go and live with Kenny, even with his mother in the house.

The pair of you would be living in sin. How could we condone such wanton disregard of decent morals?'

'We're to be married. He's already asked me.'

Alice said, 'The sooner the better in the circumstances. We'll have no bastards in this family.' Then got to her feet and hoisted her bag on her arm, as if having made this statement there was nothing more to be said on the subject.

The social worker grasped Alice by the wrist to prevent her from leaving. 'I'm sorry, Mrs Dobson, but don't you think that Dena is far too young at sixteen to be contemplating such a drastic move? What about your own situation? Has that changed? Could Dena possibly come and live with you and her uncle?'

Alice snatched her arm away and savagely shook her head, making the felt hat quiver, as if with distaste, on top of the stiff curls. 'Eric would never stand for it. He's not used to children.'

'I'm not a child any longer, I'm a woman.'

'Aye, and a loose one at that. I wouldn't dream of asking my brother to allow you to set foot over his threshold.'

'Think I'd contaminate the place, do you?'

Miss Rogers hastily intervened before the quarrel got out of hand. 'Have you thought about adoption? You could stay on at Ivy Bank until the baby is born and then a good home could be found for it. It's a perfectly straightforward process.'

'No!' Dena was horrified by the very idea, although she couldn't rightly say why; whether it was because she couldn't bear to give up this child she still hadn't properly acknowledged even existed, or simply that the thought of returning in shame to the home to face the censure of such as Norah Talbot was too terrible to contemplate.

'We seem to be running out of options. Do you love this boy, Dena, or was it simply an act done out of curiosity, or rebellion?'

The woman was far too smart for Dena's liking. Alice was making little tutting sounds at the back of her throat, and looking very much like a rabbit trapped by a poacher's torch, unable to escape. Dena wanted to shout at her to go away, to scream that she needed no one, not a mother who didn't love her. The very evidence of her disgust fired the rebellion in her all the more.

'What the devil does it matter? We had a bit of the other and now I'm up the spout. So what? Anyway, yes, if you want to know, I do love him. He's the best friend I have in the world. The only friend!'

'And you are willing to marry him?'

'Yes,' shouted Dena on a note of defiance, not stopping to think properly.

'There you are,' Alice remarked. 'The matter is settled. If this young man is prepared to make an honest woman of the girl, she can consider herself fortunate, little tart that she is.' This time she did walk away, without even a backward glance.

Dena screamed after Alice's retreating figure. 'Thanks for your support, mother!' and burst into tears. Where was the point in fighting or rebelling any more? Look where it had got her.

–

Matron, in fact, refused point-blank to allow Dena to return to Ivy Bank, stating that she was indeed beyond control and should be sent to an institution for wayward girls.

Miss Rogers was more pragmatic, putting the whole sorry episode down to loneliness and rebellion, with unfortunate consequences. Desperate to find some other solution she again visited the cafe to discuss the pros and cons of the case and on the way back, still nurturing grave reservations, she ran into Winnie Watkins.

Winnie said, 'It's none of my business but I was wondering what were happening to Dena? I heard she'd be out of that place soon.'

Miss Rogers agreed that she was indeed out of the home and related the whole sorry story, explaining that Dena was in sore need of somewhere to live, and a job, but was disappointed that the generous offer she'd hoped for had not materialised.

'Eeh, I didn't realise she was up the stick. I'd like to help myself, but I couldn't be doing with that, not babies. Anyway, I don't reckon my Donald would approve. No, no, I couldn't have her at ours if she's in that condition. Wouldn't be right, d'you see? The gossips would have a field day. I'm very fond of the lass, but…'

'I understand,' Miss Rogers stiffly remarked. People were such hypocrites. No one was prepared to help the poor girl, abandoned by her mother and now the home too, everyone is quick to censure her because she'd made one foolish mistake. 'What about employment? You once said something about a job. If I find her accommodation elsewhere, would you still be prepared to offer her work?'

Winnie looked thoughtful. 'I'd have to speak to my dear Donald, but I doubt he would object to such an arrangement.'

Miss Rogers suspected that Winnie was actually the one who ruled the roost and made all the decisions in that household, but didn't say so. 'She's a very willing girl, and bright I'd say. It's only her youth and difficult circumstances that led her down this sorry path, a wilful waywardness as her mother seems to think. In fact, the mother is part of the problem, though I really shouldn't say as much.'

'I agree with you there. Always was too high on the moral rectitude was Alice. Nosy and interfering I may be, I don't deny it, and I have me standards but I couldn't hold a candle to Alice Dobson. And it's true that I could do with a bit of help on the stall. I'm run off me feet most of the time. Folk take ages to choose which fabric they want, then there's all the measuring to be done, advice given and such like. I'm fair worn out half the time what with caring for my Donald on top of everything. He's not well, you know, not since the war.'

'Then you'll do it? You'll give her a job?'

Winnie realised she'd talked herself into this one. 'Aye, all right, you can tell Dena there's a job here for her whenever she wants one. But she can't live with me. My Donald wouldn't take to a screaming infant about the place.'

Miss Rogers grasped Winnie by both hands in a flurry of gratitude. 'Thank you so much. I really do appreciate it, and so will Dena.'

Chapter Twenty-Two

'At least you have a job to go to,' Miss Rogers told Dena, feeling pleased with herself. 'All I have to do now is find somewhere for you to stay temporarily, if that's the best we can hope for at present.'

Dena, still recuperating in hospital, felt a burst of happiness. It was all going to come right after all. She liked Winnie a lot, yet so much was happening to her and far too quickly, that she couldn't seem to get her head around how her life had so radically changed.

'What about Kenny? Is he coming to see me? Has he said he'll still marry me?'

Miss Rogers patted her hand. 'I spoke to his mother and she said he would be coming along to see you soon. As for the wedding, that's something you must discuss between yourselves.' After a small pause the older woman continued. 'Are you sure about this, Dena? You don't have to keep the baby. We can easily make other arrangements. This needn't ruin your life entirely, just when you're getting started.'

Dena looked at her in distaste. 'You think I should give my child away, don't you? Just like my mother abandoned me to that home. Well, I won't, so there. Never!'

The social worker actually smiled at her vehemence. 'Splendid! I'm delighted to hear it. But it won't be easy, Dena, even if your boyfriend does agree to marry you. People will count on their fingers and there's bound to be whispering and gossip. You can count on that!'

Kenny's first reaction when Miss Rogers informed him of the new situation, was fear. This was not at all what he'd bargained for, to father a kid at seventeen. He'd never even considered the possibility, not from just one quick screw. Dena was still the love of his life, at least, he loved her as much as he could love anyone, but how would he manage? He still didn't have a job.

Carl too was appalled, and strongly opposed to his getting involved in what he termed a shot-gun wedding. As for his mother, she viewed the entire saga as some sort of joke.

'By heck, this is the funniest thing I've heard in months. So you do have some lead in your pencil after all, lad? And here's me thinking you were a Mary Ann, and soft as butter with it.'

'I'm no Mary Ann!' Kenny spluttered, face scarlet.

'Nor is he soft,' put in Carl. 'Have you seen what he carries in his pocket? Show her, Kenny.'

The colour seemed to drain from his face in an instant, leaving Kenny white with rage. 'How the hell do you know what I've got in me pocket?'

'I make it my business to know everything about you. I'm your elder brother, responsible for you, so help me. Go on, show her the bicycle chain, and anything else you've got tucked away in that fancy jacket of yours.'

Belle's finely plucked eyebrows lifted in mock astonishment. 'Bicycle chain? Have you taken up cycling or what?' She watched dispassionately as a small tussle took place between her two sons; collars were grabbed, arms twisted and a great deal of pushing and shoving until Carl finally had Kenny pinned up against a wall. Then he roughly frisked him and pulled out the offending weapon from his pocket, along with a knuckle-duster. He tossed them both on to the kitchen table.

'There you are. That's what he gets up to when he's out wandering the streets.'

Something glittered behind Belle's eyes as she looked at her younger son. 'My word, you have grown into a big lad. Still, it's nothing to do with me what you carry in your pocket, nor yours neither, Carl. Leave the lad alone.'

Carl looked at his mother in open distaste. 'You don't care that your own son is turning into a hooligan? A Teddy boy?'

Belle shrugged her shapely shoulders and continued applying poppy-red lipstick to her full lips. She and Joe were going out tonight, miles away from Castlefield to a posh restaurant in Cheadle Hulme where they'd be unlikely to meet anybody they knew, so she really didn't have time to get involved in silly family squabbles.

'Just because he wears a fancy jacket and carries a bicycle chain doesn't turn him into a criminal. He's just a daft young stud, flexing his muscles. Proving he's a man.' Belle chuckled. 'And he's done that right enough, hasn't he? Mind you, he'll have to draw in his horns once he's wed.'

Kenny's knowing smirk at his mother's stout defence of him faded into a slight frown at these last words. 'I don't intend to be henpecked,' he said, thinking he'd best make that clear to Dena from the start.

'Have you been to see her yet?'

'N-no, not yet. I don't like hospitals.'

'Huh, some young Lochinvar you are. You'd best get yourself down there, Kenny lad. You'll be wanting to fix the date, eh? We don't want any question marks hanging over any grandchild of mine. It might be the only one I get, since some I could mention aren't making any effort at all in that direction.' She cast an accusing glance across at Carl who, disappointingly, didn't even have a steady girlfriend at the moment. 'Whatever happened to that nice red-head, Maggie, was she called?'

'What do I do about these?' Carl snapped, choosing not to go into his private life. 'Chuck 'em in the bin?'

Belle turned on him, violet eyes hard. 'Should my lovely boy ever meet trouble, he needs to be properly equipped to protect himself, don't you think?'

Kenny snatched up the offending weapons and returned them to his inside pocket, then swaggered off with a satisfied smirk on his face.

Belle called after him, 'You'd best ask her to tea on Sunday, love, then I can tell her exactly what she's letting herself in for.

I might even get the family photo album out.' And the sound of his mother's raucous laughter followed him all the way down Champion Street.

—

Kenny was suddenly overcome by doubt. What would married life be like? Would he really have to draw in his horns, stop seeing Maureen for instance? He supposed a wife might object to a husband visiting a prossy. And did he still want to marry Dena, or should he tell her to get the kid adopted and leave him out of it? He hoped she didn't expect him to deal with dirty nappies and all that messy baby stuff.

Oh, but he did still love her. He adored her. Dena Dobson was more beautiful than the new Queen in his eyes. More holy than the Virgin Mary. She was wonderful. He just wanted to set her up on a big white marble pedestal and worship her. Untouched by any other man but him, utterly perfect and without flaw. His girl! But why did his mother find the idea of him being a father so funny? Hadn't he proved that he was truly a man?

Kenny decided to go and see Maureen before calling at the hospital. She always boosted his self-confidence and he felt in dire need of some right now. And it might prove useful to discuss his problem with someone other than his own family. Kenny couldn't think of anyone better qualified to offer advice. Also, he had an urge to release some of the tension the confrontation with his family had created in him.

Maureen obligingly slipped out of her tatty old dressing gown the moment she saw him, and willingly gave herself up to pleasure. Recognising that he was all churned up with anger inside, she suggested he tie her to the bedhead so he could really let rip.

Kenny was sweating with excitement as he wound the silk dressing gown cord around her fragile wrists and knotted them to the bedpost. Then he did the same with her pretty ankles. It made him feel in control, as he so liked to be.

But then Maureen was generous, had taught him so much. His failure with younger girls had deeply affected him so that secretly Kenny had begun to worry that maybe he was indeed a Mary Ann. Maureen had proved otherwise, made him normal at last, like other men. And she was so imaginative. Best of all, she didn't require all the fuss and bother of petting and kissing. She just got right down to business.

Kenny knew in his heart that he might never have managed to make love to Dena if Maureen hadn't taken him in hand. Then she too might have found him unable to perform, just like all the rest. Although, judging by the results, it might have been better if he hadn't.

When they were finally sated and lying side by side contentedly sharing a Gold Flake, Kenny told Maureen all about his problem. Unlike his mother she didn't laugh but was deeply sympathetic. She also gently pointed out that there were other possible alternatives he could consider in order to resolve the matter.

By the time he set off for the hospital to see Dena, Kenny was feeling positively buoyant, his old self again. He arrived during afternoon visiting time, a bunch of tired-looking daisies in his hand. 'Hello, Dena. You look as pretty as a picture and not sick at all.'

She laughed. 'I'm not sick, it's just this silly ankle but I can walk a bit now, with the help of crutches. They'll be letting me out soon, anyway, now they're certain the baby is all right. Oh, Kenny, I'm pleased to see you. I thought you were never coming.'

'I've been busy.'

'Oh, yes, I suppose you must be.'

He sat on a chair beside her bed but made no move to kiss her and Dena felt a spurt of disappointment. He felt shy about showing any affection in a ward full of the noise and bustle of other people. People stared pointedly as they walked by to visit their own loved ones, no doubt taking in Kenny's Teddy boy jacket, his tight trousers and greasy quiff. Dena thought he looked very fashionable and as handsome as ever, if a bit subdued.

But then she too felt shy and awkward at this much longed for reunion.

And she was acutely aware of being watched, of faces turning in their direction, whispers behind hands. No doubt it would be even worse when she got out of the hospital and went back to the market. For the first time it occurred to Dena that she would be viewed as a fallen woman now. Disgraced and shamed.

Kenny gave her an awkward little smile but didn't seem to know what to say next. 'They'll be letting you out soon, I hope.'

Dena pulled a face. 'Tomorrow, they tell me. Not that I've anywhere to go yet. Miss Rogers is trying to find me a room somewhere. She won't let me stay at yours, nor even work in your mam's cafe. She says it wouldn't be proper. Winnie Watkins has offered me a job though, and I'm pleased about that. I like Winnie.'

Kenny cleared his throat. 'Mam says she would have liked to help but says she can't have that dragon coming round every five minutes poking her nose in where it's not wanted. We have to wait till it's all legal and above board.' He cleared his throat. 'You do still want to marry me, don't you Dena?'

Dena cocked him a cheeky grin. 'I don't remember ever saying that I would, although right now I don't seem to have much option.'

Kenny looked hurt. 'Are you saying that you don't love me any more?'

Dena was at once contrite, damping down her natural rebellion as she recognised the pain and insecurity in his sky-blue eyes. 'Oh, 'course I love you, Kenny. I'm really very fond of you, only this isn't how we meant to start off, is it?' Then added more shyly. 'I suppose Miss Rogers has told you about the baby?'

Kenny swallowed, giving a little nod. He wondered if he should ask if she really wanted to keep it, but decided that might be a bit too blunt at this stage.

He took hold of her hand and gave it a little squeeze. She looked so lovely that he wanted to climb into bed beside her and prove how much he loved her, here and now, in front of everyone. That would show them.

He had a sudden vision of what he'd been doing an hour since, and wondered how Dena would react if he asked her to play the same game. The thought shamed him. She would be his wife, above such things. He'd never treat Dena in such a way! How could he, when she was so utterly perfect? Nor did he need to, since he could still have Maureen, even after they were married. Maureen had explained that there was no reason why not, so long as Dena didn't find out. This delightful prospect banished the problem of the baby instantly from his mind.

'Mam says you're to come to tea on Sunday, so we can talk things through and start making plans.'

Dena said, 'Have you found a job yet, Kenny? I can only work for a few more months. How will we manage after that? We'll need plenty of money coming in with a new baby to feed as well as somewhere decent to live.'

'I know, I know. Don't fret. I've put some feelers out. You can safely leave all of that to me.'

He sounded irritated by the question so Dena decided to press no further on the subject, not at this point. At least he still loved and wanted her. Oh, and didn't she love him for that? Who else cared about her? Not a living, breathing soul. Not her own mother, not the home where she'd lived for the last two years. Even Miss Rogers, who'd turned out to be more human than she'd first appeared, was only doing her job.

Dena simply couldn't imagine life without Kenny beside her, her one true friend, the only person not condemning her.

He said now, 'After you've settled in somewhere, I'd like you to meet a friend of mine. She wants to help, if you'll let her.'

'That would be lovely! Any friend of yours, Kenny, is a friend of mine. Besides, I think we're going to need all the help we can get.'

Chapter Twenty-Three

Miss Rogers found Dena a room to rent on Champion Street that overlooked the fish market. It was small and dark with a bed in one corner and a sink and single gas jet on which to boil a kettle, in the other. She would have the dubious pleasure of waking up every morning to the smell of smoked haddock. 'Best I can do, I'm afraid. People go all starchy when I explain your condition, and we really can't keep it a secret for much longer, can we? Nor can we take the risk of your being thrown out with a young baby to care for. It's such a pity your uncle couldn't have been more accommodating.'

'Why should he be? He doesn't even know me. Anyway, I don't want to live too far from the market. It wouldn't be very convenient.' And Dena did not wish to live with her mother again.

Dena had received a letter from this unknown uncle of hers, stating that he was only prepared to offer her a home if she agreed either to have the baby adopted, or to marry a respectable man of his choice. She would also be required to keep out of sight until either of these happy events were brought about. Dena had torn up the letter and thrown it away.

'No, I don't suppose it would help much, living too far away, still, he is family.' Miss Rogers decided to keep her opinion to herself. She'd said too much already, was getting far too emotionally involved with this girl, which wasn't professional. Not like her at all.

Dena walked to the window to look out upon the familiar stalls with their slabs of wet fish, the colourful displays of mackerel, cod and salmon, the cries of the fishmongers calling out their special offers as they gutted and sliced, canvas flapping in the rain, people laughing and shouting back with some cheerful quip or other.

If she leaned further out she could see Barry Holmes weighing carrots, indulging in a bit of banter with a customer, which brought her some comfort at least, to have an old friend so near. It felt as if she had come home. But deep inside her, Dena felt as bleak as the weather, as cold as those poor dead fish, and just a little bit frightened. What was happening to her? How would she cope with a baby on her own? Would Kenny really marry her? Did she even want him to?

This wasn't what she'd planned to do with her life at all. What about all those dreams she'd had to get herself a good job, have money to spend on clothes and records? She'd longed to enjoy her freedom and have a good time.

Oh, she'd got herself into a proper pickle this time with her silly rebellion. Dena couldn't even make the excuse of ignorance, not since moving into Ivy Bank and listening to the other girls talk. She'd known what she was doing, and hadn't cared about the risks, believed that sort of thing only happened to girls who were at it every night, that it wouldn't happen to her!

Miss Rogers set Dena's suitcase down on to a threadbare rug that covered the green scarred lino and gave her an encouraging smile. 'Winnie says she's looking forward to seeing you on Monday morning. At least you'll have company during the day, and you'll soon have this place spruced up a bit. Clean those mucky windows for a start. Maybe she'll find you a scrap of fabric for new curtains. A bit of fresh colour would brighten the place up no end.'

They both gazed about them at the dingy room, the narrow bed, single hard-backed chair and rickety table, the flock wallpaper peeling from the walls. There wasn't even a wardrobe, just a few pegs behind the door.

Miss Rogers became suddenly brisk. 'I've brought you a few bits and pieces to start you off. A kettle and a pan, cup and saucer, plate, packet of tea and some Peak Freans biscuits. Cornflakes, a Hovis loaf and a packet of marg.' As she listed the items, she unpacked a cardboard box on to the table. 'Even a tin of rice pudding to warm up for your tea.'

'I'll be fine,' Dena said, struggling to smile.

'Right, well, I'll come and see you in a few days, to check how you're settling in.' The woman seemed reluctant to leave, paused to put a shilling next to the groceries. 'For the gas metre.' Then she was gone, and Dena was all alone.

She felt utterly bereft, as if her only friend in the world had just walked out on her, which was stupid. How could you think of a social worker as a friend, even if she was the only one willing to lift a finger and do anything for her? Although she still had Kenny, Dena was forgetting about him and the family tea, still having to face his mam on Sunday. Things weren't as bad as they might be, not even this poky bedsit. Looking about her, it came to Dena in a blinding flash of happiness that this was hers to do with as she wished. It might be tiny but she had it all to herself. No longer would she have to share a dormitory with a dozen other girls, all snoring and snuffling and weeping in the dark. She was free!

Rolling up her sleeves she found a bucket and scrubbing brush. First off, she'd give the place a good going over. Make it entirely her own. And as she struggled with the hot water geyser, she even began to hum a little tune.

–

'By heck, where's that skinny little waif gone who used to be my Saturday girl? You must have shot up six inches.'

Dena managed a chuckle, secretly pleased by Belle's astonishment. She'd felt apprehensive about meeting Kenny's mother again, wondering what her reaction might be. 'I'm still too thin, or so everyone tells me, and I've grown three inches as a matter of fact. I'm five foot four.'

Belle said admiringly, 'Well, you've grown up, that's for sure. I love your hair, it suits you. Our Kenny never mentioned that you'd turned into a beauty.'

Dena flushed. 'Now you're embarrassing me.'

Carl was embarrassing her too, just standing there staring at her, saying nothing.

Belle shook her head in a gesture of sad despair. 'I hope you know what you're letting yourself in for, taking on our Kenny. Still, I don't suppose you have much choice in the matter? This is a right kettle of fish and no mistake, a sensitive subject since you're living almost on top of the fish market these days. But you don't have to worry. We look after our own on Champion Street, so welcome to the family, love.' And to Dena's great surprise, Belle put her arms about her and gave her a warm, scented hug.

'Oh, thank you!'

Like his brother, Kenny had uttered not a single word throughout this small exchange, choosing to stand well back and keep out of the way. He too was worried about his mother's reaction. Dena was fairly stunned by it herself. She'd been expecting the worst, but then you never could be sure with Belle as she could change as swiftly as the weather. So, despite her warm, pleasant manner, Dena remained wary.

Belle led her into the living room where a welcome fire was blazing on this blustery spring day, and a table laid for tea. There was even a plateful of home-made cherry buns. No doubt baked by good old Joan Chapman at the cafe.

'You're not the first in our family who's had to make a dash for the altar. I was married myself at seventeen and my sister had two children before she was...'

'Mam! We don't need to go into all our family history,' Carl interrupted, glowering at Dena in disapproval.

'Why not? She'll be a part of it soon enough.'

'I hope not.'

Kenny jerked forward. 'What did you say?'

'I said, I sincerely hope she doesn't join our family. She's manipulated you into this situation.' Carl summed up Dena with a sneering glance. 'Look at her. Abandoned by her mother and taken into care at fourteen. Released into the world at sixteen but with no home to go to. What better than to get herself knocked up by you, idiot that you are, so she can get her feet under our table? The best in all of Champion Street. That way she gets a husband, job and a home, all in one neat package.'

Belle said, 'Eeh, I reckon that's cutting it a bit strong, lad. Girls are soft as putty where men are concerned. One smile from our Kenny and she wouldn't think at all. Isn't that right, love?'

Dena could feel the rage burning inside her, knew her expression reflected her emotions as her voice came out tight with fury. 'If you must know, when Kenny first asked me to marry him, I said no. I didn't want all that domestic stuff, but...'

'You know which side your bread's buttered,' Carl said, hissing the words out between gritted teeth. ''Course you do, and you might as well go for the jackpot eh? Make the best of a bad job.'

She wanted to smack that supercilious expression right off his handsome face. What did he know about her? Nothing! Nothing at all. But it was Kenny who again leapt to her defence.

'Keep your nose out of my business, or I'll flatten it.'

Belle held up both hands, palms gently flapping in a calming motion. 'You two are always japing over something, but we'll have none of your fisticuffs today. And for God's sake Carl, stop being such a Holy Joe and looking all poker-faced. Get the lass a nice glass of sherry. We should be celebrating my first grandchild, not engaged in argy-bargy. Come on love, sit by the fire and take no notice. You shouldn't stand too long, not in your condition. Sherry, Carl. Now, if you please!'

With an expression even more sour, Carl flung open the door of a fancy cocktail cabinet and pulled out four glasses, unscrewed the lid of a bottle of sweet sherry, and began to pour. When they'd all been served, Belle turned to Dena with a beaming smile.

'Here's to the baby, love. Isabel, after me, if it's a girl, and Frankie if it's a boy, after my father. How would that be? Good solid, English names.'

Carl grunted in disgust. 'Don't be stupid, Mam. Isabel is a Spanish name, not English at all.'

'Does it matter?' Belle snapped. 'I want her named after me. That's what's important for my first grandchild.'

Feeling bemused, Dena glanced across at Kenny, wondering what he thought about all of this, but he said nothing.

'I've told our Kenny he should count himself lucky to get you.'

'I think the reverse is more accurate, Mam,' Carl put in. 'Considering her alternatives.'

Was he always so unpleasant? Dena wondered, or did he reserve this special brand of sarcasm just for her?

Ignoring her son for once, Belle said, 'So, have you two fixed the date yet?'

Dena shook her head. 'Not yet.'

'Now then, Kenny lad, you'll have to shape yourself. Though no doubt you expect your old mam to sort it all out for you, as you do everything else.'

-

Belle continued to talk about the baby all through tea. Dena toyed with her tinned salmon and began to wonder whose baby it really was. Anyone would think it was Mrs Garside's the way she was going on about it. Despite his mother's gushing, Kenny was looking increasingly tense and Carl simply didn't speak at all. He never even glanced Dena's way, so that at the end of the meal, when the peaches and Nestlé's milk had all been finished and she offered to help clear away, Belle wouldn't hear of it.

'No love, you stay by the fire and put your feet up. Kenny can help me do the necessary. Carl, you talk to your sister-in-law-to-be. And do try to show your pleasant side for once.'

Left alone, the two of them stood for several seconds staring at each other. It was the strangest sensation Dena had ever experienced. He seemed to be looking right into her very soul, reading her unhappiness, her vulnerability. His eyes were of the darkest blue, very like his mother's, narrowed and hooded, shadowed beneath the scowl of devilishly winged eyebrows. They were telling her that she might be able to fool his stupid brother but not him. He was far more shrewd and canny. Yet even as she gazed into them, Dena noted a change in his expression, as if he suddenly became less certain and didn't know what to say to her, almost as if he were struggling to decide whether to condemn or pity her.

'You'd best sit down,' he said at last, his voice quieter, and with a gruffness to it. 'You look as if you might fall down otherwise.' He indicated she should sit on the sofa rather than in his mother's armchair.

The offer wasn't made with any sense of graciousness, nevertheless it felt almost as if he'd reached out and touched her for all he hadn't moved an inch. Dena felt a lump come into her throat and she was forced to blink very hard, finding it difficult as always to accept sympathy, however grudgingly given. 'I have been a bit sick lately, in the mornings mainly, but it's passing off.'

Carl nodded, implying he understood perfectly when really he couldn't at all, and they both fell silent once again.

They sat side by side on the sofa staring into the fire, saying nothing for some long moments, yet each acutely aware of the close proximity of the other. He was leaning forward, elbows on knees, which gave her ample opportunity to study his face in profile while he stared into the flames. He was ruggedly handsome with a square jaw, the skin smooth and darker than Kenny's. His curly black hair was rumpled from constant combing with his fingers, and Dena had a sudden longing to do the same. What would it feel like? Soft and silky, or wiry and strong?

She felt strangely content to be sitting here beside him like this, all the awkwardness vanished as if it had never been, although why should that be? It was Carl who broke the silence.

'You'll have to be patient with my younger brother. He tends to act first and think later. Likes to show off and appear the big man.'

'I'd noticed.'

179

'He's not a bad lad, but a bit headstrong and overemotional, and not always in control of himself.'

'Unlike you!' The accusation came out on a gasp, as if she wasn't able to catch her breath. What on earth was happening to her? Why did she feel all trembly and nervy inside?

He half glanced at her, then looking quickly away got up to put more coal on the fire so that it was a while before he answered. 'Let's say I prefer to take my time, and weigh things up more carefully, than jump in with two left feet.'

He came to sit beside her again and relaxed against the sofa cushions, stretching one arm along the back of it, almost touching her hair. Dena felt a tightening inside, hating herself for this instinctive response her senses were making towards him, just because he was male and good-looking, she supposed. She became aware of him studying her and turned to meet his gaze with a slight lift of her chin, determined not to show her weakness.

'At least Kenny can be warm and enthusiastic, full of fun, not cold and unfeeling like some people.'

Carl's smile, when it came, was frosty, and his eyes narrowed to dangerous slits. 'I'm sure caution is not something you would understand. But make no mistake, although Kenny and I have our differences, he's still my brother, and I'll look out for him. Were anyone to try and hurt him, for instance, or take advantage of his naivety and his good nature, I'd have something to say on the matter. If you catch my drift?'

Dena had half expected him to apologise for what he'd said earlier, not issue what sounded very like a threat. The venom in his tone shook her and her veneer of confidence crumbled as she met his icy gaze. 'I – I think so.'

'Good. I'm glad we understand each other.'

'I – I'm not sure that we do. I love Kenny, why would I want to take advantage of him, or hurt him in any way?'

'I think you might, if it suited your ends to do so, like helping yourself to all the tips, instead of sharing them?'

'Oh, but…'

At which point Kenny bounced back into the room and it was time for him to take her home. Dena was suddenly reluctant to leave. She wanted to stay and have this out with Carl, to redeem herself in his eyes, but he was already walking away. The discussion was closed.

Chapter Twenty-Four

Dena started work on Winnie Watkin's market stall first thing on Monday morning, and knew at once that she would love it. She gave the older woman a big hug. 'I'm so happy to be back home again. Thanks for taking me on. You won't regret it, I promise. I know I'll have to give up when the baby is born, at least for a while, but I intend to work for as long as I can.'

'Good for you,' Winnie said. 'I hope you don't feel offended at my not being able to offer you a home. I doubt that my Donald would care for all the mess and fuss and noise of having a baby around, d'you see?'

Dena smiled. 'I understand. I shall have to find somewhere else by the time it's born. I couldn't bring up a child in that dump but it'll do for now. Miss Rogers has done her best, so I don't complain.'

'I thought you and Kenny Garside were to be wed? Well then, won't you be living with his mam?'

This question brought her up short, despite the fact that Kenny talked of little else. Dena flushed, thinking of what Carl's reaction would be if they did move in with his mother. It would be impossible. The prospect of sharing a house with him, seeing him every day made her start to shake inside. A vivid picture of them sitting side by side on that sofa came into her mind, and something inside her clenched a jolt of emotion. It disturbed Dena just to think of him. Why was that?

Perhaps because Carl never had a good word to say for her, accusing her of stealing all the tips when she hadn't been doing that at all. It was Belle who should be blamed for taking more than her fair share, not her badly paid overworked employees.

But that was all in the past. The situation now was entirely different. Dena was in no position to take advantage of Kenny, or hurt him in any way. And why would she want to? She loved Kenny and he'd made his own feelings for her very plain.

Ever since she'd come out of the hospital not a day had gone by when he hadn't been to see her, often bearing flowers or a little love letter he'd written especially for her. And of an evening he would insist on taking her out for a drink, to the pictures, or simply a walk by the River Irwell in order to cheer her up, and celebrate her being free of the home at last. Afterwards he would walk her back to the bedsit in Champion Street, then pull her into the shadows away from the street lamps so that he could kiss her.

'You're still my girl, aren't you Dena? I'm so lucky having someone like you.'

'Why wouldn't I be?' She almost felt irritated by his constant need for assurance, his swagger and show-off manner. Dena sensed that Kenny was nowhere near as confident as he made out. He never seemed entirely sure of her, as if he considered himself unworthy of her attention. She shouldn't be so impatient with him. Wasn't this trait rather endearing?

His brother, however, wasn't in the least bit endearing. He was aggressive and antagonistic, accusing her of being on the make and only marrying Kenny in order to give her baby a name. Dreadful man! How she hated him!

Winnie's voice, still chattering on, brought her back to the present. '...so you have my heartfelt sympathy, love. Living with in-laws rarely works. Still, beggars can't be choosers, as they say.'

'I know, Winnie, but I do need to be independent, to make my own decisions and earn my own money. I worry about what will happen when the baby is born.'

She smoothed a hand over the emerging swell of her tummy, instinctively protective. Because of this baby growing inside her, people she knew well walked past her in the street without speaking, keeping their gaze fixed on some invisible spot in the far distance. She'd turned into a pariah overnight, a person to be avoided at all costs, as if having a baby out of wedlock had turned her into some sort of evil witch.

'I don't know how we'll manage if I can't find someone to look after it so's I can carry on working. We can't live on thin air. We have to eat and Kenny hasn't found himself a job yet. He says the market isn't as busy as it used to be during the war so there's less work around.'

'Well, that's true, but I expect things will change again before long. It's probably only a temporary lull. He should have tried harder with that apprenticeship of his, and it's been one job after another since. Time he shaped himself and found something permanent, since he's soon to be a dad.' Winnie's tone was impatient and she turned away and began fussing with a length of cloth, rolling it up and smoothing it as if afraid that she'd said too much.

'Yes, I suppose so.' Dena sounded doubtful, wondering why she didn't feel more confidence that Kenny would find permanent employment. In her heart, she agreed with Winnie that he wasn't trying hard enough.

'He's young enough to start afresh and learn something new, after all,' Winnie continued, unabashed.

'I was wondering…' Dena faltered, the words dying on her lips. She'd hoped to ask if she might continue working for Winnie after the baby was born, and bring it with her to work, parking the pram behind the stall. How much trouble could one small baby be, fast asleep all day? But faced with her old friend's sudden coldness, she couldn't seem to find the courage. Maybe it was too soon. She might try again in a week or two, when she'd proved her worth.

Winnie paused in her labours to turn and face her. 'What were you wondering, chuck?'

This enquiring smile was vague, not welcoming, and Dena shook her head. 'Nothing, it doesn't matter.'

Once she and Kenny were married, it would all be different. People would stop gossiping about her then, stop giving her nasty looks. She'd be respectable again. 'Right, what do you want me to do? Where shall I start?'

'You can start by helping me do a thorough stock check. I've lost track of what I've got behind this stall. Who knows what treasures I might find if we have a good sort out? And it'll help you to get to know what's what. How about it?'

'Sounds good to me.'

Dena set to with a will. Winnie had bought a small red note-book and in it she listed every roll of fabric and net curtaining, each bolt of cotton, reel of thread, yard of lace, ribbon and rick-rack trimming.

The task took every moment of her working day for the rest of the week, and in that time she didn't serve a single customer, which was a big disappointment to her. Dena liked people and had been looking forward to chatting with all her old regulars, but she got to know the stock that Winnie had for sale.

When Saturday came round and Winnie was clearly run off her feet and in dire need of a helping hand, Dena dashed to her side, eager to help. 'I'll serve Mrs Dawson, shall I Winnie?'

'No love, you carry on with what you're doing. I can manage.'

Biting back her disappointment, it came to her of a sudden that Winnie was deliberately keeping her at the back of the stall where the customers couldn't see her burgeoning bump. Anyone would think a baby was something to be ashamed of.

-

'How's it going?' Miss Rogers would ask. She visited Dena regularly twice a week; was always ready to admire Dena's efforts at sprucing up the bedsit, was interested in her job but asked the most probing questions and constantly reminded her that there were other options to marriage.

Dena always insisted that she was fine, that plans for the wedding were progressing well. In fact, Belle had taken complete charge, even to the extent of choosing an ankle-length ice blue gown for Dena to wear.

'White wouldn't be appropriate, dear.'

It was to be a quiet affair, Belle decided, and did she have anyone in mind for a bridesmaid?

'Well, there's Gwen, I suppose. My friend from the home.'

Belle sat with her notebook on her knee and pulled a face. 'Oh, I don't think so, do you, dear? We don't want any reminders of that place.'

Dena tried to protest. 'She isn't in the home now. She's training to be a nurse at Salford hospital.'

Belle chewed on the end of her pencil. 'A bridesmaid wouldn't be appropriate in the circumstances. A bit too showy, and people might make unfortunate comparisons with her slim virginal figure in comparison with your own. You are starting to show quite a bit now.'

Dena smoothed a hand over her bump and tried not to reveal the panic that was building up inside. She had a sudden desire to scream, which wouldn't do at all. With even Winnie being a bit cool and mindful of her customers sensitivities, her future mother-in-law was the only one who was the least little bit supportive and not hide-bound in prejudice, so why did Dena feel this dreadful resentment against Belle's inherent bossiness?

'I am not, however, in favour of a furtive trip to the register office. We're Catholics, so you'll have to convert. Father Dimmock has agreed all of that can be attended to quickly, in just a few short lessons.'

Dena said nothing. It was all too bewildering, but she felt a small resentment that the priest's opinion on the matter should have been sought before her own.

'Which leaves only the reception and the guest list to deal with. Not at the cafe, I think. Maybe at the Midland Hotel? No, better that I hire a room and organise the catering myself. Joan is perfectly capable of coping with a few sandwiches, sausage rolls and a cake. We don't want people seeing this as a hole-in-the-corner affair, do we? Not when I still haven't got elected on to that blasted committee. We must invite everyone from the market.

It does no harm to one's image to appear generous. Might as well get some good out of this affair. We shall have a really good do. What do you say? Oh, and what about your mother? I shouldn't think she will want to come, do you? Although I suppose we must invite her, for form's sake.'

Feeling increasingly bemused, Dena could do little more than nod or shake her head, and silently go along with Belle's plans as arrangements progressed with the speed of an express train.

Belle even started buying baby clothes, ordered a fancy cot with teddy-bear motifs, and a beautiful coach-built pram in preparation for the happy day. 'You and Kenny can live here with Carl and me, and I shall help you to look after the baby. You're far too young to take responsibility for my grandchild on your own. Don't fret about a thing, dear. It will all be taken care of.'

The banns were called and the wedding organised in three weeks flat. It was utterly amazing! Dena seemed to spend the whole of that time with not a moment to stop and think. She was either dashing to Father Dimmock for lessons or to the dressmaker for fittings; encouraging Kenny to look for work or commiserating with him when he failed. She even found herself obliged to listen endlessly to Belle's political machinations, all about her future plans and hopes for advancement in the market.

And all of this while desperately trying to keep pace with her new job and being acutely aware of Carl watching events unfold with grim-faced disapproval.

Belle insisted on taking her shopping to Kendals' department store and bought her lingerie, a beautiful nightdress, and a brand new pair of silver grey stiletto heel shoes with lovely pointed toes.

'Winkle-pickers, that's the name everyone is giving them. Very elegant dear, though do take them off as soon as the ceremony is over. We don't want to risk you falling over and damaging my grandchild, do we? Now all you need is some Goya face powder and a nice new lipstick, cyclamen pink, to put some colour into you.'

Belle even booked them a honeymoon: a week at a quiet hotel in Grasmere. 'Very romantic, dear! Think of it as my wedding present to you and Kenny.'

Dena wasn't sure that she fancied a week in the Lakes. What on earth would they do there, in the quiet green of the countryside? Walk endlessly up and down hills, no doubt, with rain dripping down their necks.

She was a city girl and would have much preferred somewhere warmer and more lively, like Blackpool or Brighton. Or London. Dena would love to go to London and see Buckingham Palace and the changing of the guard. But she'd been allowed no say in the matter. It was all organised before she was even informed. In just a few short weeks, Dena's marriage and her entire future, like the baby's name, seemed to have been taken completely out of her hands. Even Kenny seemed bemused by the speed of it all, and there was less opportunity for them to be alone together. No more trips to the flicks, no more necking in dark alleyways, and no chance for a bit of romance.

'Are you sure you want all of this?' she said to him one evening when he was walking her back to the bedsit after Belle had presented them with yet another fait accompli. On this occasion her plans for the floral decoration of the church. By the sound of it, it would surely look like Covent Garden and would cost a small fortune. Dena had tried to protest but Belle had insisted that visual impact was essential.

Oh, for a simple register office wedding!

Kenny said, 'It's not about what I want. You're my girl and must have the best.'

'But don't you think it's all getting a bit much?'

'Mam's working hard to make everything perfect for us, so the least you could do is be appreciative.' His voice had taken on a slightly huffy tone and Dena instantly back-pedalled.

'Oh, I am, I am! It's just that it all seems such a rush, and so unnecessary.'

'Aye well, we don't have much time, do we, if we're to be settled before the baby comes?'

'I suppose not.' Dena ached to have time to think, to be in charge of her own future, but Kenny was probably right. Best not to think too much and just go along with everything.

And then days before the wedding he suggested he take her round to see a friend. 'You remember I mentioned her once. She's desperate to meet you and I'm sure you'll get on famously.'

Dena tried to get out of it, protesting that she was far too busy, still with last minute details to arrange, and really tired. But he absolutely insisted.

'There's something she wants to say to you before it's too late.'

'Too late for what?'

He patted her on the shoulder and winked. 'Too late to get out of marrying me, I suppose. She just wants to help. Come on, you'll like her, I know you will.'

Chapter Twenty-Five

The moment Kenny ushered her into his friend's parlour, Maureen offered them a glass of beer, which Kenny accepted but Dena refused. She did accept an offer of tea and wondered why he'd brought her here; what all this was about.

The woman looked too old to be one of Kenny's friends, being in her early thirties, maybe even older. She was fashionably dressed in a knee-length black pencil skirt and an emerald green sweater that revealed a slim but shapely figure and set off her titian red hair. Attractive for her age, Dena supposed, yet there was shabbiness about her, and she wore too much make-up. Dena wasn't sure what she'd expected when he'd spoken of 'his friend', but certainly not a woman, let alone one like this.

The house was not at all what she'd expected either, being cluttered and not particularly clean. Alice would have been horrified by the state of those lace curtains, let alone the grimy windows, and the sofa whose pattern had long since been rubbed off by too many backsides sitting upon it. There was a milk bottle on the table, which her mother would never have approved of either, and Dena could see unwashed dishes in the sink in the back kitchen. Worse still.

Not surprisingly, in view of the mess, there was an unpleasant, unwashed odour about the place. Seeing her hesitation, Maureen gathered up a few newspapers that were littered about, and several items of clothes, then spread out a paisley shawl for her to sit on.

'Thank you.' Now Dena felt embarrassed.

Apart from the sofa, the furniture comprised a table covered by a chenille-fringed cloth, four velvet-backed chairs, and an old-fashioned sideboard stacked with plates and cups, none of them matching. An armchair stood by the hearth where a coal fire blazed, with a small side table and lamp bearing a crinoline lady beside it that cast a false rosy glow over the entire scene.

As Maureen bustled into the kitchen to make the tea, Dena whispered to Kenny, 'Is she a relative of some sort? An aunt, or a cousin?'

'Something of the sort,' Kenny muttered. 'She's a clever woman, with many skills at her fingertips.'

Dena wondered what these skills might be and again glanced about the room, looking for any sign of crochet-work or tapestry, or knitting. Her mother had used to be very fond of needlepoint in her younger days. But she saw nothing that offered any clue, not even a sock in the process of being darned.

Once the tea had been drunk and several ginger biscuits consumed by Kenny along with his beer, Maureen readily volunteered an explanation of the nature of her skills, and they were nothing at all to do with needlework. 'Kenny has explained about this bit of bother you're in, love, so I told him he could bring you round to see me. If you're wanting rid, I can help.'

Dena looked at her, confused. 'I – I'm not sure I understand what you mean.'

The woman smiled, clearly intending to be reassuring. 'Let's just say that I've helped many a young lass in a similar situation. How far gone are you, three months?'

'Three and a half.' Dena was stunned that this stranger should even know she was pregnant. Why on earth had Kenny told her?

'Not too far advanced then. You could come round tomorrow and this little problem would be history in a matter of minutes. You wouldn't feel a thing, I promise. It's not a proper baby, not yet, so it would slip away without any bother at all.'

'Slip away!' Dena turned to Kenny in a daze. 'Is this why you brought me here?'

'I were just trying to help.'

'And this is how you do it? This is your way of giving me the best, is it? You want me to kill my baby so you don't have to go through with marrying me?'

Kenny looked startled then boyishly contrite, flushing with guilt as if he'd been caught with his fingers in the treacle tin. ''Course I still want to marry you, you're the one who's been complaining about being rushed. I wanted you to have the choice, Dena love. You can either keep the baby and we'll get wed right away and live with me mam, or you can take up Maureen's offer which will give us time to save up and get married in our own time, instead of all in a rush like.'

Maureen said, 'I know Kenny adores you because he never stops talking about you, but this is about you, Dena, not Kenny. Don't expect him to help much, if you decide to keep it. Men never do. The question you have to ask yourself is do you want to be stuck with a child when you're just starting out? When you're both so young?'

Dena shivered, despite the stifling heat in the grubby little room and the gently persuasive voice of the woman. The prospect of what she was being offered filled her with disgust.

She stood up. 'I think I'd like to go home now, Kenny, if you don't mind. Thank you for the tea, Mrs…'

'Just call me Mo, everyone else does. Except little Kenny here, who is far too shy and polite.' She gave a throaty chuckle. 'At least in that respect.'

Dena chose not to take her up on that offer either and walked briskly to the door, expecting Kenny to follow her immediately. But she was out in the street before he came charging out, clearly annoyed.

'That's no way to thank someone when they offer to help. You were downright rude to Maureen in there.'

'If I was rude, and I should think she'd be too thick-skinned to notice, then I'm sorry. But what she was suggesting was not only illegal, but also nasty and highly dangerous. To be honest, Kenny, I was appalled by her so-called generous offer, and by her home, and by the woman herself. She isn't going to use her butcher's implements on me, ta very much.'

On which note Dena swung about and stalked off, her head held high.

'Don't you dare walk away from me!' Kenny yelled after her. 'Come back here this minute.' But she didn't. Dena kept right on walking.

-

The church was packed, Belle sitting in regal state close to the front, in accordance with her prerogative as mother of the groom. She was royally dressed in a Dior-style calf-length dress in fuchsia shantung that must have ten yards of fabric in the skirt alone, and a sweet little jacket trimmed with a white collar and cuffs, nipped in at the waist which made her appear slimmer than she actually was. Long white gloves and a wide-brimmed picture hat finished off the ensemble, making Belle feel as glamorous as Princess Margaret Rose herself. Only the high-heeled shoes were causing her problems, pinching her corns something shocking. She eased them off a little under the seat.

Joe Southworth chose this moment to approach and lean over the back of the pew to whisper in her ear. 'You look stunning, Belle. See you after, in the pub?'

She turned her face up to his, leaning back to allow ample opportunity for him to enjoy the view of her cleavage visible in the vee of her collar. 'Now why would you want to do that, Joe? Wouldn't Irma object to your absence from her side? Anyway, I thought you and me were history.'

'And whose fault is that? You're the one constantly blowing hot and cold, not me. I never know where I am with you, Belle. We had a nice time in Cheadle Hulme that time, didn't we?'

Belle flickered her eyelashes in a gesture of non-committal. 'You were wanting to talk about the new committee. It's coming up to that time of year again, I see. And they can't all be standing for re-election. Surely some committee members must have finished their term of office? Yourself, for instance?'

'I'm allowed to stand again for a second term, according to the constitution.'

'Then maybe I should stand against you, go right to the top.'

He chuckled softly as though she'd made some sort of joke. 'Don't talk daft. You need to have served time on the committee first.'

'And how could I do that, I wonder?' She kept her voice deliberately soft, since they were in church, but made no attempt to disguise its cutting edge.

Joe sighed, glancing swiftly behind him as he leaned closer. 'We've talked about this any number of times and I've already explained, there's nothing I can do. You know I can't propose you. It would raise eyebrows. It would look suspicious. God, but I've missed you, Belle. I'll come looking for you later and we'll make up for lost time, eh? See you.' And, giving her a knowing wink, he swaggered off, well pleased with himself.

'Not if I see you first,' Belle muttered.

The organ was playing 'Love Divine All Love Excelling' and she smiled as Kenny and Carl quietly took their seats in the pew in front of her. The pair of them looked so smart in their new grey suits with draped jackets and single button fastening, pristine white shirts and slim Jim grey silk ties.

Such fine boys, so handsome that any girl would be proud to have one for a husband. Kenny was the more dozy of the two, totally lacking in ambition but his heart was in the right place, Belle was sure of it. But then she would think so, being his mother. Who knew what went on in that head of his, daft young fool that he was. Belle hoped that becoming a father would be just what he needed to make him grow up and launch him on to the ladder of success.

Carl was much more complicated and would so often take the moral high ground. But he was right in a way. Dena Dobson was fortunate to be marrying into the kind of family who didn't object to her shady background. A brother dead in strange circumstances; taken into care for being out of control; and now up the duff at just sixteen. Her record wasn't unblemished and few women would welcome such a daughter-in-law.

Belle passed the time by idly studying her neighbours as they quietly entered and found their seats. She nodded and smiled at

Mr and Mrs George, the baker and his wife, and Jimmy Ramsay growing fatter by the day. She agreed with Annie Higginson that they couldn't have picked a better day, weatherwise, and felt a wave of sympathy for the way she bullied her sister into waiting while she comfortably settled herself before allowing her to even enter the pew.

There was good old Joan, looking all rosy cheeked and puffed up with self-importance because she'd been allowed to make all the food for the reception, and been rewarded with an extra day's holiday. Generous to a fault, I am, Belle thought.

Next to Joan came Alec Hall with his pink dickie-bow tie and black velvet jacket. Bit of a snob but such a gent! He'd grudgingly agreed to provide music later for a bit of a knees-up, with the help of that son of his, who always looked so sulky, like he wouldn't say 'boo to a goose'. But then the poor motherless boy must have had a hard time of it, living with such a father, who never had a good word to say for anyone, even his own son. Having been widowed when a V2 bomb dropped on his house with his poor wife inside, he'd be a catch for some likely woman would Alec. Belle had made a play for him herself once, but got nowhere. Just as well, happen. He was a bit too serious for her taste.

One by one the church filled up with friends and neighbours, with pretty well every stall on Champion St Market represented. But then no one would dare to miss Belle's big day. Even that slimy toad Barry Holmes had got himself a good seat near the front, on the bride's side she noticed, and his pink carnation was even larger and more showy than usual.

Dena's mother hadn't even bothered to turn up, silly cow. But then, she hadn't been sent an invitation.

Moments later the organist started the hymn all over again and there was a rustling among the assembled congregation, a shuffling of feet and bottoms as folk kept turning around to see who was here, and to check if the bride had arrived yet. Belle glanced at her watch. She should have arrived five minutes ago. No doubt she was going to be fashionably late, as was the bride's prerogative.

Another five minutes went by, and then another. Whispering had been added to the shuffling feet and Belle's heart was starting to pound. She'd kill the little bleeder when she did turn up. What right had she to keep their lovely Kenny waiting like this? And she was heartily sick of 'Love Divine'. Couldn't the flaming organist at least change the tune?

It was ten more agonisingly long minutes after that when the priest glided over on softly padding feet to whisper the fateful words: 'Are you sure that she is coming, Mrs Garside? She's almost twenty-five minutes late. It's looking remarkably like she's changed her mind.'

'Changed her mind? Don't be ridiculous!' Belle's cry of outrage came out louder than expected and heads turned in her direction. Dropping her voice to a hissing whisper, she continued, 'Why would the flaming tart change her mind? She needs this marriage. What else can she do?'

Glancing nervously at his mother Kenny looked white as a ghost, and Carl, beside himself with pent-up anger, thumped one fist into the palm of his other hand as if he'd like to hammer it into Dena's head.

The priest slid back to have a quiet word with the organist, who at least changed the tune to some dirge that sounded more like a funeral march than one appropriate for a wedding. Belle couldn't even bring herself to turn around now. She shrank into her seat, shamed before everyone, keenly aware that all eyes were upon her; shock and pity pulsating through the little church as everyone whispered behind their hands, gossiping about her and her stupid son.

Belle realised that she'd been made into a complete laughing stock before the entire market. Fat chance now of getting elected on to the committee!

Minutes later she heard the stealthy patter of footsteps as people crept quietly out of the church. Friends and neighbours had got the message, even if Belle and the poor deserted groom refused to accept it.

The bride had stood him up.

Shocking as it might seem, since the girl was pregnant and disgraced, after all, Dena Dobson clearly wasn't nearly so anxious to be made into an honest woman as Belle Garside might imagine. In the circumstances they might just as well all go home, take off their finery and get back to work. There would be no wedding celebration on this day.

Chapter Twenty-Six

Dena had her baby without any fuss in early September 1955: a beautiful girl weighing six pounds four ounces, with a cap of strawberry blonde hair and blue eyes whom she named Trudy. Dena chose the name because she'd looked it up in a baby book at the library, and discovered it meant 'one who is loved'. And Trudy would be that.

Dena knew what it felt like to be unwanted and unloved, a state of affairs she had no intention of inflicting on any child of hers.

Dena had managed to hang on to her job on Winnie Watkin's fabric stall until she was seven months pregnant. Since then she'd relied on the maternity benefit that Miss Rogers was able to get her.

The social worker had also stood as godmother at a quiet little christening ceremony, together with Winnie Watkins. The two women flushed with pride by the honour accorded them, for all they knew Dena had no one else to ask.

Christmas on her own had been a bleak and lonely time, passing in a blur of dirty nappies with nothing in the way of presents and good cheer. She'd almost found herself feeling nostalgic for Ivy Bank and for Carthorse, not to mention Miss Stanford and her shower of sweets.

There were days when Dena couldn't help feeling a little sorry for herself, but then she would think of those less fortunate, the starving babies in Africa, and the death of James Dean in a terrible road accident at only twenty-four. Racial riots in America, and even Princess Margaret. She too was without her lover this Christmas. Throughout the autumn Dena had watched the events of the doomed romance with pity in her heart. If a princess couldn't find happiness with her Group Captain Townsend, what hope had she?

Her New Year's resolution had been to put sadness behind her, not to think about Kenny any more or of what she'd lost, and to get herself a job. It was time to look to the future, for her child's sake as well as her own.

She was still living in the bedsit that Miss Rogers had found for her, still single, and now unemployed. Not the best start in life for her precious child, but Dena remained determinedly optimistic. Things could only get better. At least she had a healthy, beautiful baby of her own to love and care for.

There wasn't a day went by when she didn't thank her lucky stars for finding the strength to fight the prejudice she'd encountered. The thought of giving her baby away to some other, unknown woman, just because she happened to be respectably married, was too awful to contemplate.

As for Kenny's solution, Dena shuddered every time she remembered that sordid little room and his dreadful 'friend'. She'd once asked him if he was still seeing Maureen, but he'd vehemently denied it. Not that she believed a word of it, certain that he lied and was indeed still seeing her. Nor did she care any more what he did. It was nothing to do with her.

But if she could so easily forget him, why did she still worry about him? Why did she wish sometimes that they'd been able to get married without any fuss or interference from anyone?

On that fateful day, when it had become abundantly clear that Dena had no intention of going through with the wedding, he'd rushed over to hammer on her door and shout the place down. Dena had refused to let him in, begging him to go away and leave her alone. And, miracle of miracles, he did just that, though not before he'd assured her that if she should change her mind and decide to forgive him and marry him after all, she only had to call and he'd come running.

On the days when she was near to tears with loneliness and panic at the responsibilities and problems that lay ahead, Dena had been sorely tempted to say that she had, but then would remember why she hadn't married him in the first place.

What was worse, Dena was haunted by another face, one more ruggedly good-looking, with winged eyebrows that scowled at her, a square jaw set tight, and darkly curled hair she ached to touch. It was astonishing how her insides would clench then flutter like a scatty butterfly whenever she should chance to catch a glimpse of Carl out and about in the market.

Always he would turn away, deliberately snubbing her, not wanting to meet her eye.

Dena knew that he condemned her for letting Kenny down so terribly, for showing his brother up before everyone. She longed to be able to explain, to tell him that she'd needed time to think and properly consider what she was letting herself in for. Even now that Trudy was born, she still hadn't made up her mind whether she wanted to spend the rest of her life with Kenny. Did that mean she was stupid or wise, brave or immature, sensibly cautious or just plain irresponsible? Dena felt too confused even to understand her own motives and emotions.

Why should she need to explain to Carl, to anyone, how she felt? And why on earth was she behaving like a stupid schoolgirl with a crush when really she hated the very sight of him?

He'd never been anything but rude and unpleasant towards her, so why allow him to affect her in this way just because he was a good-looking male? He was nothing to her, nothing at all! She didn't even like him. Kenny might be tactless and immature, but at least he wasn't nearly so violent or aggressive as his brother.

She would cope somehow or other, without help from anyone, no matter how difficult it might be. Dena had soon discovered that dealing with a new baby on her own wasn't going to be easy. Trudy was often fretful, either refusing to suck properly, or being sick because she'd gobbled up her feed too fast, screwing up her little knees against colic and night after night screaming her head off. The tiny bedsit stank of dirty nappies, sour milk and Farex powder.

Nevertheless, despite all these problems the baby was a delight and Dena was entranced by her, could have sat all day simply gazing at her in wonder were it not for the nappies to be washed, and the baby food to prepare. She was breast-feeding but the health visitor, who called regularly to offer advice and support, was encouraging Dena to get her on to some solids as soon as possible, so that she would sleep better.

Miss Rogers too remained a regular visitor but Alice, on the other hand, never came near. Once again when Dena most needed a mother, she simply wasn't there. Even now, after four months, she still hadn't called to see her new grandchild.

Belle, however, was entirely different. She was never away. More's the pity, Dena thought at times. Day after day she would pop in to give advice, or, more accurately, to check that Dena was doing things properly and issue a lecture if something didn't suit her. At first, following the shame of being made to look ridiculous before everyone, Belle hadn't spoken to her for weeks, but when the baby was born she simply hadn't been able to resist coming to view her first grandchild and had fallen instantly in love with baby Trudy.

'Has Kenny been to see her yet?'

Dena shook her head. 'I doubt he will.'

'He will if I tell him to.'

It was a day or two later, at Belle's instigation, Kenny finally came to see his child. He stood and gazed down at her as she lay in the pram.

'Well, what do you think of your daughter? Isn't she beautiful?' Dena tried to keep the anxiety out of her voice, needing him to fall in love with her on sight, as she had. That would make everything right between them. She wanted him to see how the curl of her fingers were utterly captivating; to marvel at her shell-like fingernails; the twist of her blonde curls; the pout of her tiny rosebud mouth. To see that it was the most beautiful smile and not wind, and how bright and beautiful were her lovely blue eyes.

'Babies all look the same to me.' He turned to Dena with that all too familiar self-pitying expression on his face. 'I came to ask if you're ready to forgive me yet, and name the day.'

'I'm not sure I'm ready to think about all of that just yet, Kenny.'

He pouted. 'There's other girls would be glad of such an offer, I can tell you that for nothing.'

'I'm sure they would. But look at me. I'm a mess, like a fat plum pudding. Give me a chance to recover from the birth at least.'

The second time he called she asked him more pointedly, 'Do you still see Maureen?'

'No, course I don't! I've never set foot in the place since. That were all a bad mistake. I've said I'm sorry till I'm blue in the face, Dena. What more can I do?'

'And have you got a job yet? Can you afford to keep a wife and child?'

This was a question Kenny generally preferred to avoid. He looked shame-faced although he claimed to be following up the prospect of a job. 'I'll be set up by next week at the latest. We could be wed by the end of the month. I'll speak to the priest, shall I, and fix a new date for the wedding?'

Dena smiled, not believing a word he said. Did she still love him? Did she still want him? She must, mustn't she? He was the father of her child, and didn't she deserve a happy ending? She really shouldn't be too hard on him. All right, he'd made a mistake taking her to see that woman, but he'd apologised. What more could she ask?

Even so, Dena was in no hurry to change the situation. She'd managed this far on her own, and a part of her was beginning to wonder if she needed a husband at all. What was surely far more urgent was getting back to work and earning some money herself.

Belle came again a few days later, eager to vehemently defend her son. 'I can't understand why you're making such a fuss. Everyone has abortions these days.'

'Not me! I am trying but a part of me still can't forgive Kenny for asking me to do such a dreadful thing. You think I should just have let your grandchild, my precious unborn child, be allowed to "slip away" like some sort of unwanted tadpole?'

Belle bounced the baby on her knee, cooing happily. 'You could have said no.'

'I did say no, but Kenny doesn't seem to understand why.'

'So he's a clumsy, insensitive idiot? He's young. He'll learn. I do agree though that it's a good thing you kept this precious little mite safe. I would have told him so myself had he bothered to ask. But he wanted only what was best for you, and there's nothing wrong with that. He's apologised for his mistake, so what more can he do?'

Dena was silent for a moment, conceding this to be true. But that wasn't all that troubled her, was it? 'He could start by showing some interest in his daughter. He scarcely glanced at her when he came.' If only Belle had shown more affection for Kenny in the past, Dena thought. He might then have learned how to be a parent himself.

'That will come, give him time. He adores you, so far better to be married to a caring idiot than try to bring up a bastard alone. Isn't it time you stopped being so stubborn and set a new date, eh? For the sake of this little mite, if nothing else.' Belle leaned down to rub noses with the baby. 'Who's a pretty girl then? What is silly Mummy thinking of?'

'I'm not sure I'm ready for marriage yet, with anyone,' Dena reached for Trudy, taking her out of Belle's arms and tucking her back into her pram to sleep. 'I'm far too young.'

Belle's irritation showed in her voice. 'If you're old enough to have a kid, you're old enough to marry. You'll ruin that child by your stupid stubbornness. I've spoken to Father Dimmock and he agrees that illegitimacy will damage her soul, scar my darling grandchild for life. And don't say that she isn't my granddaughter because you cannot alter biology.'

Dena was obliged to agree that the latter at least was probably true but was all too keenly aware that Belle was more annoyed at having her 'big do' ruined, and her own reputation tarnished, than any concern over her future daughter-in-law's own happiness, or even the spiritual wellbeing of her grandchild.

And Belle's efforts to be voted on to the market committee had once again been doomed to failure, for which she blamed Dena entirely. Yet her obsession with the baby continued to intensify. At least Dena had stuck to her guns when it came to the fancy cot and brand new coach-built baby carriage, which she'd point-blank refused to accept. Miss Rogers had bought her some second-hand baby equipment, which Dena insisted were fine.

Belle had complained bitterly, saying only the best was good enough for any grandchild of hers, but Dena had remained immune to her pleas.

But there were days when she was tired and worn out from lack of sleep, when her purse was empty and she didn't know where the next meal was coming from. It was at these times that Dena wondered if she was right to be so stubborn in refusing Belle's offers of help. Perhaps she should have married Kenny after all, and given her baby a father and the respectability she deserved.

Yet on other days, when Trudy slept well and the sun shone, Dena felt grateful to be still free and independent.

-

If it wasn't for Barry Holmes, Dena didn't know how she would have managed through those first exhausting months. Barry popped in and out all the time, was forever cheerful and positive, never criticised, and every Friday evening, regular as clockwork, he arrived bearing a carrier bag full of vegetables and sometimes a bit of meat for the weekend or a few sausages from Mr Ramsay's stall.

He would sit and dangle little Trudy on his knee while Dena chatted on about such trivialities as colic and wind, and how many ounces her lovely baby had gained this week. He never seemed to be bored, always content to let her ramble on while he cuddled Trudy and sometimes spooned Farex into her ever-hungry mouth.

'She's like a little fledgling bird always wanting feeding. No sooner have I got one feed down her than it's coming out the other end, and then she's after another.' Dena chuckled as she turned steaming nappies on the clothes rack before the electric fire. 'An endless process.'

'You need to get out a bit more though, Dena, a young girl like you. Lovely as she is, what you need is something else to think about besides the babby. Does no good cutting yourself off from all your friends.'

'I don't have any friends left. I've not seen a single one of them since I was taken into care at fourteen.'

'What about that Gwen you met while you were inside, I mean at Ivy Bank? Couldn't you go out with her to the flicks once in a while? It would do you good to get out and have a laugh now and then.' He cuddled the baby closer as he held up one hand against any possible protest. 'And before you say that you can't, I'd gladly babysit for you.'

Dena couldn't ever remember going out simply to have a good time. It had been unheard of at the home, and just when she'd won her freedom from Ivy Bank, here she was saddled with a young baby. She tried not to resent that fact because she loved Trudy to bits, but felt at times as if she were growing old before her time.

'Would it make me seem like a bad mother if I had the odd evening out, do you think?'

Barry laughed. 'No, it would make you human, and since you'd be happier and more relaxed, an even better mother. It's all about moderation, Dena. A little bit of what you fancy does you good.'

'Oh Barry, you're so good to me. Like a father and a friend all rolled into one. Gwen works in Salford Hospital training to be a nurse. I'll write and ask her. See what she says.' And on a burst of happiness, she kissed him on both cheeks.

Chapter Twenty-Seven

Kenny had no particular wish to find work. He didn't care if people considered him unemployable, or if they thought him stupid. What did the clothes he wore have to do with anything? It was nobody's business but his own if he wanted to be a Teddy boy. All his mates dressed the same way, though admittedly not when they were going after a job. Daft cowards!

Besides, he was content to do odd jobs for his mother since he could largely come and go as he pleased. That way, his expenses were relatively small since he still lived at home, and he made a bob or two on the dogs, which paid for his beer. He was always on the lookout for something he could turn to his advantage: a bit of buying and selling if the opportunity presented itself. He'd often find stuff folk wanted rid of, that others were glad to get their hands on.

Kenny didn't like being tied down to fixed working hours, he preferred being out and about on the streets, having his mates around him ready to do his bidding, Chippy and Spider in particular. Sadly, Chippy now had a girlfriend of his own and was less keen to go out on the town with the lads, and Spider was spending more and more time at the club with Barry, working out and training.

Kenny hated being alone, and to have too much time to think, as he always ended up feeling depressed and sorry for himself. He had a great deal to feel sorry about: that little bitch leaving him hanging around at the altar like a prize idiot, for a start. No woman did that to him and got away with it. He hated the fact that all his mates laughed behind their hands instead of seeing him as the great stud he really was. Most of all, Kenny disliked Dena seeming to love that dratted baby more than she loved him. It made him go all hot and angry inside, left him feeling raw with jealousy to see her fawning over that bastard, when really she should be paying more attention to him.

There were days when she wouldn't even let him over the threshold, claiming that the baby was asleep and mustn't be disturbed, or that she had too much to do to stop and chat with him. Then half an hour later he'd see her leaning over the counter of Mr Ramsay's stall chatting away as if she had all the time in the world, or laughing with Marco Bertalone as he chucked her under the chin and treated her to a free strawberry ice. Fast piece, that's what she was. Anybody's for twopence. When he was getting absolutely nothing from her he'd tried sending her flowers and cards but did she appreciate it? Not bleeding likely. There he was standing before her like some prize idiot while she told him off.

'Stop wasting money. If you want to help, fetch me something good to eat once in a while, some baby food, or a packet of tea maybe. I can't eat flowers. Nor can Trudy. They're no help at all.'

Kenny really didn't understand women. Weren't they supposed to like romance and all that stuff? He told her straight that if she married him, she'd never need to worry again about where the next meal was coming from, shouted it at her and she shouted right back.

'More like your mum would provide it, not you!'

What a thing to say! Kenny didn't care for that, not one little bit. And now she'd started, she couldn't seem to stop, like a flaming floodgate opening.

'You're a big disappointment to me, Kenny Garside. Always doing the wrong thing. So selfish you only ever think of yourself. At least Carl, bad tempered and unpleasant though he might be, is trying to make something of his life. What are you doing? Nothing! You don't deserve to be the father of such a lovely baby.'

Kenny inwardly fumed, making a private vow that he'd find some way to show her what stern stuff he was made of. Big disappointment indeed! How dare she say such a thing?

She turned around at that point to pour warm milk on some baby cereal and he took the opportunity to give her precious darling a pinch on her bare toes. What a caterwauling brought Dena running. Serve her right, the selfish bitch!

–

It was one cold day in early January that Dena took Trudy to visit Winnie. She was keen to keep to her New Year resolution and approach her former employer with a hope of getting her old job back.

'She's a very good baby,' Dena was saying as Winnie stood staring down into the pram, an expression of something very like awe on her round face.

'It's none of my business but is she warm enough in that bonnet and matinee jacket? It's a raw one today. A lazy wind what won't go round but blows right through you.'

''Course she is. She's got on a full–length suit underneath with leggings and everything. Would you like me to lift her out so's you can hold her?'

'Nay, best not. We don't want her catching cold,' Winnie said, fear and panic in her voice. 'Anyway, knowing me, I might drop her. I'm not used to babies.'

The older woman was herself swathed in several layers of woolly cardigans, and the knitted hat with a bobble on top that she always wore. It was indeed cold in the market hall and Winnie didn't dare risk having any sort of electric fire behind her stall, as some of the other stallholders did, because of the swathes of fabric hanging about. She had a very real fear of fire.

A customer appeared and, reluctantly, Winnie dragged herself away from the baby to serve her. 'Are you sure you need four yards for that pattern, Mrs Jackson? Three and half should do, to my mind.'

'If you say so, Winnie, then it must be right.'

A tape measure hung around her plump neck, which she operated at lightening speed with practical, square hands. And when the length of fabric had been measured and cut, swiftly and neatly folded into a brown paper bag, the money paid and change given, Winnie sighed as she turned back to Dena.

'Do myself out of business the whole time, I do. Why didn't I just keep me trap shut and sell her the full four yards?'

'Because you care about your customers, and she wouldn't come back again if you oversold her fabric she didn't need.'

Winnie looked at Dena consideringly. 'I do miss you, lass. You were a good help to me. You're sharp, and with a natural eye for style. You could do well in this trade.'

'I was taught to sew in Ivy Bank, which might come in useful one day.'

'Nay, I don't do dressmaking, never have,' Winnie protested. 'Not that I've ever needed to.'

Dena shrugged. 'Things might change.' Trudy gave a little hiccup then a gurgle of pleasure at having made such a funny noise, and both women smiled down at her.

'She's such a happy baby. Sleeps like a good 'un and never makes a murmur,' Dena said, crossing her fingers behind her back against the white lie. Trudy was getting better, though she still had her moments.

Winnie Watkins couldn't remember the last time she'd been this close to a baby. Years ago probably, when she'd lost their Jeffrey. He'd been her second and last attempt at a family. Donald had told her she could mother him instead, but that hadn't turned out as she'd expected either.

She tentatively put out one finger and was startled to find it grasped in a firm grip. 'By heck, she's strong. Look, she's trying to eat my finger. I can feel her little gums.'

Dena laughed. 'She'll only suck it.'

'I doubt she'd find it very tasty. Though I have washed me hands,' Winnie hastened to add, in case Dena should be worried about hygiene.

Dena watched in silence for a moment, then taking a deep breath continued with her plea, determined not to give up easily.

'I'm desperate to get going again. A few hours two or three mornings a week would do for a start, just to see how she behaves. If she's a nuisance I'll take her home right away.'

'Well, that'd be no use for me, would it, having you playing box and cox? I wouldn't know where I was.' Winnie was leaning right over the pram now, muttering nonsense words. 'Coochy-coochy-coo. Who's a proper bobby-dazzler? Come on, chuck, give your Aunty Win a smile? Coochy-coochy-coo.'

Seeing Dena's doleful expression and again feeling the irres- istible tug of the tiny hand on her finger, Winnie found herself weakening. She was a pretty little thing right enough, just like her mam. And it wasn't the babby's fault, after all, that she'd been born out of wedlock and her mother was a sinner.

'Aye, well, happen I'll give it some thought. Talk it over with my Donald.'

Dena thanked her, then, swallowing carefully, cast her a sly sideways smile before adding, 'I would want to serve customers this time though, Winnie. I think we're both now fully aware of the state of your stock, and your storage room upstairs surely doesn't need any more tidying. I spent weeks on that job alone.'

Winnie grinned good-naturedly. 'Aye, happen we'll let you loose on the great British public now that you're decent again. If I decide in your favour, that is.'

'I always was decent.'

'You know what I mean. Though I'm no fan of Kenny Garside, you'd have been better off married to him than on your tod.' She waited, brows arched in gentle enquiry for Dena's response. None came. 'Aye well, my Donald wouldn't care for any hint of scandal.'

'I'd like to meet your Donald one day, Winnie. Maybe he'd feel differently if he actually met Trudy, in the flesh as it were. She's such an angelic little thing, a real sweetie, not an evil imp. Well, most of the time she is. Maybe he'd agree then to my having me old job back. I could take her round one afternoon. Today, if you like.'

'No, you can't do that!' came Winnie's swift response, far sharper than seemed necessary and Dena stiffened, hurt by what felt very like yet another rejection. A chasm yawned between the two women and Dena turned to go.

'I'd best get going then. I dare say you must have a lot to do.' Dena was annoyed at herself for swallowing her pride and begging for her old job back. All for nothing, it seemed, since there was still no definite offer of employment. Dena tugged up the little plaid blanket to Trudy's chin to keep her warm against the cold January day and let off the brake.

As she began to wheel the pram away, head held characteristically high, Winnie called after her. 'You could start with three mornings a week. Wednesday, Friday and Saturday. How would that do? Sharp at nine and don't be late.'

Dena spun about, her face wreathed in a smile of heart-stopping delight. 'Oh, that would be great, and I won't be late, I promise. I'll be there at nine on the dot. You won't regret this Winnie, not for a minute.'

'I hope I don't,' said Winnie, having difficulty speaking through a great lump suddenly lodged in her throat. 'But only if my Donald agrees, mind.'

'I'm sure he will.' Dena ran and kissed Winnie on both cheeks, and then rushed back to the pram and her baby, not noticing a tear roll down her employer's cheek.

Belle was watching the touching little scene from behind the counter in the market cafe and pressed her scarlet lips together in annoyance. After all she'd done for that child, the girl had simply upped and left to work for that Winnie Watkins who everyone knew was as mad as a hatter. At least if she'd married Kenny, Belle would have got her back working in the cafe for free.

Drat him! Drat all men.

Her little fling with Sam Beckett seemed to have fizzled out but she was still seeing Joe Southworth, for their bit of slap and tickle as he called it, whenever he could escape from Irma. Belle thought herself a soft fool since she was still no nearer to winning him round to vote her on to the blasted market committee. She was beginning to believe she never would succeed, and now it looked as if she was to lose her one and only grandchild as well. What did folk think of her? A failure, that's what.

'Kenny! Get out here. Do you never see what's going on under your own nose?'

Kenny came, wiping his hands on a tea towel and feeling very down in the dumps as he prepared himself for another lecture. Even his own mother was treating him with contempt these days, constantly ordering him to do something about getting Dena back. As if he could force the girl to marry him.

'Look, over there. It's Dena. I reckon she's been to see Winnie after getting her old job back. Run after her. Go on. That's your child too remember, not just hers.'

'I know, I know.'

'Well then, start taking some responsibility for it.'

'I will, I will.'

'We want little Trudy in the family, where she belongs. I need to know that my entire life hasn't been wasted raising you two numbskulls.'

'I'm working on it. I'll win round her in the end. Just give me time.'

The trouble was, he couldn't decide how to set about it. He watched in misery as Dena walked away, mesmerised by the swing of her hips, the tilt of her lovely head. Her chestnut hair was growing again, less of a shining cap and with more curl to it. He liked it better this way. He longed to touch it, to feel its cool silkiness between his fingers, to call her to him, but she seemed unmoved by his charm these days, wouldn't even give him a kiss let alone a bit of the other.

He still called round regular as clockwork but she absolutely refused to come out on a date with him, even to the Sandman Club where he and his mates liked to meet up of an evening to listen to skiffle, and pull the birds. He wouldn't need to bother about other women if he had Dena. She was still the one he wanted, the only woman who really turned him on, apart from Maureen, that is. But he couldn't marry a prostitute, could he? And Kenny was determined to have a woman on his arm like other men. Why wouldn't she forgive him, the daft cow?

And nobody had any sympathy for him, not his friends, nor his mam, and not his dratted brother. Thought he was 'the big I am' did Carl since he'd started that big fancy stall of his.

'Stop pining after her. She's not worth it.'

'I don't care about Dena Dobson no more,' Kenny lied. 'I reckon she's having it off with Barry Holmes.'

'What?'

'Aye, he's in and out of her house all hours of the day and night. Anyway, I've plenty of girlfriends. I don't need her.'

But he did. He needed Dena very much indeed. He'd had an idea on a new line of opportunities that he might pursue. If it worked, that would soon bring her running. He'd show Dena who was the big man round here; that Carl wasn't the only one with ambition. He'd win her back one way or another, see if he didn't.

Chapter Twenty-Eight

Dena loved being back at work. It felt wonderful, if only to escape the confines of the smelly bedsit and have some adult conversation. To show her appreciation, she worked harder than ever for Winnie. It meant getting up even earlier than usual, so that she could get on with her chores before Trudy woke for her feed. Dena liked to get the nappies out of soak and rinse them through first thing so that they had all day to dry. She always made sure that Trudy ate a decent breakfast: Weetabix, or scrambled egg and a rusk, if she could afford it, so that she didn't start grizzling too soon for her next feed while there were customers around.

Dena loved the smell of her, that sweet baby scent of warm milk and talcum powder. She would bury her nose in her tummy when she changed her to make her chuckle with delight. Oh, she was so happy! Everything was going to be all right after all. Absolutely perfect! Wasn't she the luckiest girl in the world to have such a lovely baby, and to have a friend like Winnie?

She didn't see much of Miss Rogers these days who claimed she had more urgent cases on her books these days to keep her occupied, but she'd pop in on Dena every few weeks or so, just to see how she was getting on.

'I'm getting on fine,' Dena would say, proud at getting back her job.

Oh, and she really did love her work. She enjoyed helping customers to choose the right fabric, often suggesting a different colour, a soft pink rather than a dingy green to set off a certain colouring, or a lovely electric blue satin rather than dove grey for a party dress.

'Be adventurous,' she would say. 'Jewel colours are all the rage right now.'

She knew this because she read every fashion magazine she could get her hands on, bought second-hand from Abe's stall.

How she loved the feel of fabric in her hands, but she remained fearful of losing her job. Trade wasn't exactly bustling with Winnie constantly complaining about how hard up she was. If she decided she couldn't afford to employ Dena any more, could cope just as well on her own, where would Dena be then?

'I miss the sewing machine we had at Ivy Bank,' she said one morning. 'If I had use of one, I could run up a few dirndl skirts to sell, or circular skirts too which are all the rage. You don't have one, I suppose?'

'I've got a Singer at home,' Winnie said.

Dena brightened. 'We could get some felt in, in bright primary colours. A rack of lovely coloured skirts on display might improve trade.'

'Don't worry, it'll pick up soon. It's always a bit slack in January and February,' Winnie muttered. 'Nothing much will happen till Easter, assuming we survive that long.'

'But we could give it a bit of help, couldn't we? While we're quiet, I could at least run up a few skirts in time for the spring season.'

Winnie looked thoughtful. 'Happen I'll bring it in one day and you can have a go. We'd be a bit pushed for space round the back here though, that's the only problem. I'll give it some thought.'

Surely she didn't need to ask Donald for his permission to lend Dena a sewing machine?

—

Dena's social life too had greatly improved. Gwen had eagerly written back and one evening they met up at the Plaza ballroom to go dancing, Barry doing the honours with Trudy, as he'd promised.

Dena didn't have a new frock to wear so Winnie let her have a remnant of cheap cotton printed with yellow polka dots on a white background. She'd made this into a pair of capri pants that finished just below her knee, all hand stitched, which she'd teamed with a white open-necked shirt, white socks and a cheap pair of ballerina pumps she'd got from Abe's second-hand stall. A scarf knotted about her neck, cowboy-style, and finished the look off nicely.

In truth she'd have come in sackcloth and ashes, it was such a treat to get out and about. Through all those years in the home she'd never been allowed the kind of normal, simple pleasures that other girls took for granted, and her dreams of enjoying them once she'd left had been dashed when she'd found herself pregnant with Trudy.

Not that she minded. Dena loved her child to bits although she had begun to feel like an old frump, stuck in all the time with the nappies and feeding bottles, and little in the way of conversation. Surely it could do no harm to have a break from being a mum once in a while?

The band was great, a quartet playing all the latest rock 'n' roll numbers which Dena adored: 'Rock Around The Clock', and a new Elvis Presley number, 'Heartbreak Hotel', which had everyone swooning. Then there were the slow numbers, 'Secret Love' and 'Three Coins in a Fountain'. Lots of boys asked her to dance and Dena felt reborn, suddenly young again. A teenager, instead of a mum!

A record player of her own had been another thing Dena had always longed for, and the money to go to the store and buy records like other girls. She ached to have the time and money to hang around in the music booths listening to all the latest hits and choosing which one she wanted to buy.

But buying a sewing machine was now top priority so that she could earn a bit extra making skirts and dresses. Dena felt that she was on her way up, had a job at last and some money coming in, but she must be sensible and not allow the excitement of her hard-earned independence go to her head.

If Kenny hadn't behaved so stupidly they might have been happily married by now. But was that what she wanted? Dena had been certain of it once, because she'd loved him so much. Now he'd let her down badly, taking her to see that Maureen creature. What had he been thinking of? Dena suspected he probably hadn't been thinking about her at all. That was Kenny's problem, always so full of himself.

Dena was not short of partners and it was while she was dancing with one lively lad about her own age, the pair of them acting a bit daft to 'Life could be a Dream', and singing at the tops of their voices when she caught sight of Carl across the dance floor.

He was dancing much more sedately with a pretty, dark-haired girl. Something jumped inside her, surprised that he should be here too. He hadn't seemed the dancing sort.

Their eyes met and she could sense his disapproval even from this distance. Was it so wrong for her to want to take a break and go out now and then? She was nearly seventeen, for heaven's sake! Oh, dear, what if he should come over and start going on at her about standing Kenny up? That would be so embarrassing!

Wanting to show that she didn't care, that she was glad that she was still fancy free, Dena wiggled her hips more outrageously than ever, making her partner roar with delight. She was having such a good time, why should she let miserable old Carl spoil it?

Dena was just throwing herself into a dizzying spin when Carl suddenly appeared by her side and she bumped right into him, her gaze coming on a level with his slim Jim tie. It was blue and plain with a single diagonal stripe halfway up, fastened in a wide Windsor knot at his throat. His shirt was white beneath a navy jacket and she'd forgotten how broad his shoulders were. She became aware that her hands were pressed hard against the warm firmness of his chest, and she instantly removed them.

About to turn away and make her escape Dena was prevented from doing so as he grabbed her by the wrist.

'Gerroff, this one's mine,' her partner protested, but Carl didn't seem to be listening. He was too intent on marching her from the dance floor.

'Hey! Where do you think you're taking me?' Dena spluttered, but since he didn't answer, and she had to concentrate on avoiding being trodden underfoot by other rock 'n' rollers, she had no option but to wait till they reached the perimeter of the dance floor. At which point he pulled her round to face him, his expression like thunder.

'What the hell do you think you're doing?'

'I – I beg your pardon?'

'You've no right to be out dancing. You're supposed to be looking after your child. Where is she?'

Dena's eyes opened wide. 'What business is it of yours, might I ask?'

'She happens to be my niece, that's what business it is. Don't you know you're the talk of the market? You and your paramours, don't you even care?'

Dena blinked, then laughed. 'Paramours is it now? I must be having a busy time of it and there's me not even noticing. Folk'll say anything to prove I'm a whore. Well, let them do their worst. And you're right, I don't care.'

His jaw seemed to tighten as he glared at her, the dark blue eyes glittering dangerously. 'And who's looking after her while you're here, making an exhibition of yourself?'

'I'm not making... Hang on, I've every right to go out for an evening with my friend, if I've a mind. Just because I have a baby doesn't mean I have to give up enjoying myself.'

The full sensual mouth twisted into a snarl. 'Oh, I'm sure you would make sure that you don't. Isn't that the reason you need to stay fancy free, so you can play the field?'

'Oh, for goodness sake, play another record, will you.'

Gwen chose this opportune moment to make an appearance. 'Is everything all right, Dena? Who is this?'

'This is the biggest nosy parker in all of Manchester, that's who this is. Will you please release my arm, you're leaving bruises?'

Dena snatched it away and began to rub the sore spot. 'Look, it's turning purple before my very eyes.'

Carl snorted his derision. 'Don't talk ridiculous. Are you going to answer my question or do I have to shake it out of you? While you are cavorting with men on the dance floor, who is looking after your child?'

Gwen interrupted again. 'Should I call one of the bouncers? If this man is bothering you, Dena, we can get him thrown out.'

Dena laughed out loud, finding the idea of someone trying to manually remove the hunky Carl from the Plaza dance floor highly amusing, particularly with his skills acquired in the boxing ring. 'It's a tempting thought, Gwen, but I don't think I'm really in any danger. You weren't planning on doing anything very serious to me, were you, Carl?' she challenged.

He held her gaze for a long moment, as if turning over various possibilities in his mind. 'Since you've refused to allow my brother to make a decent woman of you, I can only assume you enjoy being taken for a harlot. And I still want to know who the hell is looking after your child!'

'Oh, for goodness sake, Trudy is fine. If you must know, Barry is looking after her.'

The silence now was awesome. 'Barry Holmes?'

'The one and only.'

At which point Carl did a most extraordinary thing. He once more grasped her arm in an iron grip, and gave her a little shake as if he couldn't find the words to express the tumult of his feelings, brows drawn darkly together, seething with rage. 'I might've known. You're going home now, understand? Say goodnight to your friend.'

'What?'

He swung Dena about and practically frogmarched her towards the door, Gwen scurrying after them, almost losing her balance as she tried to run in her tight pencil skirt.

'Dena, what should I do?'

'It's all right, don't panic, I'll tell this interfering busybody where he can get off, just the minute he takes his paws off me.'

Unfortunately, that didn't happen until after he'd reached the front door of her bedsit. He pushed her unceremoniously into the front seat of his battered old Ford Prefect and drove at breakneck speed through the streets of Manchester, revving impatiently whenever the lights changed and held him up. He roared along Deansgate while Dena sat clinging to the strap, her knuckles white with the strain of hanging on, slowing down only as they turned into Hardman Street and then left into Champion Street. It was all dark and deserted at this time of night with trestle tables stacked against the wall of the market hall, canvas sheets rustling in the night breeze like ships sighing at being left in dry dock. The car screeched to a halt outside of her building.

'Key. Where's your key?' He held out one hand, impatiently flapping his fingers.

Dena firmly shook her head. 'I'm not giving it to you.'

'Then open the damned door!'

Even as Dena furiously protested that she wasn't going to allow him inside, she obediently slid the key into the lock, as instructed, and pushed open the door. Paying not the slightest attention to her discomfort as he still kept a ferocious grip on her arm, Carl surged up the stairs, dragging her behind him.

The smell of fish from the market that day was strong in her nostrils, seemingly intensified by being trapped in the well of the stairs, and for some reason making Dena feel ashamed of where she lived.

But what followed was even worse than she could have imagined. Barry was sitting quietly by the electric fire, Trudy on his knee contentedly sucking on a bottle when Carl charged into the bedsit like a bull on the rampage.

Barry had hardly got out the words, 'Hello, what are you doing back home so soon?' when Carl snatched the baby from him and thrust the startled, screaming infant into Dena's arms.

'Put the child to bed and don't ever leave her with this piece of low-life ever again.'

'Carl, stop this!'

'Dear, dear!' said Barry, rolling his eyes heavenwards. 'What a commotion! Have I offended you in some way, lad? And there's me thinking we were friends.'

'Colleagues, nothing more.'

'Colleagues! Ooh, what a fancy word. You were happy enough to seek me out when you wanted a bit of free advice, and you know that I've always cared about you and your brother. Like me own sons, you've been.' There was an intensity to his gaze as he looked into Carl's face, and a deep sadness.

'Let's just say I don't much care for you hanging around my niece.'

'Your niece is she now?'

'It would appear so.'

'Nothing to do with my being here, in Dena's bedsit, as a friend?'

Carl hissed something at Barry that Dena didn't hear, she was too busy trying to calm a crying baby, but Barry stood up.

'Well, if that's the way the land lies, I'd best make myself scarce. I'm not one for hanging around where I'm not wanted.'

'I think that would be for the best,' Carl said, in the kind of tone which implied that he'd be almost disappointed if he did leave, as he would then be deprived of the opportunity to personally throw him out of the building.

Dena tried to intervene. 'There's really no need for you to go, Barry. I don't know what's got into him but none of this is any of Carl's business, and I really think…'

'Never mind, cherub, you can tell me later.' Barry was halfway out of the door, nervous of Carl's temper. 'Ta-ra, chuck. Call me again anytime you need me.'

'I will, Barry, don't worry. I won't be bullied by this ape.' And she watched in dismay as her old friend beat a hasty retreat.

Dena was struggling to keep her temper while she cuddled and soothed her whimpering, frightened child. Nevertheless she turned on Carl, her voice seething with rage.

'How dare you march in here, start throwing your weight about and manhandling my child? Who the hell do you think you are? Get out! Get out now!'

'Dena, take my advice and...'

'I'm not taking any advice from you. I make it a policy never to listen to bullies. The fact that you've suddenly turned against Barry is your problem, not mine. He's like a father to me and I trust him implicitly. Now please leave before I call the police.'

'Dena, I warn you...'

'I mean it. *Get out!*'

The sound of the door slamming echoed for several moments long after he'd gone. After which Dena burst into tears.

Chapter Twenty-Nine

It was one Tuesday afternoon in early March when Dena was at a loose end that she took it into her head to go round to Winnie's house. She hadn't forgotten that her employer had once offered to lend her a sewing machine and Dena was keen to follow up her dream of making skirts to sell on the stall.

Winnie had kept promising that Donald would carry the machine in for her since it was a Singer electric table top model and not one of the old-fashioned treadle variety, but it had never materialised. Dena wished she could afford to buy one of her own but they cost almost ten pounds, so on this lovely sunny day with a hint of spring in the air, she had finally grown tired of waiting.

Her fingers were itching to be busy sewing, and Dena so longed to make a new dress for herself. She hoped that if Donald was home he would offer to carry it to the bedsit for her, then she could get on with the work as there was marginally more space in her single room than behind the crowded fabric stall.

Winnie lived at the opposite end of Champion Street, just before it joined the junction of Grove Street and, as she approached, it occurred to Dena that in all the time she'd worked for Winnie, she'd never been invited to visit. She should have asked first, but in this part of Manchester folk popped in and out of each other's houses all the time, so it shouldn't really matter.

As she walked, Dena admired the goods on sale, some-times stopping to admire a range of military buttons and medals displayed in little boxed frames, a selection of records in their brown paper sleeves, postcards and interesting bits of bric-a-brac, or pausing to try on a pair of boots or feel the quality of a pair of denim jeans. There was one stall festooned with lace and ribbons which always entranced her, and another cleverly draped in crochet and knitting patterns, the wool itself stacked high in great plastic boxes.

She could never resist the smell of freshly baked pies, the hot potato cart, or bacon butties from Belle's cafe, all mingling with the newly cut grass in the churchyard and the spring vegetables on Barry's market stall.

'Hiya, Barry,' she called out as she trundled past with the big pram, Trudy sitting up now in her little pink harness and new white matinee jacket and bonnet that Dena had knitted herself. She looked a picture with her rosy cheeks, blonde curls and lovely blue eyes.

'Hiya, chuck. Take care,' he called back, then rolled his eyes as he went back to serving what was clearly an awkward customer. 'No love, you don't have to buy the whole cabbage, you can buy half, or a quarter, just one leaf if you've a mind.'

Dena smiled to herself as the woman flounced off without buying a single thing. Barry could sometimes be a bit too sharp and sarcastic for his own good. But at least he still spoke to her, despite that fracas with Carl some weeks before. She'd never got to the bottom of what had enraged Carl that night. She'd always thought him friendly with Barry, them being members of the same boxing club, but something had obviously put his back up. Dena assumed it must have been her fault, something to do with her treatment of Kenny that had inflamed his temper, and she really couldn't help that.

She'd grown accustomed to people gossiping and behaving oddly towards her. Few on the market spoke to her these days. Backs would turn, or people would pretend not to have heard when she called out to them. Mostly she didn't even bother doing that any more, and would just walk on by, ignoring them as plainly as they ignored her.

Dena didn't mind so much for herself, but inside was growing a small fear as to how they might treat Trudy when she started to play out with the other children. Would they give her child the cold shoulder too?

There were one or two exceptions. Jolly Mr Ramsay, who looked just as you'd expect a butcher to look, all big and ruddy cheeked, with a fat belly swathed in a large blood-stained apron. His wife was very much the lean to his fat and far too prim and proper for her own good. She always walked away on some urgent business or other whenever Dena came near to the stall, leaving her husband to serve her. Mr Ramsay's florid cheeks would grow even redder and he'd slip her an extra sausage or a bit of stewing beef to make up for his wife's coldness.

'Cook it slow in a bit of Oxo, and it'll taste right good.'

The Bertalone family on the ice cream stall just inside the market hall had likewise remained friendly throughout. They were Italian and knew all about how difficult it was to settle when folk were suspicious of you.

And right at the back of the outside stalls, just by the rear door of the market hall stood Carl's household goods stall. He'd made a fine display, one to be proud of, with kettles and pans hanging from hooks across the top of it, sets of cutlery, mops and buckets, Ewbank carpet sweepers, Prestige pressure cookers and kitchen products and devices of all descriptions. Dena might like to have browsed among this treasure trove herself but she could hear him chatting with a customer, explaining how to use a roasting spit just like Philip Harben, the television cook. And although she knew that he saw her, he didn't speak or wave, didn't even acknowledge her presence. He really was the rudest man she knew. Dena stuck her chin in the air and walked on by.

Thank goodness for dear old Winnie, who'd warmed considerably from her earlier frostiness and now happily allowed Dena to serve customers, as well as allow her to have her illegitimate baby on proud display for all to see. A rare woman was Winnie, and always full of surprises.

Today, Dena was to discover that this was truer than she'd bargained for.

There was no answer to her knock, just the sound of a dog barking. Dena tried again to no avail, gave up and went back to the market hall where Winnie was busy serving a customer. Now that she'd fixed the idea in her head to start sewing today, she didn't want to let it go.

'What's this, wanting to work on your day off? Glutton for punishment, eh? Here, mind the stall a sec while I put the kettle on. I'm dying for a cuppa.'

So Dena put the brake on the pram and served one or two customers, measuring out curtain net for one, and a length of blue poplin for another. When all was quiet again she sat with Winnie on an upturned box and sipped her tea. 'I've just been round to yours.'

'What?' Winnie was so startled she almost dropped her mug and had to dab at the spill of tea down the front of her blue cardigan. 'What did you do that for?'

'Sorry, but since Donald has kept forgetting to bring in the sewing machine, I thought I'd pop round and get it. Balance it on the pram if he was too busy to carry it home for me, only I'm dying to get going. I've made some sketches of circular skirts, some with flowers and poodles in appliqué. I got the idea from one of Abe's old fashion mags, and I'm sure I can make them okay, and that they'd sell well.'

Winnie had gone all pink cheeked. 'You'd no right! No right at all.'

Dena was at once contrite, surprised that her friend was more concerned about her calling at the house than listening to details of her designs. 'I'm sorry. Is he ill or something? I never thought. He didn't answer the door. Your dog was barking and I assumed there was no one in.'

'I don't have a dog. That would be Molly Poulson's next door.'

'Oh, well, shall I call again later? Would that be more convenient?'

'No, it won't! I mean, I'll bring the flaming machine in for you tomorrow.'

'Oh, right, sorry to be a nuisance. I could collect it if you prefer. I don't mind how early it is.'

'I've said I'll fetch it, haven't I?'

A short, tight silence ensued. 'I'd best get going then.' Dena set down her mug of tea unfinished, took off the brake of the battered old pram and wheeled Trudy away, mystified by Winnie's sudden coldness. Just when she thought she'd been accepted, here was yet another rebuff.

—

'Here you are, one sewing machine. I've fetched it in myself since Donald isn't feeling too good.' Winnie called out as she came staggering into the market hall the following morning, weighed down with the thing and Dena rushed to help. It was raining and Winnie was soaked to the skin despite the old mackintosh she had slung over her shoulders.

'You should've said. I would've come round and helped you to carry it.' Dena was filled with guilt. 'Look, if your Donald isn't feeling too good, why don't you take the day off so's you can see to him. I don't mind doing a bit extra.'

'There's no need for that.'

'But you don't want to leave him on his own all day if he's ill. What's wrong, is it flu or something more serious?'

Winnie busied herself at the back of the stall hanging up her mack, then started pulling swatches of fabric out of her samples book, folding them up and putting them back again. 'He's never been the same since the war.'

'I see. Are you sure you wouldn't like to be with him?' Dena's soft heart went out towards her friend. How awful it must be to nurse a wounded husband year in and year out. And he must be a bit of tyrant since she always had to ask his permission for every little thing. 'I don't want paying for the extra hours. I'll do it gladly. I could get going on the machine as I doubt we'll be busy on a wet day like this.'

'No, I've already said, there's no need for me to stop at home all day,' Winnie snapped.

'But...'

'I've said there's no need!'

Dena realised it was pointless to press the matter further but she sensed a problem. She couldn't put her finger on what it was, but there was most definitely a problem. She'd never met Donald personally, couldn't actually remember seeing him out and about, but then why would she, if he was an invalid? Later, when she spotted Barry packing up his boxes at the end of another wet day, she went over to help as she often did, and asked him.

'Do you know Donald?'

He looked at her, eyebrows arched in surprise. 'Donald Watkins?'

Dena picked up a box of oranges and helpfully loaded it into the back of his van. 'Yes, Winnie's husband. He seems to be ill. I called the other day and she was most upset about it. Now she's saying he's not well, that he's never been the same since the war. Yet she wouldn't take the day off to look after him. It's a puzzle because I always thought she adored him. She never stops talking about him.'

Barry paused in his labours and gave Dena a sad look. 'Well there's not much point, is there? Donald flew Hurricanes during the Battle of Britain and went down over Northern France. Been missing presumed dead for over fifteen years.'

'Oh, my goodness, that's terrible, why?'

Barry shook his head. 'Winnie can't bring herself to accept it, I suppose. She waited years for news, hoping against hope that he'd come home one day, but he never did. Many did return so it seemed reasonable enough at the time. Then she created this fiction that her husband had come home wounded and was in need of special care. He became someone she could talk about at home who cared about her and what she does. And took the blame whenever she didn't know what to do or how to cope with life. Most people are aware of the truth, but go along with the tale for Winnie's sake. She's lonely, that's all.'

Dena was nearly in tears by the time he'd finished. 'Oh, poor Winnie, how awful! I wish I could help. I wish there was something I could do.'

Barry put a hand on her shoulder. 'You are helping, just by being there. Be patient with her though, and with her memories of Donald. They were a lovely young couple once, and madly in love, but they didn't have a good war. Winnie just can't seem to let him go.'

Dena set to work sewing the skirts, saying nothing to her employer about what she'd discovered. And when, a day or two later Winnie cheerily told her that Donald was feeling much better, Dena said, 'Oh good, I'm so pleased. Nothing worse than a bad dose of flu, is there?'

'He always did have a bad chest, my Donald.'

'Then you must take especially good care of him.'

'Oh, I do,' Winnie assured her. 'I do.' Her voice faded slightly and her gaze slipped away into the middle distance and then she abruptly changed the subject. 'Eeh, I'd best get on with unpacking this net curtaining. We don't want no slacking round here, not even from the boss lady, eh?'

Nothing more was said on the subject, and Dena got on with her sewing with increased diligence.

Chapter Thirty

Britain had moved on from the austerity of the 1940s and early 1950s, and a new prosperity was emerging. What was even more exciting was that even young people, teenagers as they were now called, were developing a fashion style of their own. It was with this group in mind that Dena started to draw up her designs. She went round the Manchester warehouses and bought a few remnants of polished cotton and seersucker to practise on. She also bought a couple of yards of buckram to stiffen the waistband, or to make into fashionably wide belts.

She'd seen pictures of skirts with poodle designs, the Eiffel tower, flowers and tropical palms. Dena decided on daisies for her own design and ran up a circular skirt in no time, then set about fashioning petal shapes from a piece of bright yellow felt she stuck close to the hem to form a large daisy, adding a long green stem that ran right up to the waistband. She would have loved to make an entire skirt out of felt but the fabric was expensive and she needed to prove herself first.

She stayed up half the night finishing three of these skirts in different colours, thankful that Trudy was sleeping well at the moment. The next morning Dena pressed the completed garments and took them into the market to show her employer.

'By heck, that's a bobby-dazzler,' was Winnie's instant reaction when Dena held up the first skirt, a pale blue finished with a yellow daisy.

'I have another here in pink with a white daisy, and one in green and yellow. What do you think? Could we hang them up and see if they sell?'

Winnie was examining the workmanship. 'You're plan is not bad at all. You finished off well and this zip is sewn in really neat. Who taught you?'

'Miss Stanford, a teacher at the home.'

Winnie gave her a wry smile. 'Some good come out of it then?'

They sold the skirts by lunchtime and before they closed for the day had taken orders for two more.

'You've started a craze. Daisy skirts. You'd best get off home and start sewing, lass. Here, take some of this blue cotton sateen, and how about the cabbage rose print? It's so pretty. Would that be suitable?'

Dena shook her head. 'Not for this design, I need plain colours. These gingham checks might do though. I could bind the hem with the same colour as the daisy. Maybe I shall make an orange daisy, or a pink one. Why not?'

'Why not indeed? I can see what you're going to be up to on your days off. Here, don't forget your money. You bought that fabric so it's all yours, and something for the extra hours. As for using fabric from the stall, we'll have to come to some arrangement. I'll have a word with Donald, see what hourly rate you should be on for the sewing.'

'And designing. Cutting out and sticking the daisy on is the fiddly part. I want to try other designs too. Bluebells, cats, who knows?'

'Aye, don't worry. He isn't a mean man, he'll take all of that into account. But he's in charge of finance in our household.'

'Yes,' said Dena quietly. 'I know.'

—

Dena was busy at her sewing machine when Kenny called round a day or two later, pushing his way in the minute she opened the door.

He stood watching, his mouth in a sulk as she slid a sleeve neatly into the armhole, clicked down the foot and expertly stitched it into place. She'd made several circular skirts and was now experimenting with a couple of blouses.

'What the devil are you doing now?'

'Trying to earn a living.'

'If you'd married me you'd be living round at mine with mum to do all the cooking and help with the baby. And you wouldn't need to work at all, save for helping out at the cafe.'

Dena cut off the thread and reached for the second sleeve, giving a soft sigh. 'Be honest, Kenny, you were never too keen on the idea of getting married. Your first reaction was utter panic, and you don't even like babies.' Dena had noticed he rarely made a move to touch Trudy, let alone pick her up.

Kenny troubled her deeply. Despite having stood him up at the altar, he couldn't seem to get it into his head that it was all over between them. At one time she'd wanted him to call, now she wished she could stop him from coming round. Yet he was her child's father so felt she owed him something at least. And she had long since forgiven him for taking her to see his 'friend' because that was Kenny all over: act first, think later.

'I'm not used to kids, that's all,' he sulkily remarked.

'Go on, give her a cuddle and see that she's waving her arms at you. Pick her up.'

Kenny reluctantly complied, holding the baby at arms length, her little feet dangling. Dena paused in her labours to laugh out loud. 'Hold her close, not like a bag of flour. Go on, be brave. She doesn't bite.'

Very tentatively Kenny sat the baby on his arm where she gurgled and chattered happily on her nonsense words, bouncing up and down with delight at this new experience.

Satisfied and pleased that she'd at last brought father and daughter together, Dena jumped to her feet and impulsively kissed him on the cheek. 'There, that wasn't so difficult, was it?'

Kenny looked at the infant in his arms and all the jealousy he felt for her boiled up inside. This child had suckled at Dena's breast, had demanded her attention around the clock, week after week, month after month, leaving her no time to even think about his needs. Even before she was born, Dena had put the dratted child first, before even their love for each other. That was the real reason she'd refused to get rid of it, the reason she wouldn't marry him, because she loved this stupid child more than she loved him.

Dena turned away, back to the sewing machine to stitch in the second sleeve, and that infuriated him too. She was even more interested in the blasted sewing than him.

She didn't see what happened next, didn't see Kenny lift one small chubby foot and pinch the baby's little toe very hard. The result was every bit as satisfactory as the first time. The baby started and let out a yelp, her great blue eyes wide with shock before opening her mouth and starting to wail very loudly, huge tears welling up and rolling down her rosy cheeks.

'Didn't I tell you,' Kenny said, almost dropping her back into the playpen. 'I'm no good with kids.'

—

Kenny never seemed to be away from her door. Night after night, just when she was at her busiest having put Trudy to bed, she would hear his rat-a-tat-tat and inwardly groan. Dena was beginning to dread the sound of it. Once she pretended she wasn't in but he just knocked louder and when still she didn't answer, hammered on the door and shouted.

'I know you're in there, Dena, because you can't go out. Not with a baby. So open up.'

She felt trapped in her own bedsit.

And when she weakened and did allow him to come him, he would start on again about being left standing at the altar, begging her to forgive him. 'I shouldn't have taken you to see that pro... that Maureen. I didn't think. I just wanted you to have the choice.'

'Forget it Kenny, will you please? It's all done with now, all in the past.'

'Not for me it isn't. Folk still talk about me behind their hands, even my so-called mates. They laugh and feel sorry for me. I can see it going on all the time.'

Dena gave a wry smile. 'You have my sympathies, really you do, but don't you think they talk about me too?'

'Well, they'd stop all of this nasty gossip if you'd only agree to wed me. You know that you love me really, so stop trying to prove something and admit it.'

Dena wasn't even sure any more that Kenny truly loved her. More likely he was in love with the idea of love, enjoyed having a girl on his arm to make him feel big and important. He wasn't interested in a family. 'I can't even think about such things right now. I'm far too busy building a new future for Trudy.'

Trudy, Trudy, Trudy, that's all he every heard from her lips these days. He even hated the name. Kenny sat on the edge of the bed in a sulk while Dena pulled a pair of pyjamas on to the child.

'Do you want to hold her for a minute while I warm her milk?'

Kenny vigorously shook his head. He really didn't care for babies. Dena laughed and sat her on the floor while Kenny continued to glare.

He said nothing more until Dena had fed her with warm milk out of a beaker, then put her down in her cot. As always it made him go all tense to watch her cuddling the child so lovingly when she wouldn't even let him kiss her.

At last, sighing with relief that the baby had been cleared away out of sight, he felt able to relax. But if he'd hoped she would then give him her undivided attention he was soon disappointed. Instead, she reached for a length of fabric and began to unroll it.

Seeing his expression she gave a small shrug of apology. 'Sorry, but I'm run off my feet.'

He'd never expected her to be this stubborn. What was wrong with the silly cow? Couldn't she see that he was panting for her, that she was the girl he needed, the only one who really turned him on. He could see the alluring outline of her breast as she held up the length of fabric examining it for flaws and couldn't resist making a grab for her, drawing her into his arms and trying to kiss her but instead of succumbing, she pushed him roughly away.

'Don't Kenny! Stop it.'

His face flushed crimson. 'Why? What's wrong? If you've forgiven me, why can't we get back together? Don't you fancy me any more? You're still my girl as far as I'm concerned.'

He made to reach for her again but she slapped at his hand, inflaming him all the more. 'Stop that! It would never work between us. It was all a big mistake.'

'A big mistake? Why was it a mistake? Why wouldn't it work between us?' He was almost shouting now, but she'd walked away from him and was holding open the door.

'It just wouldn't, that's all. Look, I don't want to talk about it any more. It's all over, right? I think it's time you left.' And he had no alternative but to go. Oh, but he wasn't done with her yet, not by a long chalk. The more she resisted, the more appealing she became.

Chapter Thirty-One

Kenny made the decision that what he was in need of was a little assistance from someone who knew Dena better than he did. He was well aware that Dena missed her mother, that she felt abandoned by her. If he could reconcile the pair of them, she'd see him in a much better light. It was worth a try.

Alice wasn't difficult to find. A few enquiries around the market soon resulted in her brother's address. Gossip had been rife at the time of the family reconciliation, and later when they'd refused to include Dena in the arrangement.

Kenny got off the train at Chorlton Station and walked down wide, tree-lined streets passed by the occasional motor car, a lady on a bicycle and a single decker bus heading back to the city. Clearly there was money round these parts, but it was a bit too quiet for Kenny's taste.

In his eyes this was where the posh folk lived, out in the suburbs far away from the city centre, away from the blitzed sites left by the war, and the old mills of the industrial revolution. Here there were still trees and meadows, olde worlde pubs like The Horse and Jockey where he stopped off for a pint to fortify his courage, and any number of big fancy houses. He was deeply impressed when he found Alice's family home, a large semi-detached house just off Lindow Road, in what he supposed they called the garden suburbs. Determined not to be intimidated, he marched up the gravel path and rattled the knocker very loud.

It was some long moments before the door was opened by a young girl, evidently the maid as she was wearing an old-fashioned pinafore and a cap pulled down low over her forehead.

As soon as she saw him standing on the garden path, she flicked out her blonde curls and gave a cheeky grin. 'If you was wanting to speak to Mr Hindle, he isn't in.'

'It was hactually his sister what hi wanted to speak to, if you would be so kind has to tell her that Mr Kenneth Garside would like a word,' said Kenny in his poshest voice, giving a big wink that made her giggle.

'Wait there a sec.' The maid shut the door in his face as she scuttled back into the house to deliver his message and again Kenny waited for what felt like hours but was probably no more than five minutes. He tried peering in through the stained yellow and red glass set in the top of the oak panelled door but could see nothing beyond a hall and hat stand, and a staircase with a polished banister.

At last the door creaked open again and this time it was Alice herself who stood there.

She looked different. She'd lost weight, he noticed, remembering her as a solid, stout woman, tall and formidable. But she was still rounded and comfortably plump you might say, which Kenny liked, and with shapely legs and trim ankles. She was also considerably better dressed than usual in a floral silk dress with a lace collar open at the throat. She wasn't wearing her spectacles and gazed short-sightedly at him through slitted lids, arms folded in that condemning way she had.

'What do you want? You've no right to come round here uninvited.'

'Hello Mrs Dobson, I'm pleased to see you looking so well.'

She drew in an impatient breath, which made her wide nose flare at the nostrils. She really was a very ugly woman with large cheekbones and a dried out grey frizz atop her round head. Where Dena had got her beauty from, he couldn't imagine. It wasn't from her mother.

'Well get on with it,' she ordered. 'State your business, and don't mess me about. I haven't got all day.'

Kenny cleared his throat. He'd given this moment a great deal of thought, not expecting to be welcomed with open arms, and had decided that the best way to gain her attention was through shock. And by taking advantage of Alice's great weakness: her high moral rectitude. If that meant stretching the truth a touch, what of it? Hadn't he read somewhere that the ends always justi-fied the means?

'I wonder if you are aware that your daughter has set herself up as a prossy, living alone in a bedsit and entertaining men like Barry Holmes so's she can feed her illegitimate baby. My child! I've offered to make an honest woman of her but she's turned obstinate and refuses, so I thought happen you might be able to help me persuade her to see sense. For the sake of her good name like, and yours too.'

The glare she gave him in response to this tale almost froze him to the spot but moments later Kenny found himself seated in the front parlour, the maid bringing him tea on a tray.

Kenny wasn't really one for tea cups, or polite chit-chat, but he did his best and really they got on surprisingly well. Alice sat silently sipping her tea while he poured out his heart to her. He kept on repeating how much he loved Dena, how devastated he'd been when she'd left him standing at the altar. 'And to this day I don't know why she did it.' Kenny judged it wise to make no mention of Maureen or the offer to rid Dena of her 'problem'.

'Always was stubborn,' Alice muttered.

He forced a tear to his eye. 'So what do I do now? I'm potty about her. She's the love of my life and I must have her. I must. I thought you might be able to help.'

Alice sniffed, looking him over with a condescending glance that hadn't warmed by even the smallest degree. 'You wouldn't be my first choice for a son-in-law, Kenny Garside, so why should I help? What have you got to offer my daughter? Have you got a good job, or a home to offer her?'

'You have, why don't you have her here?' he cheekily responded, glancing about the well-furnished room.

'I beg your pardon?' Now he'd offended her, which wasn't a good idea in the circumstances.

Kenny instantly and humbly apologised. 'Sorry, I'm that upset I let me tongue run away with me. And I can see that naturally you'd be worried about her even more than me, good mother like you, for all you've had your differences in the past. It must upset you badly seeing how low she's sunk.' On a sudden impulse he reached forward and stroked the pale cheek. It felt like dried leaves beneath his hand but her brown eyes flared at his touch, as if no one had ever done such a thing before. 'Will you help me, Alice?' he asked, in his softest, most persuasive tones.

'What could I do? She never did listen to me.'

Kenny decided to take a chance. Alice Dobson wasn't an easy woman to get round, but he'd always been able to rise to a challenge! And didn't he have a particular fondness for older women? He took her hand and gently pressed the soft flesh.

'She misses you. You're her mam, and every girl needs a mother around when she's got a youngster. I'm sure you can appreciate that? I know Dena can be difficult, that rebellious at times she'd cut her own nose off to spite her face, as they say. I realise you had a bad falling out, but then you were both cut up over your loss, so was it any wonder?'

He paused for maximum sentimental effect. Alice said nothing, simply drew her hand slowly from his grasp.

'I thought if I were to help the pair of you to mend bridges like, she might forgive me too for whatever crime I'm supposed to have committed. Dena will never be able to hold her head up on Champion Street Market till she's respectable again. You neither, I don't suppose.'

Alice grunted, which he took for assent.

'We could help each other, you and me. We could be mates.'

It was several moments before she answered but he could see the thoughts churning round in her head; and those small brown eyes, surprisingly vulnerable without her specs, told all. The woman was lonely, and as sex-starved as a rabbit who couldn't find a buck, though happen she didn't know it yet. Now there was a challenge!

It all worked like a dream. For once he seemed to have got something right. Alice met him at the corner of the market the very next day and they went together to Dena's bedsit.

'She'll not let me in,' Alice said.

But she was wrong. Dena was astonished to find them both standing at her door but pushed it open at once to allow them both inside. At least, Alice went in. Kenny had the good sense to stay out on the landing. Best to give the two women time to kiss and make up, or whatever mothers and daughters did. His chance would come later.

He just hoped they didn't end up tearing each other's hair out, and only began to relax when ten, then twenty minutes ticked by and the door remained closed. At last, after about half an hour, it opened again and Alice came out.

She gave him a quick glance, clearly warning him not to ask any questions at this juncture and Kenny simply smiled at Dena, stood back and patiently waited.

'Would you like to come in for a minute, Kenny?'

'What, me? Oh, right.' He couldn't believe his luck.

'I'll hang on here for you,' Alice said. 'You said you'd see me home.'

Kenny frowned, wishing the old bat would disappear in a cloud of smoke his nerves were jumping that much with excitement. But he must be patient. He mustn't go too fast and scare Dena off. 'Right you are,' he managed, and slipped quickly through the door before Dena could change her mind.

Once inside, he didn't know where to put himself and stood awkwardly shuffling his feet, putting his hands in his pockets, and then pulling them out again.

'You can sit down a minute, if you like.' Dena lifted a pile of folded nappies off the only chair in the room.

'It's all right, you sit and I can stand.'

'No, there's something I want to say and I'd rather stand up, if you don't mind.' She took a deep breath, and tried a tremulous smile. 'I want to thank you for fetching Mam here. I don't know how you managed it, Kenny, but I can't tell you how happy it's made me. She's even promised to come again. In fact, I think she might pop in regularly now.'

'You've made up your differences then?' Kenny said, beaming with pride at his own cleverness.

Dena frowned. 'She's not the hugging, kissing, demonstrative sort, my mam, but the fact that she came at all speaks volumes. I really do want to thank you!'

'Don't mention it. All part of the service.' Kenny grinned, and when it seemed she wasn't going to say anything else, he wiped his sweating palms down the backs of his drainpipe trousers and dusted down his velvet lapels. 'Maybe you'll let me call a bit more often an' all. Happen even come out with me one night, eh? We used to be good together, and you know in your heart that you've missed me.'

Dena felt a strong urge to laugh. 'You're as full of yourself as ever I see, Kenny Garside.'

He gave a wry smile. 'Tell me you've never thought wistfully about our little get-together under the old oak.'

'The less said about that the better. Look where it landed me.' She walked to the door but he was pleased to note she hesitated before opening it this time, her hand curled about the brass handle.

He took a step closer. 'I still fancy you like rotten, Dena Dobson, and even though I could have me pick of women, you're the only one for me. You're still my girl.'

Dena was openly laughing now. What else could she do? He was such a show off, so full of his own importance. 'You're outrageous, Kenny Garside, do you know that?'

'I can be anything you want me to be,' he told her with a grin. 'I can even be good if you like, reasonably so anyway. Honest!'

'If you are modest and unselfish, then stop showing off and bossing me about all the time?'

'All of that, I swear it, but never boring, and you weren't either in my arms. I wouldn't mind taking you dancing some time,

Dena, just so's I can hold you close again. Or the flicks, if you prefer, I don't give up easy. All you have to do is agree to a date then I can show you how sorry I am for offending you that time.'

Dena could feel herself warming towards him. It had been so sweet of him to find her mother, and how he'd managed to persuade her to visit Dena would never understand, but she was thrilled, and so very grateful.

'I'll think about it,' she said, rewarding him with a small smile. 'Who knows? Maybe I'll say yes one day, just as soon as you can prove to me that you mean what you say.'

'And how do I do that if you won't come out with me?'

'You could start by finding work.' She slanted a sideways smile up at him, and Kenny attempted to respond in kind.

He left then without another word, but inside he was livid. He'd almost had her in the palm of his hands. He'd seen her weakening, still wanting him, aching for him to kiss her like he used to. Then the shutters had come down, just like before. Who the hell did she think she was preaching to him about getting a job? He got enough of that at home from Carl.

And then he remembered the idea that had come to him weeks ago. Maybe this was the moment to give it a try.

–

The first person Dena told about this exciting new development was Miss Rogers when she came round on her next visit. 'And you say it was Kenny Garside who persuaded her?'

'Apparently so.'

'How surprising. The very young man she was determined you stay well clear of.' Miss Rogers was sitting with Trudy on her knee, letting the little girl pull all the things out of her big leather handbag. 'But I'm pleased for you, I am Dena, since I know how much it means to you to be on good terms with your mother. But don't have too high expectations,' was the social worker's cautious response.

Dena said nothing to this, but she was thoughtful. It was strange, in a way, that it had been Kenny who'd been the one to persuade her to call round.

Miss Rogers continued, 'Alice isn't an easy woman, as we well know, and with a volatile personality. You're doing so well on your own. Look at Trudy. She's absolutely blooming. You've made a marvellous mother, Dena. I'm so proud of you. And you're doing well at your job. I'd hate to see you risk spoiling what you've achieved.'

Dena looked into the woman's steady gaze. This plain, unprepossessing, busybody social worker was the real person she should thank for what she had. Miss Rogers had ensured that no one would be allowed to take away her baby. No mean achievement. 'Don't worry, I won't. I'm not half so stupid or gullible as I once was.'

At this, Miss Rogers actually smiled. 'That's not a description I would ever have levelled at you, Dena. Naïve and rebellious, but neither gullible nor stupid, but do be on your guard, that's all I'm saying. Your independence was hard won, hold it fast.'

Chapter Thirty-Two

Security was always a problem at the market, and the market hall had been broken into on a number of occasions in recent months, with several of the stalls either burgled or vandalised.

'Crying shame it is when people work hard all their lives to make a modest living, only to have it stolen from them.'

This complaint had come from Sam Beckett when he'd found his cash register had been jemmied and his float gone. Kenny had to agree with him, although Sam hadn't lost nearly as much money as he intended to claim back from the insurance. Kenny knew this for a fact, since Sam's hard-earned cash was now floating and jingling in his own pockets.

'What you need,' Kenny advised, 'is someone to keep an eye out for trouble, to tip you the wink should any dodgy characters start nosing around.'

'If only,' Sam said.

'I wouldn't mind keeping a lookout for you,' Kenny offered. 'I'm considering setting myself up in a little business, a sort of security firm like. Would you be interested? My fees would be very reasonable.'

Sam looked thoughtful. 'How much are we talking about?'

Kenny told him and he blenched. 'By heck, that's coming it a bit strong.'

'I could give you a discount, since you're me first client, and friendly with Mam like. How many tools did you lose the other night? Can you afford to lose spades, drills and shovels each week, rather than pay for proper security?'

'Too many,' Sam grumbled, then after a thoughtful pause. 'I'm prepared to give you a month's trial, with the discount you mentioned, and see how you go on.'

High on this first success Kenny went straight over to the Misses Higginson's millinery stall. The two maiden ladies had been broken into twice lately and were almost hysterical with fear, so were more than happy to sign up for Kenny's little scheme.

The Bertalone's too were keen to join since their best ice-cream-maker machine had been badly damaged. Besides, they knew better than to cross swords with the Garsides.

Alec Hall wasn't interested, not until the market hall was again broken into a few nights later and he suffered three smashed guitars and a broken trombone.

'Pity you didn't sign up sooner,' Kenny said, with a sad shake of his head. 'No one else was done.'

'Funny that,' Alec agreed, a tinge of suspicion in his voice, but he paid up without any further argument – almost satisfactory.

Kenny had always been jealous of Carl; his mother's favourite son, being the eldest. At least he'd been the favourite once. She wasn't so pleased with him when he'd given up the driving and settled on the outside market, not even happy that he seemed to be doing well. But then she'd always been a bit snobby about the stalls outside while she lorded it in the cafe.

But Kenny intended to catch his brother up, even to overtake him. He'd be rolling in dosh soon, earning far more money by doing nothing, than daft honest Carl would ever make from working all hours God sends on his poxy household goods stall. Serve him right!

–

'I hope we're doing the right thing, trusting Kenny Garside to act as a security agent for our stall,' the elder Miss Higginson said to Sam Beckett a week or so later when she saw him hanging up an array of coal scuttles over his stall.

He turned to smile reassuringly at her, if with a vague detachment. 'You've had no trouble lately, have you Miss Higginson?'

'Oh no, none at all.'

'Well then, it seems to be working. We can only give him a try.'

'But his charges are so expensive. I'm not sure we can afford to keep up the payments for too long.'

'I'm not prepared to pay him a penny,' Winnie Watkins chipped in, not wishing to be left out of this bit of gossip. 'And would advise you to, neither. Not that it's any of my business.'

'Oh, dear, I'm afraid it's too late. We already have. But my sister Clara thinks it should be Joe Southworth's job to deal with security issues,' pursing her prim mouth with disapproval. 'But he does nothing. I'm not sure he's up to the mark any more, are you?'

Sam could see a customer hovering and was anxious to escape. Once started on some hobby horse or other, Annie Higginson's complaints could turn into an endless litany.

Alec Hall strolled over, hands in pockets and a deep frown marking his handsome features. 'I share your disquiet, Annie, but we must tread softly with that young man. He could well be genuine, having turned over a new leaf, as it were. All we can do is give him a fair trial and hope for the best. If we're not satisfied after three months say, we can all agree to stop.'

'Oh, yes, that would be splendid. Absolutely splendid,' Annie Higginson agreed.

Winnie remarked that he wouldn't even get three weeks out of her, but with nothing more to be said on the matter and the market hall door already unlocked, they each hurried away to their respective stalls.

–

Alice did call again one Wednesday, just when Dena was getting ready to go to work. 'I'm not stopping,' she said, looking round for somewhere to sit. 'Is this your only chair? I suppose it will have to do then, though it doesn't look very comfortable. Have you got the kettle on?'

Alice sat ramrod straight in the chair, not bothering to take off her hat and coat and doing her utmost to look uncomfortable. Dena prayed Winnie wouldn't mind if she was ten minutes late for once and rushed to make tea. Drat, she didn't have a single biscuit in the place.

'It's just as well you're not stopping because I'm on me way to work,' Dena said, as pleasantly as she could. 'Tuesday is my day off, so if you could come on that day in future, it would be better.'

'For you maybe, but Tuesday is not convenient for me,' Alice said. 'I always do my baking on a Tuesday.'

'Baking? You've taken up baking?'

'We have to eat.'

An awkward pause while Dena tried to picture her mother baking. It was not a scene she was familiar with. Even when she was younger Alice had much preferred to buy her bread and cake from Mr George the baker. 'Couldn't you do your baking on another day, maybe Wednesday?'

'I do my shopping on a Wednesday. That's why I'm here. I could kill two birds with one stone if I used this market for a change, and pop in to have a cuppa with my daughter at the same time. I thought you could point your old mother in the way of a few bargains, or am I wrong?'

'No, not at all.'

Alice peered into the cup Dena handed her, just as if she expected to find tea leaves floating on the top, or a smear on the crockery. 'You're a bit mean with your milk, aren't you?' Dena added a drop more.

So that's what she represented to her mother: a chore to be squeezed in between the butcher and the candlestick maker. Dena tried not to show her hurt. 'You know this market as well I do, having used it for years. I doubt I could spot a bargain half so well as you. You never seemed to miss a trick.'

248

'Aye, well it takes a sharp eye and a skill for haggling, as I'm an expert.' Alice took a sip of the tea and pulled a face. 'This isn't best Yorkshire.'

'No Mam, I can't afford best Yorkshire.'

Alice sniffed. 'Don't tell me you can't afford biscuits either?'

'Sorry, I've run out.'

'Never were much of a housekeeper and you've clearly not improved with practice. We have decent shops in Chorlton. To be honest I don't bother much with markets these days. Cheap nasty places – markets are full of riff-raff and cabbage leaves all over the place. Oh, wanting to be off, are you? I don't know why I bothered coming at all. Well, don't let me stop you, if you'd rather be with your lover-boy.'

'I've got to go to work, I've just told you. And he's not my lover-boy.'

'It's poky in here. How do you stand it?' and with scarcely a pause for breath, 'So he chucked you then, that chap of yours?'

Dena was tugging on her coat, brown eyes downcast so that her mother couldn't see how upset she was. She should have known better. Alice hadn't changed a bit, still taking her biggest satisfaction in finding fault and criticising. Not once had she even asked how Dena was coping, or, more importantly, how Trudy was. She hadn't even glanced in the direction of the pram where, thank goodness, the baby was sleeping peacefully for once. 'Actually, I chucked him. I left Kenny Garside standing at the altar if you must know, and serve him right.'

'Why, what did he do?'

'I'll not talk about it, if you don't mind.' Dena picked up her bag of sandwiches, her heart heavy. 'I'm sorry to rush you but I'm late already.'

Alice slammed the mug down on the kitchen table. 'Pardon me for being such a nuisance.' And she headed for the door.

'Aw, Mam, don't go off in a huff. I've told you, Tuesday is my day off. I'd have more time for a chat then. I'm sure we could get on better if we just gave ourselves the opportunity.'

'I've told you, Tuesdays aren't convenient.' Alice sailed out of the room, the feather on her hat just skimming the door frame as she left.

–

The next time Dena opened the door it was to find Kenny standing there, a huge bunch of wilting chrysanthemums in his hand. She stifled a weary sigh. As if she didn't have enough trouble with her mother, here was yet another problem that wouldn't go away. 'Not today, Kenny, please. I've nothing more to say to you.'

'But you owe me after what I've done for you, getting your mam talking to you again. You could at least appear grateful.' He marched into the bedsit over to the kitchen table and slapped the flowers down right in the middle of a length of sunshine yellow cotton fabric stuck all over with different patterns of daisies, cats and parakeets. He picked one up and twisted it this way and that, poking at it with his finger. Dena removed the flowers and stuck them in a jam jar.

'You really don't have to do this. In fact I'd prefer it if you didn't.' Then she took the pattern from him and carefully pinned it into place before starting to cut it out.

Kenny watched, lower lip stuck out in a pout, saying nothing.

'I am grateful for your help, Kenny, truly I am. The trouble is that Mam and me just can't seem to hit it off. She did come round to see me again, only the other day but – oh, I don't know – maybe I didn't handle it very well. I was in a rush to get to work. I haven't seen her since.'

'I'm not surprised. That's all you ever think about these days,' Kenny grumbled. 'Bloody work!'

'Don't swear in front of Trudy.'

'She's bloody asleep.'

'Kenny! Anyway, my work is important to me! And I have a child to raise all on me own now.'

'And whose fault is that?'

Dena said nothing but went back to her cutting, not wishing to have him start on her apparent defection all over again.

Kenny gazed entranced at her slender arms, her nimble fingers, the way her breasts wobbled delightfully as she moved, and felt that familiar, delicious ache in his groin. Why couldn't she see that he needed her. Right now!

Dena was saying in falsely bright tones, 'Mam might surprise me and come round again one afternoon. I live in hope. I do appreciate your efforts on my behalf, Kenny, really I do, although that doesn't mean I have to marry you for God's sake!' She glanced up at him, wry amusement in her lovely chestnut eyes. 'You surely didn't think I'd sleep with you out of gratitude, did you?'

His face was a picture and for a moment Dena was stunned, for he clearly had thought that. But then she recognised the dangerous glitter in his eyes, how his mouth drooped into that all too familiar self-pitying pout and quickly changed her wry smile to one of sympathy.

'I'm sorry, really I am.' He took a step towards her but she held up one hand, palm outstretched. 'Come no closer, Kenny. I mean it, it's over between us. I've told you this a thousand times and I think it would be best if you didn't call any more.'

In her other hand, he noticed, she held a pair of scissors, so Kenny decided it would be sensible to obey this command, at least for now. Yet he wasn't prepared to admit defeat.

'You're tired, that's what's wrong with you. It's all this sewing you're doing. Why do you want to spend every minute of your time on this rubbish? You've got a good job with Winnie, isn't that enough? Why make more work for yourself?'

Dena looked away, concentrating on cutting out her pattern, trying to avoid the intensity of his gaze; keeping her voice deliberately light in tone. 'Because I'm ambitious, I mean to go places, and don't intend to spend my entire life in this poky bedsit.'

She glanced about her at the muddle, every surface piled high with finished, or part finished garments, bolts of fabric lying about the floor so that to move anywhere you had to squeeze between bed, sewing machine and a huge old playpen that Barry Holmes had got for her and took up most of the centre floor space. Then she smiled kindly at him. 'Find yourself another girl, Kenny. That would be for the best.'

There was a warm flush on her cheeks, a moistness to her mouth for all it was set firm. He watched, fascinated, as she pushed back a stray strand of hair. She'd had it cut again, he noticed, in that cropped, sophisticated style he didn't like. Despite her words, Kenny couldn't believe she'd rejected him so completely; that there was to be no chance of a quick bit of the other, which was indeed what he'd been hoping for weeks. He'd been working himself up to it ever since he'd called on Alice to help get him through the door again, following the last time Dena had banished him.

But he'd no intention of giving up.

In his mind he could see himself pushing her down on to that damn table amongst her blasted patterns, shoving his throbbing penis into her. He'd tie her to the table with the tape measure and pound into her till she screamed for mercy. That would show her how she was entirely his, to do with as he pleased.

He thought about this for a moment, revelling in the throbbing in his loins. And then slowly he became aware of how forlorn and pathetic he must appear, standing before her, unwanted and rejected. All his efforts had got him nowhere, nowhere at all.

Oh, but he'd have her in the end, see if he didn't. She couldn't escape him that easy.

–

In the weeks following, Dena made a dozen or more skirts, which sold steadily on the stall, then she moved on to capri pants, all in different colours from palest pastel to strong primary colours such as turquoise, tangerine or coral. She made some halter tops to go with them, boleros and cropped tops with scoop necks that showed off the midriff, and with summer coming they sold well.

Winnie provided a rack for the clothes, which stood in front of the fabric stall and customers would come time and time again to see what Dena had made this week.

She used the cabbage rose cotton sateen to make a full-skirted shirtwaister with a wide matching fabric belt, pointed collar and three-quarter sleeves with turn-back cuffs. It sold the moment she hung it on the rack, and so Winnie got her to make more in glorious florals, leaves or green ferns, candy striped or fresh-looking gingham checks. Diamond trellis checks and spots were also popular, some she made into dresses with scoop necks and little capped sleeves.

She would often see girls wearing the skirts or dresses she'd made at the dances she still attended with Gwen, whenever Barry was available to babysit; or else out and about around the market on a Saturday afternoon. It made her feel proud to have made such an impact on local fashion.

The new styles with full skirts needed support to make them look good and paper nylon petticoats became fashionable, particularly now that skirts were shorter, stopping just below the knee. Dena again went around the Manchester warehouses and bought in several different rolls of net in bright rainbow colours of pink, blue, green and mauve. These she made up into tiered bouffant petticoats, which swirled the skirts out delightfully; although they did prick somewhat, and needed an underslip to make them comfortable to wear. Nevertheless they made a girl feel like a prima ballerina; Dena was by this time spending every spare moment working on the machine.

'I'm not sure I can keep up with the demand.'

'It'll ease off soon,' Winnie assured her, 'once everyone has bought their summer togs. And Donald says you deserve a holiday bonus.'

Dena laughed. 'That's very kind of him, but a holiday would do me more good right now.'

'Not possible girl, not yet. Not while there are punters to please,' Winnie teased, then turning to a customer, 'Hello, Mrs

Dawson, your Lucy liked the frock, did she, and wants a pair of shorts now? Are you sure? She's a bit well blessed in the backside department is your Lucy. How about one of these nice little playsuits with the frilly skirt instead?'

Chapter Thirty-Three

Kenny arranged to see Alice again. This time they met up in the tearooms at the Midland Hotel, where he bought her tea and scones. He was astonished at himself. He was almost turning into a gentleman. But then he was a desperate man, growing increasingly frustrated and deeply resentful. No matter how often he called, however many bunches of flowers or boxes of chocolates he bought for Dena, she absolutely refused to accept him back into her life. She just kept saying they were finished. Now she'd even stopped letting him into the bedsit.

Why didn't she appreciate all he'd done for her? If Dena and her mother had fallen out again, whose fault was that? Certainly not his! He explained all of this and more to Alice. 'I can't seem to please her. I've even started me own business, got myself a little security firm going but she still holds herself aloof.'

Alice was surprised by what a very thoughtful and attentive young man he was turning into. So polite and earnest, almost charming in his way, so that she didn't mind in the least when he rested one hand on her knee. It was nothing more than a friendly gesture and if it brought a hot flush to her cheeks, well what of it? She loved the way his fair hair fell softly over his brow, and the seductive pout of his lower lip. Such a charming boy!

'Some girls don't know when they are well off. And Dena has never been one to listen to advice. She has never listened to me.'

'But you are my last hope, Alice. You don't mind my calling you that, do you, Alice? I'm pining away for love of her, and you're the only one who can help.' His light blue eyes beseeched her to understand as his hand again pressed a little more firmly upon the knee. The thigh above it was firm, he noticed, as he allowed his fingers to spread a little. 'You're a mature, handsome woman with a good deal of experience in life. No doubt men have always fallen at your feet, so you don't need me to draw a picture. I bet you were a right little rock 'n' roller in your day. Fact is, I can't hold on much longer, if you catch my drift? I'm desperate to have her.'

Alice found that her heart was racing, thought that she should upbraid him for having such a dirty mind, for saying such things to her. She should tell him how shocked she was that he dared to touch her so intimately, but the sensation of his fingers creeping up her thigh were making her feel giddy. Her cheeks were burning and there was a tightness in her chest, making her voice come out all breathy so that she thought she might be about to have one of her turns.

'You shouldn't speak so bluntly to a sad, old widow woman. It isn't fair to remind me of such long ago delights. You're a very naughty boy.'

Kenny was startled by her reaction to his words, meant only as a bit of soft flannel to flatter her, and then gave a little smirk. 'I'm sorry if I caused offence. What are you going to do, spank me?'

His eyes held hers for a long moment, and with such a challenge in them, such a delicious promise, that Alice thought she might faint clean away. Before she could speak he lifted her hand and kissed the blunt tipped, trembling fingers. Alice wished fervently that her hand was young and slender and gracious, instead of wrinkled and freckled with liver spots.

'I think you're the naughty one, teasing me like this,' he said. 'I should go now before I do something I shouldn't.'

He got to his feet but Alice did not let go of his hand. 'Can we meet again? Please? I promise that I'll speak to Dena, then we could meet up here again next week, and I'll tell you what she said. How would that be?'

He leaned close and pressed a light kiss on her papery cheek. 'I would like that very much, Alice.' Then he was gone and she was forced to reach into her bag for her smelling salts.

Alice arrived one morning at Winnie's stall and interrupted Dena just as she was measuring out net curtain material for a customer. 'I'm sure you won't mind if I just have a private word with my daughter.'

'Mother! I can't. I'm busy...'

'Winnie can take over for a minute, I'm sure.' Alice grasped Dena's arm and dragged her to one side, out of earshot of Winnie and her startled customer. 'So what have you got against Kenny all of a sudden?'

Dena was lost for words. Astonished to see her mother here at the market in the first place, and embarrassed that she should be so rude to a customer; it slipped by her that Alice was now addressing Kenny Garside by his first name alone.

'I'm not sure that is any of your business.'

'I mean to make it so. I've come to ask when you're going to wed the father of your child and make a decent woman of yourself. It's long past time you did. I'm ashamed that any daughter of mine could have such loose morals. Kenny may not be the brightest thing on two legs but he's potty about you. And Belle is worth a bob or two, so you could do worse than ally yourself with that family.'

'That's rich, coming from you. I thought you saw Belle as little less than the scum of the earth?'

'Beggars can't be choosers.'

'And you consider those good reasons for marriage, do you? A boy who is besotted and obsessed, and a mother-in-law with a bit put by.'

'He's the father of your child and desperately in love with you.'

'Then he'll just have to get over it because I'm no longer in love with him. And what's this all about anyway? Why have you suddenly taken up Kenny's cause? I don't remember you being so keen when we first started going out.'

'You were a child then. You're a mother now. An unmarried one, if you haven't noticed.'

'Oh, I've noticed all right. Folk I've known for years still walk past me in the street as if I'm a leper or something.'

'And no wonder. You ought to be ashamed of yourself, living alone, unmarried, with a baby, behaving like a loose woman. It's long past time you grew up.'

'Well, I'm sorry to disappoint you, Mother, but I won't marry just to please them, or you. I'll marry when I find the right man. Kenny is welcome to see Trudy any time, not that he has ever shown much interest in her, but him and me are finished. I've told him so a thousand times. It was all a big mistake.'

'Big mistake? The only mistake is you being too obstinate to agree to make yourself respectable.'

Alice took a steadying breath, remembering her blood pressure, and also recalling that her daughter didn't take kindly to being bullied. She clumsily patted Dena's hand. 'He's potty about you, and the last I heard you were equally besotted with him. Whatever silly quarrel you two have had can surely be put right, for Trudy's sake. You must put her welfare before your own. You know from personal experience how difficult it is for a child to grow up without a father. Look what agony it caused our poor Pete.' Alice dabbed at the corner of her eye with a hanky.

Dena was silent. This was a whole new aspect to her mother. Did she really care about Trudy, or was she simply having a bad moment over Pete? Dena still suffered these moments herself, even after all these years. 'Mam, I'm sorry, but I can't. I thought I loved him, but I was wrong. It was nothing but a silly infatuation. He was my first boyfriend and through foolish ignorance and stupid rebellion, I let him go too far. I don't see why I should pay for that mistake all my life. We wouldn't be happy. It wouldn't work and despite the gossip I'm doing fine on my own, ta very much, and mean to stay that way. Sorry, but there it is.'

'You'll regret it,' Alice snapped, as Dena went back to her customer offering profuse apologies.

'I'll just have to take that chance, won't I?'

When Alice passed on Dena's second rejection to Kenny, he was deeply upset, she could tell. They were in the Midland hotel as usual, Kenny smartly decked out in a sensible dark suit, with not a trace of Teddy boy about it. It looked expensive and very well tailored and this time it was Alice who rested a comforting hand on his knee. 'I did my best, Kenny lad, but, like I say, she wouldn't listen. Not that she ever did listen to me.'

'And what about me then?' he whined. 'Nobody cares a toss about me. Not me mam, nor me own brother who does nothing but find fault with everything I do. And I can't seem to look at another girl. They don't turn me on in the slightest. How shall I ever find love again, if I can't have Dena?'

'Maybe you're looking in the wrong place,' Alice said, giving his strong muscular thigh a little friendly squeeze. 'Do consider a more mature woman, one who can appreciate you.'

And as she slid her neatly gloved hand a little further along his thigh, Kenny experienced a most satisfactory jerk of energy. He'd been getting a bit worried as he'd seen no action in that department lately, which he blamed entirely on Dena. But unless he was very much mistaken, it was being offered to him now, on a plate. 'I never realised what a temptress you were, Alice.'

'Oh, there's a great deal you don't know about me.'

They took a room upstairs for the afternoon and by the time Kenny had peeled off Alice's skirt and directoire knickers, unpinning each serviceable stocking from its suspender to roll it down over chubby pink knees, followed by her flannel petticoat and pink corset, he was so excited he could hardly contain himself. Old she may be, but she was still a fine, handsome woman with a statuesque body. And the whole notion of bedding Dena's mother appealed to him, as it increased his sense of excitement. Wouldn't it serve her right for rejecting him?

'Oh, my, I've never been one for this sort of thing,' Alice gasped, visibly trembling as he suckled one wrinkled breast.

'I can't believe that, Alice, not for a moment. Still, it's never too late to learn,' Kenny said, not troubling to fondle her as he turned her over so that he could straddle her more easily. 'Let me show you a little trick. Lift up a bit and bend your knees.' Then after finding his way in with the minimum of fuss, he shoved himself hard into her. Alice gave a most satisfactory squeak, though whether out of pleasure or pain he wasn't sure, and really didn't care. Kenny just hung on to her hips, and hammered into her as hard as he could. Like he'd always said, the more mature woman was so much less bother. But that didn't stop him wanting her daughter as well.

–

Work didn't ease up. If anything, Dena became busier. She had by now bought her own sewing machine and was kept working at it throughout the summer, and as autumn approached girls were looking for pencil skirts and little party dresses with neat, high necklines, deep shawl collars or a more daring off-the-shoulder style. The fabric for these was glamorous and also more expensive: silk and brocade, tulle or chiffon; although Dena did make some simpler styles in brightly coloured abstract prints.

She finally got to make a line of circular skirts out of felt in all different jewel colours with a pair of cherries appliquéd just above the hem on each. Her young customers teamed these with scoop-neck blouses, wore their cardigans back to front, or with tight polo necks in black or white. Dena suggested to Winnie that they might consider stocking some of these too on the stall, but the older woman was doubtful.

'What with the skirts and the capri pants, and the petticoats you're making, not forgetting that new line of shirtwaister dresses, where would we put the darned things? We're running out of space.'

This had occurred to Dena too and she began to give the matter a great deal of thought. She was seventeen, nearly eighteen, surely far too young to go into business on her own. Or was she?

Carl Garside had started his stall when he was just nineteen, and look how well he was doing.

And there were other things she could sell if she had her own stall, bucket bags and raffia straw baskets, scarves, gloves, crocheted berets and hats, even popper beads and big white earrings, flatties and brightly coloured socks. Most of all she loved the sewing, even though it meant sitting up night after night and left her exhausted the next day, so there would be lots of lovely skirts and dresses to sell. Dena got excited just thinking about it.

Yet she had no money to set herself up with a market stall, let alone stock it. She had only one pair of hands, so how could she serve on the stall and make all the stock for it? It simply wasn't possible. This was all pie in the sky, nothing but dreams. It would be so much easier if Kenny would stay away and stop interrupting and pestering her. He simply ignored every word she said, wouldn't take no for an answer. And on top of everything, Trudy was teething so when Dena wasn't sewing or arguing with Kenny at the door, desperately trying not to let him in, she was nursing a screaming infant half the night. It was all getting to be too much.

Gwen had got herself a boyfriend, a male nurse who worked at the same hospital and was urging her to make up a foursome. He'd offered to bring a friend for Dena, as a blind date, and she was sorely tempted.

It would be a relief to get out and enjoy herself, to be a young teenager again. At first, following Carl's attack on her for leaving Trudy with Barry, Dena had stayed in for weeks on end, filled with guilt and remorse. He was right, she thought, and she was behaving irresponsibly. And she'd been nervous of running into Kenny. Everywhere she went he seemed to turn up like the proverbial bad penny, asking her to dance, following her home, even trailing after her when she walked Trudy in the park.

It disturbed her deeply and on more than one occasion Dena had told him off, even resorted to shouting at him to leave her alone. But she hated to be squabbling with him all the time; however, she refused to stay home behind locked doors, which would turn her into a recluse. She wanted to be a good mother, not repeat Alice's selfish mistakes. Yet surely it would do no harm to go out for the occasional evening? Staying in all the time was so depressing, no matter how much she loved Trudy, and enjoyed her work. Anyway, Carl had no say over what she did.

Dena decided that one night a week, Fridays perhaps, would be hers to enjoy, an evening she could be a young girl again, and Trudy would be safe with Barry. She accepted Gwen's offer of a blind date and it worked well as she didn't care much for the young men she chose, but that didn't bother Dena in the least. She was having a great time. They would go dancing, or to the pictures, but then one evening when they were at the Plaza dance hall and Dena was on her way back from the powder room, she ran into Carl.

He blocked her way so that she was forced to stop and her heart did a funny sort of somersault. Not having seen him for weeks she'd forgotten how tall he was, how powerful, and how incredibly good-looking. His hair was tousled, as always, and his mouth set in its usual grim, condemning line. Dena was instantly on the defensive, preparing herself for another lecture.

'I hear you're doing well for yourself.' Carl ran a considering glance over the dress she was wearing. It was navy and white-tailored, double-breasted, with a pencil skirt, a big white collar and three-quarter sleeves.

'I'm coping, thanks.' She wasn't going to give him the satis-faction of knowing how hard she was working, or how very tired she was. She lifted her chin and looked him straight into his eyes. 'What of it?'

Instead of answering, Carl grabbed her by the arm and marched her out of the ballroom. Here we go again, Dena thought, protesting vigorously as she wrenched her arm from his grasp. 'Look, I'm not having this. I'm surely entitled to one night out a week. I'm a good mother, so lay off.'

He held up his hands. 'Okay, it's not about Trudy, I just want to talk to you.'

There was something dark and brooding in his eyes and Dena found herself agreeing against her better judgement. He took her to a quiet part of the foyer out of the public gaze before saying his piece. 'I want to ask you to leave my little brother alone. Right? You made your decision when you left him standing at the altar, and the entire family looking like a complete laughing stock, so stay out of his life. Let him go!'

'What?' Dena's mouth dropped open in shock. 'You've got this the wrong way round. Kenny is the one who won't let go. He keeps turning up in my life like a bad penny, despite my telling him that it's all over between us. I'm not encouraging him, very much the reverse! Nor can you wonder at my actions on that unforgettable day. At least my daughter is alive and well, which is more than she would have been if I'd listened to your precious brother.'

'What are you saying?' Carl glared at her, bemused, his tone less certain.

'So Kenny hasn't told you about his "friend"?'

'What friend?'

'Maureen, or Mo as she likes to be called! He took me to see her days before the wedding because her talent, apparently, is to treat unborn babies like tadpoles and flush them down the sink.' Dena stuck her face up so close to his, she could see every pore in the smooth olive skin. She studied the fine shape of his Roman nose, the black curling lashes and her own face reflected in those deep blue eyes. It was not a little disturbing but she held her nerve. 'I don't suppose little brother bothered to mention any of that, did he?' Then she walked away, her chin held high.

Chapter Thirty-Four

'What the hell did you think you were doing?' Carl accosted Kenny the very next evening when he was on his way out, all dressed up like a dandy as usual, the quiff in his greased hair even more pronounced.

'What?' Kenny adopted a picture of innocence, not knowing what was coming but careful to be prepared.

'Have you been seeing that Maureen person, that prossy round the back of Tonman Street? Did she really offer to dispose of the kid? Was that the reason Dena left you standing at the altar? Because if so, then I'm not surprised you deserved it.'

Kenny said nothing but his expression told all.

'You disgust me. Where were you brought up? In a sewer?'

'Don't play the Holy Joe with me. Even Mam had a couple of clearouts in her youth, she told me so herself.'

'*Clearouts!* Is that what you call it? This is a human life we're talking about here. A child. Our mam, bless her sweet heart, had more men than she can rightly remember, and yes, I'm aware she admits to having had a couple of abortions. That's why neither of us has a father, or any idea who he might be, but that's no reason for you to go down the same road. I keep hoping we Garsides can salvage our reputation, grow a bit of dignity, and put our dear mother's colourful past behind us. But I never do take your lack of common sense into account. Get out of my sight before I start to wish she'd cleared you out as well.'

'I can improve,' Kenny burst out, wanting his brother to like him, needing his approval.

'Oh, and how will you manage that, may I ask? Where are you off to now for instance? Up to more bother, I'll be bound.'

'No!' Innocence shone out of him, hands spread wide. 'As a matter of fact I'm going to the flicks with me mates. We're going to see that new movie, *Rock Around the Clock*. Happen if you got out a bit more, you wouldn't get yourself into such a state.'

'I don't understand where you get your money from, when you don't even have a job. All you seem capable of is washing up in Mam's back kitchen, not what she had in mind for her younger son.'

Kenny danced back and forth in agitation, his skinny legs in their drainpipe trousers and artificially huge feet in their crêpe sole loafer shoes, somehow unable to keep still. 'Well, you're wrong, as I have got a job. I've started me own security firm looking after people. Me and my mates keep watch at night and see off any likely trouble.'

Carl's eyes widened. 'Any likely trouble? What the hell do you know about security?'

Kenny puffed out his chest. 'I keep my ear to the ground. I'm a success.'

'More likely if they pay you enough you agree not to break into the place yourself and nick their takings. Is that what you're up to?'

A crimson flush darkened his neck and Kenny took a step towards his brother, one clenched fist raised. 'If anyone else had accused me of that they'd have felt the weight of this, right?'

'Don't hold back on my account,' Carl growled. 'I would take great pleasure in taking you apart, yet again. One for the road, eh?'

'You keep your nose out of my business, right? Or brother or no, I'll break both your legs.'

'You and whose army? Does Mam know about this little scheme of yours? No wonder the market has had so many break-ins. I can see it all now, you daft cluck.'

Carl began to walk away but Kenny grabbed him by the shoulder and swung him round. 'One word to anyone and I warn you, you'll regret it. You keep your flaming mouth shut, right?'

Carl looked down on him with undisguised contempt. 'I will keep quiet, yes, but not because I'm scared of you, you little worm. If it gets out what you're up to, we'll all suffer and get tarred with the same brush. I shall speak to Mam though, and hope she can drum some sense into your stupid noddle.'

When Kenny had gone, slamming the door behind him, Carl punched his fist into the wall in silent fury. Stupid bastard! He'd get them all thrown off the market if he carried on like this, and himself in the lock-up.

—

Later that same night Carl was alerted by a neighbour. His brother had indeed been arrested for disorderly behaviour, and was being held in Minshull Street Police Station. He and a group of his mates had ended their evening at the pictures by jiving in the aisles, ripping up seats and chanting 'We want Bill', and 'rock, rock, rock.' Very nearly starting a riot until the police had swooped in to stop them.

'Next time,' Belle said, 'go and see *The King and I* instead. Deborah Kerr is lovely, and that Yul Brynner can darken my bedroom door any day of the week, but the music in that picture wouldn't drive anyone to riot.'

'No thanks, not my cup of tea.' Kenny winced as his mother dabbed Dettol on his cut lip. He'd already suffered a long lecture from his brother, now he wearily prepared himself for another.

'I don't know what this new rock 'n' roll is all about, nor do I want to know, but choose somewhere less public for your riot next time, will you? I'll never manage to climb the ladder of respectability if you keep knocking me off it.'

Belle was getting so desperate over her lack of progress in getting elected on to the committee that she'd even bought herself some of the new premium bonds, hoping she could win herself a fortune and retire instead. Now that was sad, Belle Garside starting to think about retirement.

'Sorry, Mam, eeh, but it were good. We couldn't help ourselves. Our feet just started going and we couldn't seem to stop.'

'Aye, well if you don't watch out you'll get a ball and chain attached to them dancing feet of yours. And look at them skinned knuckles. Who have you been beating up?'

Kenny shrugged. 'Some bloke who got in me way, I won't be made a fool of by nobody.'

'No, you can manage that all by yourself.' He yelled out loud as she dabbed at the open wounds with more disinfectant. 'So what's all this about a protection racket? Whose daft idea was that?'

'Mine, and it's not a daft idea. I'm raking it in. I've got most of the inside stalls signed up and I collect from them every month. Now I'm starting on the outside ones but they're a bit trickier as they don't have to lock up and leave stuff behind. But most of them have storage depots, a warehouse or garage where they keep their stock, and the last thing they want is to have it nicked. They've come to depend on me. Nobody gets done over on my watch.'

Belle's eyes narrowed as she paused to listen to her younger son's bragging. A stream of blood ran from an open cut on his head but she made no move to staunch it. 'And is that because you're good at your job or because, as Carl has suggested, you don't turn them over if they pay you.'

'That poxy brother of mine always has to throw his weight about like he's holier than thou. He thinks he's bleeding Carlton Heston.'

'Well, don't bother, as I can see the answer written in the guilt on your daft face. You'll have to be a lot cleverer at disguising your feelings, lad, if you intend taking up a life of crime.'

'Don't you start!'

'Actually, what I'm thinking is that you're in need of a bit of mature guidance. Any business that isn't pristine – shall we say – demands good cover. So why don't we set you up in something legit, then no one will ask awkward questions about what it is you do with your time? And your little security racket can be run alongside it on the QT.'

'QT?'

'On the quiet. Lord save me from thick sons. You need to disguise your under-the-table activities with an honest one that is all above board. A proper business.'

'What sort of proper business?' Kenny frowned, not sure he cared much for the sound of this.

Belle was thoughtful for some minutes as she slapped Elastoplast and Germolene on to various cuts and bruises, ignoring Kenny's cries and whimpers. 'There you are, good as new, and I think I have the answer to your problem. Alarms. You can sell burglar alarms. The perfect solution, and I'll put up the starting capital for you in the form of an interest-free loan. In return you can do something for me.'

Kenny's eyes glittered with excitement. 'I like it, but I can't afford to share the profits with you, Mam. I want a car, a Ford Zephyr. Dena would be sure to take me more seriously if I had wheels, she'd be dead impressed.'

Belle pursed her lips, for once devoid of their usual coating of lipstick, since it was so late. Then she allowed them to widen into a beatific smile. 'You shall have a car, my precious. Whatever your little heart desires. I shall buy it for you myself once you've succeeded in getting me onto that committee.'

She leaned closer, gripping his startled face between the flat of her hands, her highly polished nails glistening in the firelight. 'All you have to do is to persuade all your clients to vote me on as the next market superintendent. There, that's not too difficult, is it? You can do that small thing for your mam? You've plenty of time, as the elections aren't until April, which gives you nearly three months to work on people. Play your cards right, lad, and we'll both be in the money. Then I'll help you get your mucky little paws on Dena. Right?'

'Consider it done.'

Despite his mother's interesting offer, Kenny was more than willing to pursue Dena as he was furious with her. He knew that the only person who could have told Carl about Maureen and the offer to rid her of the baby was Dena herself. Nobody else knew. And he was not best pleased by this show of disloyalty on her part. The bitch was out of control and she really needed to be taught a lesson. What right had she to go telling tales about him behind his back, and to his own brother for God's sake?

He hammered on her door. 'Dena, I know you're in. I want to talk to you.'

'What is it now, Kenny?' She opened the door and his heart lurched at the sight of her. She was holding the baby in her arms, a towel slung over one shoulder as if she'd been bathing it, her hair all damp and tousled. Damn it but he wanted her. If it weren't for the bleeding infant in her arms, he'd push her down on the floor this minute and get on with the job.

'Can I come in?'

She shook her head. 'No, I'm sorry. We've been through all this already. Please do stop coming round, Kenny. I find it most upsetting.' And she closed the door in his face.

Kenny stamped down the stairs seething with fury. How dare she treat him so callously? She'd be sorry one day. He'd make her sorry.

It looked like Alice was Kenny's only hope. Maybe she could again try to talk Dena round, although he had grave doubts that she would succeed. He doubted anyone could make Dena come round, even her own mother. If necessary, he'd have to find some other way to win her. He'd give the matter his most serious consideration. For now Kenny turned his attention to his new security business, and to his newly appointed task of trawling the market, making it plain that he was canvassing for his mother while collecting his monthly dues. Some people were more than willing to vote for her, saying they were fed up with Joe Southworth anyway, as he did little to improve trade. Others were harder to convince and Alec Hall was stupid enough as to laugh.

'You taking up politics an' all, now lad? Nay, that I have to see.'

'It's for Mam. She's the one who wants your vote, not me.'

He laughed again. 'Nay, your mam won't expect anything from me. She had her fill of what I had to offer years ago. She's never been back for seconds.'

Kenny socked him one right on his nose and was deeply satisfied to see blood spurt out. 'I hope I've broken it, but just in case I haven't, you vote for her at the next election right, or I'll come back and finish the job.'

Annie and Clara Higginson, the two maiden ladies who ran the hat stall, may well have seen the occurrence if their nervous twittering was anything to go by. They swiftly agreed that they'd be delighted to vote for Belle. Hadn't they said all along that she was excellent committee material?

'And here is our monthly payment, as usual,' said Annie, usually the more forceful of the two. 'Not the full amount, I'm afraid, as Christmas is never our best time. We are so much busier in the spring, particularly Easter, don't you know. Yes, yes, much busier, dear boy.'

'That's not my problem. And I'm not your dear boy.'

'No, you're not. I mean… oh dear,' the poor woman flustered. 'We wondered if we could pay different rates, at different times of year, taking into account fluctuations in trade. Would that be at all possible? I can see by your expression that it would be most inconvenient for you. Well, it was just a thought. Do tell your dear mother that she will receive our vote. I'm only too happy to oblige, and if there is anything more we can do, you have only to say.'

'All you could do, love, is vote for Mam and pay me what you owe, that's all. I'll call for the balance next week.'

'Yes, dear… er, Kenny… er, Mr Garside. It will be ready and waiting, I do assure you.' And she offered up her most simpering smile before he laughingly strode away, a jaunty swagger to his step.

Next he went to see Winnie Watkins at her stall. Unfortunately, Dena wasn't there, and found that disappointing.

'Nay,' Winnie said, shaking her head, well wrapped up from the winter cold in her usual woolly bobbed cap. 'Your mam and I don't exactly see eye to eye on matters regarding market regulations. She wants to put up rents sky high, while I think they're high enough, and all we need is better value for money.'

'I expect she has her reasons,' Kenny said, not too sure what these might be.

'Aye, I dare say she has, like lining her own pocket. Joe Southworth might be a dimwit, and lazy, but he's fair, and he votes labour. I've been a paid up member all me life. Your mother, I believe, votes for the other lot, so there we are. We don't see eye to eye on a lot of things.'

Kenny stepped closer. 'I reckon, if you give the matter a bit more thought, Winnie, your views might change and you'll come to see that it's in your best interests to start seeing eye to eye, at least so far as the committee is concerned. If you catch my drift.'

Winnie straightened her spine. 'I'm not sure that I do, lad.'

'I hope I don't have to explain things more fully. That could be very uncomfortable for you, very uncomfortable indeed.'

'And I hope that isn't some sort of threat, because I remember you when you were nothing but a snivelling brat in wet britches. You're not much better now, but I'll have you know that my Donald will give you what for, if you so much as lay a finger on me or mine.'

Kenny burst out laughing. 'I shall look forward to it. Now that could be very interesting. See you later alligator.'

Winnie watched him go with a deep sense of unease.

271

Chapter Thirty-Five

Christmas was almost upon them yet again. Snow was turning to mush on the roads and buses and cars skidded and slid, spraying the unwary with sheets of wet ice. Pavements were piled high with the stuff and everyone was wrapped up well in fur-lined ankle boots, overcoats, woolly hats and scarves. There was the smell of chestnuts roasting and hot baked potatoes, home-made mint chocolate from Lizzie Pringle's Chocolate Cabin, and the sharp tang of holly and mistletoe from the wreaths hung up on Bette Hemley's flower stall.

Molly Poulson had made her special pork and ham pies for the festive season and Joe Southworth's cake and biscuit stall was doing a roaring trade. It was commonly agreed that no one could ice a Christmas cake as delicately as Irma, his wife. These were so popular you had to place your order weeks in advance.

Barry Holmes's stall glistened with heaps of oranges, tangerines and rosy red apples. He'd added bags of cob nuts and walnuts, plus a few pink pomegranates, in keeping with the season, and could often be seen giving away nuts and raisins to goggle-eyed children.

'I'm a soft-hearted fool where kids are concerned,' he told Dena when she laughed at him for giving away his profits. 'And here's a bag to put in the stocking of your little treasure.'

Dena gave him a quick kiss. 'What would I do without you?'

'Actually you seem to be doing very well without me these days. You don't ask me to babysit as often as you used to. You haven't needed me in weeks. What's up, have you given up on your dancing?'

Dena laughingly shook her head. It was true that she hadn't asked him to babysit much at all in recent weeks, not because of Carl's disapproval of him, but because Winnie was generally willing to sit with Trudy, so there'd been no need.

''Course not, though admittedly most nights I'm glued to my sewing machine, so it's felt like it at times. Anyway, Friday is still our night out, and Gwen insists we go to the Ritz for the special New Year's Eve do.'

'Splendid! Well, you'll need me to babysit then?'

'No, that's okay. You're relieved of duty. Winnie has volunteered to do the honours. She's going to sleep at mine.'

Barry frowned, looking disappointed by this news. 'There's no need to bother Winnie. You can count on me to stay as late as you like. Where would I want to go these days anyway, old fogey like me?'

'It's no trouble. I think she likes to do it. Bit of company for her I expect.'

He pulled a face. 'Well I don't suppose she gets much conversation out of Donald these days.'

'Barry, that's unkind. Poor Winnie, I worry about her, I do really. All on her own and rarely letting anyone inside her house in case they find out the truth about her poor deceased husband.'

'Aye, sorry, you're right.' He looked thoughtful for a moment.

'Anyway, I'd best be off, I'm late as it is.' She tucked the fluffy eiderdown up to Trudy's chin, took off the brake and set off again through the slush.

All the stalls, both inside and out, were trimmed with fairy lights. A Christmas tree forty feet high stood on the corner of Champion Street where the Salvation Army gathered to sing carols. The strains of 'Hark The Herald Angels Sing' or 'Silent Night', mingling with the more rousing notes of Chuck Berry singing 'Roll Over Beethoven', or 'Rock With The Cavemen' by Tommy Steele.

Today, Father Christmas was to make an appearance at the market, and Dena intended taking Trudy along to meet him and get a present with all the other children. Assuming she could sneak an hour off from Winnie's stall. There never seemed a minute even to snatch a cuppa.

This morning Dena felt exhausted before she even started work. She'd been up till three in the morning finishing off half a dozen little toreador jackets in scarlet satin, then Trudy had woken up with yet another tooth coming through and neither of them had got any sleep after that. She was still grizzling even now.

Christmas had been her busiest time so far, churning out party dresses, skirts and blouses as fast as her fingers could operate the machine. She would have loved to make some of the new swing opera coats in brocade but she really didn't have the time. Maybe she could make some cotton duster coats instead for the spring. She'd seen a picture of one in *Vogue*. They now had two racks in operation and neither seemed to stay full very long. Repeating on favourites while trying to put out something new and fresh each week was Dena's greatest challenge. She just didn't have enough pairs of hands.

Yet despite her exhaustion she was loving every minute of it. Overworked she may be, but she was at least earning a good wage and keeping her child without any help from anybody. And her little pot of savings was growing rapidly; so what if some folk did still turn their noses up when she passed by? Others, the young girls who were her main customers, would always smile and give her a cheery wave.

'Hi Dena. I'll be in on Saturday.'

'Are you getting some more of those patchwork skirts in, Dena? My friend's got one and I love it.'

Life was fun.

Trudy was only fifteen months old, too young yet to fully appreciate entirely what was going on, but Dena meant this to be a good Christmas for her, for them both. Alice had not invited them over to Chorlton for Christmas dinner, and if an invitation came now, at the last minute, Dena would refuse it.

She'd already made her plans. She would roast a chicken, which they would have with some of Mr Ramsay's best chipolata sausages, along with Brussel sprouts, roast potatoes and chestnut stuffing. She'd made a plum pudding, saved hard for weeks and bought a few presents for Trudy's stocking including a wooden truck she could hold on to when she started walking. There wasn't enough room for a tree in the bedsit but Dena had got a cheap box of crackers so they could have fun pulling them together, and each wear a silly hat as they ate their Christmas dinner.

This morning, over coffee, Dena asked Winnie if she'd like to come over and share the dinner with them. The flare of pleasure in her grey eyes warmed Dena's heart but just as quickly it faded again.

'Nay, I can't do that, what about Donald? He's not good with people, likes it best when we're on us own. I'd ask you over to my place but...'

'That's all right. I don't mind.' Dena thought for a moment. Winnie's obsession with hanging on to her husband as if he were still alive created untold problems. 'How about later in the day when Donald takes his nap? Could you pop over then, to see Trudy open the present you've bought for her, and to have a glass of sherry and a mince pie with us? I've got some in specially.'

Twin spots of colour bloomed on Winnie's round cheeks. 'Eeh, that'd be grand. I'd like that.'

'Donald won't mind? I mean, he's a Second World War hero, isn't he? And you must be so proud of him.'

A slight pause before Winnie answered. 'No, Donald won't mind. He'd be pleased that we were such good friends. We are friends, aren't we Dena?'

Dena put her arms about the soft plump little body. 'We are indeed. You gave me a job when I was down, and when nobody else would give me the time of day. And we work well together, don't you think?'

Dena was pleased that Winnie was coming over, but even if she and Trudy did have to spend much of the day alone, she meant to ensure that her baby had a wonderful time.

—

Christmas Eve dawned and once again Dena was late for work, having overslept following yet another marathon sewing session, this time making a few last minute frilly aprons, head bands and Juliet caps for people to buy as presents. She was almost running as she trundled the big old pram through the slush, Trudy whimpering unhappily. The pile of finished sewing was wrapped in an old mackintosh balanced precariously on top of the rainproof apron and just as Dena was negotiating the pram up the steps into the market hall, the whole lot slid off and dropped right into a pile of slushy snow.

'Oh no!' Dena leapt to snatch it up but in doing so forgot to set the brake and the big pram began to roll away from her. She made a grab for the handle and in her haste and exhaustion tripped over the parcel and fell flat on her face in the snow.

The pram was picking up pace, racing over the slippy ground towards the road and now Dena was screaming and shouting for all she was worth. Some people glanced across at her, puzzled but made no effort to help her up, others ignored her, or didn't even hear as her cries were drowned by the noise of traffic, the chatter and shouts of market traders, and the sound of Guy Mitchell's, 'Singing The Blues'. It reached the edge of the kerb, tilted off and lurched into the road, Trudy stunned into shocked silence by the speed of her ride. A large green bus was heading towards it and to her horror Dena saw that at any moment the pram, and her child within it, would be smashed to pieces.

And then like a miracle there was Carl. He was running, shoving and pushing his way through the crowds, brutally in some cases, and folk were yelling after him. Dena too was on her feet and starting to run, even though she hadn't a hope of reaching the pram in time. It might all have happened in a split second, but it felt as if time had switched into slow motion, and really she wasn't moving at all but still stuck fast in the huge drifts of snow.

Carl reached the pram just as the bus rounded the corner, snatched hold of the handle and swerved it perilously to one side as it raced past, brakes squealing, big wheels spraying passers-by with a great sheet of filthy slush and ice.

Carl was covered in the stuff, not that Dena paid him the slightest attention as she snatched up her terrified child and smothered her with kisses. 'Oh, I'm so sorry my sweetheart. Mummy shouldn't have let that big nasty pram go off. Oh, why didn't I put the brake on? Why did I bother about that silly parcel of sewing?'

'Why indeed?' Carl dryly remarked, brushing ice from his jacket. 'And a thank you would not be inappropriate at this point.'

Dena stared at him, seeing him properly at last, the great globs of ice and snow stuck in his hair and splattered all over his clothes, noting the scratches on his face and hands where he'd bumped and knocked into things. She was filled with shame. 'Oh, Carl, how can I thank you? I couldn't possibly find the words. Thank you so much! You saved my baby's life!'

Then still with Trudy pressed tight to her breast she leaned close and kissed him gently full on the mouth.

It was meant simply as a friendly gesture, he could tell, but her mouth was warm and still trembling from shock. It felt moist and vulnerable beneath his own and found himself parting her lips very slightly, lingering over the taste of her. Jerked to his senses by some inner voice of caution, he broke away, wanting to deny the emotion burning within him, yet knowing he could not. It blazed from his eyes, pulsated through every nerve in his body.

As leaping shards of desire roared through him like a furnace, Carl realised that in one small moment of intimacy, everything between them had changed forever.

Chapter Thirty-Six

Dena was wrapping Christmas presents later that evening when there came a knock to her door. Her heart jerked and for a moment she couldn't catch her breath. It must be Carl. Had he come to apologise for responding to her kiss of gratitude like that, or to remonstrate with her for causing the accident in the first place? She could still feel the warmth of it spreading through her like fire. Dena glanced across at Trudy, who was sound asleep in her cot. All sign of the sewing, including the machine, had been tidied away in preparation for Christmas Day, and she'd planned to have an early night. Now, smoothing down her skirt, she went and opened it.

It turned out to be Kenny standing on the landing, grinning at her with a Santa Claus hat on, and his arms full of parcels. 'Merry Christmas! I've fetched your Trudy her presents.'

It was on the tip of Dena's tongue to say that she was his daughter too, but stopped herself in time. She had no wish to remind him of this fact. Nor did she wish to invite him in, so she simply smiled, holding out her hands. 'Thank you.'

'There's one from Mam too, some clothes I think, and the big one is from me. It's a doll. Little girls like dolls, don't they? I got it cheap from Leo's toy stall.'

Dena hid a smile. 'Thank you.'

'Don't mention it, as it's Christmas after all. Carl didn't contribute. But that's my brother all over. Said he'd see to his own presents, but don't expect him to do anything. He's far too mean. I've got a present for you too. Can I come in?'

Dena shook her head, keeping the door half closed as she struggled to hold on to the parcels. 'Sorry, no, Trudy is asleep and since tomorrow is going to be an exciting day for her, I need her to have a good night's sleep. Besides, I'm pretty whacked myself. I've worked my socks off these last few weeks.'

Kenny pouted. 'I hardly see you these days. I should be the one looking after you.'

Dena let out a weary sigh. 'Don't start this now, Kenny.'

'I've turned over a new leaf, got myself a job, just like you asked me to. And I could help you with yours. I'll do anything, run errands for you, and drive you to the warehouses. I'm getting a car, a Ford Zephyr. Or I could look after you here, cook or wash up. I'm good at that.'

'Stop it, Kenny. I don't need your help. I'm doing fine on my own.' She started to close the door, but he put his foot inside to stop it from closing.

'How about the dance on New Year's Eve then? Barry says you're going with a friend. And who might that be?'

'Gwen has got tickets for us. I'm going with her. Not that it's any of your business.'

His cheeks fired red. 'Aye it is. You should've said.'

'Why should I? I don't have to ask your permission to go dancing with a friend.'

'I'm your fella. You're my girl. How many times do I have to remind you of that simple fact? You should be going to the dance with me, not your daft friend.'

Dena bridled at his tone, as well as at the insinuation that he was in control of what she did or who she saw. 'And I've told you a thousand times that you are not my fella, and I am not your girl. Not any more! But I'm not starting an argument standing at my own door on Christmas Eve. Good night, Kenny.' And seeing that he'd removed his foot in his agitation so that he could jig about in his crêpe-soled shoes, she quietly closed the door in his face.

His fist instantly pounded upon the panel and Trudy stirred and whimpered in her sleep. 'Let me in, Dena. I want you to open my present now!'

'Kenny,' Dena hissed through the closed door. 'Stop this at once and go, or you'll wake Trudy.'

She heard his footsteps pounding down the stairs and breathed a deep sigh of relief, but in her heart she knew that he would be back. He always was. Kenny didn't seem able to accept that she had a life of her own. He was jealous of her friends, of the time she spent on her sewing, even of Trudy. The more she resisted him, the more he seemed to want her.

What his reaction would be if he ever learned that she and Carl had kissed in that intimate way really didn't bear thinking about.

-

Christmas Day was a perfect, sunny, happy family day, even if there were only the two of them to share it. Dena tried not to think about how different it could have been if she'd had a proper family, or what Alice might be doing in Chorlton. She hadn't come round with a present or even a card, but her mother had made her choices and there was little point in complaining about it. No doubt she would call again, if and when it suited her to do so.

Dena helped Trudy to open her presents, laughing when she spent more time playing with the paper and boxes than the top and bricks she'd bought her, and the large doll that Kenny had brought round. Later she took her for a walk around the deserted market. It looked so sad and neglected with all the trestles folded away and the canvas flapping forlornly in the breeze. But it would be buzzing with life again just as soon as the holiday was over. That was what she loved about it, the colour, the noise, the bustle, and the people. More of them were speaking to her now, forced to do so since they wished to buy her lovely clothes. Dena knew in her heart that although her life might not have turned out quite as she'd hoped, she was happy.

On her return she found a small parcel sitting on her doormat. It was another present for Trudy, this time from Carl.

It was a beautiful little silver bracelet and Dena was stunned, not having expected anything. She really couldn't make him out. Most of the time he could barely find it in himself to be polite to her, or say a good word on her behalf. Then that kiss, now a present for Trudy. What was going on? And more importantly how did she feel about it?

Later in the afternoon Winnie appeared, all spruced up in a pillar-box red dress and a dab of lipstick. She looked younger and slimmer, without her several layers of woolly cardigans. Her soft brown hair was all fluffed up instead of hidden beneath the dreadful bob cap, revealing a glimpse of the pretty young girl she must once have been. She played with Trudy for a while then when the little girl had been put down for her nap, Dena poured out two glasses of sherry and they sat down for a cosy chat.

They talked about the stall and Christmas trade, and the success of Dena's little sideline.

'I need more space.' Dena suddenly blurted out. 'I can no longer cope with doing the sewing in this tiny bedsit, and I need more help. Looking after Trudy and helping you on the stall, as well as doing all the sewing on my own, is all getting a bit much.' She sat on the edge of her bed and tears began to run down her cheeks. It was the strange combination of happiness and loneliness on this special day, as well as her extreme tiredness. The accident that had very nearly happened yesterday, or simply the sherry, she felt suddenly overwhelmed by emotion. Dena put her face in her hands and began to cry.

Winnie was dumbfounded. Never, in all her life had she seen Dena give way to tears, and she didn't know how to handle it.

'Nay, lass, don't take on. I'm sure we can sort something out.' And she put her arms about Dena and rocked her gently, comfortingly, just as a mother would.

When the tears subsided, Winnie dabbed at her cheeks with a clean white handkerchief. 'Could you manage to work in my stockroom? I know it's right up there on the top floor of the market hall, a bit out of the way like, but happen we could organise it better and make some space for you in there. Maybe buy another machine and find someone to help. How does that sound?'

Dena was staring at the older woman in wonder. 'That sounds marvellous. Would you be prepared to let me do that?'

Winnie brushed away another tear and smiled. 'Ay, lass, it was the best thing I've done in years the day I took you on. Working with you has been right champion. You're like a daughter to me now. And I reckon you've only just started. You're going places – a blind man could see that. Come on, let's drink to a new beginning and a successful future.'

Dena was laughing, her gloom and despair gone in a trice, the burst of happiness she'd felt earlier came soaring back, restored by youth and Winnie's faith in her, and she raised her sherry glass to the toast.

It was over her second glass of sherry that Winnie began to talk about Donald. 'We met at the Ritz right at the start of the war. He was with a group of his mates, all airmen on a break between missions, and the first time he asked me to dance he was a bit the worse for drink. I told him to sober up before he dared ask me again.' Winnie smiled at the memory. 'Well, he was back in ten minutes, eyes focused, his hair wet through from the ducking he'd given himself under the cloakroom tap and doing his best to look as sober as a judge. You had to laugh. 'Course, I agreed, and in the space of one dance we fell in love. Before the night was out he'd asked me to marry him and I'd accepted.'

She paused, emotion blocking her throat and for several moments couldn't speak.

'We were so young, just turned twenty-three. I'll be forty, next year, and I love him as much now as I did then. We only had a few months together as man and wife but I'm grateful for what we had. He was a very special man.' Winnie looked at Dena then, a challenge in her gaze as for the first time she admitted the truth, speaking of Donald in the past tense.

Dena said nothing, simply stretched out a hand and squeezed Winnie's hard.

'We tried for a family but I had a miscarriage then lost one stillborn. He was a boy and I called him Jeffrey, though he was never christened. We coped with all of that then one day Donald went off into the wide blue yonder, just another mission, he said. But it proved to be his last.' Again she paused, the sherry glass forgotten in her trembling fingers. Dena set it safely to one side, overwhelmed by the thought of all that grief.

'I waited and waited. They said he was missing presumed dead, but I wasn't going to presume any such thing. How could I till I had proof? Losing the babies was one thing, losing my husband was dreadful. Others came back home, why not my Donald?'

A single tear rolled down the older woman's cheek and Dena wiped it gently away. 'Oh, Winnie, how awful! How can you bear it?'

'Aye well, that's the trouble. I refused to bear it, didn't I? I couldn't accept what had happened, that he was dead and gone, that I'd lost him too and he wouldn't ever be coming back.' She gulped on a sob then steadied herself. 'I never meant to let it go on indefinitely but it came to be a habit speaking of him in the present tense, like he was expected back any day. And then I said that he had returned just to stop folk asking after him all the time. There was no way back after that, and everyone just went along with it.'

Winnie looked down at her hands, threading a sodden handkerchief between her fingers. 'It's getting to know you that's taught me to be brave enough to face it. You're only a little lass but so full of spunk. You never let anything get you down. You just come up fighting and smiling every time. I admire that.' Winnie nodded, then blew her nose very loud.

'Winnie, I'm not brave at all, and much of the time I feel scared, but I know what it's like to lose someone you love. I lost my little brother, then my mother chucked me out and insisted I was taken into care, and it near broke my heart. Still does if I let myself dwell on it. I just have to keep on going because I have little Trudy here, and because I have you as a friend.' And this time it was Dena who put her arms around the older woman, offering comfort as they wept quietly together.

As if on cue, Trudy began to stir in her sleep and rub her eyes, giving a little gasping cry. Their moment of peace was over and they both laughed.

'By heck, chuck,' Winnie said, suddenly brisk. 'We're turning into a right pair of wet lettuces. Look at the face on this little babby, she'll think we've run mad if we don't cheer up. And it is Christmas, after all. Come on precious, come to your Aunty Win, let's 'Ride-a-Cock-Horse' while your mam puts the kettle on. We'll be drunk as mops on this sherry if we don't watch out.'

Then they were all three hugging and laughing, Trudy getting excited all over again and Dena hurried to do as she was bid.

'You could move into mine, if you like,' Winnie offered moments later over a cup of tea and a mince pie. 'You and Trudy would be most welcome, wouldn't you sweetie? It's a big house and, as you know, only me rattling around in it all on me tod.'

'Oh, Winnie, I couldn't possibly intrude. It wouldn't be right, not with all this baby clobber and the sewing. I'd still need to do some work at home when Trudy is asleep, even if I do use your stockroom during the day.'

Winnie's gaze was sincere. 'I'd appreciate it if you would at least consider it. I'd be right glad of the company, to be honest. Not that I wouldn't respect your privacy and independence. I know how important that is to you. The pair of you could have the big back bedroom and the front parlour all to yourselves, pay proper rent and everything. I'm sure we wouldn't fall out over sharing the kitchen and the lavvy down the yard.'

Dena grinned. 'I'm sure we wouldn't.' Then after a moment said, 'Are you sure about this?'

'I am.'

'All right, you're on. When shall I move in?'

'No time like the present, so how about tomorrow?'

Dena laughed. 'I think after the New Year would be better. This will be a busy week at the stall and I shall need time to pack.'

'The New Year it is then.'

And so they drank another toast with the tea, together with a second mince pie, to celebrate the cementing of a new era in their friendship.

Chapter Thirty-Seven

The dance on New Year's Eve was, in Dena's eyes, absolutely wonderful. She'd heard of the dubious reputation of the Ritz on Whitworth Street and didn't believe a word of it. Many mothers preferred their daughters to go to the Plaza, but her own didn't seem to care what she did, hadn't even bothered to give her daughter or grandchild a Christmas present, and to Dena the ballroom looked magnificent. It was all trimmed up with balloons and streamers, coloured spot lights glistening on the polished floor and the mirrored walls, and everyone in their best party frocks. Dena felt as if she'd entered paradise.

There were two bands, one was the Phil Moss Orchestra in their lovely red jackets playing all the best dance numbers from the cha-cha to the Gay Gordons, interspersed with the usual quicksteps and foxtrots and novelty dances such as the Paul Jones and Progressive Barn Dance.

The second band was a group who played nothing but rock 'n' roll. They were great fun and brought the house down, playing all the latest numbers including 'All Shook Up' and 'Hound Dog'; Little Richard's 'Tutti Frutti', and Dena's favourite – Lonnie Donegan's 'Rock Island Line'. She just couldn't stop jiving.

Her dress was of the palest aquamarine with a full bouffant skirt over yards of net petticoat, the waist pulled in tight by a broad belt and the close-fitting bodice held in place by shoestring shoulder straps. She'd pinned on a pink corsage made out of stiff organza, and her shoes were black ballerina pumps, as high stiletto heels were not allowed on the dance floor.

Dena felt young and pretty, all the tiredness evaporated away like mist in sunshine; stronger than she'd ever felt and with all her life still before her. Nineteen fifty-six had been a good year for her, and now she'd reached this new understanding with Winnie, who knew what the next year might bring? Nineteen fifty-seven would be the best yet.

Gwen had fixed her up with yet another blind date. 'I won't let you turn into a wallflower,' she'd said when Dena had protested. 'And you'll like Tom, he's lovely.'

Tom had a freckled moon face and was a little overweight. Some girls might not mind but he did not appeal to Dena. Fortunately he wasn't the sensitive sort and once they'd acknowledged that there were no sparks between them, he went off to find himself a new date and left her to it.

It was a wonderful night and Dena didn't go short of partners. One was an Italian who said he'd come to Manchester as a prisoner of war and stayed. She decided he was a bit old for her and politely declined the next dance. Another had sweaty hands so she soon got rid of him, while a third kept pressing to take her up to the balcony for coffee while Dena insisted that she really wasn't thirsty, thank you very much. She guessed he wanted much more than coffee and didn't fancy him at all.

At one point she thought she spotted a familiar figure and her heart clenched tight with emotion, but then he vanished behind one of the pillars and Dena couldn't be certain that she hadn't simply imagined him. Anyway, she really didn't want to think about Carl Garside, not since that kiss had shaken her rigid. Why he'd allowed it to go on so long she really couldn't imagine – some sort of test? Was he trying to prove that she was a loose woman? Dena blushed even now as she thought of how vulnerable he'd made her feel in that moment, how she'd melted in his arms, giving every impression that she was.

Someone asked her to dance and Dena shook these depressing thoughts away, thankful for the distraction. Best not to think of Carl Garside at all.

All too soon it was the last waltz with hundreds of lights spinning from the mirrored ball in the centre of the ceiling. Gwen and her boyfriend were wrapped in each other's arms, swaying to the music of 'Love Me Tender' and Dena felt a pang of sweet envy, even though she was pleased for her friend. How wonderful it must be to feel so loved, to have someone of your own who really cared about you.

A hand touched her arm. 'May I have this dance?' And there he was: hair brushed neat, the crazy black curls tamed for once, shoes polished, a knife edge to the creases of his fashionably tapered trousers. An unmistakable challenge in the dark blue enigmatic gaze: dance with me if you dare was his attitude.

Dena could do no more than move into his arms like a sleep-walker, which seemed to be exactly the place she ought to be. She felt a slow unfurling of pleasure as he held her that had something to do with the closeness of his cheek to her own, the scent of his skin and the pressure of his hand upon her back. What was happening to her? Had she lost her reason? This was Carl Garside, the boy she'd hated most in the world, the person bent on causing her the maximum embarrassment. She couldn't possibly be falling for him, could she?

No, she wouldn't allow it. He was the rudest, most difficult person she'd ever met. He'd done nothing but insult her from the day he believed he'd caught her fiddling the tips. His antagonism towards her had worsened from the moment she and Kenny got together, and, perversely, even more so since they parted.

'I've been trying to avoid you all evening,' he said, speaking softly against her ear.

Startled, she looked up into his face. 'Have you, why?'

'Can't you guess?'

Dena didn't answer. Could think of nothing to say. Her insides were churning with an emotion she really didn't care to name. What was he implying? What could she say?

She was saved by the music changing to that of 'Auld Lang Syne' as midnight approached. They were being pulled apart, urged to join the circle as the band leader started the countdown to midnight. Everyone joined in and on the stroke of twelve a great cheer went up as streamers were thrown, balloons popped and everyone was laughing and hugging, shouting Happy New Year and kissing each other.

Carl and Dena stood several inches apart, silent and uncompromising, neither willing to make the first move; each overwhelmed by the awkwardness of the moment. Yet Dena was aware of an instinctive need drawing them together even as she fought to resist it with every fibre of her being.

When Carl finally spoke she could scarcely hear the words for all the riotous laughter and singing eddying around them. But it didn't matter. His eyes were saying so much more.

'Happy New Year, Dena.'

'Happy New Year, Carl.'

Then he reached for her and kissed her and she was slipping her arms around his neck and kissing him back just as if it were the most natural thing in the world. She moulded herself to him so sweetly, so utterly, that it seemed as if she might never let him go.

His hold on her tightened, the kiss deepened, became more intense and she could think of nothing but the joy of that moment, her heart spilling over with emotion, just as if they stood alone in a vast empty desert not hemmed in by a crowd of noisy revellers.

'Let's get out of here,' he said, breaking the kiss at last. 'Let me walk you home.'

'All right, but I must tell Gwen.' She could hardly catch her breath, couldn't think.

Moments later Dena had collected her coat and they were walking together through the darkened streets, arms wrapped about each other, scarcely noticing passers-by calling out the compliments of the season to them.

'This is not what I meant to happen. I want you to believe me when I say that.'

'I know. I've never been anything but a nuisance in your eyes. I want you to know that I wasn't intending to steal those tips,' Dena burst out.

'Oh, Dena, not that again.'

'No, you must listen. Your mother always took a share too. Joan and I didn't think it fair since she also got the profits from the meals, so we decided to keep a bit back that Belle didn't know about. We shared that out just between ourselves and the other girls.'

He laughed. 'I see. Quite clever!'

'I wasn't cheating on the others, though I was cheating your mam a bit.'

He shook his head. 'No, you're right. She got her profit. The tips should have been yours.'

'And for Joan and the other girls.'

'I should've realised you wouldn't steal from anyone.' She saw him looking at her for a long moment and something twisted inside her. 'I didn't think you even liked me. What about that time when you shouted at me for getting a babysitter so's I could go out? Anyone would think it was the crime of the century the way you blasted off at me.'

'I shouted at you for using Barry Holmes as a babysitter.'

'Just because you don't like him?'

Carl looked a bit sheepish. 'Because Kenny said you were seeing him and you could be having an affair.'

Dena's jaw dropped open and then she burst out laughing. 'Me and Barry, having an affair?'

Carl had the grace to smile. 'Anyway, none of that has anything to do with why I've been resisting you.'

'Oh, and why is that then?' She was aware that she was openly flirting with him, and enjoying herself.

'I held off because you're Kenny's girl.'

'That hasn't been true for a long time. He thinks I am, and I keep reminding him that it's all over between us. I stood him up at the altar, if you remember?'

Dena was filled with a rush of guilt for rejecting Kenny, conflicting with the birth of a sparkling excitement, like champagne surging through her veins, as if she'd been waiting for this moment all her life. She felt overcome by utter amazement that this magical thing was even happening between herself and Carl.

Carl took her cold hands between his own and began to warm them, then kissed her cold nose, smiling as he did so. 'Mam still hasn't properly forgiven you for showing us all up that day. She's always banging on about your shameful behaviour and how you ruined all chance of her getting on that blasted market committee.'

'That's a bit rich. It was her idea to organise a big wedding, not mine. She still pops in to see Trudy from time to time, which I don't mind at all, although thankfully she seems to have finally given up hope of luring me into marriage with her younger son.'

Carl's eyebrows went up. 'Is that what she tried to do?'

Dena nodded. 'I suspect only so that she could claim Trudy as her grandchild. She loves her, I can understand that.'

Carl frowned then shook his head in bewilderment. He'd long since given up trying to understand his mother, or women in general come to that. Belle was utterly selfish, that was for sure. But he had more important matters on his mind right now. He tucked Dena's hand in the crook of his arm as they walked on. 'So what are we going to do about this?'

'I don't know what more I can do. I've already apologised for not telling Kenny sooner, like the day before the wedding at least, but it was a last minute panic on my part. I just knew that I couldn't go through with it.'

'I don't mean about the wedding, I mean about us.'

Dena slanted a sideways glance at him. 'Is there an "us"?'

'Don't play games with me, Dena. At least, you do if your response to that kiss is anything to go by, genuine and not a lie. Or were you only pretending just now?' He pulled her to a halt, challenging her to answer.

The expression in his eyes was so full of hurt and misery in that moment that she could hardly bear it. 'No, I wasn't pretending but I suppose it's knocked me for six. I never expected this to happen. I can't seem to think straight.'

He gave a genuine wide smile, the most relaxed she'd ever seen him and it was lovely. 'At least we agree on something at last.'

She grinned. 'I suppose we do.'

'A change for the better, I'd say, and a welcome improvement on previous relations between us. I confess I've been fighting this feeling for some weeks, months even. Every time I saw you I fell deeper into the mire of wanting to look after you, needing to love you, and longing to kiss you. When Kenny came home in a sulk the other night because you wouldn't go with him to the New Year's Eve dance, against my better judgement I found myself buying a ticket. I like you a lot, Dena, as a matter of fact.'

He looking deeply into her eyes and the next moment he was cupping her face between his hands and kissing her, his tongue caressing hers, demanding, wanting, and all Dena could do was surrender herself to the pleasure of it.

A long time later when they both caught their breath, he stroked her tousled curls and nestled her head against his chest. 'It isn't going to be easy, is it? Kenny isn't going to like this one little bit.'

Dena couldn't look at him, nor did she wish to. She didn't want to even think about Kenny in the magic of this moment. She needed time to sort out in her mind the implications of all he'd just said, all she'd felt in his arms. Small shivers of delight were running down her spine as he tenderly stroked her hair, threading his fingers through her short, soft curls.

'N-no, I don't suppose he will but I can't help that, can I? It just didn't work out for us, that's all. And Kenny will have to accept that fact.'

'It must be explained to him with great tact.'

She moved in his arms, looking up trustingly into his face. 'Will you tell him, or shall I?'

Carl kissed her pert little nose, each translucent eyelid, then smoothed her arms and shoulders and set her a little away from him, as if compelling himself to resist her. 'I shall. He'd be bound to guess anyway. Feeling as I do, I couldn't possibly keep it a secret. I have to see you again, Dena. You do realise that?'

She nodded, full of emotion in that moment that she didn't trust herself to speak.

'You do want to see me again?'

'I do, but Kenny has been pestering me for months. He follows me everywhere, constantly calling and asking me to go out with him. He seems to think I still belong to him, that I'm still his girl, and he won't take no for an answer. I shudder to think what he'll do when he learns about us.'

'You mustn't worry, I'll make it okay.' And, unable to resist, he lowered his mouth to hers and began to kiss her again, deeper and more demanding than ever.

Something seemed to unfold within her and, opening up to him, Dena gave herself with sweet abandon. But as his tongue sought hers a sharp pain of desire kicked in, and she had the good sense to stop the kissing before such matters got out of hand. 'It's late, I'd best get off home.'

'Leave it to me,' he murmured. 'I'll make it okay with Kenny. He won't be a problem.'

Chapter Thirty-Eight

When Dena told Miss Rogers that she was moving in with Winnie Watkins, the older woman was so delighted that her thin lips broke into a wide smile and she actually hugged her.

'Why, that's marvellous. Winnie is a wonderful woman, and has proved to be a stout friend for you. I believe you will suit each other well. You'll no longer be alone yet she'll respect your independence.'

Dena agreed. 'And she loves Trudy already.'

There was the suspicion of a tear in the social worker's eyes, as she looked down at the child, fast asleep in her cot with her thumb in her mouth. 'Who could resist her?'

Dena gave a bitter little laugh. 'Alice. You were right about Mam. She hasn't changed.'

Miss Rogers shook her head in sad despair. 'I doubt she'll approve of your decision, but don't allow her to influence you. Alice Dobson is a woman eaten up with bitterness, and there's nothing you can do to alter that. I'm so proud of your success, Dena, I feel as if I have been a part of it. A very small part, but I played a role nonetheless.'

'Oh, you did indeed,' Dena said with some fervour. 'Where would I be without you? Trudy would have been taken away and adopted, or I would be out on the streets maybe. You are my guardian angel, Miss Rogers. Always.'

The pair looked at each other for a moment, both slightly overcome by emotion, and then Miss Rogers was brisk once more, saying how Dena would no longer be requiring her regular visits, so this would be a parting of the ways.

'You have friends now, to watch out for you, should you need a helping hand. Although I consider you mature enough to look after yourself these days, Dena Dobson. But you might send me the odd note or Christmas card, to let me know how you're getting along.'

'I will,' Dena said, feeling a strange choking sensation in her throat. 'I shall never forget you, Miss Rogers!' And reaching up, she kissed the whiskery cheek, instantly flared to a blush pink.

And as she in turn leaned over the cot to kiss Trudy goodbye, there was the slightest quiver on the social worker's lower lip. After she'd gone, Dena put her hands to her face and wept a few silent tears.

—

A day or two later Dena was busily packing in preparation to moving out when Alice again appeared on her doorstep. Just the sight of the reproving look on her mother's face caused Dena's heart to drop several notches. What now?

'I thought you might have asked me to babysit over Christmas, or at least fetched the brat over to see me,' Alice said with a sniff of disapproval. 'But obviously you're so independent you don't need a mother any more.'

'I could accuse you of not even bothering to bring Trudy a present.' Pointedly looking at Alice's empty hands even now. 'And don't call her a brat.'

'Why not? That's what she is. And why should I give her presents? You chose to have her so you should provide for her. It's not for me to encourage the getting of bastards.'

Dena flushed with anger. 'Don't you dare use that word in front of my child.' Trudy was sitting in her playpen, happily banging pan lids together, oblivious of the cutting words and friction between the two women.

'You'll be getting yourself another one if you don't watch out. I hear you've been out gallivanting every night over Christmas.'

'Whoever told you that?'

'A little bird.'

'Well, it's a lie. I've been working hard on my sewing as well as serving on Winnie's stall. I went out only once, to the New Year's Eve dance at the Ritz.' Dena's heart turned over just thinking about that night and she bit down hard on her lip as she went to put on the kettle, hoping Alice wouldn't notice the telltale blush. Hadn't she learned it was fruitless to argue with her? Her mother was as slippery as an eel and would always manage to find some way to twist any argument around to suit herself.

Alice parked herself on the only chair, her spine as rigid as her morals, handbag on knee. But once she'd been served with a cup of best Yorkshire tea and a McVitie's biscuit, she made no comment at all, but approached her quarry from another angle. 'I heard you were doing a bit of sewing, making yourself useful at last, though what you know about dressmaking I shudder to think.'

Dena sipped her tea and chose not to explain how she'd acquired the skill for fear of opening up all that painful business of her being taken into care.

'You haven't even offered to make anything for me, your own mother.' Still failing to get a rise out of her daughter, she turned her attention to the pile of cardboard boxes and newspapers strewn around. 'What's going on here? Moving out, are we? Where to this time, if not with Kenny?'

Dena gritted her teeth, desperately holding on to her rapidly diminishing patience. 'As a matter of fact I'm moving in with Winnie Talbot. She's very kindly offered us a home.' Which is more than you did, was the unspoken thought that hung between them.

Alice sniffed. 'Much good that'll do you, she's got a screw loose has Winnie. Seems to think her husband is still alive when he came down with his plane in the war. She's a nutter.'

Dena walked to the door and yanked it open. 'If you've only come round to insult my child and my friends and accuse me of being a bad mother, you can leave right now before we come to blows.'

'If the cap fits.'

'What have you come for, anyway?'

'Do I need a reason to pop in for a chat with me own daughter?'

'Generally there is a reason behind your visits, yes. Go on, what is it this time? I'm listening.'

'Nothing fresh, I just wondered if you'd had a change of heart, that's all. If you felt ready yet to turn respectable and make poor Kenny a happy man.'

'Poor Kenny is it now? I've told you already, it's all over between us.'

'He'll not wait forever. You could lose him if you dally too long.'

'Good. I'll marry when I'm good and ready and not before, and when I find the right man.' Again that lurch of the heart. Could she have found him already? It had felt like it, when Carl kissed her after the dance, and she'd hardly slept a wink since for thinking about him. He'd promised to pop in later today, to help carry her stuff over to Winnie's. Dena's heartbeat quickened just at the thought of seeing him again.

'So you've no intention of retrieving your decency then? You intend to continue living as some sort of harlot with an illegitimate brat?'

Dena gave a wry smile. 'Well, I wouldn't have put it in those terms but yes, I intend to stay single, for the moment.'

Alice slammed down her cup and saucer and straightened her hat, although it hadn't moved an inch on the frizz of grey hair, before marching stiff-backed to the door. 'You're trouble is that you are too stubborn for your own good, girl. There might come a time when you regret being so independent. Then you'll be sorry.'

So long as I don't end up a bitter old crone like you, I'll cope, Dena thought uncharitably, as she silently and politely opened the door to let her mother out. 'Thank you for calling but if it was only to preach to me about my morals, or lack of them, then that's a shame. It really is time you tried to find something you liked about me. You could give the matter some thought before you call again.'

'I'm not sure I'll bother.'

'Well, if you don't, Mam, that would be a pity too. I shall always be glad to see you, whenever you're passing. We really should make an effort to get to know each other a little better, as adults, don't you think?' Dena jiggled Trudy in her arms. 'Say bye-bye. Grandma's going now.'

Alice looked at the child and sniffed disdainfully. 'I'll not be grandmother to no bastard.' Then wagging a gloved finger in Dena's face, 'Mark my words, girl, you'll live to regret this stupid obstinacy of yours.'

Dena watched her clump down the stairs with sadness in her heart, then softly closing the door went on with packing her few possessions in preparation for her move. Miss Rogers was right again.

At least Winnie liked her and enjoyed having her around. That was something, wasn't it?

-

Winnie and Dena were like a pair of schoolgirls, all silly and giggly as they settled her into her new accommodation, moving furniture about, fussing over sharing out cushions and bric-a-brac. Winnie had put up pretty new blue curtains in the rooms Dena was to have. She'd also made a hot pot for their tea, to celebrate a new beginning for them both.

'I know that we agreed you'd be independent, but I thought we could happen take it in turns to do the cooking, share the shopping and such like. It would be daft to double up.'

'I'm all in favour of that,' Dena said, tucking into the delicious food and chuckling as Trudy valiantly did the same with her spoon and pusher.

'Blow on it if it's too hot, love,' Winnie told the child.

''S good,' Trudy said.

''Course it is, pet. Who's a clever girl then? And Aunty Win has made a nice chocolate cake for afters.'

Watching the pair of them, so content together, Dena felt a warm glow deep inside. 'We are going to be so happy here. But I don't want you mollycoddling me, or spoiling Trudy too much. I must do my share.'

Winnie grinned. 'I hope you'll let me spoil you both just a little bit. It'll be a right treat for me to have someone to fuss over after all these years on me own. By the way, did I tell you that Barry came round on New Year's Eve? To wish me the felicitations of the season, he said, but I think he was feeling a bit left out and lonely, so I asked him in and we saw the New Year in together over a glass of port.'

'You sly old bird.'

Winnie flushed bright pink. 'There's nothing in it. Barry's just a friend. I really don't know what Donald would say.'

Dena put her arms around her friend. 'He would say, good for you. Barry can be very entertaining company.'

Winnie gave a girlish giggle. 'He tells such tales about his exploits in Blackpool. A star turn he is. Yet there's a sadness to him, a loneliness.'

Dena didn't say that Barry had said much the same about Winnie.

-

In no time at all a satisfactory routine was established. Dena and Trudy happily settled in the big back bedroom, where there was plenty of room for a cot beside the single bed, and a good view over the rooftops of Castlefield.

Having set up her sewing machine, tailor's dummy, books and sewing patterns, together with a few other bits and pieces in the front parlour, Dena felt she must have landed in paradise.

Winnie's house with its highly polished furniture may be a bit old-fashioned but it was big and spacious, such a contrast to the tiny bedsit, and to those painfully constricted years in the dormitory at Ivy Bank. And a vast improvement on the tiny cottage she'd once occupied with her mother and Pete in Barber's Court down by the canal.

Dena still thought about her brother, often longed to talk to him about her troubles, since young as he was he would always listen sympathetically. They'd been so close. She longed to tell him about her sewing and how well she was doing selling her dresses and skirts and things. How she dreamed of taking her little enterprise even further.

Each evening after Trudy had been put to bed, Dena would work at her sewing, running up a seemingly endless supply of skirts, tops and dresses. Or she would sit by the fire in the living room indulging in cosy little chats with Winnie while she stitched buttonholes or embroidered appliqué shapes. It felt good for both of them to have some company at last.

One of their little pleasures was to listen to the wireless, to *Mrs Dale's Diary* and *The Archers*. *The Goon Show* was a great favourite of Dena's and Winnie liked *Hancock's Half Hour*. So when the battered old Bakelite Bush radio stopped working, Dena set off to get a replacement. She couldn't afford to buy one but she could surely afford to rent a wireless set. It would be her contribution to the household entertainment.

A bored young man was sitting behind the counter picking his teeth when she entered the shop. Dena politely made her request. He leapt from his stool eager to help, talking knowledgeably about valves and how much better sound quality modern radios have now that everyone had electricity and didn't need an accumulator battery.

He brought out a form. 'You'll just have to fill this in and get your husband to sign it.'

'I don't have a husband.'

The young man stared at the baby in the pram. 'Well – your father then.'

'I don't have one of those either.'

'In that case,' said the young man, suddenly turning pompous. 'You can't rent a radio.'

Dena was incensed. 'Are you trying to tell me that because I'm not married and my father is dead, killed in the war, I'm somehow not considered to be a worthwhile, reliable person?'

The question was too long for him to follow, and he didn't attempt to answer it.

'I'll have you know I'm earning me own living, keeping my child without help from anyone, largely anyway, and I don't owe a penny to a soul. Just because I'm a girl, and I got pregnant too young doesn't turn me into a criminal?'

The young man flushed bright red, not really wanting to hear all these personal details. 'I'm sorry but it's the law. You need a man's signature for one of these new hire purchase agreements. I don't make the rules.'

'No, but I bet you could break them, since you're a man, or at least could bend them a little.' She tried to flutter her eyelashes at him, as she sensed there was no other way to get round him. Rather unsuccessfully, as it turned out.

'No can do, sorry! More than my job is worth.'

Dena was compelled to take the form round to Barry who gladly signed it for her. But it was a bitter pill to swallow.

–

Dena didn't allow these little setbacks to spoil things for her. Life was exciting. She also had the added thrill of Carl. Could he really care for her as much as he appeared to? Or was he just stringing her along, thinking she was easy? No, no, she didn't believe that was the case at all. Dena was determined not to see problems where there were none. Carl respected her. She could sense it.

But if they started to get serious, how would he feel about taking on his brother's child? Trudy's welfare must be her major concern. They might never get serious so where was the point in worrying about that till it happened? And then there was the problem of Kenny.

Carl had confessed to her the other day, when he carried her things round to Winnie's, that he still hadn't plucked up the courage to tell his brother about his feelings for her.

'I do want us to be upfront and out in the open,' he told her, 'but I must tread carefully. Kenny always was touchy and likely to fly off the handle at the slightest thing. I'd like to try and persuade him to take an interest in someone else before I spring it on him.'

Dena understood perfectly and was content to go along with whatever Carl thought best. Right now, she had more than enough change in her life to cope with: a new home, a new friend, a growing business, and a deliciously confusing new love in her life. She could ask for nothing more.

Chapter Thirty-Nine

The stockroom that Winnie rented at the market hall was duly cleaned out and tidied, and space made for Dena to work there for a few hours each day when she wasn't helping Winnie on the fabric stall. Trudy was trotting around into everything now, so it wouldn't be easy coping with a toddler, but Dena was determined to try. She thought that maybe it would be best if she left the playpen up in the stockroom, so she could pop Trudy in it when she was working.

Flushed with her Christmas profits, Dena visited the Manchester warehouses and bought the fabric she would need for the styles she'd designed for the coming spring and summer, then purchased a couple more sewing machines and began looking around for someone to help her.

Then one morning Joan Chapman popped her head round the corner of the fabric stall. 'I heard you were looking for someone to help with the dressmaking and I wondered if I'd fit the bill. I've done a bit in my time, making stuff for my own two girls, and for my nieces, but I'm willing to learn more. And to be honest, I'm sick and tired of baking pies for Belle Garside.'

Her round cosy figure was a familiar sight on the market, and Dena knew her for being hard-working and honest. Exactly what she needed. 'Joan, I'd love to have you on board but how would Belle cope without you? I don't want to be accused of poaching her staff.'

'She'll have to find someone else instead, won't she? Or get her own painted fingernails covered in dough for a change.'

Dena said, 'I'd have Trudy with me all day. And I'm still not married, so if that's a problem to a decent married woman such as yourself then...'

Joan interrupted her. 'I could start first thing Monday.'

'Right, you're on. I'll match what you were earning from Belle, and hope to improve on that as we go on.'

Joan beamed with pleasure. 'That'll do me nicely. And if you do start to expand, my sister might be interested in joining you as well. She's a dab hand with her Singer sewing machine.'

'I'll bear that in mind.'

'Eeh, I can't wait to get my hands on some lovely soft cotton instead of flour and fat. It'll be a real treat.'

Dena laughed. 'Don't you believe it! Your back will ache from all the bending you'll have to do over the machine, and your fingers will get sore and rough from being so often pricked by the needles. I hate it when I bleed on to a lovely piece of fabric I've just painstakingly stitched into place. Or if I'm so tired I can't think what I'm doing and put the left sleeve in the right armhole.'

'I'm sure I'll make mistakes of that nature at first,' Joan admitted. 'But don't worry, I'm a quick learner.'

'Just one more thing,' Dena said, her lovely young face creasing into a frown. 'How do you feel about having me for a boss? I'm a bit younger than you, after all.'

'Aye, but you're mighty clever with that needle, and with your designs. I've no problems with your age, Dena, or your circumstances, if you've none with mine. And you've got to be an improvement on our beloved Belle.'

It was later that same day that Belle Garside came over to express her displeasure, in no uncertain terms, over Dena pinching her staff. 'Not content with ruining my son's life, you're after damaging my business now, are you?'

'Belle, look, I'm sorry about this. It wasn't my idea. Joan approached me, not the other way round. She's looking for a change, that's all. It's nothing you've done, and I'm sure you'll find a replacement cook easily enough.'

'You and me both know that's not true. Nobody makes pies like Joan Chapman.'

'Molly Poulson does. She runs an entire business making excellent pies and puddings. Steak and kidney, minced beef, meat and potato, hot pot, you name it. You could always buy-in off her.'

'And lose most of my profit? Not flipping likely.' Belle wagged a scarlet nail dangerously close to Dena's face. 'Keep away from my family. I've had enough of you and your trouble-making. Do you hear me? Keep your hands off me and mine!'

–

Kenny believed that he'd thought of a way to soften Dena's heart and make her look more kindly upon him. It had risks attached but he was willing to try anything to win her over. He waited until she was settled in her new home then went knocking at Winnie's door to carefully explain how he wished to discuss a matter of great importance with her. Admittedly she didn't look too happy about him being there, but at least she allowed him over the threshold.

'If this is what I think it is, it would be better if we sent for Carl.'

Kenny looked at her. 'Why the hell would I want our Carl here?' He thought she looked bothered about something as she led him into the front parlour where there was evidence of baby stuff everywhere. It greatly irritated him, and he was forced to wait for several minutes while she carried the bath out to the kitchen to empty it, cleared away talc and bottles of lotion, baby clothes and toys. What messy creatures babies were, he thought, particularly when they started walking, as this one had. He made no offer to help but as Dena placed a kiss on the baby's head before carrying her upstairs to bed, he had great difficulty in restraining himself. He wanted to knock her away from the little brat, order her to kiss him for a change, to give him the love he surely deserved.

He was glad when she returned, her arms empty at last, leaving her free to concentrate on him. But some of his irritation must have shown in his voice because she flinched away from him as he approached.

'Look at you,' he said, 'a bag of nerves. Worn out by too much work and that child, I should imagine. Sit down for goodness' sake and take the weight off your feet. How can I talk to you while you're bobbing about all over the place?'

'It's all right, I can listen while I'm clearing away.' Then she started babbling on about her baby, all about how wonderful she was, and how she must leave the parlour door open so that she could hear if Trudy woke up. 'Mind you, she rarely does these days. She sleeps through the noise of my sewing machine, *Variety Bandbox* on the wireless, and everything. She sleeps in the big cot next to my bed, so she's always close by my side.'

Kenny didn't want to hear any of this.

Dena kept talking because she was feeling slightly edgy as she always did these days when Kenny was around. Had Carl told him about the kiss? Was that why he was here? She folded nappies, picked up Trudy's beaker, set it down then picked it up again, turning it round and round in her hands.

It was strange how her feelings for Kenny had changed so completely. From being utterly besotted she felt uncomfortable whenever he came near. It was his brother who fascinated her now. She and Carl had seen each other every night this last couple of weeks, and the more often they met, the more they wanted and needed each other.

She glanced at the little alarm clock she kept on the mantel-piece. Seven o'clock, still time to do an hour or two on the sewing machine, if only he would say what he had to say, and then leave without giving any trouble. Was that possible? At least Winnie was in the next room and would come if she called. She almost wished that Trudy would wake and cry: that might persuade him to go.

She was worrying unnecessarily. Maybe he had come to tell her that it was all right, that he'd no objection to her seeing Carl?

Oh, please let that be the case. Dena took a deep breath and stretched her lips into a smile. Best to get it over with as quickly as possible. 'So, what is it, this important matter you wish to discuss with me? I've got a lot of sewing to do so...'

'I've come to properly explain why I took you to see Maureen.'

Dena's heart sank. This was the last thing she'd expected or hoped for. 'Not that old chestnut again! I thought we were over all of that. It really isn't necessary to keep dragging up the past. I've put all of that stuff behind me now and so should you.'

'Well, I can't put it behind me. I need you to understand why I took you to see Maureen. You must listen to me, Dena. What I have to say is very important.' Kenny adopted a wounded, hurt expression; not meeting her gaze, hoping this would arouse her curiosity.

It seemed to do the trick as, giving a little sigh, she put down the baby's cup she'd been fiddling with and came to sit in the chair opposite. 'All right, get on with it. I'm listening.'

'It's because I know what it's like not to have a father.'

Dena frowned, not understanding. 'But Trudy does have a father. She has you, and I would have married you had it not been for your suggestion that I get rid of her. What sort of father would do that?'

Kenny became confused by her logic and struggled to get his story right in his head. It had all seemed so much less complicated when he'd worked it out earlier.

'What I mean is that I didn't want you to feel that you were being forced into marrying me. My real father didn't hang around, didn't want to I imagine. After he'd gone I had a succession of step-fathers, or at least various men in my mother's life. Not that any of them stayed very long either, so, like you, I know what it feels like to be rejected. And one of these men, I won't name him, did things to me. He hurt me.'

Dena was stunned, and then her heart went out to him. 'Oh, Kenny, no!'

He kept his head down, not meeting her gaze, fingers knotted tightly together, waiting for the rush of sympathy he knew would come. 'I've never told anyone about this before. I don't like talking about it even now, d'you see?'

'Yes, I do.' Dena came and sat beside him on the sofa, rested a hand on his shoulder. 'What did he do, this man? Did he beat you?'

Kenny had been trying to decide exactly what to tell her, and how much to say, then snatched gladly at her suggestion. He lifted his head and met her sympathetic gaze, his own deeply sorrowful. 'He was a real bully. Used me like a punchbag.'

'Kenny, that's dreadful. Did Belle know? Did she put a stop to it? Didn't she see the bruises? There must have been bruises. Didn't Carl do something to help?'

'They didn't know anything about it. He made sure the bruises didn't show and threatened he'd do worse if I told on him.'

'Well,' said Dena. 'These things happen, I suppose. Is that why you started to learn boxing with Barry, so you could stand up for yourself more? That was an excellent idea. You have to stand up to bullies.'

Kenny looked at her, studying her face to see if she was genuine in her sympathy. She didn't seem anywhere near as shocked or sympathetic as he'd hoped. Almost matter of fact, as if she just wanted him to say his piece and go. Kenny clenched his hands together and tried again. 'He'd take me down the cellar and give me a real pasting, and worse. Like I say, he did things that I can't ever talk about, not even after all this time.' And then his voice hardened to a deep, bitter note. 'He used me for his own twisted satisfaction. Touched me, and made me touch him.'

Kenny hadn't meant to go this far in his tale, the words had somehow sprung out of his mouth of their own volition. But now that they were out in the open, he saw with some satisfaction how she was stunned into silence, appalled by the picture conjured up by these few tragic sentences.

'Oh, Kenny, I don't know what to say.'

Dena was horrified. She understood the heartache caused by being abandoned and rejected, but how did a child feel when someone had abused them? When an adult they looked up to had taken advantage of their innocence? She thought of her own child and felt sick at the prospect. It really didn't bear thinking about. Filled with pity but unable to find the right words, she simply put her arms about Kenny and held him close.

They stayed like that for some little time while he breathed in the scent of her, feeling light-headed with relief. Being held close to her like this was blissful, and filled a deep need in his soul. Maybe she did care for him after all. All these years he'd kept this terrible truth bottled up inside himself, saying nothing to anyone, living with the shame of it, the knowledge of being dirty, of not being normal. He probably would never have mentioned the subject at all but for wanting to win over Dena. Who'd have thought that this would be the key to her heart? He felt so much better, almost as if he'd been cleansed in some way. Maybe he should play on her sympathy.

'How long did it go on?' she was asking him, her voice soft with pity.

'Too long.' He slid his arms about her waist and clung to her, letting his tears fall.

As he sobbed Dena held him, stroking his hair as if he were a child still. 'There, there, come on. You mustn't give in. The thing is not to let what happened ruin your life. The crime is this man's, not yours. You have to put it behind you. Otherwise evil has won, and that must never be allowed to happen. So chin up, blow your nose, and I'll make us a nice cup of tea. I've nothing stronger I'm afraid.'

She tried to get up but Kenny held fast to her, pleading with her not to leave him, his eyes swimming with tears, his face chalk-white, etched with pain. 'I know I made a mess of things between us but I only meant it for the best. I had to be sure that you really loved me and wanted to marry me, because I could never walk out on you, Dena. Once you take me on, you've got me for life.'

Dena looked at him, not following his logic. Was he saying that taking her to Maureen had been some sort of test because he didn't believe that she loved him, or that he still wanted to marry her, despite her leaving him at the altar. 'Kenny, I'm not sure!'

'Whether you can ever forgive me for what I did, I do understand, but now that I've told you all this stuff about myself you can understand me better, and why I need you so badly. Because you're the only person I truly love. I feel so much better when I'm with you, and I know that deep down you still love me. We're meant to be together, don't you see?'

Dena's sense of guilt and heartfelt sympathy for him caused her to hesitate. It was a bad mistake she instantly discovered.

Kenny became animated as he dashed the tears from his eyes. 'Look, why don't I take you some place grand to celebrate getting these horrors out of my head. I feel free, as if this is a new beginning. I can be better and more normal. You're the only one who truly understands me, Dena. Let me thank you, and take you out for a meal somewhere posh, as a treat. We'll go to the Midland. How would that do? This time I won't take no for an answer but don't worry, I'll behave myself. We don't want no more of them little blighters,' he said, jerking his chin at the ceiling, where the sleeping baby lay. 'This will be a very special date I shall remember always. I know you might still walk away after that, but your support means the world to me, Dena. Right now, having got all this business off my chest, I need it so much.'

Dena tried to protest but he closed her lips with the firm pressure of his fingers. How could she refuse?

Chapter Forty

Just one special date, Dena reminded herself as she got ready the very next evening. Not a commitment in any way for the future. She might very well be given the opportunity to explain about her feelings for his brother, and if Kenny gave her the slightest chance, she would take it. Surely Carl would be only too pleased if she did. Then she could walk away from Kenny once and for all, and having got those demons off his chest, he could find somebody else.

She hadn't seen Carl today, as Tuesday was the day he went round the warehouses to top up on his stock. And since he'd sold so much stuff over Christmas he'd warned her that it would be a long day, so he couldn't promise to be back in time to see her this evening either.

Dena had told him that it didn't matter as she intended to catch up on her sewing. Winnie agree to babysit and Dena felt bound to apologise for putting on her yet again.

'Nay, don't I love nothing more than to have this little treasure to myself for a change.'

In the event, Winnie didn't have her to herself at all. A knock on the door heralded another visit from Barry and he contentedly sat and watched as Winnie bathed the lively youngster.

'It must feel grand for you to have a young 'un in the house.'

'Aye, it does. I lost two of me own, you know.'

'Yes,' Barry said. 'I do know. I lost one too.'

Winnie looked up in surprise, just as she was slipping a clean nightgown over Trudy's head. 'Did you? I didn't know that.'

'Few folk do, not round here. It happened when I was living in Blackpool. I had a little girl, about Trudy's age, killed in a bombing raid. My wife too.'

'Oh, Barry, I'm so sorry.' Winnie paused to stare at him in horror. 'Why did you never say?'

'I don't like a fuss. Shall I put the kettle on, and make this little one her cocoa?'

Winnie beamed. 'Eeh, that'd be grand. Then when I've got her off to bed we could listen to *Ray's A Laugh*. I love Ted Ray, don't you?'

'Whatever you say, Winnie, whatever you say.'

–

As promised, Kenny took her to the Midland Hotel, and it was all hugely embarrassing because they absolutely refused to let him in. Unlike when he'd taken Alice, he'd dressed in his Edwardian get-up in the hope of impressing her, although Dena hadn't seemed too impressed, and the commissionaire at the door didn't even recognise him dressed like that. He just took one look and told Kenny to buzz off.

'No Teddy boys allowed in here,' the man announced in a booming voice, loud enough to turn heads and bring a deep flush of anger to Kenny's face and neck.

'What do you reckon I'm going to do? Contaminate the place with me drainpipes?'

'Be off with you afore I call the police.'

Dena tugged at Kenny's sleeve. 'Please don't make a scene. Let's go to the Italian. I love that food and we don't have to eat here.'

'Yes we do,' Kenny insisted. 'I've promised you dinner at the Midland, and you should have dinner here.' And he set off to march right in, dragging Dena with him. Unfortunately the commissionaire was big and brawny, and grasping hold of Kenny by his velvet collar picked him up easily and tossed him out on to the pavement where he fell in an ungainly heap.

'Be off with you! No doubt that's the kind of treatment you understand.'

Dena rushed to help him to his feet when another, more familiar voice said, 'What's going on here? Kenny, what the hell are you doing sprawled all over the pavement?'

Dena looked up with anguish in her eyes. Oh no, why did Carl have to turn up at precisely this moment? Wasn't he supposed to be out on a buying trip? 'It's not Kenny's fault. The commissionaire wouldn't allow us in.'

Carl glared disdainfully down at his brother. 'I'm not surprised, dressed like a prize idiot. And you were with him, were you?' A bitter accusation was strong in his tone.

Before Dena had the chance to reply, Kenny was on his feet dusting off his draped jacket, smoothing down the velvet flaps of his pockets and adjusting his bootleg tie. 'Aye, she is. I'm taking Dena out for a meal to celebrate our getting back together, then that idiot chucked me out.'

'Well, not exactly celebrating—' Dena began to say, but was allowed to go no further as Kenny interrupted her, demanding to know what Carl was doing here.

'I've just delivered some goods to the kitchen that they ordered before Christmas. I still have more deliveries to make so don't let me keep you. The pair of you must be keen to get on with your celebration.' And turning smartly on his heel, Carl strode away.

Dena watched him go with a terrible aching sadness in her heart.

–

After a largely sleepless night Dena was desperate to find Carl and explain how she'd been coerced into going out with Kenny. She also wanted to ask if this story he'd told her about being bullied and abused as a child, was correct, or simply one of his fantasies. Winnie had left for the market a good ten minutes ago, leaving Dena to wash up and tidy the kitchen. She rushed around, making sandwiches, putting nappies in to soak, gathering up her pile of sewing, at the same time trying to supervise Trudy eating her breakfast. The little girl was growing increasingly independent and had developed a desire to do everything for herself, which meant that it took twice as long.

'Eat your porridge there's a love. Mummy's in a bit of a rush this morning.' She was anxious to catch Carl before she started work.

Trudy gave her a placid grin, and turning her spoon upside down chuckled delightedly as porridge plopped on to the floor.

'Oh, no.' Dena snatched up a cloth to wipe it up, but couldn't help laughing when having watched her mummy clean the floor, Trudy did the same again. 'You're a right little monkey, you should eat your meal.'

Dena took the spoon and scooped up some porridge but Trudy turned her face away at the last moment so that it missed her mouth entirely and smeared all over her cheek. Dena groaned. It was clearly going to be one of those days. Finally, after an effort, she had Trudy fed and dressed and put her in the pram. She was getting far too big for it and Dena made a mental note to check out how much a pushchair would cost. The trouble was, with all the expense of Christmas and buying fabric for new stock, her savings were sadly depleted.

Dena negotiated the pram outside, piled high with sewing, as always, then had to run back in when she realised she'd forgotten her sandwiches.

It was a lovely bright winter's morning, with a sharp tang of frost in the air, and Champion Street already had that morning buzz to it as goods were being unpacked and laid out, canvas strapped into place and folk called out cheery greetings and ribald remarks to each other. Winnie would have her own stall open by now, and be wondering where she was. Dena was just about to lock the front door, her mind anxiously turning over what she would say to Carl, when a taxi drew up. As if this wasn't surprise enough, taxis being rare on Champion Street, Dena was astonished to see her mother step out of it. And with her came two suitcases.

'Mam, what's going on?' Dena eyed the suitcases with alarm. 'What's all of this?'

Alice paid the taxi driver and drew out yet another holdall before turning to Dena with a cool smile. 'I've come to stay with you for a bit. That's all right, I hope.'

'Stay with me, but you can't do that!'

'Why can't I? You're my daughter.'

'But this isn't my house. I'm only a lodger, and there's nowhere for you to sleep.' Dena didn't say that the last thing she wanted was for her mother to be under the same roof as herself and Trudy. But then she didn't get chance, as Alice was pushing open the door and marching down the lobby as if she owned the place.

Alice flung open the front parlour door, gave it a cursory inspection. 'You can sleep in here. Bit small but you'll manage. I'll have your bedroom. Where is it, at the front?'

Dena shook her head, bemused. 'No, the one at the back, but it's got Trudy's cot and everything in it.'

'Well, you'll have to move that out. I can't have my sleep disturbed by a screaming baby.'

'But I need space for my sewing and…'

Alice paused, halfway up the stairs. 'Your precious uncle and I have had a falling out so I decided I was no longer prepared to stay with him, and since you told me yourself you were moving in with Winnie, I thought I'd join you. You'd surely not see your old mum homeless? Fetch them suitcases in before someone runs off with all the possessions I have left in the world.'

And, sighing, Dena did as she was bid, closed the front door and followed her mother up the stairs.

-

It was half an hour later before Dena managed to extricate herself. And only then after a long argument over the fact that she absolutely refused to move a thing until she'd spoken to Winnie, saying that it wasn't her decision to make. By this time she was late for work so speaking to Carl would have to wait for another time.

Winnie, when she heard the news, was startled but resilient. 'She's your mam so we can hardly leave her to kip on the pavement. We'll all have to hutch up and make room.'

Particularly me, Dena thought. She was late getting out for her dinner break, feeling the need to make up to Winnie for taking an hour off that morning, and by the time she was free there was no sign of Carl. He had been there, Lizzie Pringle told her, but half an hour ago he'd packed away his stall and gone. Lizzie didn't know where.

She meant to go round to his house that evening but the entire time was taken up with moving cots, clothes and sewing equipment around, and making up beds. She felt so sad to have lost not only her bedroom and work space, but her privacy and independence. At one time she would have welcomed living with her mother, but not any longer. She'd grown used to her own freedom, and what had her mother ever done for her? It was typical of Alice that she'd chosen the larger of Dena's two rooms, even demanding that supper be brought up to her on a tray. Anything for a peaceful life, Dena thought. No mention had been made about her contributing a share of the rent. Dena spent a cramped and uncomfortable night among the muddle of her sewing equipment in the front parlour, with Trudy fretful over the change. Fortunately, because of her disturbed night on the sofa, she was first up the following morning and out of the house before her mother had stirred. Now she could at least put things right between herself and Carl. Heart in her mouth, Dena approached his stall.

Carl didn't even glance her way, although she could tell by the way he deliberately turned his back that he was well aware of her presence.

Dena felt sick. How stupid of her to allow Kenny to talk her into going out with him. Why hadn't she sympathised with his problems and left it at that? She should have stuck to her guns that it was all over between them, instead of trying to make him feel better about himself. As a result of this stupid, soft-hearted weakness on her part she'd damaged a growing relationship with

Carl at a very delicate stage, and would probably have Kenny calling round night after night and being a pest all over again.

She waited patiently for him to finish serving a young woman, for whom he was giving a long drawn-out demonstration of a new Hoover vacuum cleaner. He spread some dust on a strip of carpet then brushed it up with a dustpan and brush. Next he scattered more dust and this time used the vacuum cleaner to suck it all up. After that, he proved his case by showing how the dust was now safely in the bag and how easy it was to empty this into a dustbin. By the time the demonstration was complete he had an audience and one old woman called out, 'You had the dust in that bag already. It's a con trick.'

'I do assure you madam that it is no such thing,' Carl said in his most polite, salesman's voice. 'See, the carpet is perfectly clean, and all the pile neatly brushed up.'

The younger woman must have been convinced because she brought out her purse and purchased one there and then. 'I've been promising myself one of these things for months and now, at last, I can afford one, thanks to Champion Street Market.'

'You've been robbed, missus,' insisted the old woman.

Carl smiled confidently at the younger one. 'If you're not highly delighted with your purchase, please bring it back within seven days and you can have your money fully refunded. I'm sure you'll be pleased with it though, it's an excellent model.'

This offer so astonished his audience that he sold two more, including one to a young man who said his wife deserved a bit of help in the house. 'Good thinking, sir,' Carl grinned. 'Then she'll have more time to spend with you.'

Only when the crowd had dispersed, leaving the odd browser searching through his bargain box of wooden spoons, tin openers and nut crackers, did Dena take a deep breath and launch into her carefully prepared speech. 'Are you angry with me?'

'Sorry?' He looked at her blankly. 'I don't know what you're talking about.'

'Yes, you do. You've every right to be angry after what took place between you and me, I mean.' As Dena struggled to say what was on her mind, Carl kept on moving about his stall, dusting down the Tala kitchenware, tidying the packets of Lux Flakes and Eucryl tooth powder, neatly stacking the Nugget shoe polish and constantly improving the displays.

Dena lost patience. 'Will you please stand still and let me explain?'

Carl glanced at her, his brows raised in polite disinterest. 'I really don't think there's much point, as you're perfectly entitled to go out with whoever you please. And I can see the attraction of dinner at the Midland. I doubt I could equal such a treat, not on a regular basis. Obviously my young brother must have greater resources than I, or else he holds the key on how to win your heart.'

'Oh, for heavens sake, stop being so pompous. He came to see me last night and I felt it difficult to refuse when he talked me into it.'

Carl pressed a hand to his chest. 'Ah, yes, I can see how pity for his lovelorn soul could easily sway you into accepting an expensive meal, even with a man you claim has been harassing you for weeks on end.'

'Stop talking like a clichéd character out of *The Scarlet Letter* and listen to me please, Carl, without interrupting. I need to explain...'

He turned away to serve a customer. 'Thank you, madam, that will be two and sixpence. Lovely day, isn't it now that the snow has gone and the sun is shining? Never put the cheese grater away wet, or it'll go rusty. Here you are, just two bob for you, a special offer as I see you each week. Happy New Year! Oh, Dena, are you still here? I thought you'd have gone by now. What was it you wanted to say to me again?'

Dena turned on her heel and stamped away.

Chapter Forty-One

Kenny had shrugged off the embarrassing incident as of no account and was happily organising the purchase of a new consignment of burglar alarms. He meant to start the new year on a high note, and sell twice as many per week as before. Things were going well for him at last. He had regular money coming in each month as a result of his security business, and his mother's plan to provide cover for this more risky venture was now nicely in place with the legitimate trade he was building up selling burglar alarms. He'd sold half a dozen already. Easy money!

Best of all, Dena seemed to have finally decided to stop being difficult. He intended to take her to the flicks tonight. He wanted to see Jayne Mansfield in *The Girl Can't Help It*. He wouldn't mind rock 'n' rolling with Jayne Mansfield, so he would enjoy the film even if Dena didn't. Not that he'd told her yet that they were going, but he'd no reason to suppose she'd refuse. And later, if he kept her in a good mood, who knew how far they might rock and roll together? This was a new beginning for them both. Before January was out he'd have her in his bed or his name wasn't Kenny Garside. By summer he'd have her standing at the altar as his wife, and he'd be a happy man.

He was mortified when Dena turned him down, claiming she had too much work to do, as was ever her excuse. Some yarn about her mother moving in so that she needed to sort out furniture and her sewing stuff to make proper space.

'Well, how about tomorrow then?' Kenny said, irritated at having his plans spoiled and not really interested in her domestic arrangements, although he did feel pride in the fact that he was the one who'd helped her and Alice get back together.

'No thanks, Kenny! Going out with you the other night may have been a mistake. I'm sorry about your troubles, and I'll always be ready to listen if you want to talk any time. But that's all. Like I keep telling you, it's over between us. I'm not your girl any longer.'

He stared at her blankly, not taking in a word she said, he smiled. 'You're excited over your mam moving in, aren't you? This isn't the right time to talk about us, and you think you might lose me. That's what's bothering you, eh? Don't fret, as you won't lose me. I can wait. I'm a patient man.'

'Oh, for goodness sake, Kenny, why won't you listen? It's over. I'm sorry, but there it is.' She walked into the house and closed the door, leaving him standing on the pavement looking a complete nincompoop.

Women, he thought, what a pet they got into over nothing. It was a shame though, about him missing the picture. He'd been looking forward to drooling over Jayne Mansfield. Still, he could always ring Jenny, she might be available. Dena would come round in the end, as she had before, once things settled down between her and her mother. Right now, she was obviously tired and feeling a bit fraught.

He started to stroll away, and brightened as a new thought struck him. At least Alice was handy now that she'd moved into Champion Street. That was a bit of good news. Kenny licked his lips at the prospect of continuing to enjoy the mother, only until he finally got his hands on her luscious daughter. What would Dena think if she ever got wind of this little dalliance with her mam? Happen it would be a good thing if she did. She'd be green with jealousy. It might stop her taking him so much for granted.

Kenny got out his comb and began to preen himself. Dena was only playing hard to get, he could tell. She wouldn't be able to resist him for much longer. She was weakening already. Why else would she have agreed to go out for a meal with him to the Midland Hotel? He pushed back his padded shoulders and swaggered off, chuckling at his own cleverness.

Kenny was determined to pay no attention to Dena's little outburst. His chief concern now was that he must make enough money to buy them a decent house. He had no intention of living with his mam longer than was absolutely necessary. He wouldn't enjoy that any more than Dena would. His monthly trawl of the stalls to collect his dues took no time at all, apart from the usual haggle with Alec Hall and Sam Beckett.

'There's no need to pay security to you any more,' Sam announced. 'Joe has asked the police to keep a better watch on the place. He's even talking about employing a security guard to occupy the building at night.'

'I wouldn't rely on Joe Southworth, if I were you. He'll be history by the spring. My mam will be in charge by then, and can rely on your vote, I trust, Sam?'

'She'll never manage to get elected.'

'I wouldn't be too sure about that. There are ways and means.'

'Well, count me out. Joe's also promised to speak to the council about the litter problem, and enquire about the possibility of extending the market. He's getting his act together at last, so I'll stick with the devil I know. Besides, I don't care for all this talk of Belle's about putting up the charges. I'm paying a fair whack as it is. I can't afford any more.'

'I doubt you can afford not to, security being the problem that it is. 'Course, if you want to take the risk of something nasty happening, that's up to you.' Kenny allowed his voice to taper off, finishing with a sad little smile. 'Neither Joe Southworth nor any new security guard, if he ever gets round to employing one can guarantee that your stall will remain safe.'

There was a small silence. 'That sounds very like a threat.'

'Sounds more like common sense to me.' Kenny slid the bicycle chain from his pocket and swung it nonchalantly about, twining it between his fingers as a menacing smile played about his lips. 'Still, like I say, it's up to you.'

The following morning he called on Sam again, commiser-ating him over the sad fact that during the night someone had broken in and wrecked an expensive display of light fittings. 'These terrible things will keep on happening. You're so unlucky,' Kenny sympathised.

Sam paid up, as did Alec Hall. No one else had the courage to defy him, not even big Molly Poulson who glowered over her stack of meat pies at him as she peeled off notes with her podgy fat fingers.

The Higginson sisters were easy meat, more than willing to hand over several pounds in cash, including the cost of a new burglar alarm.

'We're still having trouble you see, Kenny,' Annie complained in her high-pitched whine. 'Some months we have no bother at all, yet just before Christmas we were broken into twice. The thieves stole several of our best hats and all the Christmas takings from that little safe I'd had fitted under the counter. It's so distressing. How do they even get into the building, that's what I'd like to know? I mean, the council has had a wrought iron gate fitted, in addition to the old Victorian doors.'

Kenny had been annoyed about the gate. It had taken some considerable effort on his part, and no small amount of clever negotiating with his mother, to get his hands on the key for it. It did prove that her sleeping with that old po-face came in handy now and then. Joe never noticed that she'd borrowed it and Kenny had a copy cut that same night. His mam had slipped it neatly back in the pocket of Joe's trousers long before he thought to put them on again. Far too interested in getting his leg over to pay proper attention.

Kenny smiled at the two sisters and sadly shook his head. 'There are windows on the upper floor, so it wouldn't be too much trouble for a clever thief to shimmy up a drainpipe.'

'Who would think of doing such a thing?' said Clara, round-eyed.

'Someone utterly ruthless and heartless, which is why you need me, dear ladies. I do hope you can afford to pay the full amount this month. After what you've just told me, you can't risk any more bad luck, can you? Oh, and I'd change the combination on that safe, if I were you. Now, let's think of a more complicated number this time. When are your birthdays?'

'Oh, Kenny,' Annie fluttered. 'What would we do without you?'

They handed over the money sweet as you please. It was really ridiculously easy.

—

Dena decided to hold a fashion show in the spring. Apart from being good for business, she thought that it might be good for her too. It would give her something else to think about besides Carl. The misery of losing him was tearing her apart. She should have realised from the start that it couldn't possibly work between them. They'd never been anything but at odds since they'd first met years ago. Just because they'd taken a shine to each other in the excitement of a New Year's Eve dance didn't mean they could hope to have any sort of future together. They'd have been at each other's throats in no time.

All the same she missed him dreadfully, missed his wry smile, the dangerous excitement of his kisses, and the tender way he held her in his arms. Dena couldn't seem to get him out of her mind. The only way she could cope was to devote every waking minute to making clothes for a spring show. That way she'd be so exhausted at the end of the day, she'd at least get some sleep.

The January afternoon was quiet, most folk having spent up over Christmas and she and Winnie were taking it in turns to mind the stall. This was Dena's afternoon for duty while Winnie had volunteered to do some baking and catch up with the ironing. She had no idea what her mother found to do all day, beyond sit in her room and read magazines. It never seemed to occur to Alice to help with any of the chores. Even Dena's request that she might sometimes mind Trudy, had been met with a strident refusal.

'It's not my place to babysit bastards.'

Dena had nearly bitten her tongue off in her efforts to keep quiet after that remark, but was determined not to fall out with Alice. A part of her resented her mother's presence, feeling it was too late for them to mend fences. She'd preferred it when there'd just been herself and Winnie and Trudy in the house, living companionably together. But then Dena would be filled with guilt. She really shouldn't feel this way about her mother. Wasn't this the perfect opportunity for them to get to know each other better and learn to be friends, as she had always wanted? It would just take a little time.

Dena settled herself in a corner with a notepad and pencil and began to make plans for her fashion show. She could hold it at the co-operative rooms. They wouldn't charge too much, surely. She'd need to make posters and stick them up all around the market. That wouldn't be too difficult. The biggest problem would be finding girls to model the clothes. Now who did she know who was still speaking to her? Besides Gwen, that is.

So many of her old friends had drifted away. Some had married while others simply ignored her. Not that she allowed herself to worry about that. She had her regular customers, the ones who came time after time to buy her skirts and dresses. A thought occurred to her. Why not ask a few of them to act as mannequins? At least they liked her stuff.

Although there were times when Dena pondered on how different life could have been if she'd never got involved with Kenny Garside, in the main she was content with her lot. She'd seen him only once since the evening he'd come round trying to bully her into going to the pictures with him to see Jayne Mansfield, one of his favourite actresses apparently. And didn't she know why? Dena had thought she'd managed to put him off for good, but no. He turned up again like a bad penny, just a few nights later.

This time she'd been sensible enough not to let him through the door, and, in the end, hearing voices raised in anger, Winnie had come to stand beside her to offer support. Arms folded across her plump little body she'd given him a mouthful. 'Your problem lad is that you don't know how to take no for an answer.'

'You keep your face out of my business,' Kenny rudely responded.

'Don't talk to Winnie like that.' Dena scolded. 'I'm not coming out with you again, not ever. No matter how much you might try to convince yourself otherwise, I'm not your girl, and that's final.'

Winnie jabbed a finger in his chest just below his Dodge City string tie. 'Don't start with your threats, you, or come round pestering Dena any more, do you hear? Or we'll have the police on you for harassment.' She slammed the door in his face. 'That'll larn him,' she remarked, deep satisfaction in her tone.

'I very much doubt it.'

Now Dena chewed on her pencil, worrying over whether he had indeed learned to take no for an answer. Kenny Garside seemed to have a knack of only hearing what he wanted to hear.

By the time the market hall clock struck five, she was pulling down the shutters and snapping the padlocks into place. She'd had a most profitable afternoon, if not in custom, at least with regard to plans for her spring show, and she felt excited and optimistic about the future. She'd spent hours browsing through a new pile of magazines from Abe's stall, sketching new styles, as well as going over plans for the show itself.

It had been hard at first to keep her mind on the task in hand as it kept straying back to Carl, and she'd often found herself staring into space, drawing nothing, seeing only his face. In the end she'd made a vow not to allow herself to think about him, nor to dream of him any more. Her relationship with both Garside boys was over, never to be referred to again.

Making this decision brought immense pain. Just the thought of not seeing Carl again tightened her chest, leaving her breathless. Right now, if she let her mind dwell on him too much, she would weep for what she'd lost. She gave no sign of her distress when she called goodnight to Molly Poulson, to Alec Hall and the Higginson sisters. At least she could hold on to her pride.

Most of the other traders had already packed up and gone home, Dena noticed, even Barry Holmes. The outside market was deserted, but then it was far too cold to hang about waiting for customers, who, if they'd any sense, would be snug by their firesides on a bitterly cold day like this. She gave a cheery wave to Lizzie Pringle who was locking up the Chocolate Cabin just as Dena left the building. 'Bye, Lizzie.'

'Bye Dena, take care.'

In her basket she'd got half a dozen crumpets to toast for their tea and she set off down the street with a spring in her step, if not in her heart. It was as she passed the last empty stall that she heard the snap of a footstep on ice behind her, and realised she was being followed. She swung about, alarmed. 'Oh, Carl, I didn't realise it was you behind me. You scared me half to death.'

'I'm sorry, only I needed to speak to you.'

'What about?' Dena managed to calm herself, wanting to keep her manner slightly cool. After all, he'd made it very plain that he was no longer interested in her, and she'd vowed never to think about him any more.

'It occurred to me that maybe I'd been a bit dismissive of you earlier by not even allowing you to explain.'

'Really?'

He smiled, not in the least put off by her icy tone. 'I got to thinking that it is my brother we're talking about, and I, more than anyone, should understand how "persuasive" he can be. Beneath that gentle charm, he's really something of a bully. So can we talk?'

Dena couldn't help but return the smile. 'All right, why not?' What did she have to lose?

Chapter Forty-Two

They sat in the corner of a coffee bar sipping espresso steam-frothy coffee out of glass cups. Carl offered to buy her a sandwich or slice of cake but Dena really didn't feel like food right now. Her heart was too full, the fear inside too hard to bear. Would he forgive her for going out with Kenny, or use the date as further proof of her loose morals? The Seeburg jukebox was playing Ronnie Hilton singing 'No Other Love' and Dena's stomach clenched. In her heart she felt that to be true of herself and Carl. She'd been so certain they had something special between them, although he may think differently.

His first words, therefore, were a delicious shock. 'I thought we had something special, you and me.'

'Oh Carl, that's just what I was thinking!' He still wasn't smiling though, and Dena took a deep breath. 'Will you let me explain? It will have to be quick, as they'll be expecting me home.'

Carl agreed and before she'd got halfway through retelling Kenny's tale of abuse, his mouth had tightened to a thin line, jaw set rigid, every muscle of his face taut with anger. 'I should've realised that something was badly wrong. He seemed to change for no reason when he was about nine or ten, suddenly withdrawing into himself and going all quiet and peculiar. He was only a young lad and we thought he was simply going through a difficult phase.'

'Oh, Carl, I'd forgotten that Kenny had kept it a secret from you. But you can surely understand why. He feared that it might get worse if he told.'

'Did he say who it was, which of Mam's many man friends did those terrible things to him?'

Dena shook her head. 'I'm afraid not. But by the time he'd finished relating what was obviously a painful story for him, I didn't have the heart to refuse when he suggested we go out for a meal to celebrate getting these horrors out into the open at last. That's how he described it. Why he now feels free and cleansed.'

'Poor Dena, I can see it would be very difficult for you to refuse after that. But then you're too soft-hearted for your own good.' Carl touched her cheek, cradling it in the palm of his hand and she leaned into it.

'Do you forgive me?'

'How could I not? Dena, you know what this means, don't you? I simply can't tell him about us, not just yet. He'll think you've deserted him because of what he's told you, and the guilt of it will hurt him even more.'

'Oh, I hadn't thought of that.' Dena was mortified. The situation seemed to go from bad to worse. 'But I still don't want to go out with him.'

'All I'm saying is that he needs to be let down gently. You must go on saying no, explaining that it's got nothing at all to do with what he told you, but that you can't change your mind just because of something that happened to him years ago. So long as he doesn't see you with anyone else for a while he'll soon grow bored and take up with one of his old flames again.'

'I wouldn't bank on it.'

''Course he will. And once he's done that, we can tell him the truth about us.'

'Does that mean I won't see you in the meantime?' The record had finished, to be followed by Tab Hunter and 'Young Love'.

Carl groaned. 'How could I bear it? There's no way I could stop seeing you. We'll just have to keep our meetings secret. We can manage that for a few weeks, can't we? I'll try to encourage Kenny to start seeing other girls, Jenny or Jeannie, or whoever. Once he has another girl dangling, then we can confess and he won't feel so let down. You know what a show off he is.'

Dena was so relieved that he liked her, and that he still wanted to see her, she didn't bother examining the details of the plan too closely. Something warm and delicious was unfurling inside her. He did still care for her, after all. She hadn't lost him.

'Oh, yes, Carl. I'm sure everything will be fine. We can keep our feelings secret for a little longer.'

—

Winter continued to bite and a stroll in the park or along the canal towpath was, of necessity, short, and fraught with the fear of discovery. But no matter what the risk, they had to see each other. The very thought that Carl might pop over to the fabric stall to chat with her between customers left Dena feeling constantly sick with anticipation. She only had to see his familiar figure striding towards her for her heart to start performing emotional somersaults. She was often tempted to find any lame excuse to linger by Carl's stall, eager to share a few precious moments with him. Dena felt so alive when they were together, as if a part of her was singing.

These precious stolen moments brought pleasure to them both. The two lovers would always have to be well wrapped in woollies and coats, scarves and hats on their long walks, more often than not accompanied by Trudy. Fortunately she was too young to reveal their secret, but her presence allowed little opportunity for lovemaking beyond a few lingering kisses. She could only hope and pray that Kenny would be too busily occupied selling burglar alarms to notice them.

Dena loved to touch his hand to feel an ache of yearning fire. Even the touch of his warm breath on her cheek would make her instinctively turn to him, her mouth moist and ready, eyes dazed with longing. She longed to have him love her but knew that if ever they started to kiss, they would surely never be able to stop, and strove to be content that at least they were together. Carl even seemed to have taken to Trudy. He would tickle and tease the little girl, bounce her up on to his broad shoulders and give her piggy backs, galloping along, making her laugh out loud in delight.

Sometimes, of an evening, Carl would call at Winnie's place to see how she was, although he never came in as it didn't seem right when it wasn't Dena's house. She too was nervous of her mother spotting him, because Dena and Alice had more than sufficient grounds for argument and confrontation, and she really didn't want to give her the excuse for any more.

They would stand at the door chatting, huddled together against the cold as they sneaked a few kisses and exchanged a few whispered words of love; Carl constantly glancing over his shoulder to make sure they were unobserved.

Dena was running out of excuses to keep Kenny at bay, had refused countless offers to go with him to the pictures or to a dance, and both herself and Carl knew that this situation couldn't go on for much longer.

Kenny too would often stroll over to the stall, interrupting when she was trying to help a customer choose a dress pattern or fabric, or else chatting in a big loud voice while she measured out a curtain length. It was so annoying and he paid not the slightest attention as she tried to shush him or make him go away so that she could concentrate. He would appear at her side when she was least expecting him, often insisting on walking her home, even the few yards down the street from the market. When, on one occasion, Dena told him that she really didn't need an escort, the next day she became aware of him trailing some distance behind her, most disturbing.

Following this experience, she plucked up the courage to carefully and tactfully remind Kenny that while she appreciated being the one he had chosen to confide his troubles to, nothing, in fact, had changed between them. Just in case he hadn't been paying attention the last time she'd explained all of this.

'Nothing's changed, Dena. You're still my girl,' was his stubborn response, and he continued to speak of their "fresh start", of how much she'd helped him to shake off the troubles of his past.

'Oh, Kenny, if only you would listen. You wouldn't want me to go out with you simply out of pity, would you? It really is time you found yourself someone new who you deserve to be loved by.'

But he just laughed and shook his head, then with a sly grin casually reminded her that she was, after all, the mother of his child. Dena came close to hating him in that moment.

–

Being confined to the house with her mother's constant presence became something of a problem. Alice's habit for caustic remarks had not diminished in the slightest and she would constantly find fault with Winnie, let alone Dena. Either it was too warm in the house, or it was too cold. She couldn't see to read her *Woman's Own*, or the overhead electric light was hurting her eyes. She considered having an indoor bathroom a great boon, claiming it was what she'd come to expect after living with her brother in Chorlton, but really didn't care for the green linoleum.

'Blue and cream is so much more sophisticated.'

'Why didn't you stay at your brothers then?' Winnie asked. 'Since his lino is so much better than mine.'

And when Winnie bought a new Cannon cooker for her tiny kitchen, Alice said it was a waste of money and refused to touch it.

It was true that even Winnie was having problems with it. She would put a pan on one of the twirly rings and they'd all sit waiting for their supper to cook before realising that nothing was happening because she'd switched on the wrong ring. Or they'd suddenly smell burning because Winnie had again underestimated how much electricity could cook a stew in comparison with the old solid fuel kitchen range, and had turned up the heat too high.

And then she burned her hand on the hot hob and Alice claimed that the new cooker was a dangerous piece of equipment, and should be removed.

'It's my house, my cooker, and I think it's glorious,' said Winnie stoutly. 'I'll fettle the damn thing, don't you worry. Marguerite

Patten says it'll take a twenty pound turkey, what more could you ask for?'

Dena had to giggle at this. 'I don't think we'll ever need to cook a twenty pound turkey, Winnie.'

'That's not the point,' Winnie said, grinning nonetheless. 'And it's so much cleaner than all that dust we used to suffer, so we must just get used to it. All of us!'

'Good gracious me! You can't possibly expect me to cook,' Alice said, looking shocked.

'I don't see why not. This isn't a hotel, tha' knows.'

At which point Dena crept away. She would try to avoid her mother by spending more time sewing in the front parlour, now doubled as her bedroom, claustrophobic though that might be. During the long cold winter, Dena had returned to the shop where she'd rented the radio and this time asked to rent a television set. The young man clearly remembered her for he asked if she had a husband yet. 'Actually no, I haven't, and my father is dead but a friend will sign your form, if you insist upon it.'

'The law has not changed,' stated the young man, pompously.

'Silly me, not appreciating that only married people can rent TV sets.'

At least having the television gave them momentary respite from Alice's constant carping, though she did still manage to find fault with jolly Jimmy Edwards in *Whack-O!* and even with *Muffin the Mule*, complaining that she could see the puppet's strings.

'Does it matter?' Dena remarked, thinking that if poor *Muffin the Mule* couldn't get it right, what hope had she got?

–

It was one Sunday afternoon after Dena had been talking to Carl for some time at the door, making their lingering farewells, when Winnie took her to one side and said, 'Why don't you ask your young man in? He could stop for tea maybe. Your mam's gone out for tea to the Midland, living it up again, so you're safe.'

Dena gazed at her in alarm. 'What young man?'

'Nay lass, I'm not blind. Those lovely cheeks of yours aren't flushed a rosy pink just because of this cold weather. He's all right is Carl, let the lad come in. Apart from anything else, you'll catch your death standing at that door, as well as entertaining half the neighbours.'

'No one can see us, we've been most careful.'

Winnie gave her an old-fashioned look. 'Aren't you aware how your little face lights up whenever he comes near? And at the market you snatch any opportunity to do a walkabout, taking twice as long as normal to post a letter or fetch us a sandwich, just so's you can stop and have a chat with him on the way back. Don't think I haven't noticed, and if I've guessed how things are between you, then others must too.'

'Oh, Winnie, I hope Kenny hasn't. We're trying so hard not to hurt him. If I could only convince him that it's all over between us, but he simply won't listen.'

'Well, this isn't the way to go about it. If neither you nor Carl are prepared to tell him, then someone else will do that task for you, sure as night follows day.'

'Oh, goodness, we never considered that possibility.'

'Then it's long past time you did. Go on, the poor lad will only be halfway down the road by now. Go and fetch him back and give him a hot cuppa at least.'

Dena ran, catching up with Carl just as he was about to turn the corner into Hardman Street. He was at once alarmed by the sight of her, all out of breath and rosy with excitement.

'Dena, what is it, what's happened?' His reaction seemed to indicate how much they were living on their nerves.

'Winnie says you're to come to tea. Will you? Apparently I light up, presumably like a firework, whenever you come near.' Dena giggled.

Carl couldn't help but laugh. 'Then I'd best come at once. It could be utterly entertaining watching you go off like a Roman candle, or do you whizz round like a spinning wheel?'

'My head is spinning right now. Winnie thinks we should tell Kenny together, and confront him with the truth.' He gathered

333

her face in his hands so that he could kiss her. 'Do you think we should?'

'Oh, not yet, let's not think about Kenny. We'll just be normal and have tea.'

Hand in hand they ran back to Winnie's house, so wrapped up in each other they didn't even see a shadowed figure slip back into a doorway.

Chapter Forty-Three

It was wonderful to sit in her parlour with Carl. They'd enjoyed one of Winnie's special Sunday teas of boiled ham and salad, then together they'd put Trudy to bed, Carl helping by reading the little girl a story while Dena warmed her cocoa. Now they sat cuddled together on the sofa in the front room, which also doubled as Dena's bed, a fire blazing in the hearth and the little girl fast asleep in her cot beside them.

'I think this could go to my head, having you all to myself. Maybe I'll be the one going off like a fire cracker, whooping with delight.'

Dena giggled and kissed his chin, all she could reach nestled so close to his chest.

There was a long silence and then he said, 'I suppose you do realise that I love you.'

Something turned over inside her, and then there really was an explosion of pure joy, just like fireworks, going off in her head. 'Oh Carl, and I love you too.'

He kissed her soft mouth, the arch of her throat, caressing her silky skin and holding her tightly to him as if he might never let her go. She made no protest when he slid open the buttons of her blouse, and she helped him with the fastening of her bra, her heart beating so fast she could hardly breathe. 'I'm not sure we should be doing this.'

'I love you,' cupping her face in his hands to kiss her some more. He was a gentle and considerate lover and when he kissed the buds of her breasts, their passion ignited. Dena couldn't remember ever experiencing anything more wonderful. His tender touches, his kisses, melted her heart. Her own fingers had pulled open Carl's shirt, were exploring the hard plain of his chest, running up into the wiry curls of his hair. More than anything Dena wanted him to make love to her. Whatever she had felt for Kenny had been nothing but calf love compared to this.

And the thought came to her that if she wanted to let him, she could. Why not? It would not be out of rebellion this time, but from pure love. Surely there could be no better reason for giving herself to a man?

But then she remembered Trudy, sleeping so innocently beside them, and knew that it wouldn't be right. She didn't care that people still turned their back on her, but how it hurt when they did that to her baby. She'd been a child herself when she'd got pregnant. But she was now a woman.

Hot and tousled Dena pulled herself free and sat back to smile at him, her breathing shallow and rapid, eyes glazed with desire. 'We have to stop this. You know we do as it's going a bit fast.' She thought he might be annoyed with her for stopping him, but he only grinned.

'You're right, as always. The last thing I want is to rush you, or hurt you in any way, dear Dena.'

'Oh, Carl.' She felt cherished and loved, deeply secure, knowing that they did indeed belong together. 'I'm sorry, only I daren't take the risk, not after – you know.'

'You don't have to explain, I understand. I got a bit carried away.'

She lay in his arms and he stroked her hair, both breathing deeply, trying to contain their emotion.

'I do want to have children with you, Dena, but I agree, this isn't the best way. We'll wait until after we're married. You will marry me, won't you Dena?'

She looked up at him, her face a rosy glow of delight. 'Oh Carl, I would like nothing better. But I already have a child. What about Trudy? Do you mind that she isn't yours?' Dena asked the question shyly, her heart in her mouth, knowing she could never marry a man who couldn't love her child as much as she did.

His reply came, sure and firm. 'I don't mind. Kenny has never seemed particularly interested in being a dad. He would hopefully give permission for me to adopt Trudy, so that I can be a proper father to her. I'd like that very much.'

For a long moment no more words were possible as she wept silent tears of joy on his shoulder. 'I can't believe this is happening. It's all so wonderful, so unexpected, just like a fairy tale.' Dena scrubbed at her eyes, tried to restore order to her tumbled curls, to calm the emotion bubbling inside. 'I love you so much and yet you were once so grumpy towards me. So bad tempered and mean.'

Carl laughed, still with that dangerous glitter in his dark blue eyes. 'I think I've always loved you, and hated to see you with Kenny.'

'You were jealous?'

'I'm afraid so.'

Dena was at last convinced that she was loved, and most content to be so. 'We should tell him. Shall we do it together, as Winnie suggests?'

Carl shook his head. 'No, I'll do it. I owe him that much at least. I don't want you upset by this any more than necessary.'

'When will you do it?'

'Soon, don't worry. It'll be fine.'

And she snuggled close, deeply content, not imagining for a moment that everything by then might well have changed.

–

Alice still wasn't making things easy for Dena, nor for Winnie, who revealed herself as having the patience of a saint, for all she frequently claimed that she'd gladly throttle Alice if she could.

'She leaves her laundry in a bag at her bedroom door, just as if I'm the flaming maid. Where does she think she is, the Midland Hotel? And that's another thing. Not that it's any of my business but do you know how often she goes there? Teas, lunches, she must be spending a small fortune feeding her face in that place.'

'Really?' Dena was startled, wondering where on earth her mother got the money.

Winnie lowered her voice as she slapped a plate on the draining board for Dena to dry. 'I don't wish to probe and you can tell me to mind me own business, but is she paying her share of your rent?'

Dena shook her head, looking thoughtful. 'No, but if she can afford to treat herself to meals at the Midland, maybe it's time we had a little chat.' She chose to broach the subject that evening, as soon as supper had been cleared away. Guessing what was coming Winnie made herself scarce. 'I'll go and read a story to our little treasure. You can put your feet up and have a rest for a change.'

Dena took a deep breath, knowing this wasn't going to be easy. 'I was wondering, Mam, how long you were thinking of stopping? Because if it was going to be for quite a while, I thought maybe you'd consider making a donation towards your keep.'

'You want me to pay rent, for staying with my daughter? I've never heard of such a thing.'

'You aren't staying with me, not strictly speaking. This is Winnie's house and it all costs money to run. Coal, electric, gas, and I know we're off rationing now. But that chicken pie you've just eaten still has to be paid for, and even the crinkle cut chips take time and effort.'

'Crinkle cut chips? I never saw anything so common in my life.'

'They're not common but most sophisticated. Winnie likes to keep up with fashion. She's planning on having the kitchen done up, new cupboards with formica tops and everything, to go with the new Cannon cooker, and the Hoover Twin Tub she's recently bought. But Winnie isn't here to do your laundry, or wait on you hand, foot and finger. You can learn to use it yourself, Mam, it's not difficult.'

Alice's jaw dropped. 'You want me to operate that thing? Never! I won't lower myself to use any new fangled machine. I wash everything by hand.'

'No, you don't. You get other people to do your laundry for you. Well, that's fine, but you'll have to pay for it in future. It's only fair!'

'Really? I never thought to hear a daughter of mine say such things to her mother. I must say you've turned greedy and selfish. I suppose it's got something to do with this new man friend of yours.'

Dena went cold, and tactfully remarked. 'What are you talking about? I don't have any new man.'

Alice lowered her chin so that she could peer condescendingly down at her daughter from above her spectacles. 'I saw you the other day walking with a man. It was raining and he was all muffled up, and I wasn't near enough to see who he was, but I saw him kiss you. Really, Dena, you are so cheap.'

'I'm not staying here to listen to this.' Dena was on her feet, ready to make a dash for it, thankful that Carl must have been too muffled up in coat and scarf for her mother to recognise him. Nevertheless, Alice was determined to have the last word.

'I should think the way you're going on, you'll have a house full of bastards before you're done.'

Emotion welled up in her throat and for a second Dena was a child again, constantly belittled and criticised and put upon by her dreadful mother, and then she heard Trudy's laughter from the front room where Winnie was reading her a story. Dena remembered that she was a mother herself now, a young woman not a child, and really didn't have to tolerate this kind of bad mouthing.

'Mam, that's the last time you use that word in this house or I'll personally throw you out of it. Do you understand?' Dena turned away in disgust, but then remembered the point of their discussion. 'Oh, and your share of the rent will be fifteen shillings. I'll let you off back rent, you can think of that as a holiday with your daughter but from now on rent is due on a Friday, right?'

'Well, I never!' said Alice. 'Over my dead body.'

Dena actually laughed out loud. 'If you don't start doing your own laundry I reckon Winnie might oblige you with that too, free and gratis.'

–

Dena managed to avoid spending too much time in the proximity of her mother by concentrating entirely upon sewing her new designs in preparation for the fashion show. The co-op had agreed to loan her their rooms for a modest fee and the local paper had promised to come along and do a piece on the show, even take a few photos. The resulting publicity, Dena knew, would be good for trade and hopefully bring in a rush of new orders. She had a dream of supplying other retail outlets, besides Winnie's stall, now that she had Joan to help her. The show would be her best chance to gain new orders.

For weeks now she'd spent half of every day up in the eerie of Winnie's stockroom, squeezed into a corner with Joan, the pair of them whirring the machines so fast they barely had time to draw breath let alone chat.

Today, however, it was bitterly cold on the market, snow and flu were rife. It was turning into an epidemic with several of the stallholders off work, including Joe Southworth and Belle Garside, which was giving his wife Irma pause for thought. Winnie had been sneezing her head off all morning and Dena insisted she go home early and get the fire going. 'Take a couple of aspirin and keep yourself warm. I'll mind the stall and see that it's all locked up safely.'

'I'll take little Trudy home with me then, shall I?' Winnie offered. 'I can keep an eye on her while she plays on the rug and I sit and feel sorry myself.'

Dena laughed. 'All right, but don't give her your cold, will you?' She'd given up all hope of her mother helping, considering herself blessed to have Winnie as a friend.

'If you'll tell me how to avoid it, I'll see that I don't.'

'No kisses and cuddles.'

'Oh, all right, but it's going to be hard. She's cruel your mam, isn't she, love?'

Trudy held out her arms to be picked up, then gave a big sneeze, and they all laughed, most of all Trudy, who thought she'd done something very clever.

'Keep her warm too. I'll bring home something tasty for tea and medicine for you both.'

It was another quiet afternoon Dena spent working on her designs for the fashion show that she hoped to hold around Easter time in April. She and Joan had hardly stopped for weeks, and had already got a little collection together. Even so, there was still a great deal of work to be done.

On this afternoon though, she decided to close early to check on her patients. She was worried about Trudy, the little girl hopefully too young to catch flu.

Dena sensed the moment she entered the front parlour, that something wasn't right. The first thing she noticed was that all her notes and plans were scattered all over the floor, as if a door had been opened and a blast of wind had blown them about. But since it hadn't been windy today, this was most odd. Looking more closely she saw that small things had been touched or moved. Her hairbrush for instance, and a book she'd been reading. It was as if someone had picked them up and put them back in the wrong place. A blouse she'd left on a coat hanger hooked over a cupboard door to air after ironing, had been left tossed on the sofa in a crumpled heap. Something Dena would never do. She was certain that she'd pinned pieces of cut-out cloth from the pattern on to her dressmaker's dummy, but instead they were stuffed in her work basket, one section torn.

Walking into Winnie's living room she found it empty and she quickly stoked up the fire, putting on more coal to warm the place up. All the doors and windows were still closed and locked but Winnie's knitting was no longer on the chair by the fire where she'd left it. Could she have felt well enough to come down for it?

Dena went into the kitchen to put the kettle on then heard a banging upstairs. Winnie must be awake. Oh, it could be her mother. For a moment she'd forgotten that Alice might be in the house too, and decided she'd better pop upstairs to check on her patients, then find out if her mother needed supper, or if she'd eaten already. Dena had hoped that she'd already made it clear that meals were not going to be provided for her every day. She realised it was too much to expect Alice to have prepared a meal for her, even if Winnie and Trudy were both ill.

She reached the landing and was about to turn towards Winnie's room when she saw that her mother's bedroom door was ajar. The banging was coming from there. Creeping closer she took a peep and saw there was someone in there. A man! What was he doing? Dear lord, was he trying to rape Alice? Dena heard a low moan and realised that, far from being assaulted, her mother was actually revelling in the sex session, and savouring every moment.

She had her hands clasped tight around the iron bed rail, head thrown back, bare legs wide open and stuck up high in the air while the naked figure of a man pumped hard into her. Dena could see his skinny backside as it bucked rhythmically up and down, making the whole bed shake and bang and squeak. If it hadn't been so shocking she would have laughed out loud.

He heard her sharp intake of breath and Dena found herself looking straight into a pair of clear blue eyes, all too disturbingly familiar.

Chapter Forty-Four

Dena was grateful that she had no time to think over the next few days as she was fully occupied nursing a grizzling child and a sick, grumpy woman. At least she was able to leave Joan in charge of Winnie's stall, open mornings only since it was a quiet time of year and many other people were also off with flu. Alice had packed her bags and gone, presumably to beg her brother to take her back. Dena really didn't care if she never set eyes on her again. How could she? Kenny Garside with her own mother!

Sex had never been something Dena would have associated with her puritanical, straight-laced mother. All that nagging about morals, all that hypocrisy and posturing, trying to make herself out to be whiter than white, while having her own daughter taken into care for being beyond control because of a few dates with Kenny. And now Alice had slept with him. It was unbelievable! If she hadn't seen them together with her own eyes she never would have believed it.

Yet again Dena had found herself vomiting down the lavatory, just as she had done years ago after identifying the body of her little brother. Why was it that she'd been saddled with such a heartless, unfeeling mother?

She would never treat Trudy so cruelly.

Right now she was almost thankful not to have time to think as she was completely occupied with her own precious daughter who was ill. To Dena's great distress the little girl began hallucinating, and she had to sponge her with cold water to bring her temperature down. It was so frightening. The doctor came the next day and gave out medicine together with a few crisp words of advice.

'One spoonful, three times a day. Rub some Vic on her chest at night and hold her head over a steaming bowl of water with a drop or two of eucalyptus oil in it, if she can't breathe properly. Otherwise, keep her warm and give her plenty of fluids. Can you cope with all of that? You're really far too young to be a mother.'

'I can cope. I have this far.'

'Hm, that's a matter of opinion. You should have listened to my advice the last time I gave it, Dena, and finished your education, but no, you did as so many silly girls do and got yourself into this pickle.'

'I got myself a lovely child,' Dena tartly replied and showed him out.

Nursing her patients allowed her no time to speak to Carl, or any opportunity to tell him what had happened as she spent most of her time running up and down stairs with warming drinks, cough medicine and hot water bottles. Joan Chapman popped in from time to time to do shopping for her, as well as keeping Winnie's stall going.

'Oh, Joan, I don't know what I'd do without you.'

'What are friends for? I've finished those razzle-dazzle skirts, what shall I make next?'

Dena was so grateful for Joan's help and whenever she could find five minutes to sit down, she found great consolation in keeping herself occupied stitching her new designs for the planned fashion show. Ideas that were progressing well! 'Have you seen Carl lately? I wonder if you'd give him this letter. It's about Kenny. It's very important, please do see that he gets it?'

Joan took the note and slipped it into her pocket. ''Course I will, love. Now I'd best be off, or we'll lose what few customers we have left.'

Carl wasn't at his stall when Joan passed by later. Leo, who was keeping an eye on it from his neighbouring toy stall, said he'd slipped across to a warehouse, but he'd give him the letter as soon as he got back. Leo was sneezing badly, his long face smothered in a large khaki handkerchief he'd had since his army days.

'You sound just like Winnie Watkins. You should watch that cold of yours.'

'Don't I know it? I'm shivering like a virgin on her wedding night.'

Unfortunately, before Carl had returned, Leo had succumbed to the dreaded influenza, packed away his stall and gone home to be nursed by his wife. He forgot all about the letter in his jacket pocket.

—

Later that same afternoon Kenny happened by his brother's household goods stall and wondered if he should mention how Dena had surprised him by coming home early the previous afternoon. He was completely unfazed by having been discovered in what he termed 'a moment of indiscretion' with Alice. Serve Dena right if she was jealous. She'd had her chances in the past. She surely couldn't expect him to turn into a bleeding monk. And what if he was with her mam? She was a right little mover, that Alice. Knew all about how to shake, rattle and roll. But what a dingdong row had followed. She'd stormed off into the night, flinging all her goods and chattels into the back of a taxi, yelling at him in her whining, complaining voice that he was useless, and didn't even have a car to give her a lift back to her brother's house in Chorlton. Kenny had felt affronted.

Wasn't his mam going to buy him a Ford Zephyr, just as soon as he'd got her elected onto the market committee, only a week or two away now. Eeh, but what a lark! The tale might give Carl a laugh. 'Hey up, have you heard the latest? Want a bit of a giggle?'

'I'm not in the mood for your jokes today, Kenny. I do want a word though, if you've got a minute.' It occurred to Carl that this was as good an opportunity as he was likely to get. Far better, he decided, to tell Kenny in public, in between serving customers. That way they might avoid coming to blows. He really had no taste for scrapping with his own brother, and once he started down that road Carl was aware that he didn't know his own strength.

Barry Holmes had trained him well in the amateur boxing ring. Too well!

Much safer, he thought, to tell him out in the open. Even Kenny wouldn't risk a scene in the middle of the market. He was wrong.

Carl said what he had to say, albeit with some hesitation and apology, but as kindly and diplomatically as he could, with all due regard to Kenny's feelings. Nevertheless it was the most difficult thing he'd ever done in his life. Always, before, he'd tried to protect his younger brother, now he had to say things he knew would hurt him. Almost as soon as the words were out of his mouth he could see the fury building behind his brother's eyes.

In the silence that followed his halting announcement, Carl waited, hardly daring to breathe. Should he explain further, or had he said too much?

Before he had time to decide, Kenny went into action and let out a great roar and with one sweep of his arm cleared the front of Carl's stall, sending pans, buckets, toasters, cake tins, brushes and mops flying everywhere. The din was tremendous. Folk stopped to stare in horror, and were forced to duck or flee for their lives when pots and pans were sent hurtling in their direction. A packet of OMO smashed on to the cobbles, sending soap powder scattering over everyone like a shower of blue snow.

Carl had never heard or seen anything like it.

Even then Kenny wasn't satisfied. He picked up the trestle tables and heaved them upwards as if they were no more than matchwood, sending the stuff stacked up at the back of the stall crashing to the ground. He turned his attention to Carl, his face twitching with fury, upper lip curled back in a scornful sneer as he drew back one fist preparatory to punching him.

'Don't even consider it!' Carl held up a staying hand and for one long timeless moment the two brothers glared at each other in silent rage.

Kenny seemed to relax, dropped his stance and half turned away as if he'd thought better of it, before suddenly whirling about and flinging the punch right at Carl's jaw.

Carl ducked, missed the blow by a whisker, and catching Kenny off balance, grappled him to the ground. Within seconds the pair of them were sprawling amidst the dust, Kenny desperately throwing punches, and Carl doing his utmost to defend himself. They might well have killed each other had not Mr Ramsay and Alec Hall heard the commotion and come running. Even then it took the assistance of several onlookers before they managed to drag the two brothers apart.

'So help me, I'll see her dead before ever she lies with you,' were Kenny's parting words as Alec hustled him away.

—

Dena was greatly upset by the news of the fight brought to her by Joan. Strangely, her first instinct was to rush to Kenny and apologise for having hurt him and to beg his forgiveness, but then she remembered how much he had hurt her. If he'd taken no for an answer months ago, none of this would have happened. And she was sure that he looked on sleeping with her mother as some sort of perverted revenge.

When she described to Carl what she'd seen in the bedroom, he was incandescent with rage. Dena feared for a moment that his anger might spurn another fight. But they both realised that there was nothing more to be said, or done. Like it or not, Kenny and Alice were adults and could do as they pleased. And Kenny must now face the mess he'd got himself into.

But Carl, who had nurtured and cared for his younger brother all his life, found it hard to let go. 'He has to learn that he can't use and abuse people in this way. He can't just take and have everything he wants like a kid in a sweet shop. He has to learn responsibility and care.'

'It's not our place to teach him though, and how can we if he doesn't want to learn? Anyway, what he does with Alice isn't important, not any more. It's you and I that count.'

'We're still okay then, you and me?'

347

And when she simply nodded, he took her in his arms and they held each other close.

Dena no longer cared about Alice, refused to even call her mother. Any chance of healing the cracks in their relationship had long since been lost. Now relations had broken down between Carl and Kenny too. If only he'd accepted that what Dena had been saying was true, that she wasn't his girl. It was all too clear now, that she was Carl's.

—

Dena arrived at the market hall at nine as usual the following morning, calling out a cheery hello to everyone as she happily ran up the stairs. Her arms were full of the previous night's sewing that she'd done at home while Trudy was sleeping, and she was at first unsurprised to find the stockroom door wide open, thinking that Joan must have got there before her. But then she saw that it was hanging half off its hinges and a strange smell hung in the air. Someone had forced the lock and she didn't even need to step inside to know that disaster awaited her.

The room looked as if it had been hit by a tornado. All the beautiful new dresses, blouses, skirts and jackets she and Joan had so painstakingly stitched; weeks and weeks of work had been torn to shreds. They lay scattered everywhere like a rainbow of scrap paper, all trampled underfoot by somebody's muddy boots. Not only that, but the two Singer sewing machines had been smashed to pieces. Someone had taken a hammer to them both. They would never work again.

The dressmaker's dummy stood forlornly in the midst of it all, the lovely cobalt blue satin evening gown they'd so carefully tacked into position the day before, now slit to ribbons with a thousand cuts.

In one sickening moment of revelation, Dena recognised who the culprit must be, and in that instant knew she was ruined. How could she possibly recover from this, or find the time and money to start again and remake every garment in time for the show?

Kenny had taken his revenge. Her dreams were as dust, ripped apart along with her new designs.

–

'You did this and have ruined me!' Dena stood with hands on hips when she confronted Kenny; her normally soft brown eyes a blaze of gold and hot with rage.

Kenny smirked, as if she'd said something amusing.

'Well, aren't you at least going to tell me why?'

'You know that you've been two-timing me, you little whore.'

'How dare you call me that? I've been telling you for months that you and I are finished. But would you listen? Would you hell! I'm amazed you've the cheek to even say such a thing after what you did with my mam.'

'She was more than willing.'

'I don't want to hear. If you must know, Carl and I only got together at the New Year's dance and I have tried to tell you it was over between you and me, any number of times. Leaving you standing at the altar should have been a big enough hint. But you just kept right on pestering me, trailing after me everywhere, being an absolute nuisance. You never seem to leave me alone.'

She half turned away, then went back to him, jabbing her finger in his chest, unable to control her anger as a new thought occurred to her. 'Before you went upstairs to screw my mother while *my* child, your daughter, lay sick in the adjoining room, did you rummage through my personal belongings? Was it you who scattered my plans and designs all over the floor?'

'What if it was? I needed to know what you were up to. What you were doing that was so much more important than seeing me.'

'How dare you? And how did you even get into the house? Did Alice let you in?'

Kenny's lip curled into that all too familiar sneer. 'No, I got in with a key, what else? I'm no common burglar. I'm clever, me. I borrowed your key from your bag behind the stall when you were busy serving a customer one day, and had another one cut. I've got several, as a matter of fact. One never knows when they might come in useful.'

Dena was shocked to the core. It would never have occurred to her that anyone, even Kenny Garside, would stoop so low to rob it from her. What a slimy toad he was. How many times had he sneaked into the house, during all these long months of following her? The thought made her feel sick. 'I shall have the locks changed first thing in the morning, and I shall tell everyone else to do the same, just in case. You're worse than a burglar, Kenny Garside, you're a sneak thief.'

'I didn't take anything.'

'You stole our privacy. You took away our sense of security in our own home. And now you've ruined my workshop. Not only weeks of work but you've destroyed my future, my relationship with my mother, and my life!' She was very nearly in tears by this time and Dena struggled to harden her heart, knowing she must get away from him before she broke down completely. 'You're despicable! Is it any wonder I chose your brother instead of you? I regret the day I ever clapped eyes on you.'

As she turned to go, he grabbed her by the arm and held her in a vice-like grip. 'Don't think that brother of mine is innocent either, because he isn't. He's the one who killed your little brother.'

Chapter Forty-Five

They were sitting in the bus shelter beside the old horse trough at the corner of the market; had been there for a good half hour while Dena told Carl of Kenny's ridiculous accusation. She'd expected him to laugh it off, to dismiss it instantly as vengeful nonsense, but he hadn't done that at all. At first he'd gone strangely silent, and then started asking all manner of odd questions. 'Why won't you trust me and believe what I say? I had nothing to do with your brother's death.'

'Why should I believe you when you're being so evasive?'

'What did he tell you exactly? Did he say what had happened, and how it all came about?'

Dena shook her head, tears standing bright in her eyes. This discussion was getting worse, and she simply couldn't understand why. 'He told me to ask you, so that's what I'm doing. You tell me, Carl, how it all came about.'

'I can't. I've already said that I wasn't there.'

'But you must be able to remember what you were doing that night.'

'Are you saying I need an alibi?'

'I'm saying give me some proof, otherwise I've only your word for it.'

He turned to stare at her and his dark blue eyes were strangely blank. 'You'll take Kenny's word, not mine?'

Dena began to feel desperate, her heart brimming with fear, sure she was about to vomit. Why didn't he sound more reassuring instead of this defensive, troubled note in his voice? 'You say you weren't the one responsible for Pete's death but you won't explain why Kenny would accuse you of such a terrible thing.'

'Isn't that obvious?'

'Oh, come on, he may well be prepared to ruin my business but this is all a bit far-fetched even for Kenny. I don't believe he'd go so far as to accuse his own brother of murder, just because I've chosen you in place of him.'

Carl's reply came swift and sharp. 'It wasn't murder. It was never meant to go that far!'

The silence that followed this statement was appalling, stretching endlessly between them as Dena stared at Carl in a state of numbed disbelief. She had told no one, not even the police, that any third person or persons were involved. No one knew that they had been attacked, only that Pete had drowned, and she had failed to save him. She could see, by the horror dawning in his eyes, that he had recognised his mistake. The implication was clear. He'd just admitted that he knew more than he was saying. Dena's voice, when she found it, was dangerously soft. 'Are you admitting that Pete didn't simply fall in the canal and drown?'

'I'm saying nothing.'

'But you're aware we were attacked?'

'I heard a rumour.'

'From where, and who told you this rumour?'

'Does it matter?'

'It does to me because I never told anyone, not the police, not even my own mother. I took the coward's way out and pretended Pete had been messing about in the dark, then simply slipped and fell in. I've had to live with that guilt ever since. Not only did I fail to protect him but I should have done more to find the culprit, to seek justice for my little brother's death. So, tell me, Carl. If you know all of this, what else do you know? Who were those thugs? And why did they attack us?'

'I've already told you that I know nothing about it. Just leave it,' then he got up from the bench and walked away.

Dena watched him go with a pain in her heart that she was sure would split her in two. Could this really be happening? Carl hadn't laughed off the accusation at all. He'd been deliberately evasive and his behaviour decidedly suspicious. Dear Lord, what on earth should she do now? Had she fallen in love with her brother's killer?

—

Later that day Dena went to see Barry. As always in times of trouble she needed someone to be on her side. Dena sat on an upturned orange box patiently waiting while he weighed out two pounds of cox apples for a customer, only half listening as he joked about her own cheeks being rosy as apples. When the woman had gone, Dena said, 'I suppose you've heard the latest.'

He turned innocent eyes upon her. 'And what might that be, chuck?'

'Don't play games with me, Barry. The entire market is talking about Carl and me, and about that fight. The latest is that Kenny has wrecked my machines and ripped all my finished dresses to shreds. He's ruined me.'

Barry's jaw dropped open. 'Nay lass, I hadn't heard that. Oh, Dena, that's dreadful. Poor love, what will you do?'

'Stick my head in the gas oven?'

Barry gave a harsh little laugh that held no amusement in it. 'Stick Kenny's head in the gas oven, more like. Come on, you're no quitter. What are you doing sitting here? You should be out buying new machines, picking yourself up and starting all over again.'

'There isn't the time and I'm not sure I have the will, or the energy, let alone the money to start again.' Tears pricked the backs of her eyes and she felt unable to stop them from rolling down her cheeks.

'Self-pity doesn't suit you, love. Na then, what can I do to help? I could lend you a bob or two, mind Trudy while you get back to work.'

'Oh, Barry, you're so sweet but I can't borrow money from you, and I've got Winnie to help with Trudy, don't forget.'

'I never forget that you don't need me around as much, not now you've got Winnie,' he said, pulling a long face.

Dena frowned, realising instantly that without meaning to, she'd hurt his feelings. 'You're my good friend, I shall always need you, and you know that you can come and see Trudy any time. Winnie tells me that you often pop in. Come tomorrow, if you like. She's over the flu and very bored. She could do with a bit of spoiling and petting.'

Barry visibly brightened. 'You don't mind my taking an interest?'

'I not only don't mind, Barry, I need you around to help give my lovely daughter at least the illusion that she has a loving family.'

'I'm your man, and you'll think about a possible loan?'

'I'll give it due consideration.' She turned to go then paused to smile back at him. 'You really like children, don't you Barry?'

'I'm more used to lads these days,' he said, as he turned away to restack his pile of apples. 'But I've a soft spot for little girls too.'

–

In the days following she never seemed to have a moment to herself as she cleaned and scrubbed out the devastated workroom, which was just as well in the circumstances. Against all odds, Dena held onto the hope that Carl was innocent. It had occurred to her that he might be covering up for his younger brother. Hadn't he always protected Kenny? Although there was little comfort in that thought, since Kenny was the father of her child. Whichever brother had done the deed, it was a sorry mess. But Dena loved Carl, and prayed that he wasn't the one responsible for Pete's death, and that one day he would admit to her who was.

Easy-going Joan was not oblivious to how things stood with regard to the Garside brothers. Even if she was unaware of the goings-on in Alice's bedroom she'd heard about the fight, as had the rest of the market, and seemed to understand what it had all been about. Somehow it didn't surprise her that Kenny should choose to take revenge in this way.

'We'll just have to start over,' she said, and set about not only borrowing more sewing machines and roping in her sister to help, but also a couple of friends as well.

'Oh, Joan, I'm not sure if we can.'

'Well, we won't find out by standing about feeling sorry for ourselves, will we?'

At least Winnie was back at her stall and helping to care for Trudy, sometimes with Barry's help. Dena had finally agreed to take the loan and dashed around the Manchester warehouses replacing all the fabric Kenny had ruined. Having done that, she spent every minute she could frantically sewing.

'At least we know what we're doing this time,' Joan pointed out, ever optimistic. 'It'll only take half as long now that I know every bit of each pattern off by heart.'

'Joan, you're an absolute treasure.'

'You're not so bad yourself.' Her homely face beneath the boyish crop of dark hair grinned good-naturedly.

Mutual praise was all very well, but would their second efforts carry the care and freshness of their first? Dena didn't dare to think otherwise. She had her mind set on that fixed date in her calendar, the one shouting at her from every poster she'd stuck up, so she kept her head down and sewed. The work at least served to keep her mind off Carl. She missed him so much. If she saw him around the market she would find her heart would stop beating, leaving her unable to breathe. Sleep was impossible and her machine would continue to whirr in Winnie's front parlour long into the small hours, until Dena fell into bed with exhaustion. The benefit of her mother's departure, was that she and Trudy had their own bedroom back again.

A day or two following the fight, Joan said, 'I saw Belle earlier and she'd like a word, when you've got a minute.'

'Oh, what about? Did she say?' As if Dena couldn't guess. It surely wouldn't be about Alice, but she might have heard Kenny's version of the fight.

'All I know is that you should watch out for Belle Garside, love. She'll not take this upset over her two precious lads lying down. She might be all glamour, gloss and lipstick on the outside, but she has a heart like a clever calculating machine operated by gears. That works entirely for her own selfish ends. You'd do well to remember that, Dena.'

'I will, don't worry. But maybe I'll avoid her for the moment, at least until I'm able to speak to Carl about it.' Dena frowned, wondering if Carl would ever speak to her again. 'We couldn't help the way we felt about each other. I was too young when Kenny and I first got together.'

'You don't have to explain to me, chuck.' Joan lifted the foot of the machine and swivelled the half finished blouse round, before efficiently sliding the next seam under. 'Carl would always get my vote, difficult and sombre though he might be at times. But then there's never been a lot of time for fun in that household, what with an endlessly changing supply of step-fathers or courtesy uncles. Belle ran off with Barry Holmes once, you know.'

'You're joking.'

'No, I'm not. The social threatened to take the childer into care, only she came to her senses, and was back on the market within forty-eight hours, a saner and wiser woman. But if it hadn't been for young Carl, fourteen or fifteen at the time, it might have been a different story. He minded his younger brother and persuaded the authorities to wait and give her a second chance. He loves his mam, though he bears his responsibility of being the man of the house a bit too seriously. Always has, poor lamb.'

Dena listened to all of this enthralled, who would have thought it? Belle and Barry! Was that why Carl had such a prickly relationship with him? She wondered if she should ask Joan about the other men in Belle's life, the courtesy uncles. Would it help if Carl knew who had hurt Kenny? She decided to keep out of it. It was none of her business, after all, and she had enough problems on her plate right now. Besides, she had no wish to upset Belle, who'd never actually done anything to hurt her, so far as she was aware.

'Let's not worry about it just now, Joan. We have too much work to do and I so want this show to be a success.'

'We'll make sure that it is,' Joan agreed. 'There, that's another blouse done. I'll get right on with the next, and press everything later. You do realise that if it is a success, you'll need to expand this business of yours and take on more staff to help with the sewing? Even Winnie's stockroom might not be big enough then. You'll need to put it on a proper footing.'

'Oh, Joan, do you think so?'

'Aye, lass, I do. You're going places, girl. I can see that.'

—

Later that day Dena went over to Carl's household goods stall, in the hope of speaking to him about Belle, but he deliberately turned his back on her. He didn't even have a customer to serve he just strolled away from her to talk to an embarrassed Leo. Dena was left standing red-faced and humiliated before everyone.

Barry gestured for her to come over, and he gave her a big hug. 'How are you doing, lass? I've heard all about you and Carl having your first lover's tiff.'

A dark shadow crossed her face. 'How did you know we were going out?'

Barry shrugged. 'I didn't. You managed to keep that little secret very much up your sleeve, but Kenny is slagging you both off, telling everyone how he's been betrayed by his own brother who's slept with his girl.'

Dena flushed bright crimson. 'I never did, it's a lie. Anyway, it doesn't matter now, Carl and me are through.'

Barry looked shocked. 'Nay, chuck, just because of one little tiff?'

'It wasn't a little tiff. It was so awful and all Kenny's fault for throwing accusations about. A lot of nonsense about our Pete, and Carl being involved, at least I hope it is nonsense. I think Kenny is just out for revenge over various difficulties we've been having lately. He couldn't seem to accept it was over between us. But I don't believe a word of what he said about Carl, really I don't. He'd never do anything so terrible to my Pete, I know he wouldn't.'

The smile on Barry's face seemed to have frozen. 'By heck, Dena, your life is more lively that the flicks.'

Dena would have laughed at the joke if she'd felt in a happier frame of mind. 'He did react very oddly when I told him, and in no time at all I found myself accusing him too. It was dreadful! Awful! I didn't mean to, it just happened.'

'Have you any proof?'

She shook her head. 'None, only something Carl said about the attack. The truth is, Barry, our Pete didn't just fall in, and nobody knew that fact except me, because I didn't tell anyone that he was thrown in by a bunch of thugs. Oh, I wish I knew who they were.'

'Oh, Dena, love, what a thing to have to live with, and you think Carl might know who was responsible?' Barry's voice had dropped almost to a whisper, all sign of joking gone.

'I think he might be covering up for someone and taking the blame himself.'

There was a silence.

Dena felt so uncomfortable in her remembered pain and guilt that she suddenly and desperately wanted to change the subject. Grasping at the first thing that came into her head she decided to tease him about the story Joan had told her earlier. 'I know there's not much love lost between you and Carl. I've heard all about how you and Belle had a bit of a fling a few years back. You're a dark horse, not letting on.'

Barry looked startled, as well he might, but answered her question nonetheless. 'It wasn't even that, not a proper fling anyway. She'd been having a bad time, needed a break and a bit of excitement in her life. Belle's like that, can never be content with boring routine for long, so she hooked onto me to supply a few much needed thrills. It wouldn't have gone anywhere.'

'But you were forced to rush back from your dirty weekend so she didn't lose the children?'

Barry pulled a face. 'Something of the sort, but who told you, Carl?'

'No, not Carl. It doesn't matter, just gossip. This market is rife with it.'

'What does Belle say about all of this – this other business?'

'I don't know. I haven't spoken to her yet. But if she ever starts preaching at me for bringing all this mess upon myself, or accusing me of playing one of her sons off against the other, it might help if I had a bit of ammunition of my own to fire back. Do you mind?'

Barry had the grace to smile, for all it looked a bit stiff and forced. He was saying, 'It's all dirty water under the bridge so far as I am concerned. You've not given up on him then, young Carl?'

Dena wondered if she'd broken some sort of taboo by mentioning the rumour, and should have kept her mouth shut. She shook her head, a stray tear sliding down her cheek. 'I live in hope after all I've been through.'

A strangely sad expression darkened his face. 'I'm right sorry about what happened to Pete. You're a good lass who didn't deserve any of it. But no one should ever underestimate you, Dena. You're a rebel too, at heart.'

'I'm a survivor,' Dena said, kissing him on the cheek before striding away.

Barry watched her go until she was out of sight.

Chapter Forty-Six

Belle folded her arms across her voluptuous bosom and considered Dena with a thoughtful frown. 'I've a bone to pick with you, madam.'

'I thought you might have.'

'Stealing Joan Chapman from under my nose has left me in a right pickle. I've been driven to doing the baking myself for weeks, so you'll understand I feel a bit put out by that. I've got someone now, a plain but reliable girl to take Joan's place. Mind you, she's not prepared to start as early, or work half as many hours. Joan was one of the old school. No complaints and got on with the job, no questions asked. Today's young are another breed altogether. You can't get decent staff these days. Loyalty is dead.'

Dena said nothing, waiting patiently for Belle to get to the point, knowing she'd already had her say about losing Joan some time ago, and that there was another matter entirely on her mind. Although it was typical of her to first make an issue over a matter that most affected her personally.

Belle took her time, shaking a cigarette from a packet of Kensitas, lighting it from a gold cigarette lighter and blowing a stream of blue smoke in Dena's face. 'Speaking of loyalty, what's all this I hear about you and our Carl?'

Here it came! It always paid to give herself pause for thought where Belle was concerned. 'What have you heard?'

Belle drew hard on her cigarette, flicking away the ash with an air of disdain. 'I hear your loyalty has suffered a remarkable sea change, first one of my boys, then the other. So why should I believe you won't treat my elder son the same way you treated his brother, by dumping him at the altar too? Because if that's what you have in mind, girl, you'd best think again. It was bad enough to be shamed once, I'll not stand by and see it happen all over again. We Garsides have our pride.'

'I realise that, Belle. But what I feel for Carl is entirely different.'

Belle made no mention of the battle royal Kenny was conducting, and Dena too said nothing.

'What of our Kenny? He's upset to have lost you. What are you going to do about him?'

Dena could wait no longer. She took an eager step forward. 'Belle, I'm sure you've heard what's happened. It's like open warfare that Kenny is throwing punches and wild accusations about. He's picked a fight with Carl and...'

'Take no notice of that, my boys are always japing over something. Been doing it ever since they were small.'

'And he's wrecked my sewing room, attempted to ruin my hopes for a spring fashion show. Joan and her sister are doing their best to help salvage something out of the mess but I'll be lucky if we can get it finished in time, so late in the day, and it won't be anything like as good. You've always been fair with me, Belle. Believe me when I say that I didn't let Kenny down on purpose. It was just one of those things. Will you try and explain that to him?'

'Why should I?'

'Because I don't want to hurt him but it's Carl I love, and I believe he loves me. Well, anyway, we did our best not to hurt Kenny but it's happened, and there it is. Please try to make him see that I'm still fond of him, as a sister, that he can see Trudy any time he likes, if he's a mind to. And she'd still be in the family, if Carl and me got back together, that is.'

Belle's frown cleared a little. 'Well, that would be one good thing to come out of this muddle, I suppose. But whether I can calm him down now that he's in one of his rampages, is another matter altogether. When did a lad ever listen to his mother?'

'But you'll try?'

Without even pause for thought, Belle gave a very firm shake of her head. 'No, lass, I make it a policy in life not to interfere with either of my son's affairs. And I expect the same respect in return from them. I won't do anything to stop your plans with our Carl, but I'll not do anything to help you either. You'll just have to hope for the best where our Kenny is concerned, that he'll be satisfied with this little tantrum and let the matter drop.'

'Little tantrum? But he's smashed my machines.'

'I don't want to know,' Belle interrupted. 'Don't tell me any more. Like it or not, you'll just have to live with the consequences of your action.'

This wasn't the result Dena had hoped for, yet she had no choice but to accept Belle's decision. It could have been worse, she supposed. At least Belle wasn't intent on making life any more difficult for her than it already was.

Belle's attention had already moved back to her own personal concerns, and she was busily applying a thick coat of crimson lipstick. 'Now where's my bag? The election is only days away and I really must get out and about and on with my canvassing. I can rely on your vote, I trust, Dena?'

'Of course,' Dena said. What else could she say?

–

Kenny was feeling mighty pleased with himself as he went around the market collecting his dues, knowing it was only a matter of time before Dena came running back to him. How could she not after such a revelation? He should have done it long since. But while he waited for that to happen, it was vital that he went on with his plans to make as much money as he could, so that he could properly provide for her, as she deserved. Besides, the elections were due at the end of this week and Kenny felt it incumbent upon himself to ensure that everyone had got the message about who they were expected to vote for.

He didn't trouble himself with the Higginson sisters. They were so nervous of him they'd have voted Adolph Hitler on to the committee had he still been around and Kenny had instructed them to do so. It was a great pity others weren't as obedient.

Lizzie Pringle stared at him blankly from her stance inside the Chocolate Cabin, saying nothing as he explained again the importance of her vote. Then, just to emphasise his point, he picked up a rum truffle and popped it in his mouth. 'Wouldn't pay for you to be obstinate, Lizzie. You do see that?'

'Yes,' Lizzie said. 'I do.'

'Good. I'm glad we understand each other.' Then he hawked and spat on the rest of the box of truffles and sauntered off, well pleased with himself.

The Bertalones were a walkover, ever fearful of being sent back to Italy, Kenny supposed. They were so polite to him it was almost nauseating, even gave him a raspberry dash as a treat. But then they didn't much care for the way he eyed up their youngest daughter, Katrina, so that might have something to do with it. Kenny was willing to use any trick he thought appropriate, even though the girl didn't appeal to him in the slightest.

Jimmy Ramsay, Sam Beckett and Alec Hall had long since accepted that he was in control. He could tell when he spoke to them that they didn't like being told what to do, but realised it was pointless trying to fight him. Far too expensive on their respective businesses, Kenny thought with a chuckle as he counted the notes they'd given him before clipping them safely to the wad he'd already collected.

Molly Poulson and the rest of the stallholders were easy to talk round, taking the minimum of effort. But then there was Barry Holmes.

Kenny paused, propping himself against the horse trough while he lit up a Gold Flake to consider the matter. How would Barry react to him telling him what to do? Wasn't he, in a way, the cause of all his problems? After careful thought how best to play it, he stubbed out the cigarette with the heel of his crêpe-soled shoe, thrust back his padded shoulders and strolled over to Barry's stall. He was a man too now, not some snotty-nosed kid, and what he had to say proved far easier than he'd expected.

Barry just looked at him and nodded. 'Whatever you require, Kenny.'

Winnie, however, was proving to be a very obstinate, difficult old woman indeed. He watched her all of that day and the next, choosing to make his approach the night before the election when she was on her way home. She was late, as luck would have it, and dusk was falling, so Winnie didn't instantly recognise him when he approached.

'Who's there? Who's following me?'

He could hear the nervousness in her voice and it was an enormous satisfaction to him that when he announced himself, she didn't appear relieved. One could almost say that she was frightened.

'I just wanted to remind you of the elections tomorrow, Winnie. You promised to vote Joe Southworth out of office, if you remember, and put my mam in his place.'

'I did no such thing. You've got that all wrong, lad.'

'I'm sorry to hear you say that, Winnie. It's a great pity indeed that you can't find it in your heart to be more obliging. I was hoping you might have seen sense by this time.' She was standing four-square before him, a large bag on her arm and knitting needles in hand as if she was ready to clout him with one and stab him with the other. An amusing thought, which almost made him laugh out loud.

'Don't try your bullying on me, Kenny, lad. I'm no wilting violet. It may have escaped your notice but this is a secret ballot and I intend to keep it that way. How I vote is me own business, not yours.'

'I'm afraid not, Winnie. That isn't how it works. You'll vote for Belle Garside, my mam, if you know what's good for you. And you don't want any further trouble, like your stall going up in flames, or your house burned to the ground with Dena and that bastard child of hers tucked up in their beds.'

He saw how the colour drained from her cheeks. 'You'd never do such a wicked thing!'

'Are you prepared to take the risk? That's the more sensible question you should be asking yourself? Don't try to fight me, Winnie, or you'd be bound to lose. Just put your cross against my mother's name, that's the safest way.'

'Go to hell!'

He hit her then, punched her straight in the face as he'd learned to do as a boy in Barry Holmes's boxing ring. Then he kicked her in the stomach as she lay crumpled on the ground, and kicked her again and again. By the time he'd got his temper back under control and stalked off, it was clear that Winnie wouldn't be voting for anyone.

—

Dena first became concerned when Winnie did not appear for tea. By seven-thirty, unable to sit still and wait any longer, she gathered Trudy in her arms and went back to the market hall to look for her. She found it all locked up and in darkness. So where was she? Surely Winnie hadn't taken it into her head to go off somewhere, visiting a friend without telling her? She would never do that. And she'd known that Dena would have the tea ready by six. Something was wrong, she was sure of it.

It was then that she saw Joe Southworth. He came striding towards her across the cobbles and the expression on his face told her everything. A great lump of fear rose in her chest, almost stopping her from breathing. 'Joe, what is it, tell me!'

'Now don't start panicking, Dena.' He explained that Winnie had apparently been found an hour earlier by two young boys playing out on their bikes. Fortunately they'd had the good sense to call Joe, and he had rung the ambulance at once. 'They've taken her to the infirmary where she's to have an operation to remove her spleen. She's still unconscious but holding her own, and we can but pray she continues to do so. If you come with me, love, I'll run you over there in my car.'

Dena sat by Winnie's bedside all night, very much against the rules but the young night nurse was kind. She'd even found a little bed to tuck Trudy into and the little girl was asleep in minutes. Despite her exhaustion Dena couldn't rest. She sat holding her friend's hand, praying, pleading, and begging with God not to take this dear woman from her, whom she loved so much.

Just before dawn and despite all her best efforts to stay awake, Dena must have slipped into an uneasy slumber because the young nurse was suddenly shaking her shoulder and calling her name. 'Dena, wake up. Wake up, and look.'

'What happened?' she sat up, startled, her heart pounding with fear.

'By heck lass, you look like you've got two holes in your head where your eyes should be. What have you been doing to yourself?'

'Oh Winnie, thank God you're awake!'

Chapter Forty-Seven

The day of the elections dawned and Belle was up bright and early. She had a ten o'clock appointment at Joyce's hair stylist on the corner of Champion Street to have her hair done, all back-combed and bouffant and well lacquered against any stray wind. It was vital that she look her best when they made the announcement. She'd also bought herself a new dress especially for this most important day. It was in her favourite fuchsia with a dash of orange thrown in, a lively number so that nobody could miss seeing her up there on the platform. The skirt just skimmed her knees and though she said it herself, she didn't have bad legs. The white court shoes would set them off a treat.

She wondered if Marco Bertalone would approve. Age had done nothing to take away his good looks and she wouldn't be against testing his loyalty to that plump, pudding-faced wife of his. There was a faded prettiness about her but the poor woman had cropped too well, having produced five children, or was it six? And lost her figure as a result. She didn't make the best of herself, not a mistake Belle would ever make.

Belle was very excited as she slapped Max Factor pancake all over her face, in no doubt that she was going to win this time around, not only get elected on to the committee, but be in complete control, ousting Joe Southworth from power at last. She would be so glad not to have to occupy his bed any more. His appeal had long since palled. Taking her eyebrow pencil she carefully plucked a line on each brow. Oh, and hadn't she loved all the campaigning, and canvassing? She might consider standing for the local council in due course.

She spat on to her block of mascara, rubbed in the brush then began to apply it to her long lashes, congratulating herself that she'd definitely got it right this time. Kenny too had turned up trumps. Real dark horse, he'd turned out to be, with far more gumption to him than she'd ever given the lad credit for. People were actually stopping her in the street, assuring Belle that she could count on their vote, and would she please tell Kenny that. He was a good lad, but Belle felt a bit sorry for him, having lost Dena in the end. She hadn't made up her mind whether she approved of these goings-on, or not. Carl was saying nothing on the subject, had been very sullen these last few days, keeping his opinions very much to himself. But that was Carl all over, shutting himself away, keeping his own counsel.

Poor Kenny was the one really suffering though. For the lass to shame him once at the altar was bad enough. It was surely adding insult to injury for her to choose his brother instead? Belle paused in her thoughts to rummage through her make-up bag and search for the right shade of lipstick. Had she used up all her fuchsia? Ah, here it was. Her eyeliner was now good, to widen her dazzling violet eyes.

One advantage was that she was delighted the little one, her grandchild, would remain in the family. Kenny didn't have it in him to make a good dad. Carl had always played that role, so it was no bad thing. And it was no skin off her nose which of her sons the lass was sleeping with. What difference did it make? Although Belle had to admit she would have preferred both of them to look for a girl with more power, a good family background and a deal of money, the lass was nobody's fool and going places with that little business of hers.

As Belle patted Goya powder over her nose and then clipped on a pair of large white daisy earrings, she wondered if she could persuade Dena to make one or two bits and pieces for her future mother-in-law, in her spare time. She had a fancy for a smart little suit, something in turquoise or aquamarine. It was then that the door burst open and Carl came striding in with news.

Belle was duly elected, leaving a disgruntled Joe Southworth with no option but to offer his congratulations and stand down. No one seemed particularly happy about this decision and many were already beginning to regret their weakness. There were going to be many changes in the market. For a start, all the rents immediately went up. Belle bludgeoned this through the committee within days of taking over.

Not only that but traders were expected to pay for a full fifty-two week year, irrespective of whether they chose to trade in every one of those weeks, and that every stallholder must personally attend at least one in every month. This brought forth an outcry of objections, particularly from farmers who used the market only when they had produce to sell.

'That's your problem,' Belle told them. 'We need reliable stall-holders, not simply those who come when they feel like it.'

There was some support for this argument so it went through without further challenge, although there were a few murmurs when she pushed through an amendment. If regulations weren't followed, suspensions or fines could be imposed.

'And who would benefit from such fines?' cried one outraged stallholder. 'How much spare cash would find its way into your back pocket?'

'The committee would benefit, and through them the entire market,' Belle responded, tight-lipped with anger. 'What are you accusing me of? Fraud? Malpractice? It takes money to run this market and pay for cleaning, the new electric lighting we're going to install, as well as the purchase of better equipment. I have plans for many improvements and a new development in the future. Money has to be found from somewhere.'

To her credit, Belle did have some good ideas. She planned to build a more solid row of stalls for the fish and meat market, and promised to approach the council for a grant to help pay for it. 'You shouldn't have canvas flapping about where fresh food is concerned.'

Jimmy Ramsay, for one, heartily approved of this idea.

But when she started to talk about controlling new licences, only issued to the sort of business the market needed to attract and not more of the same type of stall, she came up against some stiff opposition.

'That smacks of censorship,' Alec Hall remarked.

'It's common sense. Would you want another music stall in competition with yours?'

'I believe in competition so I suppose I'd have to live with it. This market used to be a free market, one to which anyone could come along, put up a stall and start trading. All right, those days are long gone, but that doesn't mean that we have the right to pick and choose who is allowed to trade and who isn't. If there's space to expand, if a vacancy exists, then that should be the only criteria, not the nature of the stall.'

Belle did not agree and argued the point at length, with some degree of support, though little success. She lost this particular vote, vowing to return to the subject at a later date when the extensions were complete.

Abe Johnson was heard to remark that while he personally had no wish to see a load of other second-hand stalls moving in to compete with his, he did agree with free choice and didn't think for a minute that Belle would stick by the committee's decision. 'She's her own woman, that one. And now that she's got her hands on some power, she'll exercise it in her own way, whatever the rights and wrongs of the case.'

'There's no way she can go against a committee decision,' Alec protested.

'You think so?' Abe shrugged. 'We'll see. Only time will tell.'

–

Dena was now fully aware that Kenny had been the one responsible for Winnie's injuries, and for once had no idea how to deal with the matter. Winnie insisted that she say nothing, and was in fact adamant on the subject.

'Didn't you always say it was far safer to remain invisible? Setting yourself up against Kenny Garside might not be such a good idea. He would only exact even more punishment.'

'Yes, I was wrong. You should always seek justice, and most definitely always speak up when you're being bullied. That's important because if we don't stop him, he'll go on and do it to other people too.'

'Aye, but his mam is a powerful lady on this market, and your future mother-in-law.'

'There's little danger of that happening now. Carl hasn't spoken to me in days. He goes out of his way to avoid me. It's so awful!' Although Dena admitted that they'd had a bad quarrel, she wouldn't tell Winnie what it had been about. Not until she'd worked out the true significance of his reaction to Kenny's accusation in her own mind, she really had no wish to talk about it any further. Even talking about it to Barry had been a mistake, and she'd bound him to secrecy. She couldn't bring herself to believe that Carl was the one responsible for Pete's death. Could it have been Kenny? Was Carl protecting his brother?

Winnie's next words seemed to give some credence to this theory. 'You do know that Kenny has been running a protection racket?' She raised her eyebrows in a rueful acknowledgement of her own foolishness in standing up to him. 'That's why he thumped me, because I wouldn't *kowtow* to his bullying. He claims to offer security, including one of his expensive burglar alarms, in return for a regular monthly payment. And if you don't pay up, then your stall suffers from a mysterious number of break-ins. You don't have to be 'Brain of Britain' to work out why.'

'Oh, my goodness, Winnie, I'd no idea. But I thought this security business of his was all legal and above board.'

'Pigs might fly.'

'Why didn't you tell me this before?'

Winnie gave a sigh. 'I didn't want to put any more worries on your shoulders. I thought I could handle him, daft cluck that I am. The Higginson sisters are paying him a small fortune every month, as are many of the other stallholders. He even controls the combination they use on the new safe they had fitted. The poor souls are so hard up they're actually talking of selling up and leaving the market.'

'Oh, but that would be dreadful, to be driven from a job you love because all your profits are being stolen from you. That's appalling! He's not getting away with this. We have to do something.'

'What can we do?'

Dena frowned. What indeed? Hadn't Kenny already proved the depth of his desire for vengeance? Not only had he wrecked her work room and destroyed all the new designs for her fashion show, he'd also destroyed her relationship with Carl. And look what he'd done to Winnie? She was fortunate that Joan and her crew were willing to start all over again on very little pay, but there seemed to be nothing she could do to win back Carl. To risk annoying Kenny further could result in even more mayhem and mischief being wreaked on all their heads. Yet what was the alternative? To allow Kenny to continue to bully and shove folk around? Not if she had any say in the matter.

Dena stiffened her spine and her voice took on a new firmness. 'There's always strength in numbers. We need to call a meeting of all the stallholders involved, and none of the Garside family should be invited.'

Winnie's eyebrows shot up in utter disbelief. 'You'd never manage it, not in secret. Belle would be sure to get wind of such a meeting. She sees herself as queen of the market now, and she'd view any alternative group as a sign of rebellion. She wouldn't like that one little bit and be certain to take retaliation. Haven't you heard of the new fines and suspensions she intends to inflict on folk? She might even decide to turn us off altogether, and let our pitches to newcomers. Folk won't want to take the risk of losing their livelihood. There are other risks too, particularly for you.'

'You had the courage to stand up against Kenny, why shouldn't I?'

'I'm saying folk are afraid the Garsides will fight dirty.'

'Then I must make sure that they don't. I refuse to stand by and do nothing when people are being bullied, particularly when I might well be the cause of Kenny's nasty campaign. He's gone too far this time.'

Chapter Forty-Eight

The meeting was held in Winnie's front parlour one night after the market closed. The little room was packed with stallholders, some of whom were more than a little sceptical about the wisdom of taking on such a fight against the Garsides. However, no one was in any doubt that they wanted Kenny stopped.

'Question is,' said Jimmy Ramsay, rubbing one hand over the stubble of his broad chin. 'How do we set about it?'

'We should all refuse to pay. We should call his bluff,' Alec said.

The two Misses Higginson visibly trembled. 'And what if he robs us all, or sets fire to the place?'

There was a small silence before Dena chipped in. 'He may be a bit wild, but even Kenny wouldn't go that far.'

'How can you be sure, Dena?'

She couldn't. There had been a time when she'd thought she knew and understood Kenny. Now he was behaving oddly, as was Carl, who was deliberately avoiding her, having gone off into one of his huffs, making it very plain it was all over between them.

Lizzie Pringle cleared her throat, then suggested in her gentle voice that they should consider Belle's role in all of this. 'She must have known what he was about because someone supplied him with the capital to set up in business selling those burglar alarms. I would guess they were meant simply as a cover for his less edifying business dealings. And since Kenny brought pressure to bear on us all to make us vote for Belle, was the election even legal?'

'That's a good point,' said Alec. 'It just wasn't fair.'

'Belle has some good ideas,' Sam Beckett put in, 'this market needed a shake-up and she'll certainly give it that.'

There was much more discussion in the same vein with everyone talking at once, somebody pointing out that Sam would be bound to take Belle's side, since he was sharing her bed. Sam took great exception to this, fervently denying the accusation, and heated words were exchanged until Molly Poulson pounded one fat fist on the table and shouted for order.

'This isn't getting us anywhere. We can talk in circles for hours but we have to stand firm. That's the vital thing. Otherwise, Kenny will keep on upping the ante and we'll be helpless.'

'We wanta no dictators here,' shouted Marco Bertalone, getting very excited. 'We have hada too many of those already. We wanta no more.' His round, doe-eyed wife, who scarcely spoke a word of English but recognised when her husband was getting agitated, briskly shushed him.

Alec agreed. 'Marco's right. That's exactly how Kenny is behaving, like some tin-pot bloody Hitler. We haven't fought a war to be dictated to by some slip of a lad in our own back yard.'

That did it. A vote was taken and the result was unanimous. Belle might have some good ideas for the market, amongst her more radical proposals, but she had won the election unfairly. Consequently, it must be declared null and void and a new one held. As for Kenny, a small delegation was appointed, comprising Jimmy Ramsay, Alec Hall, and Dena, who absolutely insisted she be included, and would undertake to clearly explain to him that security was no longer an issue. No further protection payments would be made. Not by anyone.

'Not even us,' said Clara Higginson on an unusually brave note, and without even checking with her sister Annie first.

A cheer went up all round and the meeting was declared closed.

—

Belle was not at all happy about the decision, and absolutely refused to go along with it when it was made clear that she hadn't, in fact, won the election fair and square; that no one else was happy about it, not even her most stalwart supporters.

Jimmy Ramsay told her in his calm, authoritative way that she had no alternative. 'We have to hold another election, Belle, otherwise we'll have nothing but trouble from now until "kingdom come". We can hold it the same time next month. That gives any alternative candidates ample time to get their act together, but there's no reason to hang around any longer than that. The important thing is that it must be seen to be carried out fairly, and you would be wise to have a quiet word with that young lad of yours, and curb his over-enthusiasm.'

'I never interfere with my boys.'

'Aye, you do,' Jimmy continued, puffing out his considerable chest. 'You boss 'em around summat shocking, so don't deny it. We'll have no more being messed about, Belle. You bring young Kenny to heel, or others may do it for you.'

And she had to be content with that.

Kenny was less amenable when it was forcibly pointed out to him that now everyone had bought their burglar alarms, and new security measures were being brought in, no further payments would be made to him.

'You'll regret it,' he shouted, losing his temper.

'I don't think so,' Alec said. 'We'll all stand by each other, should any unexpected trouble occur. We've agreed to take turns and keep watch until a new security guard has been appointed. Joe Southworth had that one right, at least.'

Dena rested a quiet hand on Kenny's arm. 'You must accept this, Kenny. It's called progress. And people don't care to be bullied.'

'Don't you start!' he shouted, almost spitting in her face, then stormed away, though not before picking up one of Alec Hall's most expensive guitars and smashing it against the wall.

Leaping to her feet in shock, she would have run after him but Alec prevented her. 'Leave it, Dena. He's just in a paddy because he hates to lose. We've made our stand.'

The day of the fashion show finally arrived and despite all the difficulties they'd had to endure, the new designs were ready. Dena, with the help of good old Joan Chapman and her stalwart crew, had managed to salvage something out of the mess. Anything that hadn't been too badly damaged was painstakingly taken apart and put back together, sufficiently repaired to at least pass muster for the show. A new one could always be made later if the design was sold. But most were too far gone for such remedial measures and every ruined dress, skirt, blouse or coat had been carefully remade.

Dena thought it all an absolute miracle and knew she could never have succeeded without the help of her friends. Barry had scarcely been away since Winnie had come home from the hospital, helping to nurse her as well as minding Trudy for much of the time. 'You're an absolute star,' Dena told him.

But he simply grinned and placed a plate of hot dinner before her. 'Eat! You need to keep your strength up, girl.'

The models were all lined up ready, picked from her regular, and most attractive, customers. They were a lively group of girls plus two older women, who were excited about the thrill of modelling Dena's clothes, even if they were a bit nervous about their first time on the catwalk. They spent all day getting the rooms ready. Abe had lent her a length of carpet, second-hand but well brushed and with a lovely beige pattern that didn't clash with any of the dresses. Chairs were arranged along each side and refreshments provided for afterwards. Now that she was almost recovered, Winnie had put herself in charge of those, albeit with Barry's help.

There'd been a little tussle over that at first, since both Dena and Barry thought it was too soon after her operation only a few weeks before, but Winnie had been adamant. 'Personally I thought we'd go for something a bit sophisticated. I could manage to chop squares of cheese and pineapple chunks and stick 'em on sticks, if I sit up to the table. I thought we'd have fancy little sausages and some of Fanny Craddock's gourmet canapés. What do you think?'

'We'll let you organise the food only if I do all the running around,' Barry said. And so it was agreed.

'It all looks wonderful, Winnie. Thank you.'

'We make a good team,' Barry said, a twinkle in his eye.

'You're getting a bit above yourself, lad. Look at me, stuck in this thing like a flipping invalid.'

'You are an invalid. At least we can control you in that.'

Winnie had been so determined to attend the show that Barry had borrowed a wheelchair and insisted she could only attend if she agreed to stay in it. Much against her will Winnie finally conceded to do that, but the arguments between them continued, though largely in good spirit. She sat up very straight, ordering everyone around, smartly attired in a knitted suit with her hair neatly brushed and no sign of the old woolly bob cap.

Dena's own suit was in zingy lemon linen with a box jacket and pencil skirt, teamed with stiletto-heeled shoes in the palest cream she could find. She'd even elected to wear a tiny pill-box hat and gloves to match, to give herself confidence.

–

Half an hour before the show was due to start Dena was a bag of nerves, convinced that no one would come. 'How many tickets have we sold, any at all? People might just have bought a ticket out of good manners to be polite, with no intention of coming at all. Oh no, it's started to rain. Now everyone will decide to stay at home and watch *Emergency – Ward 10* instead.'

'Dena love, shut up, and stop getting your knickers in a twist. There you are see, your first customer.'

By seven o'clock, the time the show was meant to begin, the room was packed and people were still coming in. They had to borrow extra chairs from the next room to accommodate them all.

There was Belle right at the back, and beside her sat Kenny. Good heavens! He wasn't the only male in the room, several women had brought their husbands, no doubt with cheque books to hand, but the sight of him put her momentarily off her stroke. She could see Jimmy Ramsay, Sam Beckett and Alec Hall, all there to offer support.

Even Miss Rogers had come alone. She gave Dena's hand a little squeeze as she took her seat. 'Turning up in your life again, though I hope not like a bad penny.'

Dena laughed. 'I'm delighted to see you.'

There was no sign of Carl.

When everyone was at last settled, Dena took her place at the podium, her heart pounding. Taking a deep breath to steady her nerves, she welcomed everyone to her first fashion show. And they were not disappointed. There were some wonderful clothes on show. Several sheath dresses, and some cut into the fashionable princess line with boat-shaped necks. Jazzy skirts and neat little tops. Playsuits and shorts, sundresses in bright floral cotton and her trademark daisy skirts and capri pants in a kaleidoscope of colours.

The local press were there, dazzling everyone with their flash cameras as they snapped pictures of the outfits.

Dena had made some of her favourite duster coats out of crisp sailcloth, with dresses to match. For these she chose a colour scheme of canary yellow, ice blue and pale straw. She also produced an identical style of coat in silk brocade jewel colours she called opera coats. She'd so longed to make them that first Christmas, now she had.

'Perfect for that special occasion.'

Out came a model in a stunningly different day dress that made the audience gasp. It was a waistless chemise that Dena informed everyone with great authority would be the coming thing. She was taking the gamble that waists would be less of a feature by next season. The range was neatly styled in muted, pastel shades with straight-cut necklines.

'And here we have one or two trapeze line dresses for those of you wishing to be even more adventurous. I believe long swinging skirts are now history, and skirts are creeping shorter for girls, and could be fun for gentlemen.' This brought forth a flurry of laughter.

Tiny waists were still a feature in her evening wear and there were lots of glamorous, feminine, low necked, and boned strapless dresses in taffeta or satin. There were several strappy cocktail dresses in blues and soft pink chiffon, a killer scarlet number that would make anyone look like Diana Dors, plus a selection of smart little black sheaf dresses, which could be worn anywhere.

The *pièce de résistance* was a strapless ball gown divided into four alternating sections of peach and ivory silk.

Dena thanked everyone for their support and closed the proceedings with an admission: 'I would have loved to have concluded my first show with more ballgowns, and with a bridal gown, but there simply hasn't been time. And to be honest I wasn't convinced that I possessed the necessary skills to do proper justice to something important, maybe next time.'

There were cheers along with the rapturous applause, and it seemed everyone had far more confidence in her skills than she had in herself. Dena was thrilled with her success and the accolades came thick and fast.

'That was wonderful! Marvellous. So exciting! Well done, Dena.'

Several reporters asked if they could interview Dena later and the girls all trooped out again in their final outfits to take their share of the praise. Joan too, who'd spent all evening dressing them and running around backstage in a lather of terror that something might go wrong, was brought out and made to take a bow. She was flushed with pride, her short hair standing on end, no doubt from much combing with agitated fingers. And Joan's sister, stationed by the door collecting tickets, was now busily engaged taking orders. It was all so exciting, and as everyone agreed, a huge success.

'Wasn't that wonderful?' Dena said, as people finally began to make their way home.

Winnie hugged her tight. 'What a little champion you are love.'

—

They'd rolled up the carpet and swept the floor, all the clothes were packed away in their cardboard boxes ready for collection in the morning, and the models, far too excited to go home had gone off for a brandy and Babycham at a nearby pub, chattering happily over their success. Some were even considering a new career. Joan and Winnie had gone along with them, urging Dena to come too but she was still embroiled in her last interview.

Laughing, she waved them off. 'I'll be with you shortly. I'm sure we're nearly done here.'

Ten minutes later she'd said goodnight to the last reporter, then took one final look around the co-operative rooms, making sure that everything was in order before securely locking the big double doors.

It was past nine o'clock and dark outside, save for the orange glow of the street lights but it was only a short walk to the pub just a few yards along the street. Dena chuckled to herself. From the sound of it, they were having something of a party in there.

The figure stepped out in front of her without warning. 'Hello Dena!'

'Kenny!' Dena stopped in her tracks, surprised and a little alarmed.

'I thought you might need a bit of help carrying your stuff.'

'No, I've left most of it to be collected in the morning. I can manage, thanks.' She made to walk past him but he stopped her with the gentlest of touch on her arm.

'I liked your show. It was brilliant.'

She made no mention of what she believed he had previously ruined. 'Thanks, I was surprised to see you there. Didn't think it would be your sort of thing.'

'I wanted to see what it was you'd been doing these recent weeks. What had taken up so much of your time.'

Dena stifled a small sigh. Surely he wasn't still showing signs of jealousy. Would his resentment towards her never end? She forced a smile. 'Well, I'm glad you enjoyed it. Now, if you'll excuse me, I'm meeting the rest of the team for a drink and a bite of supper. See you, Kenny.' And this time she did walk right past him. She could see the door of the pub standing ajar, light streaming out, and had very nearly reached it when he grabbed her.

Chapter Forty-Nine

Dena came round in the pitch dark, with not even street lamps to lift the gloom. But by the smell of the damp and rotting vegetation, she guessed at once where she was. Down by the canal, where this whole sorry mess had begun over four years ago.

Kenny was hunkered down, propped against an old stone wall a few yards away. 'Sorry I had to hit you, Dena. It was the only way. I realised that you'd never have come with me willingly.'

Dena pushed herself up into a sitting position, feeling her head swim as once it had before after a severe beating. Her new lemon linen suit, she noticed, was smeared with mud, there was no sign of her hat and shoes; her knees were bleeding and her nylon stockings scarred with ladders. Not that she cared about the state of her clothes, as all she wanted was to go safely home. A nub of fear was growing inside her. At one time she would have laughed at the very idea of being afraid of Kenny Garside, but no longer. He had done too many terrible things. Nevertheless she must strive to appear brave.

'Kenny, what is this all about? Why are you still angry with me? I've told you a thousand times that it's all over between us. What more can I do to convince you?'

He got to his feet and strolled over towards her, smoothing his breast pocket with one hand as if checking its contents. 'Dena, what you don't seem to understand is that this isn't your decision to make. How many times must I make it clear that I am the one who will say whether or not you're still my girl? You should understand that's because I'm a man and you're only a woman.'

'Don't be ridiculous! That attitude went out with the ark.' Dena gave a small laugh, a little foolish in the circumstances.

Kenny crouched down beside her, his face coming to within inches of her own. She could see the curl of his upper lip, the sweat on his brow, every pimple on his chin and the deep anger in his vivid blue eyes. His tone was entirely matter of fact and Dena wondered if this was a good or a bad thing.

'Carl doesn't want you any more. You and my brother are history. He realises he should have kept his nose out of my affairs, so you can stop lusting after him.'

'It's not lust, I love him. I can't help how I feel, Kenny, although I agree Carl may not want me now after I accused him of killing our Pete.' She looked up into his eyes. 'But that was you, wasn't it? I can remember seeing your eyes glaring at me from out of that balaclava.'

'I'm sorry you've remembered that, Dena. It's a real shame. Now I'm going to have to do something about that.' He was on his feet towering over her as he drew out his bicycle chain and began to swing it menacingly close to her face like the bully he was.

Dena was on her feet in an instant, every nerve tingling as she desperately ignored what he might do to her, all her senses alert and suddenly she wasn't afraid any more. 'You don't scare me, Kenny Garside, not one little bit. You can follow me around like Mary's flaming little lamb, as much as you like. You can rip every dress I ever make, smash my machines, do your worst but you can't make me love you! I don't even like you any more. In fact, all of that stuff you do has the opposite effect. Did that never occur to you, you stupid lad?'

She thumped him hard in the chest and he staggered back, almost losing his balance. 'You bullied my little brother. I know you did. Carl knows it too. You tried to shift the blame on to him and I almost believed you, went along with it for a while despite the fact that I love him. Now he won't even speak to me. You beat up my little brother and threw him away in the cut as if he were nothing more than a piece of rubbish!'

'I didn't like the little bleeder and he got what he deserved.'

'You're the one who's rubbish, nothing but a piece of shit! Do you know that, Kenny Garside? You're no better than the muck I used to knock off me boots when I was a kid. Well, I'm not a kid now, I'm a grown woman and you can't bully me, even if you did bully my little brother!' She was jabbing him in the chest with her finger while she issued these accusations.

'Don't talk to me like that you whore! I had a harder time than you when I was a kid. You don't know how well off you were. Haven't I told you already what I had to suffer?'

'Oh, shut up. Stop your whining and complaining. You're a born liar and a bully, Kenny Garside. I don't believe a word you say any more.'

'It's true. If Barry flipping Holmes had played fair by my mam and married her instead of chucking her over, she would never have gone off with all them other chaps, including the one who hurt me.'

'Look, Kenny, I'm sorry for what happened to you as a boy, if it really did, but you can't let that sort of bitterness scar you for life. You can't take revenge on everyone else for something they aren't responsible for. That's why my mam is the mess she is. You're a good pair, both wallowing in self-pity.' She spread her hands in despair, pale face etched in pain. 'But why hurt our Pete, for God's sake? What had he ever done to you? Just tell me that. Why did you do it?'

'He was one of Barry's favourite, always winning trophies in the ring.'

Dena stared at him, wide-eyed. 'You were jealous of our Pete? Just as you were jealous of me when I made a new life for myself, as well as Trudy and even Carl, your own brother.'

'Particularly Carl, my flaming Holy Joe brother. Anyway, it wasn't just that. Your Pete saw me nick something from Woolies and threatened to tell.'

'What are you saying? That you killed my little brother because he saw you shoplifting?'

Kenny avoided her accusing gaze. 'That was the trouble with your Pete. He was a blabbermouth, always up to something yet forever coming up smelling of roses. Barry Holmes could see no wrong in him, and I knew once Pete started blabbing to Barry that I'd never hear the last of it. Barry would tell Mam, and then where would I be? Me and Chippy got a few of the lads together to give him a going over and teach him a lesson. We never meant it to go that far, but the lads started to enjoy themselves a bit too much. They weren't supposed to touch you at all. You were expected to run for it. And we thought your Pete could swim.'

'He was unconscious, so how could he swim? They knocked him senseless! Beat him to a bloody pulp.'

Kenny looked at her. 'I know. I'm sorry.'

'You're sorry? You think that makes it all right because you're claiming to be sorry!' Of their own volition her hands began to slap at him. She couldn't seem to stop herself. Dena slapped him all around his head and shoulders, sobbing as if her heart would break, reliving all the pain and hurt of that terrible time. 'Why the hell would I run away when you big bullies attacked my little brother? I couldn't save him! I was supposed to protect him and he drowned because of you! So why don't you try to do the same to me? Go on, show me how big and clever you are.'

Dena fully expected him to rise to the challenge and make a grab for her, pick her up and toss her in the canal as he had done with Pete. She mentally prepared herself for the shock of hitting the cold water while reminding herself that she could swim, that she'd surely be safe, but then seeing the bicycle chain still in his hand, realised he could hit her, or beat her senseless with his knuckle-duster as his mates had done once before.

Fortunately, he didn't touch or hit her with the bicycle chain. He didn't do any of those things. Kenny sank to his knees and began to cry. He sobbed like a child, although more out of self-pity for himself rather than guilt over his crime.

She looked down at him with contempt. 'No wonder I love your brother and not you. What the hell am I going to do with you now, you snivelling coward?'

A voice came from out of the darkness. 'You could call the police, Dena, that's what you should do.'

'Carl!' Dena swirled around as he stepped quietly out of the shadows.

'I'm sorry to startle you, Dena, only everyone was concerned about your non-appearance at the pub and I came out looking for you. Someone told me they'd seen our Kenny helping you along the street. They'd assumed you weren't feeling well, and he was taking you home.'

Carl likewise looked down at his brother. 'I've protected you all your life, but I can't save you this time. You're going to have to face your punishment like a man, and by doing so learn to be more sensible.'

–

Dena knew she had one last hurdle to face. Consequently, she asked the social worker if she would be the one to tell Alice what had truly happened to her son. 'She's not going to like it, so it would be better coming from you, not me.'

Miss Rogers gave a wry smile. 'If she shoots the messenger, I get all the flack?'

'Something of the sort, and do tell her I'll call and see her sometime. She is still my mother, after all.'

Miss Rogers shook her head in disbelief. 'She really doesn't deserve you for a daughter.'

Days later the furore over Kenny's arrest had died down. Belle had come to terms with it, greatly assisted by the hope that the charge was likely to be one of manslaughter, not cold-blooded murder. Dena and Carl at last found time to talk, and she felt unaccountably nervous, fearful of saying the wrong thing and losing him for good.

'How long had you been standing there, listening to our conversation, before you intervened? Long enough to hear me tell Kenny about my reason for preferring you?'

'Does it matter?'

'It does to me.' Dena drew in a shaky breath. 'I can't deny it, I still love you.'

He looked at her, his expression solemn. 'But you didn't trust me, did you?' Carl reminded her. 'You didn't believe in my innocence. Your first reaction when Kenny told you that I was the one guilty of your brother's death was to believe him, despite everything he'd done, all the harassment and trouble he'd caused you.'

Dena hung her head in shame, tears choking her throat. She feared he was going to walk away, and could feel it coming. How would she live if he did? She looked into his eyes, her own pleading with him to understand and forgive her. 'Actually, I can't explain how shocked and confused I felt in that moment. I was still reeling from the destruction of my work room and all my dreams. But that's no excuse. I tried to laugh it off when I told you, but you didn't react as I expected. You were too concerned with protecting your own brother to own up to the fact that you too suspected him. Even when you refused to speak to me, I swear that I continued to believe in your innocence. Ask Barry! I told him that all I had left was hope. That I would hold on to my faith in you.'

Tears hung on her lashes and Carl brushed them gently away with the tip of his little finger. 'I'm sorry, Dena. I felt so ashamed, not only of the fact that my brother was probably the one responsible for the death of your own brother, but that I'd been unable to stop him. I should have controlled him better, and somehow prevented it from happening.'

Dena stretched out a hand, but then withdrew it before it touched him. 'How could you do that? You can't watch him every minute of the time. Kenny has a will of his own and makes his own choices in life. But I can understand the guilt that you feel. Somehow we'll both have to learn to live with the fact we let our brothers down, not out of malice or inadequacy on our part, but because we're young and only human. We did our best.'

There was a silence. 'I still love you, Dena. Is it possible that despite everything, we could start again? Could we make a go of it, do you think?'

Her eyes blazed with the passion of her emotion. 'Oh, I do hope so, Carl. I'm willing to give it a try if you are.'

He grinned at her then, a wide, generous smile that filled her with joy as well as hope. 'Barry tells me that he's going to ask Winnie if she'll name the day?'

'What?' Dena's eyebrows shot up. 'Winnie never said anything to me.'

'I don't think he's plucked up the courage to propose to her yet, but he fully intends to. Says he's never been so happy in his life as he has since he became friendly with you and Winnie. That goes for me too. I expect she'll be asking you to design her outfit. Then you could get round to making that wedding gown, the one you didn't get time to make for the fashion show.'

'You were there, weren't you? You must have heard me say that.'

'I was hiding in the kitchen, peeping through a crack in the door. Wouldn't have missed your big event for the world, Dena. So how about it, are you going to make it, that special wedding gown?'

Dena frowned. 'Why would I do that?'

'Well you can't walk down the aisle in sackcloth and ashes, now can you? And I really don't care whether it's white, ice blue or sky-blue pink. I reckon you should choose your own gown and style of wedding this time, and not let Mam have any say at all.'

Dena gazed at him, her heart in her mouth. 'Are you saying what I think you're saying?'

'Come here. Maybe you'll believe me if I show you.'